# Life or Death

## ALSO BY MICHAEL ROBOTHAM
## FROM CLIPPER LARGE PRINT

# Life or Death

## Michael Robotham

W F HOWES LTD

This large print edition published in 2015 by
W F Howes Ltd
Unit 4, Rearsby Business Park, Gaddesby Lane,
Rearsby, Leicester LE7 4YH

1 3 5 7 9 10 8 6 4 2

First published in the United Kingdom in 2014
by Sphere

A CIP catalogue record for this book is available
from the British Library

ISBN 978 1 47129 707 6

Typeset by Palimpsest Book Production Limited,
Falkirk, Stirlingshire

Printed and bound by
www.printondemand-worldwide.com of Peterborough, England

This book is made entirely of chain-of-custody materials

For Isabella

Life can be magnificent and overwhelming
– That is its whole tragedy. Without beauty,
love, or danger it would almost be easy to
live.

ALBERT CAMUS


To be, or not to be: that is the question.

WILLIAM SHAKESPEARE

# CHAPTER 1

Audie Palmer had never learned how to swim. As a boy when he went fishing with his father on Lake Conroe he was told that being a strong swimmer was dangerous because it gave a person a false sense of security. Most folks drowned because they struck out for shore thinking they could save themselves, while those who survived were found clinging to the wreckage.

'So that's what you do,' his daddy said, 'you hang on like a limpet.'

'What's a limpet?' Audie asked.

His daddy pondered this. 'OK, so you hang on like a one-armed man clinging to a cliff while he's being tickled.'

'I'm ticklish.'

'I know.'

And his daddy tickled him until the whole boat rocked from side to side and any fish in the vicinity swam into dark holes and Audie spotted his pants with pee.

This became a running joke between the two of them – not the pee, but the examples of holding on.

'You got to hold on like a giant squid hugging a sperm whale,' Audie might say. 'You got to hold on like a frightened kitten on a sweater,' his daddy replied. 'You got to hold on like a baby being breastfed by Marilyn Monroe.'

*And so it went on . . .*

Standing in the middle of a dirt road some time after midnight, Audie recalls these fishing trips with fondness and thinks how much he misses his daddy. The moon is blooming overhead, pregnant and white, creating a silver path on the surface of the lake. He can't see the far side, but he knows there must be one. His future lies on the distant shore, just as death stalks him on this one.

Headlights swing around a bend, accelerating toward him. Audie plunges down a ravine, turning his face to the ground so it won't reflect the light. The truck hurtles past, kicking up a cloud of dust that balloons and settles around him until he can feel it on his teeth. Getting to his hands and knees, Audie crawls through the tangle of brambles, dragging the plastic gallon containers behind him. At any moment he expects to hear someone shouting and the telltale click of a bullet sliding into a chamber.

Emerging at the edge of the lake, he scoops mud in his hands and smears it over his face and arms. The bottles knock emptily against his knees. He has tied eight of them together, lashing them with scraps of rope and strips of torn bed sheet.

2

He takes off his shoes, laces them together and hangs them over his neck. Then he knots the calico laundry bag around his waist. There are cuts on his hands from the razor wire, but they're not bleeding badly. He tears his shirt into bandages and wraps them around his palms, tightening the knots with his teeth.

More vehicles pass on the road above him. Headlights. Voices. Soon they'll bring the dogs. Wading into deeper water, Audie wraps his arm around the bottles, hugging them to his chest. He begins to kick, trying not to create too big a splash until he gets further from shore.

Using the stars to navigate, he tries to swim in a straight line. Choke Canyon Reservoir is about three and a half miles across at this point. There's an island roughly halfway, or maybe less, if he survives that long.

As the minutes and hours pass, he loses track of time. Twice he flips over and feels himself drowning until he hugs the containers tighter to his chest and rolls back above the surface. A couple of the bottles drift away. One springs a leak. The bandages on his hands have long ago washed loose.

His mind wanders, drifting from memory to memory – places and people, some he liked, others he feared. He thinks of his childhood, playing ball with his brother. Sharing a Slurpee with a girl called Phoebe Carter who let him put his hand in her whiter-than-white panties in the back row of the cinema when he was fourteen. They were watching *Jurassic Park* and a *T. rex* had just eaten a blood-sucking lawyer who was trying to hide in a port-a-potty.

Audie doesn't remember much else about the film, but Phoebe Carter lives on in his memory. Her father was a boss at the battery-recycling plant and drove around West Dallas in a Mercedes when everyone else had beat-to-shit cars with more rust than paint. Mr Carter didn't like his daughter hanging out with boys like Audie, but Phoebe wouldn't be told. Where is she now? Married. Pregnant. Happy. Divorced. Working two jobs. Dyeing her hair. Turned to flab. Watching Oprah.

Another shard of memory – he can see his mama standing at the kitchen sink singing 'Skip to My Lou' while she washed the dishes. She used to make up her own verses about flies in the buttermilk and kittens in the wool. His father would come in from the garage and use the same soapy water to wash the dirt and grease from his hands.

George Palmer, dead now, was a bear-like man with hands the size of baseball mitts and freckles across his nose like a cloud of black flies had swarmed into his face and got stuck there. Handsome. Doomed. Men in Audie's family had always died young – mostly in mining or rig accidents. Cave-ins. Methane-gas explosions. Industrial accidents. His paternal grandfather had his skull crushed by a twelve-foot piece of drilling pipe that was thrown two hundred feet by a blast. His uncle Thomas was buried with eighteen men. They didn't bother trying to bring the bodies out.

Audie's father had bucked the trend by living to fifty-five. He saved enough money on the rigs to buy a garage with two gas pumps, a workshop and a hydraulic lift. He worked six days a week for twenty years and put three kids through school, or would have done if Carl had bothered trying.

George had the deepest, softest voice of any man Audie had ever met – like gravel turning in a barrel of honey – but he had less and less to say as the years rolled by and his whiskers grew white and cancer ate away at his organs. Audie wasn't there for the funeral. He wasn't there for the disease. Sometimes he wondered if a broken heart had been the reason, rather than a lifetime of cigarettes.

Audie rolls beneath the surface again. The water is warm and bitter and comes in everywhere, in his mouth and throat and ears. He wants to fight for air, but exhaustion drags him under. Legs burning, arms aching, he's not going to make it across. This is where it ends. Opening his eyes, he sees an angel dressed in white robes that billow and ripple around her as though she's flying rather than swimming. She spreads her arms to embrace him, naked beneath the translucent cloth. He can smell her perfume and feel the heat of her body pressed against his chest. Her eyes half open, her lips parted, waiting for a kiss.

Then she slaps him hard across the face and says, 'Swim, you bastard!'

Thrashing to the surface, gasping for breath, he clutches at the plastic containers before they float away. His chest heaves and water spurts from his mouth and nose. Coughing. Blinking. Focusing. He can see a reflection of the stars on the water and the tips of dead trees silhouetted against the moon. So he kicks again, moving forward, imagining the ghostly shape below him in the water, following him like a sunken moon.

And at some point, hours later, his feet touch rocks and he drags himself ashore, collapsing on a narrow sand beach, kicking the bottles away. The night air has a dense feral odour, still radiating heat from the day. Mist hangs on the water in wisps that could be the ghosts of drowned fishermen.

He lies on his back and looks at the moon disappearing behind the clouds that seem to be floating in deep space. Closing his eyes, he feels the weight of the angel as she straddles his thighs. She leans forward, her breath on his cheek, her lips close to his ear, whispering, 'Remember your promise.'

# CHAPTER 2

The sirens are sounding. Moss tries to go back to his dream but heavy boots are ringing on the metal stairs; fists grip the iron railings and dust shivers on the treads. It's too early. Morning count isn't normally until eight. Why the siren? The cell door opens, sliding sideways with a dull metallic clang.

Moss opens his eyes and groans. He'd been dreaming about his wife Crystal and his boxer shorts are tented with his morning glory. *I still got it*, he thinks, knowing what Crystal would say: 'You gonna use that thing or spend all day looking at it?'

Prisoners are ordered from their cells, scratching at navels, cupping testicles and wiping grit from their eyes. Some emerge willingly while others have to be encouraged with a swinging bat. There are cells on three levels enclosing a rectangular yard with safety nets to stop people from attempting suicide or being thrown off the walkways. The ceiling has a tangle of pipes that gurgle and knock as though something sinister lives inside them.

Moss hauls himself up and out. Barefoot. He stands on the landing with his face to the wall. Grunts. Farts. He's a big man, softening in the middle, but solid across the shoulders due to the push-ups and chin-ups he does a dozen times a day. His skin is a milk-chocolate brown and his eyes seem too big for his face, making him look younger than his forty-eight years.

Moss glances to his left. Junebug is leaning his head on the wall, trying to sleep standing up. His tattoos leap and snarl on his forearms and chest. The former meth addict has a narrow face and a moustache trimmed into wide wings that stretch halfway across his cheeks.

'What's happening?'

Junebug opens his eyes. 'Sounds like an escape.'

Moss looks in the other direction. Along the length of the landing, he sees dozens of prisoners standing outside their cells. Everyone is out now. Not everyone. Moss leans to his right, trying to peer inside the next cell. The guards are coming.

'Hey, Audie, get up, man,' he mutters.

Silence.

From the upper level he hears a voice ring out. Someone arguing. A scuffle develops until the Ninja Turtles storm up the stairway and dish out a beating.

Moss steps closer to Audie's cell. 'Wake up, man.'

Nothing.

He turns to Junebug. Their eyes meet, silently asking the question.

8

Moss takes two steps to the right, aware that the guards could be watching. He peers into the darkness of Audie's cell and can make out the rack bolted to the wall. The basin. The toilet. No warm body or cold one.

A guard yells from above. 'All present and accounted for.'

A second voice comes from below. 'All present and accounted for.'

The hats and bats are coming. Inmates flatten their bodies against the walls.

'Up here!' yells a guard.

Boots follow.

Two of the uniforms are searching Audie's cell as though there's somewhere he could possibly be hiding – under a pillow, or behind the deodorant. Moss risks turning his head and sees Deputy Warden Grayson reach the top of the stairs, sweating from the climb. Fatter than Albert, his belly hangs over his polished leather belt and more rolls of skin are trying to smother his collar.

Grayson gets to Audie's cell. He looks inside and takes a breath, making a sucking sound with his lips. Unhooking his baton, he slaps it into his palm and turns to Moss.

'Where's Palmer?'

'I don't know, suh.'

The baton swings into the back of Moss's knees, dropping him like a felled tree. Grayson is standing over him.

'When did you last see him?'

9

Moss hesitates, trying to remember. The end of the baton is driven into his right side, just below his ribs. The world flushes up and down in his eyes.

'Chow time,' he gasps.

'Where is he now?'

'I don't know.'

A shimmer seems to rise off Grayson's face. 'Lock the place down. I want him found.'

'What about breakfast?' an officer asks.

'They can wait.'

Moss is dragged into his cell. The doors close. For the next two hours he lies on his rack, listening to the prison buildings quiver and groan. Now they're in the workshop. Before that it was the laundry and the library.

From the next cell, he hears Junebug tapping on the wall. 'Hey, Moss!'

'What?'

'You think he got out?'

Moss doesn't answer.

'Why would he do something like that on his last night?'

Still Moss remains silent.

'I always said that sonbitch was crazy.'

The guards are coming again. Junebug goes back to his rack. Moss listens, feeling his sphincter opening and closing. The boots stop moving outside his cell.

'On your feet! Against the back wall! Spread 'em!'

Three men enter. Moss has his wrists cuffed and

looped through a chain that is wrapped around his waist, while another tethers his ankles. He can only shuffle. His trousers are undone and he doesn't have time to do up the buttons. He has to hold them up with one hand. Prisoners are whooping in their cells and hollering messages. Moss walks through shafts of sunlight and catches a glimpse of police cars outside the main gates where stars of light reflect from their polished surfaces.

When he reaches the administration wing, he's told to take a seat. Guards on either side say nothing. Moss can see their profiles, the peaked caps, sunglasses and tan shirts with dark-brown epaulettes. He can also hear voices inside the adjacent meeting room. Occasionally one utterance rises above the others. Accusations are being made. Blame apportioned.

Food arrives. Moss feels his stomach cramp and his mouth fill with saliva. Another hour passes. Longer. People leave. It's Moss's turn. Using short mincing steps, he shuffles into the room, keeping his eyes lowered. Chief Warden Sparkes is dressed in a dark suit that already looks crushed where he's been sitting down. He's a tall man with a mane of silver hair, a long thin nose, and he walks like he's balancing a book on his head. He signals for the officers to step back and they take up positions on either side of the door.

Along one wall is a table covered with plates of half-eaten food: deep-fried soft shell crab, spare ribs, fried chicken, mashed potato and salad. The grilled cobs of corn have black skillet marks and are glistening with butter. The warden picks up a spare rib and sucks the meat from the bone, wiping his fingers with a moist towelette.

'What's your name, son?'

'Moss Jeremiah Webster.'

'What sort of name is Moss?'

'Well, suh, my momma couldn't spell Moses on my birth certificate.'

One of the guards laughs. The warden pinches the bridge of his nose.

'Are you hungry, Mr Webster? Grab a plate.'

Moss glances at the feast, his stomach rumbling. 'Are you fixing on executing me, suh?'

'Why would you think that?'

'Meal like that could be a man's last.'

'Nobody is going to execute you . . . not on a Friday.'

The chief warden laughs, but Moss doesn't think the joke is very funny. He hasn't moved.

*Maybe the food is poisoned. Warden's eating it. Maybe he knows which bits to eat. Hell, I don't care!*

Shuffling forward, Moss begins heaping food onto a plastic plate, piling it high with ribs, crab claws and mashed potato, trying to perch a cob of corn on the top. He eats with both hands, leaning over the plate, the juices smearing his cheeks and dribbling down his chin. Meanwhile, Warden Sparkes picks up another spare rib and takes a seat opposite, looking vaguely repulsed.

12

'Extortion, fraud, drug dealing – you were caught with two million dollars' worth of marijuana.'

'It was only weed.'

'Then you beat a man to death in prison.'

Moss doesn't answer.

'Did he deserve it?'

'Thought so at the time.'

'And now?'

'I'd do a lot of things different.'

'How long has it been?'

'Fifteen years.'

Moss has eaten too quickly. A piece of the meat is lodged halfway down his throat. He thumps his fist on his chest, making his cuffs rattle. The warden offers him something to drink. Moss swallows a full can of soft drink, fearing they might take it away. He wipes his mouth. Belches. Eats again.

Warden Sparkes has sucked the spare rib clean. He leans forward and plants the bone into Moss's mashed potato where it sticks upright like naked flagpole.

'Let's start at the beginning. You are friends with Audie Palmer, is that correct?'

'I know him.'

'When did you last see him?'

'Yesterday evening at chow time.'

'You sat with him.'

'Yes, suh.'

'What did you talk about?'

'Usual stuff.'

The warden waits, his eyes expressionless. Moss can feel the butter from the griddled corn coating his tongue.

'Roaches.'

'What?'

'We were discussing how to get rid of roaches. I was telling Audie to use AmerFresh toothpaste and put it in the cracks in the wall. Roaches don't like toothpaste. Don't ask me why, they just don't.'

'Cockroaches.'

Moss talks between mouthfuls, eating around his mashed potato. 'I heard a story about a woman who had a cockroach crawl into her ear while she was sleeping. It had babies that burrowed right into her brain. They found her dead one day with roaches coming out her nose. We fight a war against them. Some niggas will tell you to use shaving cream, but that shit don't last through the night. AmerFresh is best.'

Warden Sparkes eyeballs him. 'We have no pest-control problems in my prison.'

'I don't know if the roaches got that memo, suh.'

'We fumigate twice a year.'

Moss knows all about the pest-control measures. The guards show up, order prisoners to lie down on their racks, while their cells are sprayed with some toxic-smelling chemical that makes everyone feel poorly, but has zero effect on the roaches.

'What happened after chow time?' asks Sparkes.

'I went back to my cell.'

'Did you see Palmer?'

'He was reading.'

'Reading?'

'A book,' says Moss, in case any further explanation were needed.

'What sort of book?'

'A thick one without any pictures.'

Sparkes doesn't see any humour in the situation. 'Did you know Palmer was due to be released today?'

'Yes, suh.'

'Why would a man escape the night before he was due to be released?'

Moss wipes grease from his lips. 'I have no idea.'

'You must have some inkling. The man spent ten years inside. One more day and he's a free man, but instead he makes himself a fugitive. When he's caught he'll be tried and sentenced. He'll get another twenty years.'

Moss doesn't know what he's supposed to say.

'Are you hearing me, son?'

'Yes, suh.'

'Don't tell me you weren't close to Audie Palmer. Don't tell me that for a second. This ain't my first rodeo and I know when someone is crow-hopping me.'

Moss blinks at him.

'You shared the next cell to Palmer for – what – seven years? He must have said something to you.'

'No, suh, honest to God, not a word.'

Moss has reflux. He burps. The chief warden is

still talking. 'My job is to keep prisoners incarcerated until such time as the federal government says they're eligible for release. Mr Palmer wasn't eligible for release until today, but he decided to go early. Why?'

Moss's shoulders rise and fall.

'Speculate.'

'I don't know what that word means, suh.'

'Give me your opinion.'

'You want my opinion? I'd say that Audie Palmer was dumber than shit on a biscuit for doing what he did.'

Moss pauses and looks at the uneaten food on his plate. Warden Sparkes takes a photograph from his coat pocket and puts it on the table. It's a picture of Audie Palmer with his puppy-dog eyes and floppy fringe, as wholesome as a glass of milk.

'What do you know about the Dreyfus County armoured truck robbery?'

'Just what I read.'

'Audie Palmer must have mentioned it.'

'No, suh.'

'And you didn't ask?'

'Sure, I did. Everybody asked. Every guard. Every nigga. Every visitor. Family. Friends. Every sonbitch in this place wanted to know what happened to the money.'

Moss didn't have to lie. He doubted if there was a man or beast incarcerated in Texas who didn't know the story of the robbery – not just because

16

of the missing money, but because four people died that day. One escaped. One got caught.

'And what did Palmer say?'

'Not a damn thing.'

Warden Sparkes fills his cheeks with air like he's blowing up a balloon and then releases it slowly.

'Is that why you helped that boy escape? Did he promise you some of the money?'

'I didn't help nobody escape.'

'Are you cocking your leg and pissing on me, son?'

'No, suh.'

'So you want me to believe that your best friend escaped from prison without saying a word to you?'

Moss nods, his eyes searching empty air above the warden's head.

'Did Audie Palmer have a girlfriend?'

'He used to talk about a girl in his sleep, but I think she was long gone.'

'Family?'

'He has a mother and a sister.'

'We *all* have a mother.'

'She writes him regular.'

'Anyone else?'

Moss shrugs. He isn't revealing anything that the warden couldn't find in Audie's file. Both men know that nothing important is going to come out of the interview.

Sparkes stands and paces, his shoes squeaking on the linoleum floor. Moss has to twist his head from side to side to keep him in view.

'I want you to listen carefully, Mr Webster. You had some discipline problems when you first arrived, but they were just kinks and you ironed them out. You won privileges. Gained them the hard way. That's why I know your conscience is bothering you, which is why you're going to tell me where he's gone.'

Moss looks at him blankly. The warden stops pacing and braces both his hands on the table.

'Explain something to me, Mr Webster. This code of silence that operates among people like you, what do you think it achieves? You live like animals, you think like animals, you behave like animals. Cunning. Violent. Selfish. You steal from each other. You kill each other. You fuck each other. You form gangs. What's the point of having a code?'

'It's the second thing that unites us,' says Moss, telling himself to hold his tongue even as he ignores his own advice.

'What's the first thing?' asks the warden.

'Hating people like you.'

The chief warden upends the table, sending plates of food clattering to the floor. Gravy and mashed potato slide down the wall. The guards wait for the signal. Moss is hauled to his feet and pushed out the door. He has to shuffle quickly to stop himself falling. They half carry him down two flights of stairs and through a half-dozen doors that have to be unlocked from the other side. He's not going back to his cell. They're taking him to the Special Housing Unit. Solitary. The Hole.

18

Another key slides into a lock. The hinges barely squeak. Two new guards take custody. Moss is ordered to strip down. Shoes. Pants. Shirt.

'Why you in here, asshole?'

Moss doesn't answer.

'He aided an escape,' says the other guard.

'I did no such thing, suh.'

The first guard motions to Moss's wedding ring. 'Take it off.'

Moss blinks at him. 'The regulations say I can keep it.'

'Take it off or I'll break your fingers.'

'It's all that I got.'

Moss closes his fist. The guard hits him twice with the baton. Help is summoned. They hold Moss down and continue to hit him, the blows sounding oddly muted and his swelling face wearing a strange look of astonishment. Falling under the blows, he grunts and gargles blood as a boot presses his head to the floor where he can smell the layers of polish and sweat. His stomach lurches, but the ribs and mashed potatoes stay down.

When it's over they toss him in a small cage of woven steel mesh. Lying on the concrete, not moving, Moss makes a wet noise in his throat and wipes blood from his nose, rubbing it between his fingertips where it feels like oil. He wonders what lesson he's supposed to be learning.

Then he thinks of Audie Palmer and the missing seven million dollars. He hopes Audie has gone for the money. He hopes he spends the rest of his life sipping pina coladas in Cancun or cocktails in Monte Carlo. Screw the bastards! The best revenge is to live well.

# CHAPTER 3

Just before dawn the stars seem brighter and Audie can pick out the constellations. Some he can name: Orion and Cassiopeia and Ursa Major. Others are so distant they're bringing light from millions of years ago, as though history were reaching across time and space to shine upon the present.

There are people who believe their fates are written in the stars, and if that's true then Audie must have been born under a bad sign. He's not a believer in fate or destiny or karma. Nor does he think that everything happens for a reason and that luck evens itself out over a lifetime, falling a little here and there like it comes from a passing raincloud. In his own heart he knows that death could find him at any moment and that life is about getting the next footstep right.

Untying the laundry bag, he takes out a change of clothes: jeans and a long-sleeved shirt that he stole from one of the guards who left a gym bag in his unlocked car. He pulls on socks and laces his feet into his wet boots.

After burying his prison clothes, he waits until

John ~ Rond

the eastern horizon is edged in orange before he begins walking. A creek crosses a narrow gravel wash, feeding the reservoir. Mist clings to the lower ground and two herons stand in the shallow water, looking like lawn ornaments. The mud banks are pockmarked with holes made by nesting swallows that flit back and forth, barely brushing the surface of the water. Audie follows the creek until he comes to a dusty farm track and a single-lane bridge. He sticks to the road, listening for vehicles and watching for clouds of dust.

The sun comes up, red and shimmering above a line of stunted trees. Four hours later, water is a memory and the blazing orb is like a welder's flame against the back of his neck. Dust cakes every wrinkle and hollow of his skin and he's alone on the road.

Past midday, he climbs a rise, trying to get his bearings. It looks like he's crossing a dead world that some ancient civilization has left behind. The trees are huddled along the old watercourses like herded beasts, and heat shimmers off a flatland that is threaded with motorbike tracks and turkey trails. His khaki pants are hanging low and there are hoops of sweat beneath his arms. Twice he has to hide from passing trucks, slipping and sliding down loose rocks and shale, crouching behind brush or boulders. Stopping to rest, he sits on a flat rock and remembers the time his daddy chased him around the yard because he caught him stealing milk money from people's doorsteps.

'Who put you up to it?' he demanded to know, twisting Audie's ear.

'Nobody.'

'Tell me the truth or I'll do worse.'

Audie said nothing. He took his punishment like a man, rubbing the welts on his thighs and seeing the disappointment in his daddy's eyes. His older brother Carl watched from the house.

'You did good,' Carl said afterwards, 'but you shoulda hid the money.'

Audie climbs back onto the road and continues walking. During the afternoon he crosses a sealed road with four lanes and follows it from a distance, taking cover when traffic blows past. In another mile he comes to a dirt track curving north. In the distance, along the rutted road, there are mud tanks and pumps. A derrick is silhouetted against the sky with a flame burning from the apex, creating a shimmer in the air. At night it must be visible for miles, standing atop a mini-city of lights like a fledgling colony on a distant planet.

Studying the derrick, Audie fails to see an old man watching him. Stocky and brown, he's wearing coveralls and a wide-brimmed hat. He's standing next to a boom gate with a painted pole and a weighted end. Nearby is a shelter with three walls and a roof. A Dodge pickup is parked beneath a lone tree.

The old man has a pockmarked face, flat forehead and wide-set eyes. A shotgun rests in the crook of his arm.

Audie tries to smile. Dust cracks on his face.

'Howdy?'

The old man nods uncertainly.

'Wondered if you might spare me some water?' says Audie. 'I'm parched.'

Resting the shotgun on his shoulder, the man steps to the side of the shed and opens the top of the water barrel. He points to a metal ladle hanging on a nail. Audie dips it into the barrel, breaking the still surface, and almost inhales the first mouthful, bringing water up through his nose. He coughs. Drinks again. It's cooler than he expects.

The old man takes out a crumpled packet of cigarettes from the pocket of his coveralls and lights one of them, drawing the smoke deep into his lungs, as though seeking to replace any fresh air.

'What are you doing out here?'

'Had a row with my girlfriend. Bitch drove off and left me. I figured she'd come back – but she didn't.'

'Maybe you shouldn't be calling her names if you want her to come back.'

'Maybe,' says Audie, ladling water over his head.

'Where did she dump you?'

'We were camping.'

'By the reservoir.'

'Yeah.'

'That's fifteen miles from here.'

'I walked every one of them.'

A tanker rumbles along the track. The old man

leans on the weighted end of the boom gate, making it lift skywards. Waves are exchanged. The truck drives on. The dust cloud settles.

'What are you doing out here?' asks Audie.

'Guarding the place.'

'What are you guarding?'

'It's a drilling operation. Lots of expensive equipment.'

Audie holds out his hand and introduces himself, using his middle name, Spencer, because the police are less likely to have released it. The old man doesn't ask for anything more. They shake.

'I am Ernesto Rodriguez. People call me Ernie because it makes me sound less like a spick.' He laughs. Another truck is approaching.

'You think one of these drivers might give me a ride?' asks Audie.

'Where you heading?'

'Anywhere I can catch a bus or a train.'

'What about your girl?'

'I don't think she's coming back.'

'Where do you live?'

'I grew up in Dallas, but I've been out west for a while.'

'Doing what?'

'Bit of everything.'

'So you heading anywhere and you do a bit of everything.'

'That's about it.'

Ernie gazes south across flatlands that are scratched by ravines and dotted with rocky outcrops. A fence runs away from them and seems to dip off the edge of the earth.

'I can give you a ride as far as Freer,' he says, 'but I don't finish for another hour or so.'

'Much obliged.'

Audie sits in the shade and takes off his boots, gingerly fingering his blisters and the cuts on his hands. More trucks pass through the gate, leaving full, returning empty.

Ernie is a talker. 'I used to be a short-order cook until I retired,' he says. 'I make twice that now, because of the boom.'

'What boom?'

'Oil and gas, it's big news. Ever heard of Eagle Ford Shale?'

Audie shakes his head.

'It's this sedimentary rock formation, runs right under South and East Texas, and its full of marine fossils from some ancient ocean. That's what makes the oil. And there's natural gas trapped down there in the rocks. They just got to dig it up.'

Ernie makes it sound so easy.

Just before dusk a pickup truck arrives from the other direction. It's the night guard. Ernie hands him the keys to padlock the boom gate. Audie waits in the Dodge. He wonders what the two men are talking about and tries not to get paranoid. Ernie returns and climbs behind the wheel. They negotiate the rutted track and swing east onto Farm to Market Road. The windows are open. Ernie dips his head to light a cigarette, holding

26

the wheel with his elbows. He yells above the rushing air, telling Audie how he lives with his daughter and his grandson. They got a house just outside of Pleasanton, which he pronounces 'Pledenten'.

To their west a jungle of clouds has swallowed the sun before it dips below the horizon. It's like watching a flame burn through a soggy piece of newspaper. Audie leans his elbow on the windowsill and keeps watch for roadblocks or police cruisers. He should be clear of them by now, but he doesn't know how long they'll keep looking for him.

'Where are you fixing on spending tonight?' asks Ernie.

'Haven't decided.'

'There's a few motels in Pleasanton, but I never stayed in any of 'em. Never had the need. You got cash?'

Audie nods.

'You should call your girl – say you're sorry.'

'She's long gone.'

Ernie drums his fingers on the steering wheel. 'I can't offer more than a bunk in the barn, but it's cheaper than a motel and my daughter is a good cook.'

Audie makes noises about declining, but knows he can't risk checking into a motel because they'll ask him for identification. Police will have posted his photograph by now.

'That's settled then,' says Ernie, reaching for the radio. 'You want to listen to some music?'

'No,' says Audie, too abruptly. 'Let's just talk.'

'Fair enough.'

A few miles south of Pleasanton, the truck pulls up in front of a gaunt house beside a barn and a stunted grove of cottonwood trees. The engine dies clumsily and a dog wanders across the dirt yard, sniffing at Audie's boots.

Ernie is out of the truck, mounting the steps, calling out that he's home.

'We got a guest for supper, Rosie.'

In the depths of an open hall, a light shows from the kitchen where a woman is standing over the stove. Broad-hipped with a round, pretty face, her skin is a milky brown and her eyes elongated, more Indian than Mexican. She's wearing a faded print dress and bare feet.

She looks at Audie and back to her father. 'Why are you telling me?'

'He'll want to eat and you're doing the cooking.'

She turns back to the stove where meat hisses in a frying pan. 'Yeah, I do the cooking.'

The old man grins at Audie. 'Best get you washed up. I'll find you some clean clothes. Rosie can wash those later.' He turns to his daughter. 'Where do you keep Dave's old clothes?'

'In that box beneath my bed.'

'Can we find sumpin' for this fella?'

'Do what you like.'

Audie is shown to the shower and given a fresh set of clothes. He stands under the hot spray for a long time, letting the water turn his skin pink.

Luxuriating. Daydreaming. Prison showers were truncated, regulated and dangerous activities that never made him feel cleaner.

Dressed in another man's clothes, he combs his hair with his fingers and retraces his steps along the hallway. He can hear a TV. A reporter is talking about the prison escape. Audie looks cautiously through the open door and sees the TV screen.

*'Audie Spencer Palmer was nearing the end of a ten-year sentence for an armoured truck robbery in Dreyfus County, Texas, in which four people died. Authorities believe he scaled two fences using bed sheets from the prison laundry after short-circuiting one of the alarm systems with a chewing gum wrapper . . .'*

A young boy is sitting on the rug in front of the TV. He's playing with a box of toy soldiers. He glances up at Audie and then at the screen. The story has changed. A weather girl is pointing to a map.

Audie squats on his haunches. 'Howdy.'

The boy nods.

'What's your name?'

'Billy.'

'What game are you playing, Billy?'

'Soldiers.'

'Who's winning?'

'Me.'

Audie laughs and Billy doesn't understand. Rosie calls from the kitchen. Supper is ready.

'You hungry, Billy?'

He nods.

'We best hurry or it might all be gone.'

Rosie makes a final survey of the table, putting a knife, fork and plate in front of Audie, her arm brushing his shoulder. She sits and motions to Billy to say grace. The boy mumbles the words, but says 'amen' clearly. Plates are passed, food spooned, speared and consumed. Ernie asks questions, until Rosie tells him to 'be quiet and let the man eat'.

Occasionally, she sneaks a glance at Audie. She has changed her dress since before dinner. This one is newer and hugs her a little tighter.

When the meal is finished, the men retire to the porch, while Rosie clears away the table and washes and dries the dishes and wipes the benches clean and makes sandwiches for tomorrow. Audie can hear Billy reciting his alphabet.

Ernie smokes a cigarette and props his feet on the porch railing.

'So what are your plans?'

'I got kin in Houston.'

'You want to call them?'

'I went west about ten years ago. Lost touch.'

'Difficult to lose touch with people these days – you must have really made an effort.'

'Guess I did.'

Rosie has been standing inside the doorway listening to them. Ernie yawns and stretches, saying he's about to hit the sack. He shows Audie to the bunkhouse in the barn and wishes him goodnight. Audie spends a moment out of doors looking at the stars. He's about to turn away when he notices Rosie standing in the shadows near a rainwater tank.

'Who are you really?' she asks, accusingly.

'A stranger who appreciates your kindness.'

'If you're fixin' to rob us, we don't have any money.'

'I just need somewhere to sleep.'

'You told Daddy a pack of lies about your girl-friend running off. You been here three hours and you haven't asked to use the phone. Why are you really here?'

'I'm trying to keep a promise to someone.'

Rosie makes a scoffing noise. She is motionless, half in shadow and half out.

'Who do these clothes belong to?' Audie asks.

'My husband.'

'Where is he?'

'He found someone he liked better 'n me.'

'I'm sorry.'

'Why? It ain't your fault.' She looks past Audie into the darkness. 'He said I got fat. Didn't want to touch me any more.'

'I think you're beautiful.'

She takes Audie's hand and places it on her breast. He can feel her heart beating. Then she raises her face, pushing her lips against his. The kiss is hard, hungry, verging on desperation. He can taste her hurt.

Breaking her grip, Audie holds her at arm's length, looking into her eyes. Then he kisses her forehead.

'Good night, Rosie.'

# CHAPTER 4

Prison tried to kill Audie Palmer every day. Awake. Asleep. Eating. Showering. Circling the exercise yard. Through every season, scorching in summer, freezing in winter, rarely in between, prison tried to kill Audie Palmer, but somehow he survived.

To Moss's mind, Audie seemed to exist in a parallel universe where not even the worst of deeds could alter his demeanour. Moss had seen movies about people returned from Heaven or Hell because something in their life had been left undone. He wondered if maybe Audie had been sent back from Hell because of some glitch in the devil's bookkeeping or a case of mistaken identity. If that was so, a man might appreciate penitentiary life because he had witnessed so much worse.

Moss first set eyes on Audie when the young man walked up the ramp with all the other new arrivals. As long as a football field with cells on either side, the ramp was a cavernous place with a waxed floor and fluorescent lighting that buzzed overhead. The mainline prison population watched from the cells, catcalling and whistling at the fish.

All at once the cell doors opened and people spilled out. This only happened once a day when it was like rush hour on the subway. Prisoners were settling accounts, placing orders, collecting contraband or looking for targets. It was a good time to draw blood and get away with it.

It didn't take long for someone to discover Audie. Normally, he'd be news because he was young and good-looking, but folks were more interested in the money. There were seven million reasons to befriend Audie or to beat the shit out of him.

Within hours of his arrival, his name had spread on the prison grapevine. He should have been shitting bricks or begging to get into The Hole, but instead Audie calmly paced the exercise yard where a thousand men had paced a million paces before. Audie was no gangster or wiseguy or killer. He didn't pretend otherwise and that was always going to be his problem. He had no pedigree. No protection. To survive in a penitentiary, a man needs to form alliances, join a gang, or find a protector. He can't afford to be pretty, or soft, or rich.

Moss watched all this from a distance, curious but with no skin in the game. Most fish tried to make a statement early, marking territory or warning off predators. Kindness is seen as a weakness. Compassion. Benevolence. Toss food in the trash before you let another man take it from you. Never offer your place in the queue.

The Dice Man tried it on first. He offered to

get Audie some prison hooch. Audie declined politely. The Dice Man tried a different approach. He upended Audie's chow tray as he walked past his table. Audie looked at the puddle of gravy, mashed potato and chicken. Then he raised his eyes to the Dice Man. Some of the other cons laughed. Dice Man seemed to grow six inches. Audie didn't say a word. He crouched down and began scooping up the mushed-up food, putting it back on his tray.

People cleared back a little, sliding along benches. They all seemed to be waiting for something, like passengers in a stopped train. Audie was still squatting on the floor, picking up food, ignoring everyone. It was like he inhabited a space of his own creation, outside the thinking of other folks, a place that lesser men can only dream of reaching.

The Dice Man looked at his shoes. Gravy had splashed on them.

'Lick it off,' he said.

Audie sighed wearily. 'I know what you're doing.'

'What's that?'

'You're trying to goad me into fighting or rolling over, but I don't want to fight you. I don't even know your name. You've started something and you think you can't back down, but you can. Nobody is going to think less of you. No one is laughing.'

Audie stood up. He was still holding the tray.

'Do any of you think this man is funny?' he shouted.

He asked the question so earnestly Moss could see people giving it some serious thought. The Dice Man looked around like he'd lost his place on the page. He swung a punch at Audie because that was his usual fall-back position. In the blink of an eye, Audie had swung the tray into the side of the Dice Man's head. Of course that only provoked him. He roared forward but Audie was faster. He drove the corner of the tray into the Dice Man's throat with such force that he dropped him to his knees where he curled onto the floor, struggling to breathe. The guards arrived and took the Dice Man to the prison hospital.

Moss thought Audie had some sort of death wish, but that wasn't the case. Prison is full of people who believe the world doesn't exist apart from in their own minds. They can't imagine life outside the walls, so they bring their own world into being. A man is nothing inside. He's a grain of sand under somebody's shoe, a flea on a dog, a pimple on the buttocks of a fat man. The biggest mistake a man can make in prison is to believe he matters at all.

Each morning it began again. Audie must have fought a dozen men the first day and another dozen the second. By lockdown, he'd been bashed so badly that he couldn't chew and both of his eyes were like purple plums.

On the fourth day, the Dice Man had sent word from the prison hospital that he wanted Audie Palmer dead. His gang made the arrangements.

That evening, Moss took his chow tray to the table where Audie was sitting alone.

'Can I sit down?'

'It's a free country,' mumbled Audie.

'It's not though,' replied Moss. 'Not when you've been in prison as long as I have.'

The two men ate in silence until Moss said what he came to say. 'They're going to kill you in the morning. Maybe you should ask Grayson to put you in The Hole.'

Audie raised his eyes above Moss's head as though reading something in the air, and said, 'I can't do that.'

Moss thought Audie was being naïve or stupidly brave or maybe he wanted to die. This wasn't a struggle over missing money. Nobody in prison can spend seven million dollars – not with the worst drug habit or need for protection. And it wasn't about the small stuff like chocolate bars or extra soap. In prison, you fuck up, you die. You look at a person the wrong way . . . you die. You sit at the wrong table at chow time . . . you die. You walk on the wrong side of the corridor or the exercise yard, or make too much noise when you're eating . . . you die. Petty. Stupid. Unlucky. Fatal.

There were codes to be lived by, but these were not to be mistaken for any sense of camaraderie. Incarceration put people close together but it didn't *bring* them together, it didn't unify.

The next morning at eight-thirty the doors opened and the ramp filled. The Dice Man's troops were waiting. They'd given the job to a newcomer, who had a fibreglass shank hidden up his sleeve. The others were stationed as lookouts or to help him ditch the weapon. The fish was going to be gutted like a fish.

Moss didn't want any part of it, but there was something about Audie that intrigued him. Anybody else would have surrendered or kowtowed or begged to be put in solitary. Anybody else would have looped a bed sheet around the bars. Audie was either the dumbest sonbitch in history or the bravest. *What did he see in the world that nobody else did?*

Prisoners had spilled out of the cells and pretended to be doing business but mostly they were waiting. Audie didn't appear. Maybe he'd taken his own way out, thought Moss, but then came the crashing symbols and a thumping baseline of 'Eye of the Tiger' turned up loud, blaring from Audie's cell.

He appeared, bare-chested, dressed in boxer shorts, long socks and trainers darkened with bootblack. Dancing on his toes, throwing shadow punches, he had a sock on each fist stuffed with toilet paper to look like enormous boxing gloves. With his face beaten to a pulp, he looked like Rocky Balboa coming out to fight Apollo Creed in the fifteenth round.

The kid with the shank didn't know whether to laugh or cry. Audie danced and jabbed, ducked and weaved, wearing those ridiculous gloves. But then a strange thing happened. Niggas started laughing. Niggas started clapping. Niggas started singing. When the song finished playing, they carried Audie above their heads like he'd won the heavyweight title of the world.

That's the day that Moss best remembers when he thinks of Audie Palmer – watching him dance out of that cell, throwing punches at phantoms, ducking and weaving at shadows. It wasn't the beginning of something or the end of something, but Audie had found a way to survive.

Of course folks still wanted to know about the money, even the guards, who had grown up in the same dirt-poor projects as the men they were watching, which left them open to bribery and smuggling contraband. Some of the female correctional officers suggested Audie transfer funds into their bank accounts in return for sexual favours. These were women who could eat their own weight in burgers, but who started looking mighty fine after a few years inside.

Audie refused their offers. Not once in ten years did he ever mention the robbery or the money. He didn't lead anyone on, or make any promises. Instead he conveyed a sense of calm and equanimity, like a man who had banished from his life all superfluous sentiment, all longings and all patience for the nonessential. He was like Yoda, Buddha and the Gladiator all rolled into one.

# CHAPTER 5

A beam of sunlight settles on Audie's eyelid and he tries to flick it away like an insect. The light comes back and he hears a giggle. Billy is holding a small mirror and angling the sun through the open barn door.

'I can see you,' says Audie.

Billy ducks down and giggles again. He's wearing tattered shorts and a T-shirt that's too big for him.

'What time is it?' Audie asks.

'After breakfast.'

'Shouldn't you be at school?'

'It's Saturday.'

*So it is*, thinks Audie, rising to his hands and knees. At some point during the night he rolled off the bunk and curled up on the floor, which felt more familiar than a mattress.

'Did you fall out of bed?' asks Billy.

'I guess I did.'

'I used to fall out of bed but I don't any more. Ma says I outgrowed it.'

Audie emerges into the sunlit yard and washes his face at a pumpjack. It was dark last night when he arrived. Now he can see a clutch of small, unpainted houses surrounded by rusting vehicles, spare parts, a water trough, a windmill and a woodpile stacked against a crumbling stone wall. A small black boy is riding a bicycle that's too big for him, sitting on the frame to reach the pedals, navigating between fluttering chickens.

'That's my friend Clayton,' says Billy. 'He's black.'

'I can see that.'

'I don't have many black friends, but Clayton's okay. He's little but he can run faster than a bike unless you're going downhill.'

Audie cinches the belt on his trousers to stop them falling down. On the porch of a neighbouring house he notices a thin man in a checked shirt and black leather vest watching him. Audie waves. The man doesn't wave back.

Rosie appears. 'Breakfast is on the stove.'

'Where's Ernie?'

'Work.'

'He starts early.'

'Finishes late.'

Audie sits at the table and eats. Tortillas. Eggs. Beans. Coffee. There are glass jars of flour, dried beans and rice on shelves above the stove. He can see Rosie through the window hanging washing on a line. He can't stay here. These people have been kind to him, but he doesn't want to bring them trouble. His only hope of staying alive is to follow the plan and keep hidden for as long as possible.

When Rosie reappears he asks her about getting a lift into town.

'I can take you at midday,' she says, rinsing his empty plate in the sink. She brushes a strand of hair from her eyes. 'Where are you heading?'

'Houston.'

'I can drop you at the Greyhound Depot in San Antonio.'

'Is that out of your way?'

She doesn't answer. Audie takes money from his pocket. 'I'd like to pay you something for the lodgings?'

'Keep your money.'

'It's clean.'

'If you say so.'

It's thirty-eight miles into San Antonio, heading north on Interstate 37. Rosie drives a small Japanese-made car with a broken exhaust and no air conditioning. They travel with the windows open and the radio turned up loud.

At the top of the hour, a newsreader lists the headlines and mentions a prison break. Audie begins talking, trying to make it sound natural. Rosie interrupts him and turns up the volume.

'Is that you?'

'I'm not fixing to hurt anyone.'

'That's good to know.'

'You can drop me off right here if you're worried.'

She doesn't answer. Keeps driving.

'What did you do?' she asks.

41

'They said I robbed an armoured truck.'

'Did you?'

'Hardly seems to matter any more.'

She sneaks a glance at him. 'Either you did or you didn't.'

'Sometimes you get blamed for things you didn't do. Other times you get away with things you did. Maybe we finish up even at the end.'

Rosie changes lanes, looking for the exit. 'I don't have a lot of moral authority since I don't go to church any more, but if you've done something wrong you shouldn't run away from it.'

'I'm not running away,' says Audie.

And she believes him.

Pulling up outside the bus station, Rosie looks past Audie at the row of buses heading to distant cities.

'When you get caught, don't mention what we did for you,' she says.

'I won't get caught.'

# CHAPTER 6

Special Agent Desiree Furness walks across the open-plan office on her way to see her boss. Anyone glancing up from a computer screen would see only her head above the level of the desks and think perhaps a young child had wandered into the building to visit a parent or sell girl scout cookies.

Desiree had spent most of her life attempting to grow taller, if not physically then emotionally, socially and professionally. Her mother and father were both short and the genetic numbers had come up on the lowest percentile for their only child. According to her driver's licence, Desiree was five foot two, but in reality she needed high heels to reach such lofty heights. She wore the same heels through college, almost crippling herself, because she wanted to be taken seriously and to date basketball players. That was another cruel twist of fate, her attraction to tall men – or perhaps she harboured some innate desire to have lanky progeny, dealing her children a different genetic hand. Even now, aged thirty, she still got asked for her ID at bars and restaurants. For most women this might have been flattering but for Desiree it was an ongoing humiliation.

When she was growing up, her parents would say things like 'Good things come in small packages' and 'People appreciate the little things in life'. These sentiments, however well-meaning, were hard to accept for an adolescent who still shopped for clothes in the kiddie section. At college, where she studied criminology, it had been painfully embarrassing. At the academy it had been mortifying. But Desiree had belied and defied her stature, topping her graduating class at Quantico, proving herself fitter, brighter and more determined than any of the other recruits. Her curse had been her motivation. Her size had made her reach higher.

Knocking on Eric Warner's door, she waits for his summons.

Grizzled and prematurely grey, Warner has been in charge of the Houston office ever since Desiree was posted to her home city six years ago. Of all the powerful men that she's met, he has genuine authority and charisma, along with a natural easy scowl that makes his smiles look ironically sad, or just sad. He doesn't make fun of Desiree's height or treat her differently on account of her gender. People listen to him, not because he shouts but because his whisper begs to be heard.

'The escapee at Three Rivers – it was Audie Palmer,' says Desiree.

'Who?'

'The armoured truck robbery in Dreyfus County. 2004.'

'The guy who should have ridden the needle?'

'That's him.'

'When was he due out?'

'Today.'

The two agents look at each other, thinking the same thing. What sort of moron escapes from prison the day before he's due to be released?

'He's one of mine,' says Desiree. 'I've been keeping an eye on the case since Palmer was transferred to Three Rivers for legal reasons.'

'What legal reasons?'

'The new US Attorney was unhappy with the length of the original sentence and wanted him retried.'

'After ten years!'

'Stranger things have happened.'

Warner rattles a pen between his teeth, holding it like a cigarette. 'Any sign of the money?'

'Nope.'

'Take a drive. See what the chief warden has to say.'

An hour later, Desiree is on the Southwest Freeway passing Wharton. The farmland is flat and green, the sky wide and blue. She's listening to her Spanish language tapes, repeating the phrases.

*¿Dónde puedo comprar agua?*

*¿Dónde está el baño?*

Her mind drifts to Audie Palmer. She inherited

his file from Frank Senogles, another field agent who had moved further up the food chain and was tossing his scraps to Desiree.

'This one is colder than a well digger's asshole,' he told her when he handed over his case notes, looking at her breasts instead of her face.

Cold cases were normally divided up between active agents with newbies getting the oldest and the coldest files. Periodically, Desiree checked for new information, but in the ten years since the robbery none of the stolen money had been recovered. Seven million dollars in used banknotes, unmarked and untraceable, had simply vanished. Nobody knew the serial numbers because the cash was being taken out of circulation and destroyed. It was old, soiled and torn, but still legal tender.

Audie Palmer had survived the robbery despite being shot in the head, and a fourth gang member – believed to be Palmer's older brother Carl – had got away with the money. Over the past decade there had been false alarms and unconfirmed sightings of Carl. Police in Tierra Colorado, Mexico, reportedly arrested him in 2007 but they released him before the FBI could get a warrant for his extradition. A year later an American tourist holidaying in the Philippines claimed that Carl Palmer was running a bar in Santa Maria, north of Manila. There were other sightings in Argentina and Panama – most of them anonymous tip-offs that led nowhere.

Desiree turns off the Spanish lesson and gazes

at the passing farmland. *What sort of idiot escapes the day before his release?* She had already considered the possibility that Audie might have fled to avoid a reception committee. Surely he could have waited one more day. Under the reoffending policy in Texas he could get another twenty-five years.

Desiree had been to Three Rivers FCI once before to interview Audie and to ask him about the money. It was two years ago and Audie hadn't struck her as being an idiot. He had an IQ of 136 and had studied engineering at college before dropping out. Getting shot in the head could have changed his personality, of course, but Audie had come across as polite, intelligent and almost apologetic. He called her ma'am and didn't comment on her height, or become annoyed when she accused him of lying.

'I don't remember much about that day,' Audie told her. 'Someone shot me in the head.'

'What *do* you remember?'

'Being shot in the head.'

She tried again. 'Where did you meet the gang?'

'In Houston.'

'How?'

'Through a distant cousin.'

'Does your cousin have a name?'

'He's *very* distant.'

'Who hired you for the job?'

'Verne Caine.'

'How did he contact you?'

'Telephone.'

'What was your job?'

'Driving.'

'What about your brother?'

'He wasn't there.'

'So who was the fourth member of the gang?'

Audie shrugged. He did the same when she mentioned the money, spreading his arms as though ready to be searched then and there.

There were more questions – an hour of them – taking them in circles and over hurdles and through hoops until the details of the robbery were a tangled mess.

'So let me get this straight,' said Desiree, not hiding her frustration. 'You only met the other members of the gang an hour before the robbery. You didn't know their names until afterwards and they all wore masks.'

Audie nodded.

'What was going to happen to the money?'

'We were going to meet up later and divide it up.'

'Where?'

'They didn't tell me.'

She sighed and tried a different approach. 'You're doing it tough in here, Audie. I know everybody wants a piece of you – the screws, the cons. Wouldn't it be easier if you just gave the money back?'

'I can't.'

'Doesn't it bother you that people are out there spending it all, while you're rotting away inside?'

48

'The money was never mine.'

'You must feel cheated. Angry.'

'Why?'

'Don't you begrudge them getting away?'

'Resentment is like swallowing a poison and waiting for the other person to die.'

'I'm sure you think that's very profound, but to me it sounds like bullshit,' she told him.

Audie smiled wryly. 'Have you ever been in love, Special Agent?'

'I'm not here to talk about . . .'

'I'm sorry. I didn't mean to embarrass you.'

Recalling the moment, she experiences the same emotion again. Blushing. Desiree couldn't remember ever meeting a man, let alone a prisoner, who was so self-assured or accepting of his fate. He didn't care if his stairs were steeper or if every door was closed. Even when she accused him of lying, he didn't get annoyed. Instead he apologised.

'Will you stop saying you're sorry.'

'Yes, ma'am, I'm sorry.'

Arriving at Three Rivers FCI, Desiree parks in the visitors' area and stares out of the windshield, her eyes travelling across the strip of grass to the double line of fences strung with razor wire. Beyond she can see guards in the towers and the main prison buildings. Zipping up her boots, she steps out of the car and straightens her jacket, preparing for the reception rigmarole – filling out forms, surrendering her weapon and handcuffs, having her bag searched.

A handful of women are waiting for visiting hours to begin – girls who ended up with the wrong guys, or the wrong criminals, the ones who got caught. Losers. Bunglers. Swindlers. Throwbacks. It's not easy to find a good criminal or a good man, thinks Desiree, who has decided that the best of them are usually gay, married or fictional (the men if not the criminals). Twenty minutes later she is ushered into the chief warden's office. She doesn't take a chair. Instead she lets the warden sit and watches him grow more and more uncomfortable as she moves around the room.

'How did Audie Palmer escape?'

'He scaled the perimeter fences using stolen sheets from the prison laundry and a makeshift grappling hook made from a washing-machine drum. A junior officer had let him into the laundry out of hours to collect something he left behind. The officer didn't notice that Palmer failed to return. We believe he hid in the laundry until the tower guards changed shift at 2300 hours.'

'What about the alarms?'

'One of them triggered just before eleven, but it looked like a fault with the circuit. We rebooted the system, which takes about two minutes. He must have used that window of time to go over the fences. The dogs tracked him as far as Choke Canyon Reservoir, but we think that was probably a ruse to throw us off the scent. Nobody has ever escaped across the lake before. Most likely Palmer had somebody waiting for him outside the fence.'

'Does he have any cash?'

The warden shifts in his chair, not enjoying this. 'It has been ascertained that Palmer had been withdrawing the maximum amount of $160 bi-weekly from his prisoner trust account, but spending virtually nothing at the commissary. We estimate he could have as much as twelve hundred dollars.'

Sixteen hours has passed since the escape. There have been no sightings.

'Were there any unfamiliar cars in the parking lot yesterday?'

'The police are checking the footage.'

'I need a list of everyone who has visited Palmer in the past decade along with any details of correspondence he may have had by mail or email. Did he have access to a computer?'

'He worked in the prison library.'

'Does it have an internet connection?'

'It's monitored.'

'By whom?'

'We have a librarian.'

'I want to talk to them. I also want to speak to Palmer's caseworker and the prison psychiatrist, as well as any member of staff who worked closely with him. What about other inmates – was he close to anyone in particular?'

'They've already been interviewed.'

'Not by me.'

The warden picks up the phone and calls his deputy, speaking like he has a pencil clenched between his teeth. Desiree can't hear the conversation, but the tone is clear. She's about as welcome as a skunk at a lawn party.

Warden Sparkes escorts Special Agent Furness to the prison library before taking his leave, saying he has calls to make. There is a foul taste in his mouth that he wants to wash away with a shot of bourbon. On better days than this one he drinks too much and has to draw the blinds and cancel meetings, claiming to have a migraine.

He pulls a bottle from the drawer of a filing cabinet and pours a shot into his coffee mug. He has been chief warden at Three Rivers for two years, having been promoted and transferred from a smaller low-security facility because he came in under budget with minimal reportable incidents. This gave a false impression of his skills. If men like these could be controlled, they wouldn't be locked up.

Warden Sparkes has never troubled himself with the debate about whether nurture or nature is primarily to blame for criminal behaviour and the degree of reoffending, but he does believe it's society's failure, not the correctional system. This sentiment doesn't fit with the times in Texas, a state that treats offenders like livestock and gets the dumb beasts it deserves.

Audie Palmer's prison file is open on his desk. No

history of narcotics or alcohol abuse. No penalties. No suspension of privileges. He was hospitalised a dozen times in his first year following altercations with other prisoners. Stabbed (twice). Slashed. Beaten. Strangled. Poisoned. Things settled after that, although periodically somebody would make an attempt on his life. A month ago a prisoner sprayed lighter fluid through the bars of Audie's cell and tried to set him ablaze.

Despite the attacks, Palmer had never sought to be isolated from the general prison population. He had not asked for special treatment or courted favours or tried to bend the rules to suit his circumstances. As with most prison files, there was little by way of background. Maybe Audie grew up in a shithole. Maybe his father was an alcoholic or his mother was a crack whore or he was unlucky enough to be born poor. There are no explanations or revelations or red flags, yet something about this case makes the warden itch in a place he can't politely scratch. It could have been the two unfamiliar cars he saw in the visitors' parking lot this morning, one of them a dark blue Cadillac, the other a pickup truck with a bull bar and spotlights. The man inside the Cadillac didn't bother coming to the visitors' gate but occasionally got out and stretched. Tall, thin and hatless, he was dressed in a tight-fitting black suit and heavy boots; and his face was a queer bloodless colour.

The second driver had arrived at 8 a.m. but hadn't made his way to the reception area until three hours later. Powerfully built, although thickening around the middle. His hair was neatly trimmed above prominent ears and he wore a sheriff's uniform that had sharp creases from a hot iron.

'I'm Sheriff Ryan Valdez of Dreyfus County,' he'd said, offering a hand that was cool and dry to the touch.

'You're a long way from home, Sheriff.'

'Yes, sir, I reckon I am. You've had a busy morning.'

'And it's still early. What can I do for you?'

'I'm here to help you look for Audie Palmer.'

'I appreciate your offer, but the FBI and local police have everything under control.'

'The Feds know shit!'

'Pardon?'

'You're dealing with a cold-blooded killer who should never have been allowed into a medium-security facility. He should have gone to the chair.'

'I don't sentence them, Sheriff, I just keep 'em locked up.'

'How's that going for you?'

Colour drained from the warden's cheeks and a throbbing red cloud of burning cinders drifted across his eyes. Ten seconds. Twenty. Thirty. He became conscious of blood thumping in his temples. He finally managed to speak. 'A prisoner escaped on my watch. I take responsibility for that. It's an exercise in humility. You should try it some time.'

Valdez opened his palms and apologised. 'I'm sorry we got off on the wrong foot. Audie Palmer is of special interest to the Dreyfus County Sheriff's Office. We arrested him and prosecuted him.'

'I accept that, but he's no longer your concern.'

'I believe he may try to return to Dreyfus County and hook up with his former criminal associates.'

'Based upon what evidence?'

'I'm not at liberty to share that information, but I can assure you that Audie Palmer is extremely dangerous and well connected. He owes the state seven million dollars.'

'It was federal money.'

'I believe you're splitting hairs with me, sir.'

Warden Sparkes studied the younger man carefully, noticing his lack of sleep and the acne scars that pocked his cheeks.

'Why are you really here, Sheriff?'

'I explained myself.'

'We only announced Audie Palmer was missing at seven o'clock this morning, by which time you'd already been parked outside for at least an hour. So I figure you either knew he was going to escape or you came here for some other reason.'

Valdez got to his feet and tucked his thumbs in his belt. 'Warden, do you have a problem with me?'

'You might make a better impression if you pulled your head out of your ass.'

'Four people died in that robbery. Palmer was responsible for their deaths whether he pulled the trigger or not.'

'That's your opinion.'

'No, that's a fact. I was there that day. I stepped over body parts and through pools of blood. I saw a woman burned alive in her car. I can still hear her screaming . . .'

Any pretence of camaraderie had vanished like a fish spitting a hook. The sheriff smiled without showing his teeth. 'I came here to offer my services because I know Palmer, but it seems you're not interested.'

He placed his hat on his head, adjusted the brim, and left, pushing the door instead of pulling the handle, muttering under his breath. The warden watched from the office window until he saw Valdez emerge from the front gate and cross the parking lot to the pickup truck. Why would a county sheriff drive two hundred miles to tell a chief warden how to do his job?

# CHAPTER 7

Moss has spent a sleepless night in The Hole, nursing his ego more than his bruises. He doesn't blame the guards for giving him a beating. By losing his temper, he gave them a reason. He 'enabled them', his shrink would say. Anger management has always been a problem for Moss. Whenever he's put under pressure or suffers from stress he feels as though a small bird is trapped inside his head, humming away, trying to get free. He wants to crush that bird. He wants the sound to stop.

The moments when he completely loses his temper are almost euphoric. All his hate, fear, anger and pride, his triumphs and failures, come together and his life seems to mean something. He's freed from a world of darkness and ignorance. He feels alive. Intoxicated. Untouchable. But now he understands how destructive this force can be. He's worked hard to control his temper and escape his past, to become a different man.

Rubbing his finger where his silver wedding band should be, he thinks about Crystal and what she'll say when she visits him next. They've been married twenty years (and he's been inside for fifteen of them) but some unions are written in the stars . . . or not. Crystal was seventeen when he met her at the San Antonio Rodeo. She was on the arm of a boy with buck teeth and a face like a pepperoni pizza, but she seemed to be looking for someone more interesting, although maybe not quite as interesting as Moss turned out to be.

Her mother had always warned her about boys like Moss, but that only made Crystal more curious. She was a virgin, Moss discovered. Once or twice she'd wanted a boy to fling her onto the bed and teach her what it was all about, but she kept hearing her mother's voice in her ear about lust being a deadly sin and teenage pregnancy a life-wrecker.

Moss had gone to the rodeo to check out the security and recce the gate takings, but gave up on the prospective job when he saw how many state cops were on duty. So he bought himself a corndog and shot a dozen metal ducks in the shooting gallery, winning a Pink Panther. Later he saw Crystal watching the rodeo parade. She was nowhere near as pretty as some girls he'd known, but there was something about her that heated his blood.

Her boyfriend had gone to get her a soft drink. Crystal floated off with Moss, laughing at his flattery and listening to the music. He wanted to show off. At the shooting gallery and coconut shy he won her a Daffy Duck, two helium balloons and a doll on a stick. They sat together to watch the rodeo. Moss knew what effect it would have on Crystal – seeing cowboys riding bulls and horses. In his opinion, more pregnancies could be blamed on rodeos than almost any other form of entertainment, except maybe for male stripper revues. Crystal was giddy with excitement and Moss knew that he had her. She would do anything for him. He would take her back to his place, or they would do it in the car, or even a quick knee-trembler behind the haunted house.

But he was wrong. Crystal kissed him on the cheek, ignoring his best lines, and gave him her phone number.

'You will call me tomorrow evening at seven o'clock. Not a minute before or a minute after.'

Then she walked away, swinging her hips like a metronome, and Moss knew he'd been played like a cheap ukulele, but in the same breath he realised that he didn't care. She was smart, sexy and spirited. What more could a man want?

A guard hammers on the door. Moss gets to his feet and faces the wall. They shackle him again and take him to the showers and then to the reception area – not the main visitors' block, but a small interview room normally used by attorneys visiting their clients.

The prison shrink, Miss Heller, is waiting outside the room. The inmates call her Miss Pritikin because she's the only woman in the prison who weighs less than two hundred pounds. Moss sits and waits for her to say something.

'Am I supposed to start?' he asks.

'You're not here to see me,' she replies.

'No?'

'The FBI wants to talk to us.'

'About what?'

'Audie Palmer.'

Miss Heller had always reminded Moss of a speech therapist who took him for elocution lessons when he started high school because he couldn't roll his 'r's or pronounce a 'th' sound. The therapist was in her twenties and would stick her fingers in his mouth, showing him where to put his tongue when he said particular words. One day Moss got an erection but the therapist didn't get angry. She gave him a shy smile and wiped her fingers with a paper towel.

A door opens and a caseworker leaves, nodding to Miss Heller, who is next in line. Moss waits, his legs splayed, eyes closed, head against the wall. Convicts are experts at killing time because they age in dog years. They can read the same magazines and books over and over; watch the same movies, have the same conversations and tell the same jokes, making months and years disappear.

He thinks about Audie and tries to picture him enjoying freedom, sleeping with a Hollywood starlet or tossing empty champagne bottles off the back of a yacht. Unlikely, he knows, but the mental images curl the corners of his lips.

After Audie survived his 'title fight', he began sitting with Moss at chow time. They rarely spoke until they'd finished eating, and then it was usually small talk and observations rather than ruminations on life. Audie was still a target because he was young and clean and the money preyed on men's minds. It was only a matter of time before somebody else tried to break him.

An inmate called Roy Finster, who called himself Wolverine on account of his lupine facial hair, bailed up Audie outside the shower block and began swinging punches. Moss leapt onto Roy's back and rode him to the ground like a lassoed steer before putting his knee across his neck.

'I need the money,' Roy said, wiping his eyes. 'My Lizzie is gonna lose the house if I don't do sumpin'.'

'What's that got to do with Audie?' asked Moss.

Roy pulled a letter from his shirt pocket. Moss gave it to Audie. Lizzie had written to say the bank was going to foreclose on the house in San Antonio and that she and the kids were moving back to Freeport to live with her folks.

'I won't get to see 'em if they move to Freeport,' sniffled Roy. 'She says she don't love me no more.'

'Do you still love her?' asked Audie, still breathing hard.

'What?'

'Do you still love Lizzie?'

'Yeah.'

'Do you ever tell her?'

61

Roy took umbrage. 'You saying I'm soft?'

'Maybe if you told her she might try harder to stay.'

'How do I do that?'

'Write her a letter.'

'I'm not real good with words.'

'I'll help you if you'd like.'

So Audie wrote a letter for Roy and it must have been something special, because Lizzie didn't take the kids to Freeport and she fought to keep the house and they all kept coming to visit Roy every other week.

A door opens and a guard kicks the back of Moss's chair, telling him to wake up. Climbing to his feet, Moss shuffles slowly into the room, hunching his shoulders so he appears smaller. Humbler. There is a teenage girl waiting in the interview room. Not a girl, a woman with short bobbed hair and studs in her ears. She flashes a badge.

'I'm Special Agent Desiree Furness. Should I call you Moss or Jeremiah?'

Moss doesn't answer. He can't get over her size.

'Is there something wrong?' she asks.

'Did someone put you in a tumble dryer 'cos I swear you been shrunk about five sizes?'

'No, this is my normal size.'

'But you're so itty-bitty.'

'You know the biggest problem with being short?'

Moss shakes his head.

'I have to look at assholes all day.'

He blinks at her. Grins. Sits. 'That's a good one.'

'I got loads of them.'

'Yeah?'

'Willy Wonka called and said he wants you to come home. Ding dong, didn't you hear the witch was dead? Weren't you in *The Lord of the Rings*? If you were Chinese, they'd call you Tai Nee . . .' Moss is rocking on his chair laughing. His manacles rattle. '. . . I'm so short I tread water in the kiddie pool. I need a ladder to get to the bottom bunk. I hit my head on the ground when I sneeze. I need a running start to reach the toilet. And no, I'm not related to Tom Cruise.' She stops. 'Are we done now?'

Moss wipes his eyes. 'I didn't mean no offence, ma'am.'

Desiree goes back to the folder, unmoved by his apology.

'What happened to your face?' she asks.

'Car accident.'

'You're a funny man.'

'It helps to keep a sense of humour in a place like this.'

'You were friends with Audie Palmer.'

Moss doesn't answer.

'Why?' she asks.

'Why what?'

'Why were you friends?'

It's an interesting question and not one Moss had ever really contemplated. Why are we friends with anyone? Shared interests. Similar backgrounds.

Chemistry. None of these things applied to him and Audie. They had nothing in common except for being in prison. The Special Agent is waiting for his answer.

'He refused to surrender.'

'What does that mean?'

'Some men rot in a place like this. They grow old and bitter, convincing themselves that society is to blame and they're just victims of shitty childhoods or unfortunate circumstances. Or they spend their time railing against God or searching for him. Some paint or write poetry or study the classics. Others pump iron or play handball or write letters to girls who loved them before they threw their lives away. Audie didn't do any of these things.'

'What did he do?'

'He endured.'

She still doesn't understand.

'Do you believe in God, Special Agent?'

'I was raised a Christian.'

'You think he has a grand plan for each of us?'

'I don't know about that.'

'My father didn't believe in God but he said there were six angels – Misery, Despair, Disappointment, Hopelessness, Cruelty and Death. "You'll meet every one of them eventually," he told me, "But hopefully not in pairs." Audie Palmer met his angels in pairs. He met them in threes. He met them every day.'

'You think he was unlucky?'

'That boy was lucky when he *didn't* get bad luck.'

Moss drops his head and runs his fingers over his scalp.

'Was Audie Palmer religious?' asks Desiree.

'I never heard him pray, but he did have deep philosophical discussions with the jail preacher.'

'What about?'

'Audie didn't believe he was unique or that he had some sort of destiny. And he didn't think Christians had a monopoly on morals. He used to say that some of them could talk the talk, but their walk was more John Wayne than Jesus. Know what I'm saying?'

'I think so.'

'That's what happens when you spend two thousand years lawyering the Bible, trying to justify bombing the shit out of people when the Book says you're supposed to be loving thy neighbour and turning the other cheek.'

'Why did he escape, Moss?'

'I honestly don't know, ma'am.'

Moss rubs his hands over his face, feeling the bruises and swelling. 'Places like this run on contraband and rumours. Every nigga will tell you a different story about Audie. They say he got shot fourteen times and lived.'

'Fourteen?'

'That's what I heard. I seen the scars on his skull. It must have been like putting Humpty Dumpty back together again.'

'What about the money?'

65

Moss smiles wryly. 'Folks say he bribed the judge to escape the chair. Now they'll be saying he bribed the guards to let him escape. Ask around – every nigga got a different story. Some say the money is long gone, or that Audie Palmer owns an island in the Caribbean; or he buried the cash in the East Texas oilfields, or his brother Carl is living the high life in California married to a movie star. Place like this is full of stories and nothing fires the blood like a fortune in untraceable bills.' He leans forward. The ankle chains rattle against the metal legs of his chair. 'You want to know what I think?'

Desiree nods.

'Audie Palmer don't care about the money. I don't think he cared about being in here. Other men counted the hours and the days, but Audie could stare into the distance like he was looking across an ocean, or watching sparks floating above a campfire. He could make a cell seem like it had no walls.' Moss hesitates. 'If it weren't for the dreams . . .'

'What dreams?'

'I used to lie on my rack listening, wondering if one night he might suddenly blurt out where he hid the money, but he never did. Instead I used to hear him sobbing. It sounded like a child lost in the corn, yelling for his mama. I used to wonder what made a grown man cry. I asked him, but he wouldn't talk about it. He wasn't ashamed of crying. He didn't fear the weakness it bespoke.'

The Special Agent looks at her notebook. 'The two of you worked in the library. What did Audie do there?'

'Studied. Read. Stacked shelves. He educated himself. He wrote letters. He prepared appeals for other people, but never himself.'

'Why?'

'I asked him that.'

'What did he say?'

'He said he was guilty.'

'You know he was due to be released yesterday?' she asks.

'I heard.'

'Why would he escape?'

'I've been thinking about that.'

'And?'

'You're asking the wrong question.'

'What should I be asking?'

'Most guys in here think they're tough, but they get reminded every day that they're not. Audie spent ten years trying to stay alive. Barely a week went by when guards didn't visit his cell and beat him like a redheaded stepchild, asking the same questions that you're asking. And during the day it was the Mexican Mafia, or the Texas Syndicate or the Aryan Brotherhood, or whatever stupid, craven punk wanted a piece of him.

'There are also people in here with particular compulsions that have nothing to do with greed or power. Maybe they saw something in Audie they wanted to destroy – his look of optimism or

67

sense of inner peace. Scum like that don't just want to hurt other men, they want to consume them, they want to rip open their chests and eat their hearts until the blood runs down their faces and their teeth are stained red.

'Whatever the motivation, there was a contract out on Audie from day one and it was doubled a month ago. That boy was stabbed, strangled, beaten, glassed and burned, but he never showed hatred or remorse or weakness.'

Moss looks up, holding her gaze.

'You want to know why he escaped, but that's the wrong question. You should be asking why he didn't do it sooner.'

# CHAPTER 8

udie doesn't catch the first available bus. Instead he wanders the streets of San Antonio growing accustomed to the blur of movement and the noise. The high-rise buildings are taller than he remembers. Skirts shorter. People fatter. Phones smaller. Colours duller. People don't make eye contact. They push past, hurrying somewhere: mothers with strollers, businessmen, office workers, shoppers, couriers, schoolchildren, delivery drivers, shop assistants and secretaries. Everybody seems to be trying to reach somewhere or to be running away from it.

He notices a billboard perched on top of an office block. Two images, side by side: the first shows a woman in a business suit, spectacles, hair tied up, working on a laptop computer. The second shows her in a bikini on a white sand beach, with water the colour of her eyes. Underneath are the words: *Lose Yourself in Antigua*.

Audie likes the look of the islands. He can picture himself on that beach, slowly going brown, rubbing suntan oil into some honey's shoulders, letting it dribble down her back into the nooks and crannies. How long had it been? Eleven years without a woman. One woman.

Each time Audie resolves to catch a bus, something distracts him and another hour passes. He buys a cap and sunglasses, along with a change of clothes, a pair of running shoes, a cheap watch, shorts and a hair trimmer. At a phone shop an assistant tries to sell him a sleek, rectangular prism of glass and plastic, talking about apps, data bundles and 4G.

'I just want one that calls people,' Audie says.

Along with the cell phone he buys four pre-paid SIM cards and stows his new purchases in the pockets of a small rucksack. Afterwards he sits in a bar opposite the Greyhound depot, watching people come and go. There are soldiers in uniform carrying kitbags, transferring in or out of one of the military bases dotted around this part of Texas. Some of them are chatting up the pavement princesses, who are hooking out of nearby motel rooms.

Studying his cell phone, Audie contemplates calling his mama. She'll know by now. The police will have visited. Maybe they're bugging her phone or watching the house. After his daddy died, she moved in with her sister Ava in Houston. It's where she grew up and couldn't wait to escape, but now she's right back where she started.

Audie's mind wanders. He remembers squeezing through the window of Wolfe's liquor store at age six to steal cigarettes and packets of gum. His brother Carl had lifted him up to the window and caught him when he jumped out. Carl was fourteen and Audie thought he was the coolest older brother a boy could have, even though he was rough sometimes and a lot of kids were scared of him. Carl had one of those rare smiles that you come across only a handful of times in life. In an instant it came across as reassuring and likeable, but the moment that smile vanished he became another person.

When Carl went to prison the first time, Audie wrote him letters every week. He didn't get many replies, but he knew Carl wasn't much of a reader or a writer. And later when people told stories about Carl, Audie tried not to believe them. He wanted to remember the brother he idolised, the one who took him to the state fair and bought him comic books.

They used to go fishing in the Trinity River, but they couldn't eat anything they caught because of the PCBs and other pollutants. Mostly they snagged shopping trolleys and dumped tyres while Carl smoked dope and told Audie stories about the bodies that were sunk in the murky depths.

'They weigh 'em down with concrete,' he said matter-of-factly. 'They're still down there, trapped in the mud.'

Carl also told stories about famous gangsters and murderers like Clyde Barrow and Bonnie Parker, who grew up less than a mile away from where Audie was born. Bonnie went to the Cement

City High School, which had been renamed by the time Audie sat in the classrooms, looking out on different factories but the same houses.

'Bonnie and Clyde spent barely two years together,' said Carl. 'But they lived every damn minute like it was their last. It was a love story.'

'I don't want to hear about the kissing,' said Audie.

'One day you will,' said Carl, laughing at him.

Leaning forward, talking softly, he recounted the final ambush as though telling a ghost story around a campfire. Audie could picture the misty predawn scene, the isolated road outside of Sailes, Louisiana, where police and Texas Rangers ambushed the couple on May 23, 1934, opening fire without warning. Bonnie Parker was only twenty-three. She was buried in Fishtrap Cemetery, not a hundred yards from where Audie and Carl grew up (although later they moved her body to Crown Hill Cemetery to be with her grandparents). Clyde was buried a mile away at Western Heights Cemetery, where people still visited his graveside.

Carl went to prison the first time for mail fraud and cash-machine scams, but drugs were his undoing. He developed a habit at the state penitentiary in Brownsville and never lost the taste. Audie was nineteen and at college when Carl got released. He drove to Brownsville to pick him up. Carl walked out wearing a green-striped shirt and a pair of polyester trousers and a leather overcoat that was too heavy for the weather.

'Aren't you hot in that?'

'I'd rather wear it than carry it,' he said.

Audie was still playing baseball and had been hitting the weight room.

'You look good, little bro.'

'So do you,' said Audie, but it wasn't true. Carl looked washed out, gaunt and angry; needing something that was out of reach. People said that Audie got the brains in the family – making it sound as though intelligence arrived by FedEx and you had to be home on the day or the package got returned. But it's got nothing to do with intelligence. It's about courage, experience, desire and a dozen other ingredients.

Audie drove Carl around the old neighbourhood, which was more prosperous than Carl remembered, but there were still strip malls, chain stores, derelict buildings, drug dens and girls hooking out of cars on Singleton Boulevard.

At a 7-Eleven, Carl stared at a couple of high-school girls who came in to get Slurpees. They were wearing cut-off denim shorts and tight T-shirts. They knew Audie. Smiled. Flirted. Carl made some comment and the girls stopped smiling. That's the moment Audie studied his brother and recognised something new in him: a sharp, almost fearful streak of self-loathing.

They bought a six-pack and sat beside the Trinity River, under the railway bridge. Trains rumbled over their heads, on their way to Union Station. Audie wanted to ask him about prison. What was it like? Were half the stories true? Carl asked him if he had any weed.

'You're on parole.'

'It helps me relax.'

They sat in silence, watching the brown currents swirl and eddy.

'You really think there are bodies down there?' asked Audie.

'I'm sure of it,' said Carl.

Audie told Carl about his scholarship to Rice University in Houston. They were paying his fees, but he had to cover his living expenses, which is why he was working double shifts at the bowling alley.

Carl liked to tease him about being 'the brainiac in the family', but Audie thought his brother was secretly proud.

'What are you going to do?' asked Audie.

Carl shrugged and crushed a beer can in his fist.

'Daddy says he can get you a job labouring on a construction site.'

Carl didn't reply.

When they finally drove home, the reunion was full of hugs and tears. Their mama kept grabbing Carl from behind like he was going to escape. Their daddy came home early from the garage, which he rarely did. He didn't say much, but Audie could tell he was happy to have Carl home again.

A month later, Audie started his second year at

college in Houston and didn't get back to Dallas until Christmas. By then Carl was squatting at a house in the Heights and doing various unspecified jobs. He'd broken up with his girlfriend and was riding a motorbike that he was 'minding for a friend'. He seemed on edge. Jumpy.

'Let's play poker,' he suggested to Audie.

'I'm trying to save money.'

'You could win some.'

Carl talked him into it, but kept changing the rules, saying it was how they played in prison, but all the changes seemed to favour Carl and Audie lost half the money he'd been saving for college. Carl went out and came back with beer. He also had some crystal meth and speed. He wanted to get blasted and couldn't understand why Audie chose to go home.

The following summer, Audie worked at the bowling alley and at the garage. Carl used to drop round, trying to borrow money. Their sister Bernadette had started dating a guy who worked for a bank downtown. He had a new car and nice clothes. Carl wasn't impressed.

'Who does he think he is?'

'He's not doing anything wrong,' said Audie.

'He thinks he's better than we are.'

'Why?'

'You can see it. He acts all superior.'

Carl didn't want to listen to anyone telling him that some people worked hard to live in a nice house, or drive a new car. He preferred to resent their success. It was like he was standing outside someone else's party with his nose pressed to the window, watching the swirling skirts and pretty girls dancing to the music. He didn't just watch with envy. His eyes were questioning. Indignant. Hungry.

Late in the summer Audie got a call about ten one evening. Carl was in a bar in East Dallas. His bike had broken down. He needed a ride home.

'I'm not coming to get you.'

'A guy mugged me. I don't have any money.'

Audie drove across town. Parked out front. The bar had a glowing Dixie Beer sign and wood floors covered in cigarette burns that looked like crushed cockroaches. There were bikers playing pool, hitting the cue ball so hard it sounded like a whip cracking. The only woman was in her forties, dressed like a teenager, drunk dancing in front of the jukebox while a dozen men watched.

'Stay for a drink,' said Carl.

'I thought you had no money.'

'I won some.' He pointed to the pool table. 'What do you want to drink?'

'Nothing.'

'Have a 7Up.'

'I'm going home.'

Audie started to leave. Carl followed him into the parking lot, angry at being shown up in front of his new friends. His pupils were dilated and he missed the door handle with his first two attempts. Audie drove home with the windows open in case

Carl got sick. They travelled in silence and Audie thought Carl had fallen asleep. But then he spoke, sounding like a lost child.

'Nobody is going to give me a second chance.'

'Give it time,' Audie told him.

'You don't know what it's like.' Carl sat up straighter. 'All I need is one big score. Then I'd be set. I could blow this place and start somewhere new with nobody prejudging me.'

Audie didn't understand.

'Help me rob a bank,' said Carl, making it sound obvious.

'What?'

'I can cut you in for twenty per cent. All you got to do is drive. You don't have to come in. Just stay in the car.'

Audie laughed. 'I'm not going to help you rob a bank.'

'You only have to drive.'

'If you want money, get a job.'

'That's easy for you to say.'

'What's that supposed to mean?'

'You're the blue-eyed boy, the favoured one. I wouldn't mind being the prodigal son – give me my share early and you won't see me for dust.'

'We don't have shares.'

''Cos you got it all.'

They went back to their folks' house. Carl slept in his old room. Audie woke up thirsty during the night and went looking for a glass of water. He found Carl in the kitchen, sitting in the darkness except for the refrigerator door that was propped open. His face was shining.

'What have you taken?'

'Just a little sumpin' to help me sleep.'

Audie rinsed out his glass and turned to leave.

'I'm sorry,' Carl said.

'What are you sorry about?'

He didn't answer.

'World hunger, global warming, evolution, what are you sorry for?'

'Being such a disappointment.'

Audie went back to Rice and topped nearly all of his classes that second year. He worked nights at a twenty-four-hour bakery and came to lectures with flour dusting his clothes. One particular girl, who looked like a cheerleader and walked like a catwalk model, gave him the nickname 'Doughboy', which seemed to stick.

When he came home that following Christmas he discovered his car was missing. Carl had borrowed it and hadn't bothered bringing it back. He wasn't living at home any more. He was at a motel off the Tom Landry Freeway, living with a girl who looked like a hooker and had a baby. Audie found him sitting by the pool, dressed in the same leather overcoat that he wore when he left Brownsville. His eyes were glazed and crumpled beer cans were scattered beneath his chair.

'I need the keys to my car.'

'I'll bring it around later.'

'No, I want it now.'

'It's out of gas.'

Audie didn't believe him. He got behind the wheel and turned the key. The engine died. He threw the keys back at Carl and caught the bus home. He picked up his baseball bat and went down to the cage and hit eighty pitches, taking out his frustration.

It was only later that Audie pieced together what happened that evening. After he left the motel, Carl had filled the tank with a can of gas and driven to a liquor store on Harry Hines Boulevard. He took a six-pack of beer from the refrigerator and picked up packets of corn chips and chewing gum. The attendant was an old Chinese man, wearing a uniform with a name on the badge that nobody could pronounce.

The only other person in the store was in the far aisle, crouching down, looking for a particular flavour of Doritos that his pregnant wife wanted. He was an off-duty police officer, Pete Arroyo, and his wife Debbie was waiting outside, eating an ice cream because she was craving something sweet as well as savoury.

Carl walked up to the attendant and pulled a .22 Browning automatic from his overcoat and held it against the old man's head, telling him to empty the cash register. There were lots of pleadings in Chinese that Carl didn't understand.

Pete Arroyo must have seen Carl in the disc-shaped mirrors angled above the aisles. Creeping closer, he reached behind his back and took out his pistol. He crouched, aimed and told Carl to put his hands in the air. That's when Debbie pushed open the heavy door, her baby bump sticking out like a jack-o'-lantern. She saw the gun. Screamed.

Pete didn't fire. Carl did. The officer fell and squeezed off one round, hitting Carl in the back as he climbed into the car and it drove away. Paramedics spent forty minutes working on Pete Arroyo, but he died before he reached the hospital. By then witnesses had given police a description of the shooter and said there could have been somebody with him, sitting behind the wheel.

# CHAPTER 9

The bus leaves for Houston at 7.30 p.m. Audie boards at the last possible moment and takes a seat near the emergency exit. He pretends to fall asleep, but watches the concourse through cracked eyelids, expecting to hear sirens and see a blaze of flashing lights.

'This taken?' asks a voice.

Audie doesn't answer. A fat man manoeuvres a suitcase into the overhead rack and dumps a bag of takeaway food on the tray table.

'Dave Myers,' he says, extending a big red-freckled hand. He's sixtyish with sloping shoulders and a roll of flesh instead of a jawline. 'You got a name?'

'Smith.'

Dave chuckles. 'Good as any.'

He eats noisily, sucking salt and sauce from his fingertips. Then he flicks on the overhead reading light and unfurls a newspaper, snapping the pages.

'I see they're gonna cut the border patrols again,' he says. 'How they gonna keep illegals out of this state? Give them an inch and they'll take the whole nine yards.'

Audie doesn't respond. Dave turns the page and grunts. 'We've forgotten how to fight a war in this country. Look at Iraq.' (He pronounces it Eye Rack.) 'If you ask me they should nuke the whole lot of them Muslim countries, know what I'm saying, but that ain't gonna happen with a black man in the White House, not with a middle name like Hussein.'

Audie turns his face to the window and looks at the darkened landscape, picking out the dotted lights of ranch houses and navigation beacons on the distant peaks.

'I know what I'm talking about,' says Dave. 'I fought in Nam. We should have nuked them slant-eyed gooks. Agent Orange was too good for them. Not the women. Those gook girls could be mighty fine. They might look twelve but they cum like flapping fish.'

Audie makes a noise. The man pauses. 'Am I bothering you?'

'Yeah.'

'Why's that?'

'My wife is Vietnamese.'

'No shit? I'm sorry, man, I didn't mean no disrespect.'

'Yes you did.'

'How was I to know?'

'You just insulted an entire race of people, an entire religion and women in general. You said you wanted to fuck 'em or nuke 'em, which makes you a racist and a scumbag.'

Dave's face grows red and his skin tightens as though stretched over a bigger skull. He stands and reaches for his suitcase. For a moment Audie thinks Dave could be looking for a gun, but he moves along the aisle, finding another seat, where he introduces himself to someone new and complains about the 'intolerant assholes' you meet on long-distance coaches.

After stopping at Seguin and Schulenburg, they reach Houston just before midnight. Despite the hour, the concourse is populated by random clusters of people, some sleeping on the floor and others lying across seats. There are buses marked for LA, New York, Chicago and places in between.

Audie goes to the restroom. He turns on the tap and splashes water on his face, scratching the stubble on his jawline. His beard is growing too slowly to give him a disguise and sunburned skin is starting to peel from his nose and forehead. When he was in prison he used to shave every morning because it filled five minutes of his day and showed that he still cared. Now he sees a man in the mirror instead of a boy: older, skinnier, hard in a way he never was.

A woman and young girl enter the restroom, both blonde and both dressed in jeans and canvas shoes. The woman is in her mid-twenties with her hair bunched on the back of her head in a high ponytail. She's wearing a Rolling Stones T-shirt that hangs on the points of her breasts. The little girl looks about six or seven, with a missing front tooth and a Barbie backpack looped over her shoulders.

'I'm sorry,' says the mother, 'they've closed the women's restroom for cleaning.'

Setting a bag of toiletries on the edge of the sink, she takes out toothbrushes and toothpaste. She wets paper towels, peels off her daughter's T-shirt and washes under her arms and behind her ears. Then she leans her over the sink and wets the girl's scalp with running water, using soap from the dispenser to wash her hair, telling her to keep her eyes closed.

She turns to Audie. 'What are you staring at?'

'Nothing.'

'Are you some kind of pervert?'

'No, ma'am.'

'Don't call me ma'am!'

'Sorry.'

Audie leaves hurriedly, wiping his wet hands on his jeans. In the street outside the bus station there are people smoking and loitering. Some are dealers. Some are pimps. Some are predators looking for runaways and strays; girls who can be sweet-talked; girls who can be shot up; girls who stop yelling when hands close over their throats. *Maybe I'm jaded*, thinks Audie, who doesn't usually look for the worst in people.

Circling the block, he finds a McDonald's, brightly lit and decorated in primary colours. He buys himself a meal and a coffee. A little while later he notices the mother and daughter from the restroom.

They're sitting in a booth making sandwiches from a loaf of bread and a jar of strawberry jelly.

Audie's enjoying the scene when the manager approaches them.

'You're not allowed to eat here unless you buy sumpin'.'

'We're not doing any harm,' the woman says.

'Y'all making a mess.'

Audie takes his tray and walks to the booth. 'Hurry up, girls, what did you decide you wanted?' He slides onto the bench seat opposite and looks at the manager. 'Is there a problem?'

'No, sir.'

'Good to know, maybe you could get us some extra napkins.'

The manager mumbles something and retreats. Audie cuts his hamburger into quarters and slides it across the table. The girl reaches for the food but gets a slap on the wrist from her mother. 'You don't take food from a stranger.' She looks at Audie accusingly. 'Are you following us?'

'No, ma'am.'

'Do I look like an old maid?'

'No.'

'Then don't call me ma'am! I'm younger 'n you are. And we don't need your charity.'

The girl lets out a squeak of disappointment. She looks at the burger and then at her mother.

'I know what you're doing. You're trying to win my trust so you can do terrible things to us.'

'You have a paranoid mind,' says Audie.

85

'I'm not a junkie or a prostitute.'

'I'm glad to hear that.' Audie sips his coffee. 'I'll go back over there if you want.'

She doesn't say anything. The bright neon lights show up the freckles on her nose and her eyes that are – what? – green or blue or something in between. The little girl has managed to sneak a quarter of the burger and is eating it behind her hand. She reaches out and takes a French fry.

'What's your name?' asks Audie.

'Thcarlett.'

'Did you get something for that tooth, Scarlett?'

She nods and holds up a Raggedy Anne doll, which looks pre-loved but much-loved.

'What do you call her?'

'Bethie.'

'That's a pretty name.

Scarlett covers her nose with her sleeve. 'You thmell.'

Audie laughs. 'I'm fixin' to have a shower real soon.' He holds out his hand. 'I'm Spencer.'

Scarlett looks at his outstretched palm and then at her mother. She reaches out. Her whole hand fits inside his fist.

'And who might you be?' Audie asks the mother.

'Cassie.'

She doesn't take his hand. Despite her prettiness, Audie can see a hard shell around Cassie like scar tissue covering an old wound. He can imagine her growing up in a poorer quarter, conning boys into buying her snow cones for a flash of her knickers, using her sexuality but never quite understanding the dangers of the game.

'And what are you ladies doing out so late?' he asks.

'None of your business,' says Cassie.

'We're thleeping in our car,' says Scarlett.

Her mother hushes her. Scarlet looks at the floor and hugs her doll.

'Do you know of any cheap motels nearby?' asks Audie.

'How cheap?'

'Cheap.'

'They're a cab-ride away.'

'Not a problem.' He slides out of the booth. 'Well I best be off. Nice meeting you.' He pauses. 'When was the last time you had a hot shower?'

Cassie glares at him. Audie holds up his hands. 'That came out the wrong way. I'm sorry. It's just that somebody stole my wallet on the bus and I'm going to have trouble getting a motel room without identification. I got plenty of cash, but no ID.'

'What's that got to do with me?'

'If you booked the room – I'd pay for it. I'll pay for two rooms. You and Scarlett can have one of them.'

'Why would you do that?'

'I need a bed and we both need a shower.'

'You could be a rapist or a serial killer.'

'I could be an escaped convict.'

'Right.'

Cassie focuses hard on his face as though trying to decide if she's about to make a stupid decision. 'I got a taser,' she says suddenly. 'You try anything funny and I'll zap you.'

'I don't doubt it.'

Her car is a beaten-up Honda CRV, parked in a vacant lot beneath a Coca-Cola sign. She rips a ticket from beneath the wiper blades and crumples it into a ball. Audie is carrying Scarlett in his arms with her head resting against his chest. Asleep. She feels so small and fragile that he's frightened she might break. He remembers the last time he carried a child – a little boy with eyes so brown they gave the word brown meaning.

Cassie leans into the car, shoving sleeping bags into corners and clothes into a suitcase, rearranging their possessions. Audie slides Scarlett onto the back seat and puts a pillow beneath her head. The engine turns over a couple of times before it fires. The starter motor is almost shot, thinks Audie, remembering the years he spent in the garage watching his daddy working. The chassis scrapes on the kerb as they reach the deserted street.

'How long you been living in your car?' he asks.

'A month,' says Cassie. 'We were staying with my sister until she kicked us out. She said I was flirting with her husband but he was the one doing the flirting. Couldn't keep his hands to himself. I swear there's not one decent guy in this freakin' city.'

'Scarlett's father?'

'Travis died in Afghanistan, but the army won't pay me a pension or recognise Scarlett because Travis and me weren't married. We was engaged, but that don't count. He got killed by an IED – you know what that is?'

'A roadside bomb.'

'Yeah. I didn't know when they told me. Amazing what you learn.' She scratches her nose with her wrist. 'His parents treat me like some sort of welfare witch who popped out a baby just to get a government handout.'

'What about your parents?'

'Don't have no momma. She died when I was twelve. Daddy kicked me out when I got pregnant. Didn't matter to him that me and Travis were gonna get married.'

She keeps talking, trying to overcome her nerves, telling Audie that she's a qualified beautician with 'a diploma and everything'. She holds up her nails. 'Look at these.' She's painted them to look like ladybugs.

They take an exit onto the North Freeway. Cassie sits high in her seat with both hands on the wheel. Audie can picture the person she expected to be – going off to college, spring break in Florida, wearing bikinis and drinking mojitos and roller-blading along the beachfront; getting a job, a husband, a house . . . Instead she's sleeping in a car and washing her kid's hair in a restroom sink. That's what happens to expectations, he thinks. One event or wrong decision can change everything. It could be the popping of a car tyre or stepping off a sidewalk at the wrong moment or driving past an IED. Audie doesn't hold to the view that a person makes his own luck. Nor does he even consider the notion of fairness, unless you're talking about a skin colour or someone's hair.

After about six miles, they take an exit onto Airport Drive and pull into the Star City Inn, where palm trees are standing sentry by the main doors and the parking lot glistens with broken glass. A handful of black guys in baggy jeans and hoodies are loitering outside one of the ground-floor rooms. They study Cassie like lions looking at a wounded wildebeest.

'I don't like this place,' she whispers to Audie.

'They won't bother you.'

'How do *you* know?' She makes a decision. 'We get one room. Twin beds. I'm not sleeping with you.'

'Understood.'

A single room on the first floor costs forty-five dollars. Audie puts Scarlett in one of the double beds, where she settles into sleep, sucking her thumb. Cassie carries a suitcase into the bathroom and fills the tub with hot water, sprinkling in washing powder.

'You should get some rest,' says Audie.

'I want these to be dry by the morning.'

Audie closes his eyes and dozes, listening to the gentle sloshing of water and clothes being wrung out. At some point Cassie crawls into bed next to her daughter and stares across the gap at Audie.

'Who are you?' she whispers.

'Nobody to fear, ma'am.'

# CHAPTER 10

The ballroom is crowded with a thousand guests – men in black tie and women in high heels and cocktail dresses with swooping necklines or exposed backs. These are professional couples, venture capitalists and bankers and accountants and businessmen and property developers and entrepreneurs and lobbyists, and they're here to meet Senator Edward Dowling, newly elected, grateful for their support, *their* man in the Texas upper house.

The Senator is working the room like a seasoned professional, with a firm handshake, a touch of the arm, a personal word for each and every guest. People seem to hold their breath around him, basking in his reflected glory, yet despite his gloss and obvious charm there is still something of the used car salesman about Dowling's interactions, as though his boundless self-confidence has been learned from self-help tapes and motivational books.

Ignoring the trays of champagne, Victor Pilkington has found himself an iced tea in a frosted glass. At six foot four, he can look over the sea of heads, making a note of which alliances are being formed or who's not talking to whom.

His wife Mina is somewhere in the crowd, wearing a flowing silk gown that plunges in elegant folds down to the small of her back and between her breasts. She's forty-eight but looks ten years younger, thanks to tennis three times a week and a plastic surgeon in California who refers to himself as the 'body sculptor'. Mina grew up in Angleton and played varsity tennis for the local high school before going to college, getting married, divorcing, trying again. Twenty years on, she still looks good, on the court and off, whether playing mixed doubles or flirting with younger men in the Magnolia Ballroom.

Pilkington suspects she's having an affair, but at least she's discreet. He tries to be the same. They sleep in separate rooms. Lead separate lives. But keep up appearances because it would be too expensive to do otherwise.

A man brushes by him. Pilkington raises his hand and grips the passing shoulder.

'How are things, Rolland?' he says, to Senator Dowling's chief of staff.

'I'm a bit busy right now, Mr Pilkington.'

'He knows I want to see him.'

'He does.'

'You said it was important?'

'I did.'

Rolland disappears into the crowd. Pilkington gets himself another drink and makes small talk with several acquaintances – never taking his eyes off the Senator. He doesn't much like politicians, although his family had produced a few. His great-grandfather, Augustus Pilkington, was a Congressman in the Coolidge administration. Back then the family owned half of Bellmore Parish, with interests in oil and shipping, until Pilkington's father managed to lose it all in the seventies oil crisis. The family fortune had taken six generations to build and six months to trash – such are the vagaries of capitalism.

Since then Victor had done his best to restore the family's name – buying back the farm, so to speak, acre by acre, block my block, brick by brick. But it hadn't been without personal cost. Some people succeed *because* of their parents and others in spite of them. Pilkington's father spent five years in prison and finished up cleaning hospital toilets. Victor despised the man's weakness, but appreciated his fecundity. If he hadn't impregnated a teenage shopgirl in 1955 when he raped her in the back of his vintage Daimler (specially shipped from England), Victor would never have been born.

It's strange how one family can celebrate its great-ness, tracing its genealogies back to the founding fathers of Texas, their political offices and compan-ies and dynastic marriages, while another family's principal achievement might simply be survival. It had taken bankruptcy and his father's imprison-ment for Victor to appreciate what an achievement it was to rise above the common people, but tonight, in this room, he still feels like a failure.

On the far side of the ballroom Senator Dowling is surrounded by well-wishers, sycophants and political fixers. Women like him, particularly the matriarchs. All the 'old money' families are here, including a young Bush who is telling college football stories. Everybody laughs. Anecdotes don't have to be funny when you're a junior Bush.

The doors to the kitchen open and four waiters emerge carrying a two-tier birthday cake with candles. The Dixieland band strikes up 'Happy Birthday' and the Senator presses his hand to his heart and bows to every corner of the ballroom. There are photographers waiting. Flashguns reflect from his polished teeth. His wife materialises beside him, dressed in a black diaphanous evening gown with a sapphire and diamond necklace. She kisses his cheek, leaving a lipstick imprint. That's the shot that will make the social pages of the *Houston Chronicle* on Sunday.

Three cheers. Applause. Somebody jokes about the number of candles. The Senator wisecracks back at him. Pilkington has already turned away and gone to the bar. He needs something stronger. Bourbon. Ice.

'How old is he?' asks a man leaning next to him, his bowtie unfurled and dangling down his chest.

'Forty-four. Youngest state senator in fifty years.'

'You don't seem that impressed.'

'He's a politician, he's bound to disappoint eventually.'

'Maybe he's going to be different.'

'I hope not.'

'Why's that?'

'That'd be like finding out there was no Santa Claus.'

Pilkington has had enough waiting around. Moving through the crowd, he reaches the Senator, interrupting him mid-anecdote. 'I'm sorry, Teddy, but you're wanted elsewhere.'

Dowling's face betrays his irritation. He excuses himself from the circle.

'I think you should be calling me Senator,' he tells Pilkington.

'Why?'

'It's what I am.'

'I've known you since you were jerking off over your momma's JC Penney catalogue, so it might take me a while to get used to calling you Senator.'

The two men push through a door and ride the service elevator down to the kitchens. Stainless steel pots are being scrubbed in the sinks and dessert plates are lined up on benches. They step outside. The air smells of recent rain and yellow slicks of moonlight reflect from the puddles. Traffic is backed up in both directions on Main Street.

Senator Dowling undoes his bowtie. He has fine, feminine hands that match his cheekbones and small mouth. His dark hair is trimmed neatly and wet-combed to create a part on the left side of his scalp. Pilkington takes out a cigar and runs his tongue over the end, but doesn't attempt to light it.

'Audie Palmer escaped from prison the night before last.'

The Senator tries not to react, but Pilkington recognises the tension in the younger man's shoulders.

'You said this was under control.'

'It is. Tracker dogs followed his trail to the Choke County Reservoir. It's three miles across. Most likely he drowned.'

'What about the media?'

'Nobody has picked up on the story.'

'What if they start asking questions?'

'They won't.'

'What if they do?'

'How many people did you prosecute as a district attorney? You did your job. That's all you need to say.'

'What if he's not dead?'

'He'll be recaptured and sent back to prison.'

'And until then?'

'We sit tight. Every lowlife in the state is going to be searching for Palmer. They're going to string him up and pull out his fingernails trying to find out what happened to the money.'

'He could still hurt us.'

'No, he's brain-damaged, remember? And you keep telling people that. Tell 'em Audie Palmer is a dangerous escaped convict who should have gone to the chair but the Feds fucked it up.' Pilkington clenches the cigar between his teeth, sucking on the chewed leaf. 'In the meantime, I want you to pull a few strings.'

'You said everything was under control.'

'This is extra insurance.'

# CHAPTER 11

Three guards drag Moss from his rack and make him kneel, half-naked, on the cold concrete floor. One of them swings a baton across Moss's back for no reason other than vindictiveness or spite or whatever sadistic streak seems to infect men who are put in charge of prisoners.

Dragged upright, Moss has a bundle of clothes thrust into his arms before being marched along the landing, through two doors and down the stairs. His cheap cotton boxer shorts are losing their elasticity and he has to hold them up with one hand. Why is he never wearing decent underwear when he gets invited out?

A guard tells him to get dressed. His wrists and ankles are cuffed and linked to a chain around his midriff. Without any explanation, he is taken down the ramp to where a prison bus is parked in the central courtyard. A handful of other inmates are already on board, segregated in cages. He's being transferred. It always happens this way – in the dead of night when there's less chance of trouble.

'Where we heading?' he asks another prisoner.

'Somewhere else.'

'I worked that much out.'

The door closes. Eight detainees are isolated in heavy-gauge metal cages, which have floor drains, security cameras and side seats. A US marshal is seated with his back to the driver's cabin, nursing a shotgun on his lap.

Moss calls out, 'Where we heading?'

No answer.

'I got my rights. You got to let my wife know.'

Silence.

The bus pulls out of the gates and heads south. The other detainees are dozing. Moss watches the road signs and tries to work out where he's being taken. Night transfers are usually interstate. Maybe that's his punishment. They're going to send him to some shithole prison in Montana, fifteen hundred miles from home. An hour later the bus pulls into the West Gaza Transfer Unit near Beeville. Everybody else is taken out except for Moss.

The bus leaves again. Moss is the only detainee. The US marshal has gone and the only other person on board is the driver, silhouetted behind a dirty plastic screen. They head northeast on US 59 for a couple of hours before reaching the outskirts of Houston and turning southeast. If they were transporting him out of state they'd have driven him to an airport. This doesn't smell right.

Just before dawn, the bus pulls off the four-lane and takes a number of turns before stopping in a deserted rest area. Peering through the steel mesh, Moss can make out the shadows of trees. There are no prison lights or guard towers or barbed-wire fences.

The uniformed driver walks down the centre aisle of the bus and stops outside the cage.

'On your feet.'

Moss turns and faces the window. He listens as the padlock is keyed and the bolt slides open. A hessian sack is pulled over his head. It smells of onions. Moss is pushed forward, nudged with a baton or the barrel of a gun. He tumbles down the stairs, landing on his hands and knees. Gravel digs into his palms. The air smells fresh and cool like a new day is about to begin.

'Stay here. Don't move.'

'What's gonna happen?'

'Shut up!'

He hears the footsteps fade, insect sounds, his own blood pumping in his ears. Hours seem to pass in the following minutes. Moss can make out vague shapes through the loose weave of the bag. Headlights swing across him. Two vehicles. They circle the bus and pull up at a distance.

Doors open and close. Two men walk on gravel. They are standing in front of him. Moss can make out their shapes. One of them is wearing a pair of polished black shoes. Formal wear. He's overweight but when he stands erect he gives the impression of a trimmer man. The guy with him is fitter, possibly younger, dressed in cowboy boots and brown trousers. Nobody seems in a hurry to talk.

'Are you gonna kill me?' asks Moss.

'I haven't decided,' says the older man.

'Do I get a say?'

'That depends.'

Moss hears the sound of a handgun being unholstered and the safety removed.

'You don't say a word unless I ask a direct question, is that clear?'

Moss doesn't answer.

'*That* was a direct question.'

'Oh, yeah, I'm clear.'

'Where's Audie Palmer?'

'I don't know.'

'That's a shame. I was hoping you might be somebody I could do business with.'

The pistol is placed at Moss's head, digging into the depression below his right ear.

'I can do business,' says Moss.

'Give up Audie Palmer.'

Moss hears the trigger edge back.

'I can't tell you sumpin' I don't know.'

'You're not in prison any more. You got no reason to hold your mud.'

'If I knew I'd tell you.'

'Maybe you're just being loyal.'

Moss shakes his head. He can see colours dancing in front of his eyes. Maybe this is what people mean when they talk about seeing the light, or having their lives flash before their eyes when they're about to die. Moss is disappointed. Where are the women, the parties and the good times? Why can't he picture them instead?

The younger man pivots and drives his fist into Moss's stomach. Deep and unexpected, the blow reaches a soft place right under his sternum. His mouth opens. Air out. None in. He might never breathe again. A boot swings into his back, pitching him forward, pressing his face into the leaf litter. Spittle drips down his chin.

'How long is your sentence?'

'All day.'

'Life, eh? How many years you done?'

'Fifteen.'

'Chances of parole?'

'I live in hope.'

The older man is squatting on his haunches beside Moss. His voice and diction are melodic and almost hypnotic. He's a southern gentleman. Old school.

'I am going to offer you a deal, Mr Webster. It's a good one. You could call it a once-in-a-lifetime deal because the alternative is watching a bullet come out of your eye socket.'

There is a long pause. The bag has bunched up and Moss can see a few inches of grass. A caterpillar is crawling towards his mouth.

'What's the deal?' asks Moss.

'I'm givin' you time to think about it.'

'But I don't know what it is.'

'Fifteen seconds.'

'You haven't told me . . .'

'Ten, nine, eight, seven, six, five—'

'I'll take it!'

'Good man.'

Moss is dragged to sitting. The smell of urine fills his nostrils and he can feel the sticky wetness soaking the crotch of his trousers.

'When we leave here, you're going count to a thousand before you take that sack off your head. You'll find a pickup truck parked over yonder. Keys are in the ignition. In the jockey box you'll find a thousand dollars, a cell phone and a driver's licence. That cell phone has a GPS tracking device. If you turn it off, or lose it, or if someone else answers that phone when it rings, the local police will inform the FBI of your escape from Darrington Prison Farm in Brazoria County. I will also send six men to your wife's home – yes, I know where she lives – and they will play house with her in a way that you have not been able to for the past fifteen years.'

Moss doesn't respond, but he can feel his fists clenching. The suited man has crouched down again. The cuffs of his trousers rise up to show pale hairless ankles above his black socks. Even without being able to see the man's eyes, Moss knows that they are fixed on him with all the intensity of a baseball catcher ready for anything that comes in fast or kicks out of the dust.

'In return for being granted your freedom, you are going to find Audie Palmer.'

'How?'

'By using your connections in the criminal underworld.'

Moss has to stop himself laughing. 'I been fifteen years inside.'

The comment draws a swift kick. Moss is growing tired of being hit.

'Is this about the money?' he asks, riding the pain.

'You can have it. We're only interested in Audie Palmer.'

'Why?'

'He was responsible for people dying. The only reason he escaped being prosecuted for murder was because he took a bullet to the head.'

'And if I find him, what happens?'

'You contact us. The number is programmed into that phone.'

'What happens to Audie?'

'That's not your concern, Mr Webster. You swung three times and struck out. Now you have a chance to step up to the plate and get back in the game. Find Audie Palmer and I will make sure your remaining sentence is commuted. You'll be a free man.'

'How do I know I can trust you?'

'Son, I just got you transferred out of a federal prison to a state prison farm that doesn't even know you're coming. Think of what else I can do. You fail to find Palmer and you'll serve the rest of your sorry life in the toughest, meanest penitentiary in Texas. Do you understand?'

The man leans closer and tosses the soggy end of an unlit cigar near Moss's face.

'You have only one choice, Mr Webster, and the sooner you realise that the easier it's going to be. Remember what I said about that cell phone. Lose it and you're a wanted man.'

# CHAPTER 12

Every time Audie closes his eyes he falls in love again. For a dozen years it has been this way – from the moment he first set eyes on Belita Ciera Vega and she slapped him hard across the face.

Belita had been carrying a jug of water from the kitchen along a baking cement path to fill the water trough in a birdcage that held two African grey parrots. The jug was heavy and water sloshed from side to side, spilling down the front of her thin cotton dress. She looked barely out of her teens, with long hair that was so dark it had a purple tint like satin under a black light; and it was plaited like a horse's tail, reaching down to the small of her back, where her dress was tied with a bow.

Audie hadn't expected to meet anyone coming around the side of the house and neither had Belita. The cement was hot and she hadn't worn her sandals. She danced from foot to foot, trying to stop her feet from burning. More water spilled until the front of her dress was plastered to her skin and her nipples stood out like dark acorns beneath the fabric.

'Let me help you,' said Audie.

'No, señor.'

'It looks heavy.'

'I am strong.'

She spoke Spanish and Audie knew enough to understand her. He pried the jug from her fingers and carried it to the birdcage. Belita folded her arms to cover her breasts. She stood in the shade, away from the hot cement. Waiting. Her eyes were brown with golden flecks like you sometimes see on a boy's marble.

Audie gazed across the gardens and the swimming pool to the dramatic cliffs. On a clearer day he could have seen the Pacific.

'That's some view,' he said, whistling quietly.

Belita looked up at the same moment that Audie turned. His eyes dropped from her face, to her throat and her breasts. She slapped him hard across the left cheek.

'I didn't mean *those*,' he said.

She gave him a pitying look and turned back to the house.

He tried again in broken Spanish. '*Lo siento, señorita. No quería mirar . . . um . . . ah . . . your . . .*' He didn't know the word for breasts. Was it *tetas* or *pechos*?

She did not answer. He did not exist. She walked away from him, her dark hair swinging aggressively from side to side. The screen door slammed shut. Audie waited outside, holding his trucker cap in his hands. He sensed that something had happened,

107

some kind of revelation, but he couldn't fathom the meaning. He glanced back along the concrete path where the damp patches had evaporated. There was nothing left to show of the incident beyond what survived in his memory.

When she reappeared she was wearing another dress, even more threadbare than the first one. She stood behind the screen door and spoke this time in broken English.

'Señor Urban he not home. You come back.'

'I'm here to pick up a package, a yellow envelope. *Sobre amarillo.*' Audie mimed the dimensions. 'He said it was in the study on the side table.'

She looked at him scornfully and disappeared again. Audie watched the fabric swaying as her hips moved. It was effortless, like water sliding down a sheet of glass.

She returned. He took the envelope from her.

'My name is Audie.'

She locked the screen door and turned away, disappearing into the dark cool of the house. Audie stood there dumbly. There was nothing left to see but he kept looking anyway.

According to the red numbers on the digital clock it is just after eight, but light has been leaking from the edges of the curtains for the past hour. Cassie and Scarlett are still asleep. Rising quietly, Audie goes to the bathroom. As he passes the small desk he notices the car keys on the veneered wood. The key chain has a pink rabbit's foot.

Pulling on his jeans and a sweatshirt, he lowers the lid of the toilet and sits to write a note on motel stationery.

*I've borrowed your car. I'll be back in a couple of hours. Please don't call the police.*

Outside he slips behind the wheel and takes a ramp onto Interstate 45, heading north out of Houston. The freeway is quiet on a Sunday morning and within half an hour he's clear of the city and taking exit 77 along Woodlands Parkway past golf courses, lakes and streets with rustic names like Timber Mill and Doe Run Drive and Glory Bower. He pictures the map in his mind – the one he committed to memory when he searched for the address using a computer at Three Rivers Prison.

Pulling into the empty parking lot of the Lamar Elementary School, Audie gets changed into shorts and laces his new running shoes. He starts off slowly, jogging along bike paths beneath oak, maple and chestnut trees. There are stop signs at each intersection and the houses are set back from the road, with watered lawns and flowerbeds. A newspaper boy rides past him on a bicycle pulling a trailer. He tosses each paper like a tomahawk, spinning it end over end, until it slaps onto porches or front paths. Audie had a newspaper route when he was in his teens, but he never delivered to a neighbourhood like this one.

Sunlight shines through the trees, creating dappled shade on the asphalt as he runs. He sees men on the golf course, fat as pharaohs, riding in gleaming white buggies. This is their enclave, white, clean, law-abiding – a semi-reclusive retreat full of trophy houses with flagpoles and porch swings and their backs permanently turned to their neighbours.

Audie pauses and props his leg on a fire hydrant, stretching his hamstrings. He sneaks a look at a two-story house with a gabled roof and sashayed porch on three sides. There is a teenage boy riding a skateboard on a square of concrete outside the garage's triple doors. Olive-skinned and dark-haired, the boy moves with an easy grace. He has made a ramp from a sheet of plywood and two breezeblocks. Kicking off on the skateboard, he puts in a couple of powerful strides before launching himself off the ramp, spinning the board with a flick of his feet and landing the jump.

The boy looks up, shielding his eyes from the glare, and Audie feels a breath catch in his throat. He should keep running, but now he's rooted to the spot. He bends until his forehead almost touches his shin. Behind him, a car pulls into the driveway, the tyres crunching over pecan husks. The boy flips the skateboard with his foot and catches it in his fist. He steps aside as the garage door opens and the car pulls inside. A woman emerges from the interior carrying a brown paper sack of groceries. She's wearing blue jeans, flats and a white blouse. She hands the groceries to the boy and walks down the driveway toward

Audie. For a moment he almost panics. She bends to pick up the newspaper and then spies him, noting the loops of sweat under his arms and the lock of hair stuck to his forehead.

'Nice morning for a run.'

'Yes it is.'

She brushes a blonde ringlet aside, showing her green eyes. Diamond studs glint in her earlobes.

'You live locally?'

'Just moved in.'

'I didn't think I'd seen you round here before. Where are you staying?'

'Riverbank Drive.'

'Oh, that's nice. Do you have kin?'

'My wife died a while back.'

'I'm sorry.'

She runs her tongue over her small white teeth. Audie looks across the ample lawn. The boy is doing pirouettes on the skateboard. He loses his balance and almost falls. Tries again.

'What made you move to the Woodlands?' she asks.

'I'm working on a company audit. Should only take a few months, but they found me a house. It's too big, but they're paying.' He can feel the sweat drying on his back. He motions to the house. 'Not as nice as this place.'

'You should join the country club. Do you play golf?'

'No.'

'Tennis?'

Audie shakes his head.

She smiles. 'That rather limits your choices.'

The boy calls to her, yelling something about being hungry. She glances over her shoulder and sighs. 'Max couldn't find milk in the fridge if it mooed at him.'

'Is that his name?'

'Yes.' She holds out her hand. 'I'm Sandy. My husband is the local sheriff. Welcome to the neighbourhood.'

# CHAPTER 13

Moss pats the pocket of his shirt, checking on the envelope of cash. Satisfied, he studies the laminated menu, swallowing the saliva that is pooling in his cheeks. He looks at the prices. When did a burger cost six bucks?

The waitress is dark-eyed and honey-skinned, wearing white shorts and a red blouse. She has the sort of preppy enthusiasm that must get her lots of tips.

'What can I get you?' she asks, holding a small black box instead of an order pad.

Moss rattles off his selections. 'Pancakes. Waffles. Bacon. Sausages. Eggs scrambled, poached, fried and what's that creamy sauce?'

'Hollandaise.'

'Yeah, some of that, along with hash browns, beans, biscuits and gravy.'

'Are you expecting company?'

'Nope.'

She looks at the order again. 'Are you sassing me?'

He looks at her nametag. 'No, Amber, I'm not.'

'You're gonna eat all that food?'

'Yes I am. I'm gonna waddle out of here carrying my stomach.'

Amber wrinkles her nose. 'Y'all want sumpin' to wash it down with?'

'Coffee and orange juice.' He pauses, thinking. 'Got any grapefruit?'

'Yeah.'

'I'll start with that.'

Amber goes to the kitchen and Moss picks up the cell phone. He marvels at how small it is. Cell phones used to be bricks carried around by spies and men in suits. Now they look like pieces of jewellery or cigarette lighters. He's seen them in movies and on TV – wheedling like petulant children – and how people tap on the front like they're sending messages in Morse code.

Who should he call? Crystal for starters, but he doesn't want to get her mixed up in this. It's been fifteen years since he held her properly. Ordinarily, they spoke through a Perspex screen, not even holding hands, spending an hour together before Crystal drove back to San Antonio where she works as a dental nurse.

What if they're listening to his calls, he wonders. Can they do that? Are they going to keep their bargain if he finds Audie Palmer? Probably not. They're going to grinfuck him either way – tell him one thing while doing the opposite, all the time smiling.

There might be another way out if he can find the money. Seven million bucks can buy a man a kingdom or an island or a new identity or a new life. It can buy him a ticket out of Hell if he knows the devil's travel agent.

He and Audie have been friends for a long time, but what does that mean when your life is at stake? In prison friendship is about survival and mutual benefit, not respect or loyalty. Why didn't Audie tell him he was going to escape? Moss had kept him alive. He had watched his back. He had got him a job in the prison library and arranged for them to have adjoining cells so they could play chess at night, writing each move on scraps of paper and casting them along the concrete floor. Audie should have told him. He was owed that much.

The cook emerges from the kitchen. He's a squat dark-skinned Mexican whose cheeks are so scarred with acne he looks like a chewed pencil. The waitress points out Moss. The cook nods, seemingly satisfied, and Amber brings Moss his coffee and orange juice.

'What was that about?' he asks.

'Boss wants you to pay up front.'

'Why?'

'He thinks you'll skip out before the check arrives.'

Moss takes the envelope out of his pocket, counting out three twenties.

'Let's see how far that gets me.'

Amber is looking at the envelope, her eyes wide. Moss gives her another ten. 'That's for you.'

She slips the money into her back pocket, her voice a little lower now, almost husky. Moss feels an ancient stirring. He's old enough to be her father, but a feeling's a feeling. There's nothing bitter or rancorous about this girl, no life taint, no tattoos or piercings, nothing faded or worn-out or tired. He can imagine her breezing through high school, popular with the boys, waving pompoms on the football field, doing cartwheels and flashing her knickers and her brightest smile. Now she's in college, working part-time, making her parents proud.

'You got a payphone?' he asks.

Amber glances at his cell but doesn't comment. 'Out back, between the restrooms.'

She gets him some loose change. Moss punches in the number. Listens to it ringing. Crystal picks up.

'Hey, babe, it's me,' he says.

*'Moss?'*

'The one and only.'

*'You don't normally call on a Sunday.'*

'You'll never guess where I am.'

*'Is this a trick question?'*

'I'm sitting in a diner about to have a fine breakfast.'

There are two beats of silence. *'Have you been drinking the Kool Aid?'*

'No, baby, I'm stone cold.'

*'Did you escape?'*

'Nope.'

*'What happened?'*

116

'They let me go.'

'Why?'

'It's a long story – I'll explain it when you get here.'

'Where are you?'

'Brazoria County.'

'Are you coming home?'

'Not until I finish a job.'

'What job?'

'I got to find a guy.'

'Who?'

'Audie Palmer.'

'He escaped! I seen it on the news.'

'They think I know where he is.'

'Do you?'

Moss laughs. 'Not a clue.'

Crystal doesn't see the funny side. 'Who are these people who asked you to find him?'

'My employers.'

'Do you trust them?'

'No.'

'Oh, Moss, what have you done?'

'Chillax, babe, I got things under control. I need to see you real bad. I got a hard-on so big it would make Dumbo jealous, know what I'm saying?'

'Now you're just being crude,' she scolds.

'I mean it, babe, I got a hard-on so big I don't have enough skin left to close my eyes.'

'Hush now.'

Moss gives her his cell phone number and tells her that he'll meet her in Dallas.

'*Why Dallas?*' she asks.

'It's where Audie Palmer's mama lives.'

'*I can't just drop everything and drive to Dallas.*'

'Have you been listening? I got a hard-on so big . . .'

'*Okay, okay.*'

# CHAPTER 14

On the day his brother Carl shot the off-duty police officer, Audie didn't get home until past dinnertime. He'd been hitting balls in the cage at the high school before walking to a friend's house to borrow a mower. He planned to make some extra money cutting lawns before he went back to college.

Pushing the mower along the broken pavement, Audie turned the corner into his street and crossed the road to get away from the Hendersons' dog, which bust a gut barking whenever anybody walked past the house. That's when he noticed the police cruisers and the flashing lights. Audie's battered Chevy was parked against the curb, the doors and trunk open.

Neighbours were standing outside their houses – the Prescotts and the Walkers and the Mason twins – people Audie knew, who were watching a tow truck winch the Chevy onto its back wheels.

Audie shouted at them to stop but saw a deputy crouch over the hood of the car, arms outstretched, holding his gun in a two-handed grip, one eye closed.

'HANDS IN THE AIR! NOW!'

Audie hesitated. A spotlight blinded him. He took his hands off the mower and grabbed two fistfuls of sky. More deputies scurried crablike from the shadows.

'GET ON THE GROUND.'

Audie knelt.

'ALL THE WAY DOWN.'

He lay on his stomach. Somebody sat on his back. Another braced their knee across his neck.

'You have the right to remain silent and refuse to answer any questions. Do you understand?'

Audie couldn't nod because they were kneeling on his neck.

'Anything you say may be used against you in court, do you understand?'

Audie tried to speak.

'If you cannot afford an attorney, one will be provided for you without cost.'

His hands were cuffed. They turned him over and checked his pockets. Took his money. They put him in the back of a cruiser. A sheriff got in beside him.

'Where's your brother?'

'Carl?'

'Got any other brothers?'

'No.'

'Where is he?'

'I don't know.'

They drove Audie to Jack Evans Police Headquarters in South Lamar Street and kept him waiting for two hours in an interview room. He asked for a drink of water and to use the restroom and to make a phone call, but nobody would listen. Finally a detective arrived and introduced himself as Tom Visconte. He had curly hair like a cop from a 1970s TV show, with sunglasses perched on top. He sat opposite Audie and closed his eyes. Minutes ticked by. Audie thought the detective might have fallen asleep, but then his eyes fluttered open and he mumbled, 'We want to take a sample of your DNA.'

'Why?'

'Are you refusing?'

'No.'

A second officer entered and took a swab from inside Audie's cheek, putting the budded stick into a glass test tube with a stopper.

'What am I being held for?'

'Accessory to murder.'

'What murder?'

'The one at Wolfe's liquor store this afternoon.'

Audie blinked at him.

'That's a good look. Might play well with the jury. Your car was seen leaving the liquor store.'

'I wasn't driving my car.'

'Who was?'

Audie hesitates.

'We know Carl was with you.'

'I didn't go to the liquor store. I was hitting balls at the cage.'

'If you were hitting balls, where's your bat?'

'At my buddy's house – I went to borrow his mower.'

'And that's your story?'

'It's the truth.'

'I don't believe it,' said Visconte. 'I don't think you believe it either, so I'm gonna give you a minute to remember.'

'Won't change anything.'

'Where's Carl?'

'You keep asking me that.'

'Why did he shoot Officer Arroyo?'

Audie shook his head. They kept going around in circles. The detective would tell Audie what happened as though they had the case sewn up tight with footage and eyewitnesses. Meanwhile, Audie would shake his head and say they were mistaken. Then he remembered bumping into a girl he went to school with. Ashleigh Knight. He helped her put air in her tyres at the gas station. She asked him about college. Ashleigh was working at Walmart and going to beauty school.

'What time was that?'

'About six o'clock.'

'I'll check that out,' said Visconte, not believing him. 'But let me tell you it looks bad for you, Audie. People go the chair for killing a cop, even as an accomplice. Jury isn't gonna differentiate between which one of you pulled the trigger – unless of course you're the one who cooperates with the police and gives up the other.'

Audie began feeling like a broken record. No

matter how many times he told the same story, they twisted his words and tried to trip him up. They told him Carl had been shot. He was bleeding. He could die without medical help. Audie could save him.

Thirty-six hours later, the questioning ended. By then Visconte had talked to Ashleigh and studied the footage from the gas station. Audie had no money. He walked home. His mother and father hadn't left the house for two days. There were reporters outside, littering the lawn with coffee cups and shoving microphones in people's faces.

Nothing was said around the supper table. Food was passed. Knives and forks scraped on plates. A clock ticked on the wall. Audie's father seemed to be diminished, like his skeleton was shrinking inside his skin. Bernadette drove from Houston when she heard the news. She had just finished her nurse's training and found a job in a big city hospital. The ranks of reporters had thinned by the fourth day. Nobody had heard from Carl.

That Sunday Audie arrived late for work at the bowling alley because he had to catch two buses and walk the last half a mile. The police hadn't returned his Chevy, which was still Exhibit A in the homicide.

Audie apologised for being late.

'You can go home,' said the owner.

'But I got a shift today.'

'I filled it.'

He opened the cash register and gave Audie twenty-two dollars in back pay. 'I'm gonna need that shirt back.'

'I don't have anything to change into.'

'Not my problem.'

The owner waited. Audie took off the shirt. He walked the seven miles home because the bus wouldn't take him without a shirt. On Singleton Boulevard, opposite Gary's Car Yard, a pickup truck pulled over. A girl was driving, Colleen Masters, one of Carl's druggy friends. Pretty, with bleached hair and too much mascara, she was fidgety and nervous.

'Get in.'

'I'm not wearing a shirt.'

'I'm not blind.'

He slid onto the passenger seat, self-conscious about his bare chest, which was winter-pale and splotchy. Colleen pulled into the traffic, glancing in her mirrors.

'Where are we going?'

'To see Carl.'

'Is he in the hospital?'

'Will you stop asking questions?'

They didn't talk again. She drove the rattling truck to a junkyard in Bedford Street beside the railway tracks. Audie noticed a brown paper bag on the seat. Bandages. Painkillers. Whisky.

'How bad is he?'

'See for your own self.'

She parked under a spreading oak and handed

Audie the bag. 'I'm not doing this any more. He's your brother, not mine.'

She threw Audie the truck keys and walked away. Audie found Carl in the office, curled up on a bunk bed, blood leaking through the bandages. The smell made his stomach heave.

Carl opened a bloodshot eye. 'Yo, little bro', did you bring me sumpin' to drink?'

Audie put the bag down. He poured whisky into a cup and held it to Carl's lips. His skin had a sickly yellow sheen that seemed to cling to Audie's fingertips.

'I'm going to call an ambulance.'

'No,' Carl sighed. 'Don't do that.'

'You're dying.'

'I'll be fine.'

Audie looked around the shed. 'What is this place?'

'Used to be a junkyard. Now it's a just a yard full of junk.'

'How did you know about it?'

'Buddy of mine used to work here. He always hid the keys in the same place.'

Carl began coughing. His whole body heaved and collapsed. He grimaced and showed blood on his teeth.

'You got to let me get help.'

'I said, no.'

'I'm not going to watch you bleed to death.'

Carl pulled a pistol from beneath his pillow and pointed it at Audie's head. 'And I'm not going back to prison.'

'You won't shoot me.'

'You sure about that?'

Audie sat down again. His knees were touching the edge of the bunk. Carl reached for the bottle of whisky and looked in the brown paper bag.

'Where's my stuff?'

'What stuff?'

'Traitorous bitch! She promised. Let me give you some advice, little bro, never trust a junkie.'

Carl's hands were shaking and sweat prickling on his forehead. He closed his eyes and tears squeezed from the delta-like wrinkles.

'Please let me call an ambulance,' said Audie.

'You want to make the pain go away?'

'Sure.'

'I can tell you what to buy.'

'I'm not buying you drugs.'

'Why? You got money. What about that cash you been saving? You could gimme that.'

'No.'

'My need is greater.'

Audie shook his head. Carl sighed and took a rattling breath. For a long while nothing was said. Audie watched a fly crawling across the fetid bandage, feeding on the pus and dried blood.

Carl spoke. 'Remember when we used to go fishing at Lake Conroe?'

'Yeah.'

'We stayed at that wood cabin near Wildwood Shores. It weren't much to look at, but you could catch fish right from the dock. Remember that time you caught that 15lb bass? Man, I thought that fish was gonna pull you right out of boat. I had to keep hold of your belt.'

'You were yelling at me to keep the line tense.'

'I didn't want you to lose it.'

'I thought you were angry with me.'

'Why?'

'It should have been your fish. You gave me your rod to hold while you got Daddy a beer from the cooler. That's when it bit.'

'I wasn't angry. I was proud of you. That was a state junior record. They wrote you up in the newspaper and everything.' He smiles, or it could be a grimace. 'Man, they were great days. The water was so clear. Not like the Trinity River, which is only fit for bodies and garfish.' He took a rattling breath. 'I want to go there.'

'Lake Conroe?'

'No, the river, I want to see it.'

'I'm not taking you anywhere except a hospital.'

'Take me to the river and I promise, after that, you can do whatever you like.'

'How am I supposed to get you there?'

'We got the truck.'

Audie looked out the window at the railway yard and the rusting freight cars that hadn't rolled in twenty years. The tattered curtains were billowing like apparitions. What was he supposed to do?

'I'll take you to the river but then we're going to the hospital.'

★  ★  ★

127

Audie's mind drifts back to the present. He's standing beneath the drooping branches of a willow tree, secretly watching the same house and wondering about the boy. She said his name was Max. He looked about fifteen, fine-boned with a wedge-shaped face and wide-set brown eyes. Eighth grade. What do fifteen-year-old boys like? Girls. Action movies. Popcorn. Heroes. Computer games.

It's midday Sunday and the shadows are bunched beneath the trees as if avoiding the hottest part of the day. Max leaves the house and kicks along the pavement riding his skateboard, jumping the cracks and weaving around a woman walking her dog. Crossing Woodlands Parkway, he heads north to Market Street and The Mews where he buys a can of soda and sits in bright sunshine on a bench in Central Park, rocking the skateboard beneath his sneakers.

Looking over a shoulder, both ways, he puts a cigarette to his lips and cups his hands around a lit match before waving the matchstick in the smoky air. Audie follows his gaze to a girl working on the window display in one of the shops. She's putting a dress on a mannequin, pulling it over the bald plastic head and shoulders and hourglass curves. The window dresser is about Max's age, maybe a little older. When she bends her skirt rides up and he can see almost to her panties. Max picks up the skateboard and puts it on his lap.

'You're too young to be smoking,' says Audie.

'I'm eighteen,' says Max, spinning around, trying to drop his voice an octave.

'You're fifteen.' Audie takes a seat and opens a carton of chocolate milk.

'How do you know?'

'I just do.'

Max stubs out the cigarette and looks hard at Audie, trying to work out whether he's someone who might know his parents.

Audie holds out his hand and introduces himself, using his real name. Max stares at the outstretched palm. 'You were talking to my mom this morning.'

'That's right.'

'Are you gonna tell her I smoke?'

'No.'

'Why are you sitting here?'

'I'm resting my legs.'

Max goes back to looking at the shop window where the girl is putting a chunky necklace on the mannequin. She turns and looks out the window. Waves. Max waves back self-consciously.

'Who is she?'

'A girl from school.'

'What's her name?'

'Sophia.'

'Is she your girlfriend?'

'No!'

'But you like her?'

'I never said that.'

'She's pretty. Ever talked to her?'

129

'We hang out.'

'What does that mean?'

'We're in the same group – sort of.'

Audie nods and takes another swig of chocolate milk.

'When I was about your age, I liked this one girl, Phoebe Carter. I was always too scared to ask her out. I thought she just wanted to be friends.'

'What happened?'

'I took her to see *Jurassic Park*.'

'Everybody's seen that.'

'Well, it was new back then and pretty scary. And when Phoebe got scared, she jumped into my lap. I don't remember anything else about that film.'

'That's lame.'

'I bet if Phoebe Carter jumped in your lap you wouldn't think it was lame.'

'I bet I would 'cos Phoebe Carter must be old by now.'

Audie laughs and so does Max.

'Maybe you should ask Sophia to see a movie.'

'She's got a boyfriend.'

'So what? You got nothing to lose. I met a woman this one time and she had a really bad boyfriend. I tried to get her to leave him but she didn't think she needed rescuing, but she did.'

'What was so bad about him?'

'He was a gangster and she was a slave.'

'There ain't no slaves any more. They were emancipated in 1865.'

'Oh, that was just one type of slavery,' says Audie. 'There are plenty more.'

'So what happened?'

'I had to steal her away from him.'

'Was he dangerous?'

'Yeah.'

'Did he come looking for you?'

'Yes and no.'

'What's that mean?'

'I'll tell you the story one day.'

A uniformed cop is watching them from fifty yards away. He's eating a sandwich. Finishing the last mouthful, he wanders over to the bench, brushing crumbs off his shirt.

Max looks up. 'Hi, Deputy Gerard.'

'Where's your old man?'

'Working today.'

The deputy looks at Audie with curiosity. 'Who's this?'

'Max and me are just shooting the breeze,' says Audie.

'You live in the area?'

'I just moved in around the corner from Max. Met his mother this morning.'

'Sandy.'

'She seemed very friendly.'

The deputy agrees and tosses his sandwich wrapping in the bin. He touches the edge of his hat with his finger as a final salute. Audie and the boy watch him leave.

'How did you know my name?' asks Max.

'Your mother told me,' says Audie.

'And why do you keep staring at me?'

'You remind me of someone.'

The teenager looks back at the shop window. Sophia has gone.

'Remember what I said,' says Audie, getting to his feet.

'About what?'

'Asking her out.'

'Yeah, right,' says Max sarcastically.

'In the meantime – do me a favour and quit smoking. It's not good for your asthma.'

'How do you know I have asthma?'

'I just do.'

# CHAPTER 15

Cassie punches Audie hard in the stomach.
'You stole my car!'
'I borrowed it,' he gasps.
'Don't bullshit me, mister. It's not borrowing if you don't ask first.'
'You were asleep.'
'Let's see how that holds up in court. Do I look stupid to you?' Cassie flexes her hand. 'Christ, that hurt! What are you made of, cement? Where did you go?'
'I had to get my credit cards replaced.'
'It's Sunday. Banks don't open.'
'I had people to see.'
'Who?'
'My sister lives in Houston.'
'Your sister?'
'Yeah.'
'Why aren't you staying with her?'
'I haven't seen her in a while.'
Cassie isn't buying any of this. She holds up the taser. 'You want a dose of this?'
Whatever softness Audie had once seen in Cassie has disappeared beneath a shell of anger and

resentment, her natural defences. Turning away, she drags her suitcase onto the bed where Scarlett is lying on her stomach watching the Disney channel.

'Come on, we're leaving.'

'But I like it here,' says Scarlett.

'Do as you're told!'

Cassie is collecting damp washing from the bathroom, shoving the clothes into a suitcase.

'I'm really sorry about the car,' says Audie. 'It won't happen again.'

'Damn straight.'

'Let me take you to dinner – we'll go somewhere nice.'

Scarlett looks at her mother expectantly.

'Did you use all my gas?' Cassie asks.

'I filled up the tank.'

'OK. Dinner and then we're leaving.'

Cassie chooses the restaurant. They drive to a Denny's where the laminated menu has pictures of all the dishes. 'I like seeing what I'm gonna eat,' she explains, ordering a steak and jacket potato. Scarlett has spaghetti and meatballs and between each mouthful she colours in a drawing using a box of broken crayons. When they've finished eating and the plates are cleared and dessert is under discussion, Cassie seems to have mellowed.

'What would you do if you had a million dollars?' she asks Audie, as though this had been their ongoing conversation.

'I'd buy my mother a new kidney.'

'What's wrong with her old one?'

'It doesn't work so good.'

'How much would it cost to buy a new kidney?'

'I'm not sure.'

'But you'd have some money left over, right? It wouldn't cost a million – not just for one kidney?'

Audie agrees and asks what Cassie would do with a million dollars.

'I'd buy a house and some nice clothes and a new car. I'd open up my own salon – maybe a whole string of 'em.'

'Would you go and visit your daddy?'

'Only to rub his face in it.'

'People say a lot of things they don't mean in the heat of the moment.'

Cassie falls silent, running her finger through a ring of condensation on the table. 'Who is she?'

'Pardon?'

'Last night when you were sleeping, you kept saying a woman's name.'

Audie shrugs.

'Must be someone. Your girlfriend?'

'No.'

'Wife?'

Audie changes the subject and talks to Scarlett about her drawing, helping her choose the colours. After he pays the bill they wander through the night stalls, picking up trinkets and putting them down again.

Back at the motel he goes to the bathroom, locks the door and studies his reflection in the mirror.

135

He takes the hair trimmer from his bag and runs it back and forth across his scalp like he's mowing a miniature lawn. Dark locks float into the sink. Afterwards, he stands under the shower, spreading his arms and turning his face to the spray. When he emerges he looks like he's joined the army.

'Why'd you cut your hair?' asks Scarlett.

'I wanted a change.'

'Can I feel?'

She stands on the bed and runs the palm of her hand over the short spikes, giggling. She stops suddenly. 'What are thosth?'

She's seen the scars. They're more visible now that his hair is cut so short. Cassie crosses the room and grabs Audie's head in both hands, turning it towards the lamp. It's as though his skull was shattered and glued back together like a busted vase. There are more scars on his forearms, flattened grey worms that wrap around his muscles. Defence wounds. Prison souvenirs.

'Who did that to you?'

'I didn't get his number.'

Cassie pushes him away and goes to the bathroom. She runs a bath for Scarlett and doesn't come back until the girl is playing in the tub. Sitting on the opposite bed, she holds her hands in her lap, staring at Audie, who has put on a long-sleeve shirt to hide his forearms.

'What's going on here?'

Audie looks up at her, trying to understand the question.

'You wear those dark glasses and the baseball cap and every time you pass a camera you lower your head. Now you've cut your hair. Are you a fugitive?'

Audie exhales, almost relieved. 'Some folks are looking for me.'

'Are they drug dealers, gangsters, repo men, police?'

'It's a long story.'

'Did you hurt anyone?'

'No.'

'Did you break one of the Ten Commandments?'

'No.'

Cassie sighs and puts one foot on top of the other as a little girl might. Her hair is so fair that her darker eyebrows look stark and painted on, rising and falling as she talks.

'It's bad enough that you lied to me and stole my car . . .'

'I'm not a criminal.'

'You act like one.'

'It's not the same thing.'

Wrapped in a towel, Scarlett appears in the doorway of the bathroom. Steam has flattened her curls.

'I don't want to thleep in the car, Mommy. Can't we thtay here?'

Cassie hesitates and pulls her daughter closer, hugging her with her legs and arms as though clinging to a tree in a flooded river. She glances at Audie over the girl's bare shoulder.

'One more night.'

137

# CHAPTER 16

Ryan Valdez doesn't usually drive the cruiser home. He prefers taking the pickup because it's less conspicuous, albeit downmarket for The Woodlands where most of his neighbours are driving BMWs or Mercedes or luxury SUVs.

Sandy says he looks like a redneck when he drives the pickup.

'Maybe I *am* a redneck.'

'Don't say that.'

'Why not?'

'Because you'll never fit in.'

Fitting in is important to Sandy, and Valdez sometimes feels that his wife is more embarrassed by his uniform than the car he drives. It's not that their neighbours don't respect the police and feel they perform a vital function, but that doesn't mean they want to socialise with a county sheriff. It is one degree too close – like dining with your proctologist.

Valdez had taken almost a year to get membership of the country club, and that was only after his uncle, Victor Pilkington, pulled some strings. Before then, Ryan and Sandy had hosted barbecues and wine appreciation nights and Sandy had started a book club, but it didn't open doors or lead to invitations. Living in Woodlands was like being back in high school, but instead of nerds, jocks, band geeks and cheerleaders, now there were socialites, empty-nesters, country clubbers, Republicans (patriots) and Democrats (socialists). Valdez didn't know where he fitted in.

Pulling into the drive, he waits for the garage doors to open and glances at the glorious erection of shingles and brick that cost him more a million dollars. The tall arched windows are reflecting the afternoon sun and shadows spill across the lawn like pools of oil.

Walking through the house, he calls out and thinks nobody's home. He gets a beer from the icebox and steps onto the patio. That's when he notices the boy doing laps, crawling down the pool with an easy stroke. Max turns onto his back and stares skywards as he backstrokes, water rolling off his shoulders. When he reaches the far end, he stops. Stands.

'Hi.'

Max doesn't answer.

'Where's your mom?'

He shrugs.

Valdez tries to think of another question. When did talking to Max become so difficult? The teenager pulls himself out of the water and wraps a towel around his midriff, tying it like a sarong. The late sun is casting a yellow glow across the

139

lawn. Max takes a seat on a lounger and sips on a luridly coloured can.

'Did she mention dinner?' asks Valdez.

'Nope.'

'I'll sort something.'

'I'm going out.'

'Where?'

'Toby's. We're doing a biology project.'

'Why can't Toby come here?'

'He's got the stuff.'

'Do I even know Toby?'

'I don't know, Dad. Do you know Toby? I'll have to ask him.'

'Don't talk to me like that.'

'Like what?'

'You know what I mean.'

Max shrugs as though he doesn't have a clue. Something snaps inside Valdez and he grabs a fistful of the boy's hair, wrenching him upright. His vision has narrowed and he seems to be looking at the world through a stained-glass window.

'You think you can talk to me like that. I put a roof over your head. I put food in your stomach. I pay for that phone you carry and the clothes you wear and that computer in your room. You treat me with respect or I'll drown you in that fucking pool. Do you understand me?'

Max nods, holding back his tears.

Valdez pushes him away, immediately embarrassed and wanting to apologise, but the teenager is already walking to the cabana where he closes the door and he turns on the shower. Cursing himself, Valdez hurls his can of beer halfway across the lawn, where it bounces and foams at the mouth. The boy goaded him. He had no goddamn right! Now he's going to tell his mother and cause even more problems. She'll take Max's side like she always does. If only the kid would just ease up. Show some more respect. There's no common ground any more. They don't watch Rangers games together or play Xbox or tease Sandy about her cooking.

An earlier image of Max is summoned from his memories – a little boy dressed in a cowboy hat, holding the sheriff's hand. They were best friends. They were father and son. They were partners in crime. They were close. His anger drains away. It's not Max's fault. He's fifteen. It's what teenagers do – rebel against their parents, test the boundaries. Valdez had a fractious relationship with his own father when he was about the same age, and his old man didn't brook any backchat or smartass comments.

According to Sandy it's a stage kids go through. Hormones. Adolescence. Peer pressure. Girls. Why doesn't Max just masturbate four times a day like every other teenage boy? Better still, Valdez could take him to a brothel – one of the cleaner places – and put the kid out of his misery. Sandy was always saying he should do more father–son stuff. He smiles to himself. She'd throw a fit if he got Max laid.

He hears a sliding door open and turns. Sandy steps onto the patio and puts her arms around him. Her hair is tousled and she smells of something sexy and sweaty.

'Where you been?' he asks.

'At the gym.'

Somewhere above them he hears a hawk cry out, or possibly an osprey. He raises his chin and shields his eyes, but can only make out the silhouette.

'I tried to call you today. You didn't have your cell turned on,' he says.

'I put it down last night and couldn't find it.'

Max emerges from the cabana and crosses the lawn. He kisses Sandy on the cheek. She rearranges his wet hair. How was school? Any homework? Toby's? No problem. Don't be home late.

Later Valdez sits at the kitchen bench and watches Sandy prepare a meal. Her hair is cut short, curled at the ends, blonde, and her blue-green eyes have a mysterious quality that causes men to stare at her longer than they should. How did he ever convince her to marry him? He hopes it was love. He hopes it still is.

'I thought I might take Max away camping next weekend.'

'You know he's not a big fan of the outdoors.'

'Remember that holiday we took to Yosemite? Max must have been about seven. He loved that trip.'

Sandy kisses the top of his head. 'You have to stop trying so hard.'

Valdez looks out the patio doors to where two ducks have landed in the pool. He doesn't *want* to stop trying. If he could just reset the clock and go back to when Max was happy to kick a ball or play catch . . .

'Give him time,' says Sandy. 'He doesn't like who he is right now.'

'Who do *you* think he is?'

'He's our son.'

When the meal is finished they sit side-by-side in the porch swing. Sandy holds one brown knee in the crook of her arm and paints her toenails with a tiny brush held between her thumb and forefinger.

'How was work?' she asks.

'Quiet.'

'You gonna tell me about why you went all the way to Live Oak County?'

'I was checking up on someone.'

'Who?'

'A prisoner was due to be released. He escaped a day early.'

'Why would he do that?'

'That's not the important thing.'

Sandy puts her leg down. Turns to face him, waiting for an explanation.

'Remember the armoured truck robbery – the guy who survived?'

'The one you shot?'

'Yeah. I tried to keep him locked up but the

parole board decided to set him loose. If he hadn't escaped, he would have been out anyway. I went up to the prison to talk to the chief warden, but Palmer had gone over the wire.'

Sandy sits up straighter, her eyes narrowing. 'Is he dangerous?'

'He's probably in Mexico by now.'

Valdez gives her a squeeze and she sinks back against him, holding his forearm between her breasts and resting her head on his shoulder. He's going to let the matter rest, but reaches for his phone and scrolls through the images.

'That's what Palmer looks like,' he says, showing Sandy a recent photograph.

Her eyes widen. 'I saw him!'

'What?'

'Today. Outside the house,' she stammers. 'He was jogging. He said he just moved in around the corner. I thought it must be the Whitakers' old place.'

Valdez is on his feet, walking through the house, peering through the curtains, his thoughts fizzing. He checks the locks on the windows and doors.

'Did you see a vehicle?'

Sandy shakes her head.

'What else did he say?'

'He said he was a widower . . . doing some sort of audit. Why did he come here?'

'Where's that gun I bought you?'

'Upstairs.'

'Get it for me.'

'Now you're scaring me.'

Valdez punches a number into his phone. He's through to a dispatcher. He relays the information, putting out a BOLO on Audie Palmer and asking for extra patrol cars in the neighbourhood.

'But you said he'd be in Mexico by now,' says Sandy. 'Why would he come here?'

Valdez has collected her gun and fitted the magazine. 'From now on you carry this everywhere.'

'I'm not gonna carry a gun.'

'Do as you're told.'

He grabs his keys.

'Where are you going?'

'To get Max.'

# CHAPTER 17

The Shady Oaks Motel is just off the Tom Landry Freeway – a seventies building that is functional, utilitarian and ugly as a safari suit. Moss parks the battered blue pickup truck out front of his room and takes a shower before lying on the bed, waiting for Crystal. She arrives wearing dark glasses and a shiny black raincoat like she's hiding from the paparazzi. Moss opens the door and she runs into his arms, wrapping her legs around his waist and kissing him passionately as he carries her backward into the room.

She looks around. 'Is this the best place you could find?'

'It's got a jacuzzi.'

'You want me to get cholera?'

He grabs her hand. 'No, I want you to feel this.'

Her eyes widen. 'Now you're just spoiling me.'

'The hardness of the butter is related to the softness of the bread. And your bread is soft, baby.'

She laughs and shrugs off her coat before unbuckling his trousers. 'Where did you get the threads?'

'They were left in a car for me.'

'You got a car?'

'I have.'

She pushes him back onto the bed and straddles him. Neither of them talks until they're sweaty and spent. Crystal goes to the bathroom. Moss lies on the bed with a towel over his middle.

'Don't you get too comfortable,' he yells.

'Why not?'

'I'm gonna do that all over again as soon as my eyes uncross.'

Crystal flushes the toilet and joins him on the bed. She takes a cigarette from the pocket of her raincoat and lights it up, putting it between his lips before lighting one for herself.

'How long has it been?'

'Fifteen years, three months, eight days and eleven hours.'

'You kept count.'

'No, but it's close enough.'

She wants to know about Audie Palmer and the missing millions, listening without interrupting, although she frowns and harrumphs at chunks of the story like she wasn't born yesterday.

'Who are these people?'

'No idea, but they got some real juice to get me out.'

'And they're going to let you keep the money?'

'That's what they said.'

'And you believe them?'

'No.'

She's resting her head in the crook of his arm, with her thigh over his waist.

'So what will you do?'

Moss draws on the cigarette and blows a smoke ring, which rolls upwards until the draft from the air conditioner obliterates the ghostly shape.

'Find Audie Palmer.'

'How?'

'His mama lives in Westmoreland Heights – not a mile from here.'

'And if she doesn't know?'

'I'll ask his sister.'

'And then?'

'Jesus, woman, I'm trying not to get ahead of myself! Have a little faith. If anyone can find Audie I can.'

Crystal still needs convincing. 'What's he like?'

Moss ponders this for a while. 'Audie is clever. Book-bright, you know, but not street-savvy. I taught him to have eyes in the back of his head and he taught me stuff.'

'Like what?'

'About philosophy and shit like that.'

Crystal giggles. 'What do you know about philosophy?'

Moss pinches her for laughing. 'Well, this one day I was getting frustrated trying to write a letter to the appeals board and I said to Audie, "The only thing I know is that I know nothing," and Audie told me that I just quoted a famous philosopher – a man called Socrates. Audie says a man

148

is smart to have doubts and question everything. The only thing we can know for certain is that we know nothing for certain.' He looks at Crystal. 'Does that make sense?'

'No, but it sounds clever.'

Crystal rolls onto her side and stubs out the cigarette in the ashtray. A wisp of smoke rises from the crumpled butt. She picks up Moss's hand and notices his missing wedding ring. Sitting upright, she bends the finger backwards until he cries out in pain.

'Where is it?'

'What?'

'Your wedding ring.'

'They took it off me in solitary and didn't give it back.'

'Did you ask 'em nicely?'

'I fought for it, babe.'

'You're not trying to act single on me.'

'No way.'

''Cos if I thought you were being unfaithful, I'd slice little Moss off and throw him to the dogs. Am I making myself clear?'

'Crystal.'

# CHAPTER 18

The cell phone is bouncing across the kitchen table. Special Agent Desiree Furness saves it from toppling off the edge. Her boss is calling, hoarse and half asleep. Not a morning person.

*'Audie Palmer was seen in The Woodlands yesterday morning.'*

'Who saw him?'

*'A sheriff's wife.'*

'What was Palmer doing in the Woodlands?'

*'Jogging.'*

Desiree grabs her jacket and puts her pistol in the shoulder holster. She's still eating a piece of toast when she skips down the outside stairs, waving to her landlord Mr Sackville, who lives beneath her and keep tabs on her comings and goings through a crack in his curtains. She drives north against the rush-hour traffic and pulls up twenty minutes later in front of a large house, partially hidden by trees. A police cruiser is sitting in the driveway with two uniformed deputies inside, playing games on their cell phones.

Desiree straightens her shoulders in a familiar attempt to appear taller as she shows them her badge and walks to the front door. Her fringe is too short to be pinned up and keeps falling over one eye. She warned her hairdresser not to trim too much off, but he didn't listen.

Sandy Valdez opens the door on a security chain, speaking through the six-inch gap. She's dressed in a tight top, Lycra leggings, ankle socks and cross-trainers.

'My husband is dropping Max at school,' she says in the kind of voice you hear from educated southern women.

'It's you I wanted to see.'

'I already told the police everything.'

'I'd appreciate you being just as considerate with me.'

Sandy unlatches the chain and escorts Desiree through the house to the sunroom. She's a size ten, blonde hair, smooth skin. Pretty. The house is tastefully furnished with just a hint that the eye was trying too hard to be stylish, poring over interior design magazines without ever settling on a theme.

Refreshments are offered . . . declined. There is a brief moment when both women run out of small talk and Desiree looks around the room as though contemplating an offer.

Sandy notices Desiree's shoes.

'They must hurt your feet and your back.'

'You get used to it.'

'How tall are you?'

'Tall enough.' Desiree gets to the point. 'What did you and Audie Palmer talk about?'

'The neighbourhood,' says Sandy. 'He told me he'd just moved into a place around the corner. I said he should join the country club to make some friends. I felt sorry for him.'

'Why?'

'He said his wife had died.'

'What else did he talk to you about?'

Sandy tries to think. 'He said he was doing some audit for his company. I thought he'd moved into the old Whitaker place. You will catch him, won't you?'

'We're doing everything we can.'

Sandy nods, but doesn't look reassured.

'Did anyone else see him?'

'Max, our son.'

'Where was he?'

'Riding his skateboard out front of the garage. I came home from the store and Palmer was standing beside the driveway, stretching.'

'Did Max talk to him?'

'Not then.'

'What do you mean?'

'He saw him later at the Mews – it's not far away. Max was riding his skateboard and Palmer was sitting on a park bench. I told the other detectives all this.' Sandy is wringing her hands in her lap. 'Ryan wanted to keep Max home today, but he'll be safe at school, won't he? I mean, we're doing the right thing by acting like nothing is wrong. I don't want Max growing up thinking the world is full of monsters.'

'I'm sure you made the right decision,' says Desiree, who isn't used to having such a sisterly conversation. 'Had you ever met Audie Palmer before yesterday?'

'No.'

'Why do you think he came to your house?'

'Isn't it obvious?'

'Not to me.'

'It was Ryan who shot him – everybody knows that. Audie Palmer got one in the head. He probably should have died and saved everyone a lot of trouble. Either that or gone to the chair – not that I believe in executing people willy-nilly, but four people died, for God's sake!'

'You think Audie Palmer wants revenge?'

'I do.'

'How would you describe his demeanour?'

'Pardon?'

'Did he seem agitated? Stressed? Angry?'

'He was sweating a lot – but I figured he'd just been running.'

'And apart from that?'

'He looked relaxed . . . like he didn't have a care in the world.'

Less than two miles away, Ryan Valdez pulls through the school gates and turns off the radio. It always amazes him, the people who call into talkback shows to spout their prejudices and publicise their ignorance. Don't they have anything better to do than to bitch about the state of things, which were always better in 'the good old days', as though time had mellowed their memories, turning vinegar into wine?

'So we're clear. You wait to be picked up. You don't leave the school. You don't talk to any more strangers . . .'

Max takes out an ear-bud from his ear. 'So what did this guy do?'

'It doesn't matter.'

'I think I should know.'

'He stole a bunch of money.'

'How much?'

'A lot.'

'And you arrested him?'

'Yeah.'

'Did you shoot him?'

'He was shot.'

Max looks genuinely impressed. 'And now he's come back to get you?'

'No.'

'Why else would he come to our house?'

'Let me worry about that. And don't go upsetting your mom by asking her questions.'

'Is this Audie Palmer scary?'

'Yeah.'

'He didn't look very dangerous.'

'Looks can be deceiving. He's a killer. Remember that.'

'Maybe you should let me carry a gun?'

'You're *not* taking a gun to school.'

Max sighs in disgust and opens the door. He

joins the tide of students funnelling through the gates. Valdez watches him walk to the main doors, wondering if he'll turn back or wave. The answer is no.

When the boy disappears, he takes out his cell and puts in a call into the Dreyfus County Sheriff's Office. He talks to his most senior deputy, Hank Poljak, and tells him to contact every dispatcher in Houston and the surrounding counties.

'If Audie Palmer is sighted I want to know first.'

'Anything else?' asks Hank.

'Yeah, I won't be in the office today.'

# CHAPTER 19

The cab surfs the freeway traffic under the sun's red stare. Audie gazes out of the tinted windows at the ocean of soulless strip malls, red-tiled houses and cheap prefab warehouses with razor wire along the rooftops and bars on the windows. When did Houston start dragging its knuckles? It had always been a strange city – a collection of neighbourhoods, like Los Angeles, where people commuted from home to work, barely interacting with one another. The only difference is that Houston is a destination while LA is merely a stop-off on a journey to somewhere better.

The cab driver is foreign, but Audie has no idea where he's from. One of those tragic countries, he supposes, a land beset by dictators or fanatics or famine. He has dark skin, more olive than brown, and receding hair that seems to be slipping backward off his head. Opening the sliding window between the front and back, he tries to start a conversation, but Audie isn't interested. Instead his mind wanders back to when he left Carl on the banks of the Trinity River.

There are moments in life when important choices have to be made. If we're lucky we get to make them, but more often they're made for us. Carl wasn't at the river when Audie got back with the police and paramedics. There were no bloody bandages, no messages or apologies. Audie knew what had happened, but didn't tell anyone. It was more out of respect for his parents than for Carl. The police wanted Audie charged with wasting their time and kept him in custody for another twelve hours before they allowed him to go home.

Weeks went by and Carl's name disappeared from the headlines. In January Audie returned to college and was summoned to the Dean's office. His scholarship was being withdrawn because he was a 'person of interest' in a cop killing.

'I didn't do anything wrong,' said Audie.

'I'm sure you're right,' said the Dean. 'And when this is all sorted out and your brother is found, you can reapply and the admissions officer will assess your eligibility and character.'

Audie packed up his things and withdrew his savings and bought a cheap car and headed west, putting miles between the past and whatever was coming. The Caddie rattled and banged across fifteen hundred miles, always threatening to perish, but displaying a will to survive that people normally attribute to sentient beings. Audie had never seen the sun set over the ocean. He'd never seen anyone surf in real life. In southern California he saw both. Bel-Air, Malibu, Venice Beach – famous names, images from films and TV shows.

It was different being on the west coast. The women smelled of sun oil and moisturiser instead of lavender and talcum. They talked about themselves and were obsessed with materialism, spiritualism, therapy and style. The men were tanned, with thick shiny hair or oiled skulls, wearing hundred-dollar shirts and three-hundred-dollar shoes. They were fixers, hustlers, stoners, dreamers, actors, writers, movers and shakers.

Driving as far north as Seattle, Audie worked as a barman, a bouncer, a packer, a fruit picker and a delivery guy. He stayed in cheap motels and doss houses, or occasionally with women who took him home. After travelling for six months he walked into Urban Covic's skin joint, twenty miles north of San Diego. It was darker than a cave except for the spotlighted stage where a pale girl with flesh climbing over the rim of her panties was polishing a silver pole with her thighs. A dozen men in suits gave her encouragement or pretended not to notice. Most of them were college boys or working stiffs trying to impress their Japanese business partners.

These southern Californian girls seemed to enjoy their work, torqueing and thrusting in the time-honoured fashion, earning every note that found its way into their G-strings and bra straps.

The manager had a comb sticking out of his shirt pocket and hair slicked back in wet-looking ridges like a freshly ploughed field.

158

'Got any work?' asked Audie.

'We don't need any musicians.'

'I'm not a musician. I can work the bar.'

The manager took out his comb and ran it over his scalp, front to back. 'How old are you?'

'Twenty-one.'

'Experience?'

'Some.'

He gave Audie a form to fill out and said he could work a shift unpaid as a trial. Audie proved himself to be a hard worker. He didn't drink. He didn't smoke. He didn't sniff. He didn't gamble. He didn't try to screw the girls.

Apart from the bar and the rooms, Urban Covic also owned the Mexican restaurant next door and the gas station opposite. These attracted families and helped him launder some of the money he earned from his other less lawful activities. Audie started work at eight most nights and went through until four in the morning. They let him eat at the restaurant first. It had a rear courtyard with a grapevine trellis and stucco walls banked with wine bottles.

Two weeks into his new job, he noticed a vehicle with blacked-out number plates, three up, waiting in the parking lot. He called the police and cleared the tills, hiding the money under the spillage pans. The men came in with sawn-off shotguns and balaclavas. Audie recognised one of their tattoos. It belonged to a guy who was dating one of the dancers and would hang around to make sure that none of the punters got too touchy-feely with her.

Audie put his hands in the air. People were crouching under tables. The girl on the pole had covered her breasts and crossed her legs.

The armed men broke open the registers and grew angry at the slim pickings. The guy with the tattoo waved a gun at Audie, who held his nerve. The sirens were coming. Shots were fired. One bullet shattered the mirror above the bar. Nobody got hurt.

Urban Covic arrived in the early hours, his face still creased from the pillow. The manager told him what had happened. He summoned Audie into his office.

'Where you from, kid?'

'Texas.'

'Where you going?'

'Haven't worked that out.'

Urban scratched his chin. 'Kid your age has got to decide if he's running away from something, or running toward it.'

'I guess so.'

'You got a driver's licence?'

'Yes, sir.'

'From now on you're my driver.' He tossed Audie a set of keys to a black Jeep Cherokee. 'You pick me up every morning at ten unless I tell you otherwise. You run errands if I need 'em doing. You drop me home when I say. I'll double your salary, but you're on call twenty-four hours a day.

160

If that means sleeping in the car, you sleep in the car.'

Audie nodded.

'Right now, I want you to drive me home.'

And that is how his new career began. He was given a room above the bar. Squashed under the apex of the roof, it was barely wider than a corridor, but it came rent-free with the job. There was a skylight and a bed of rough pine. Piled in the corner were his books and a rucksack. He had kept his engineering textbooks because of some vague notion that he might finish his degree one day.

Audie ferried Urban to meetings or collected people from the airport or picked up dry-cleaning or delivered packages. That's how he met Belita – when he went to pick up an envelope from Urban's house. He didn't know that she was Urban's mistress – he didn't care – but from the moment he set eyes upon her he had the strangest feeling that his blood was running backwards, pulsing through the valves of his heart in reverse, cascading instead of climbing, reaching his extremities and rushing inward.

Sometimes you can sense when you meet the person who is destined to change your life.

# CHAPTER 20

Moss becomes conscious of birds chirping and the ringing of a bicycle bell that sounds whimsical and cheerful. For the past fifteen years he has woken to a dawn chorus of banging, burping, coughing and farting, with each new day offering no more promise of light than a small square window above his head. Waking up this way is nicer, he decides, even if the bed next to him is empty. Crystal left early, driving back to San Antonio. He can still recall the weight of her as she straddled his thighs and kissed him goodbye, telling him to be careful.

Swinging his feet to the floor, he opens the curtain a chink and studies the parking lot. The gleaming towers of Dallas are in the distance, catching the sunshine on their mirrored edges. Moss wonders if the rich aren't trying to build stairways to Heaven because it's easier than squeezing a camel through the eye of a needle.

Showered, shaved and dressed, Moss drives north into Westmoreland Heights, where most of the streets are lined with wooden cottages that are worth less than the vehicles parked out front and some of these cars are jacked up on breeze blocks or gutted by fire. There are small pockets of promise in the blighted streets – a new building or prefabricated warehouse – but every unmarked wall is an invitation to a spray-can and each unbroken window an inducement to a thrown rock.

Moss parks outside a convenience store in Singleton Boulevard. The upper-floor windows are boarded up and the lower ones are covered in metal bars that are so thick you can't read the posters stuck to the inside of the glass.

A bell sounds as he enters. There are boxes stacked from floor to ceiling, and cardboard pallets wrapped in plastic, holding cans of beans and corn and baby carrots. Some of the labels are in foreign languages. The woman behind the cash register is sitting in a large armchair covered in a tartan rug. She's watching a TV infomercial with a smiling couple feeding vegetables into a blender.

'*Throw away your old kitchen appliances, this does it all,*' says the smiling host.

'*It's a miracle, Steve,*' says the woman.

'*Yes, it is, Brianna – a* kitchen *miracle. This is the juicer God uses in Heaven.*'

The live studio audience laughs. Moss doesn't know why.

'What can I do for you?' asks the woman, without taking her eyes from the screen. She's in her fifties with sharp features that crowd in the centre of her face.

'I'm looking for directions. A friend of mine used to live around here. I think his mother still does.'

'What's her name?'

'Irene Palmer.'

Moss can't see her woman's lower half but he can tell she's reaching for something. A bell rings further inside the house.

'You're looking for Irene Palmer?'

'That's what I said.'

'I don't know anyone by that name.'

'Do you know how I can tell you're lying?' says Moss. 'You repeated the question before answering. It's sumpin' people do when they're making things up.'

'You think I'm lying?'

'See – that's another tactic – answering a question with a question.'

Her eyes have narrowed to almost nothing. 'Don't make me call the cops.'

'I'm not looking to cause any trouble, ma'am. Just tell me where I can find Irene Palmer.'

'Leave that poor woman alone. A mother ain't responsible for ev'thang her children do.'

She thrusts out her chin, almost challenging Moss to disagree with her. A man appears in the doorway wearing nothing but sweat pants and tattoos. Early twenties. Muscled. Packing attitude.

'You got a problem, Ma?'

'He's looking for Irene.'

'Tell him to fuck off.'

'I did.'

164

A big automatic pistol is tucked into the waistband of his sweatpants. It's the first thing Moss focuses upon.

'I'm a friend of Audie Palmer,' says Moss. 'I got a message for his ma.'

'You can leave it with us. We'll make sure she gets it.'

'I was told to deliver it personally.'

The bell tinkles and an old black lady enters, as wrinkled as a dead crimson rose. Moss holds the door open. She thanks him.

'What can I get you, Noelene?' asks the storekeeper.

'This young man was here first,' she says, motioning to Moss.

'He was just leaving.'

Moss decides not to argue. He walks outside and finds a spot in the shade, waiting for the old woman to reappear. She's pulling a tartan shopping trolley with hard plastic wheels.

'Can I help you with that, ma'am?'

'I can manage.'

She shuffles past him along the sidewalk, which is crumbling in places. Moss follows her for thirty yards. She stops.

'Are you fixin' on robbing me?'

'No, ma'am.'

'Why are you following me?'

'I'm looking for Irene Palmer.'

'Well, I'm not her.'

'I know that. I'm a friend of her son.'

'Which one?'

'Audie.'

'I remember Audie. He used to cut my grass and clean up the yard. His school bus ran right by my place. Bright boy. Clever, you know, and always polite. Never any trouble . . . not like his brother.'

'Carl?'

'Did you know him?'

'No, ma'am.'

She shakes her head. Her silver hair is so tightly curled it looks like a ball of steel wool clinging to her skull.

'Carl came out of the womb facing the wrong way, know what I'm saying?'

'Not really.'

'He was always in trouble. His folks tried hard. His daddy ran a garage on Singleton Boulevard. Gone now. Factories have gone, the lead smelter, good riddance to that one. Poisoning our kiddies. You know what lead does to children?'

'No, ma'am.'

'Makes 'em stupid.'

'I didn't know that.'

She struggles to pull the trolley over the broken concrete. Moss picks it up like a suitcase and carries it for her.

'What happened to Carl?'

Noelene frowns. 'Thought you said Audie was a friend.'

'He didn't talk about his brother.'

166

'Well, it's not my business to tell you. I'm not a gossip, not like some I could name.' In the same breath she starts talking about people Moss should avoid. She calls them 'no-goods'.

'We got some no-goods around here, ugly, dangerous people. You ever heard of the Gator Boyz?' Moss shakes his head. 'They recruit teenage boys to sell drugs. Their leader has this alligator on a leash – a real live one that he leads round like a pet dog. I hope that gator bites his leg off.'

She pauses to catch her breath and leans on Moss's arm. She notices his tattoos.

'You been inside. Is that where you met Audie?'

'Yes, ma'am.'

'You looking for the money?'

'No.'

She eyes him doubtfully. They've reached the front gate of a small unpainted wooden house with a neat garden. Taking her trolley, she walks along the path and bumps the wheels up the steps to a narrow porch. She takes out a key and unlocks the screen door. Just before it closes, she turns.

'Irene Palmer moved to Houston. She's living with her sister.'

'Got an address?'

'Might do. You wait here.' The old woman disappears into the dark interior. Moss wonders if she's calling the police. He looks along the shoulderless street to where a playground has been built beneath a strand of pines. The swing set is broken and

167

someone has dumped a soiled mattress beneath the jungle gym.

The screen door opens. A hand extends, holding a piece of scented notepaper.

'Irene sent me a Christmas card. This was the return address.'

Moss takes the note and bows his head in thanks.

# CHAPTER 21

The cab drops Audie outside the Texas Children's Hospital. Money changes hands and the driver looks at the cash and suggests he deserves a tip. Audie says he should be nicer to his mother and gets a reply that no mother would approve of.

After buying a coffee and a Danish from a place across the road, Audie sits on a concrete bollard and watches the front entrance of the hospital. Nurses depart in twos and threes, the night shift off to bed. Replacements arrive with wet hair and neatly pressed blue trousers and paisley shirts. Audie licks crumbs from his fingers and spies Bernadette over the lip of his paper cup. Homely and pretty, she's wearing two badges on her blouse and walks with a slight stoop because she's taller than she wants to be.

Growing up, Audie didn't have much in common with his sister, who was twelve years older and seemed like a know-it-all. He remembers Bernadette taking him to school on his first day and putting Band-Aids on his bloody knees and telling him lies to stop him misbehaving. If he played with his penis it would drop off, she said; and if he sneezed, farted and blinked at the same time his head would explode.

Keeping his baseball cap pulled low over his eyes, Audie walks into the hospital and follows Bernadette from a distance. She takes a crowded elevator to the ninth floor. Audie keeps his head down and pretends to be reading messages on his phone. When Bernadette disappears into a nursing station Audie waits at the end of the corridor, feeling exposed. Nearby is a door marked STAFF ONLY. He slips inside and finds a changing room. Tucking his cap into his pocket, he takes a doctor's white coat from a hanger and hangs a stethoscope around his neck, praying that nobody asks him to perform CPR or clear an airway. He takes a clipboard from a hook on a gurney and walks along the corridor as though he knows where he's going.

Bernadette is making up a bed in an empty room, forcefully tucking in the corners and stretching the sheets as tight as a drum. It's how their mother taught her to make a bed, and Audie remembers almost needing a crowbar to squeeze between the top and bottom sheets.

'Hi, Sis.'

She straightens and frowns, holding a pillow to her chest. Her face seems to run through the full spectrum of emotions and her head rocks from side to side, denying the evidence of her eyes. She looks frightened of him, or frightened of herself. But something melts inside her and she closes the

170

gap between them, hugging him hard. Audie smells her hair and his whole childhood seems to come flooding back.

She strokes his cheek. 'You know it's against the law to impersonate a doctor.'

'I think that's the least of my problems.'

She pulls him away from the open door and closes it. Her fingers trace the scars that are visible beneath his short-cropped hair. 'Amazing,' she says. 'How in God's name did you survive?'

Audie doesn't answer.

'The police came to see me,' she says.

'I figured they would.'

'Why, Audie? You had one more day.'

'Best if I don't tell you my reasons.'

The hum of the air conditioner is the only sound in the room. It moves a strand of hair that has pulled loose from her bun. Audie notices the flecks of grey.

'Letting yourself go?'

'Stopped using the bottle.'

'You're only, what?'

'Forty-five.'

'That's not old.'

'Walk in my shoes.'

Audie asks her how she's doing and she says fine. Neither one of them knows where to begin. Her divorce came through. Her ex-husband had been affectionate and smart and successful and a violent drunk, but mercifully the alcohol affected his aim and Bernadette knew how to handle herself. Her new boyfriend works on the rigs. They're living together. Kids are out of the question. 'Like I said, I'm too old.'

'How's Ma?'

'Sick. She's on dialysis.'

'What about a transplant?'

'Doctors don't think she'd survive one.' She goes back to making the bed, but her eyes suddenly cloud. 'Why did you come back here?'

'Unfinished business.'

'I don't believe you robbed that armoured truck.'

He squeezes her hand. 'I need your help.'

'Don't ask for money.'

'What about a vehicle?'

Bernadette crosses her arms, her eyes filled with doubt. 'My boyfriend has a car. If that were to go missing, I might not even notice for a week.'

'Where is it?'

'Parked on the street.'

'Keys?'

'Didn't they teach you anything in prison?'

'I don't know how to hotwire.'

She jots down her address. 'I'll leave 'em on the wheel.'

Another nurse has come to the door, Bernadette's supervisor. 'Is everything all right?' she asks, addressing Audie, wondering why the door was closed.

'Fine,' he replies.

She nods and waits. Audie holds her gaze until she grows self-conscious and turns away.

'You'll get me fired,' whispers Bernadette.

'I need one more thing.'

'What's that?'

'Those files I left for you – did you print them out?'

She nods.

'In a day or two, I'll call and tell you what to do with them.'

'Am I going to get into trouble?'

'No.'

'Am I going to see you again?'

'I doubt it.'

Bernadette steps away then back again, opening her arms, squeezing Audie so hard he can barely breathe.

'I love you, little brother.'

# CHAPTER 22

Cassie has packed and repacked her suitcases but still hasn't left the motel. Staring at the digital clock between the beds, she can hear it ticking inside her head, as though challenging her to make a decision.

Spencer's rucksack is tucked beneath his bed. Is that even his real name? How did he get those scars on his head? She pictures the violent force and feels something shake loose inside her.

Scarlett is watching *Dora the Explorer* on TV, lying on her front with her chin resting in her cupped hands. She's seen all these episodes before but still gets excited. Maybe kids like knowing what's going to happen next.

Cassie grabs the rucksack and begins going through the pockets, unzipping compartments and searching. She finds a notebook and takes it into the bathroom, closing the door and sitting on the toilet with her dress forming a hammock between her knees. She opens the book. A photograph flutters out. Cassie picks it up from the tiled floor. It shows a young woman, dark-skinned and beautiful, holding a bouquet of flowers. Cassie feels a stab of jealousy and can't understand why.

She slips the photograph between the pages, hard against the spine, and goes back to the beginning. There is a name written on the inside of the front cover: Audie Spencer Palmer. Below there is a price sticker and a label saying, *Three Rivers FCI.*

The pages are full of handwriting that is small and spidery and difficult to read. Cassie struggles to comprehend more than a few sentences. It looks and sounds like poetry with phrases like 'perceptions of the truth' and the 'pathos of absence', whatever that means.

Taking out her cell phone, she consults a torn page that she ripped from the telephone directory. A woman answers and seems to be reading from a script:

*'Hello, you've reached Texas Crime Stoppers – all calls are confidential. My name is Eileen. How can I help you?'*

'Do you offer rewards?'

*'We provide financial remuneration for information leading to the arrest and charging of a felony suspect.'*

'How much?'

*'That depends upon the seriousness of the offence.'*

'How much could it be?'

*'Five thousand dollars.'*

'What if I knew the whereabouts of an escaped convict?'

*'What's his name?'*

Cassie hesitates. 'I think he's called Audie Spencer Palmer.'

'*You think?*'

'Yeah.'

Cassie glances at the locked door, having second thoughts.

'*Would you like to give me your name?*'

'No.'

'*Audie Palmer has a federal warrant out for his arrest. Tell me where you are. I can get officers to come and get you.*'

'You said this call was confidential.'

'*How are we going to pay you the money, if we don't know your name?*'

Cassie pauses.

'*What's wrong?*' asks Eileen.

'I'm thinking.'

'*You're in danger.*'

'I'm gonna have to call you back.'

'*Don't hang up!*'

# CHAPTER 23

Moss drives all the way to Houston with the windows down and the radio turned up loud. Not country music. He prefers listening to classic southern blues about suffering and salvation and women who break your heart. Late afternoon he pulls up outside a white-painted Baptist church with a wooden cross on the front wall above a sign that reads, JESUS DOESN'T NEED TO TWEET.

He parks in the shade of a crippled elm with a gnarled trunk and roots that are pushing up the cement sidewalk like the world's slowest earthquake. The church doors are locked, but he follows a side path to a small wooden-framed cottage set on cinder blocks, shaded by more trees. Flowers are growing in neat beds with edges trimmed by the blade of a shovel.

Moss knocks. A big woman appears behind the screen, leaning on a walking stick.

'I'm not buying anything.'

'Are you Mrs Palmer?'

She searches for the spectacles on a cord around her neck. Looks at him. Moss steps backwards, so as not to frighten her.

'Who are you?'

'I'm a friend of Audie's.'

'Where's that other one?'

'Who?'

'He knocked earlier. He said he knew Audie. I didn't believe him and I don't believe you.'

'My name is Moss Webster. Audie might have mentioned me in his letters. I know he wrote you every week.'

She hesitates. 'How do I know that's you?'

'Audie said you hadn't been well, ma'am. He said you needed a new kidney. You used to write to him on pink paper with flowers on the border. You have a lovely hand, ma'am.'

'Now you're just trying to flatter me,' she says, telling Moss to go around the back of the cottage.

Sheets are flapping on a line above his head as he turns the corner of the house. She calls from the kitchen and gets him to carry a pitcher of lemonade and two glasses to an outside table that is covered in pecan husks. She fusses over getting it clean and Moss notices an ugly bruise-coloured bulge on her forearm like bubbles of blood are trapped beneath her skin.

'That's a fistula,' she says. 'I'm on dialysis twice a week.'

'That's too bad.'

She shrugs philosophically. 'Bits have been falling off me since I had babies.'

Moss sips the lemonade, which is sour enough to make his lips pucker.

'Are you looking for the money?' she asks.

'No, ma'am.'

She smiles wryly. 'Do you know how many people I've had visiting me over the last eleven years? Some come with photographs, some have letters they say my Audie has signed. Others come with threats. Caught one of them digging up my yard right over yonder.' She points to the base of the pecan tree.

'I'm not here about the money.'

'You a bounty hunter?'

'No.'

'Why were you in prison?'

'I did some things I'm not proud of.'

'At least you admit it.'

He pours himself another glass of lemonade. The condensation has left a ring of moisture on the wooden table. He makes a second circle and draws a wet line between them.

Mrs Palmer grows misty-eyed talking about Audie winning a scholarship to college and how he was studying to be an engineer until Carl messed it up.

'Where is Carl now?' asks Moss.

'Dead.'

'Are you speaking literally or figuratively?'

'Don't use fancy words with me,' she scolds. 'A mother knows if her boy is dead.'

Moss raises his hands. 'I know you've talked to the police, Mrs Palmer, but is there anything you didn't tell them? Places Audie might have gone. Friends.'

She shakes her head.

'What about his girlfriend?'

'Who?'

'He had a photograph he carried with him everywhere. She was a honey, but he never talked about her – except in his sleep. Belita, that was her name. The only time I ever saw Audie lose his temper was when someone stole that photograph.'

Mrs Palmer concentrates. For a moment he thinks she might remember something, but the idea is lost.

'I've only seen him twice in fourteen years – once when he was lying in a coma and they said he was going to die. Then they said he was going to be brain-damaged on account of the bullet in his head, but he proved them wrong. I saw him on the day he was sentenced. He told me not to worry. What mother isn't going to worry?'

'Do you know why Audie escaped?'

'No, but I don't believe he took that money.'

'He confessed.'

'Well if he did, he had a reason.'

'A reason?'

'Audie doesn't do anything on the spur of the moment. He's a thinker. Sharp as a tack. He didn't need to rob someone to make a living.'

Moss looks into the sky where the light is fading and three birds on the wing are etched clearly like ducks hanging on a white wall. Mrs Palmer is still speaking. 'If you find my Audie, tell him I love him.'

'I think he knows that, ma'am.'

★　★　★

As he's leaving the church grounds, Moss notices a man on the far side of the road. Wearing a black suit, one size too small, he has muddy brown hair that grows into sideburns and then into a beard that looks like a strap holding on a helmet. An old vinyl bag hangs from his shoulder, the zip broken, the inside a black hole.

He is squatting on his haunches beneath a tree, one hand draped over a knee, the other flicking at the burning end of a cigarette. Moss crosses the road. The man glances up at him and then goes back to watching a line of ants marching past his shoes. Every so often he drops his finger, creating a furrow in the dust. The ants scatter and regroup. Puffing on his cigarette, he holds the burning tip close to the line of ants, watching the insects twist in the heat. Some rear up and want to fight. Others hobble and skitter trying to repair their ruined bodies.

'Do I know you?' asks Moss.

The man looks up, letting smoke leak from the corners of his mouth, rising past eyes that have a bleak, almost vicious depth to them. 'I don't believe so.'

'What are you doing here?'

'Same as you.'

'I don't think so.'

'We're both looking for Audie Palmer. We should team up. Share information. Two heads are better than one, amigo.'

'I'm not your amigo.'

The man bites his thumbnail. Moss steps closer.

The man stands. He's taller than Moss expects and his right foot has pulled behind the left, set at an angle, the posture of someone who has martial arts training. His pupils seem to dilate to take over the whole of his corneas and his nostrils flare.

'Have you been bothering Mrs Palmer?'

'No more 'n you.'

'I want you to leave her alone.'

'I'll bear that in mind.'

Moss doesn't try to outstare him. He knows he'll lose. Instead he wants to get as far away as possible and never think about this man again. At the same time he senses it won't happen. It's like knowing that a page is about to turn and the news is going to get worse, but you're forced to read on to the end.

# CHAPTER 24

Urban Covic was a generous boss who treated Audie with respect and paid him a fair wage. Wherever Urban went in southern California he seemed to be known. The best tables were reserved at restaurants, doors were opened at City Hall and nothing was too much trouble. Yet despite his obvious wealth and influence, Urban seemed to sense that people found him odious. He wasn't a good-looking man. God had given him a dumpy body and a pigeon-toed walk and protruding eyes. 'I could have been born handsome and stupid, but I got ugly and wise,' he once told Audie. 'I prefer it that way.'

The bullies of Urban's youth had been silenced or suitably punished. To this end, he had a few trusted lieutenants who did the heavy lifting, mostly nephews or cousins, who lacked his brains but knew how to physically intimidate.

Urban had a fleet of different vehicles, all of them American because he saw it as his patriotic duty to support local jobs. Audie would pick him up every morning and Urban would tell him which car to wash and take from the garage. Urban sat in the back and when he wasn't talking on the phone he liked to read books about Greek legends and to quote headlines from the newspapers – not the *LA Times* or the *San Diego Tribune*, but the supermarket rags with shoutlines about alien abductions, celebrity miscarriages and people adopting ape babies.

'This country is so screwed up,' he'd say, 'and long may it continue.'

He also told Audie stories about how he left Las Vegas because the Nevada Gaming Control Board had made it 'too fucking hard' and most of the mobsters were forced to the fringes, running girls and illegal crap games.

'So I came here and carved out my niche.'

Audie thought it was an interesting way of describing Urban's various business interests, which took in farms, clubs, restaurants and motels.

A month passed. Despite picking Urban up every morning and dropping him home, Audie hadn't seen Belita. Urban got off the phone and asked, 'You play poker?'

'I know the rules.'

'I got a game at the house tonight. There's an empty chair.'

'I'd be out of my league.'

'If it gets too hot, pull out. Nobody is going to fleece you.'

Audie thought about seeing Belita again and said yes. He wore a new shirt, polished his boots and put gel in his hair.

The game had three other players. One of them

was a San Diego city counsellor, another a businessman, and the last looked like an Italian mobster with teeth like broken tombstones, stained with red wine and crud.

The table was set up in a dining room, which had a view over the valley but the light was so low and bright that Audie couldn't see anything except his own reflection. He could smell food cooking in the kitchen and could hear someone moving around.

Some time after nine, Urban suggested they take a break. He rang a bell on the sideboard. Belita arrived, carrying a tray of buffalo wings, spiced nuts and Texas caviar: corn chips and guacamole. She was wearing a dress and a long apron cinched tight at her waist. Her plaited hair fell so far down her back it would have touched the crack of her ass if she'd been naked.

Audie had been fantasizing about this girl for a month and felt himself blush in her presence. She didn't make eye contact with anyone. After she'd gone the mobster licked barbecue sauce from his fingers and asked Urban where he found her.

'She was picking fruit at the farm.'

'So she's a wetback,' said the businessman.

'We're not supposed to call 'em that any more,' said the counsellor.

'What should we call them?' asked the businessman.

'Piñatas,' said the mobster. 'Bang 'em hard enough and they cum all over you.'

The others laughed. Audie said nothing. They played some more. Drank. Ate. He stayed sober. Belita bought more food. The mobster put his hand on her leg and ran it up between her thighs. She flinched and looked at Audie for the first time. Embarrassed. Ashamed.

The mobster pulled her onto his lap. She raised her hand to slap him. He grabbed it and twisted her wrist until she cried out and he dumped her without ceremony onto the floor. Audie pushed back his chair, his fists bunched, ready to fight.

Urban intervened and told Belita to go back to the kitchen. The mobster sniffed his fingers. 'Can't she take a joke?'

'I think you should apologise,' said Audie.

'I think you should sit the fuck down and shut your mouth,' replied the mobster. He looked at Urban. 'You fucking her?'

Urban didn't reply.

'If you're not, you should be.'

'Let's just play,' said Urban, who dealt another hand.

By 2 a.m. the counsellor and businessman had gone home. Audie had a healthy pile of chips in front of him, but the mobster had the biggest haul. Urban was drunk. 'I hate this game,' he said, throwing down his cards.

'How's about I give you a chance to win it all back?' the mobster said.

'What do you mean?'

'One hand, all in.'

186

'I didn't make my money doubling up on a losing streak.'

'Bet the girl.'

'What?'

'Your housekeeper.' He pinched a stack of chips and let them fall onto the pile. 'If you win, you get it all back. I win, I get the girl for the night.'

Audie glanced at the kitchen door. He could see Belita packing the dishwasher and polishing glasses. Urban looked at the table. He was down five, maybe six thousand.

'Let's just call it a night,' Audie said.

'I want to play another hand,' replied the mobster. 'You don't have to play.' His lips peeled back, showing all his crumbling teeth.

'This is crazy,' said Audie. 'You don't own her.'

He was talking to Urban, who immediately bristled. 'What did you say?'

Audie tried to recover. 'I'm just saying that she's done nothing wrong. We've had a good night. Let's go home.'

The mobster pushed all his chips into the centre of the table. 'One hand – winner takes all.'

Urban began shuffling the cards. Audie wanted to upend the table and scatter the cards to the winds. Urban cut the deck. 'Texas hold'em one hand.' He glanced at Audie. 'Are you going down Pussy Lane or Man-Up Road?'

'I'm in.'

Urban called to the kitchen. Belita appeared. She kept her eyes down, wiping her hands on her apron. Her hair shone in the low-hanging light, creating a halo around her head.

'These gentleman want to bet everything on the table, but I'm out of chips,' said Urban, looking strangely energised. 'They're suggesting I put you up as collateral.'

She didn't understand.

'If I lose, one of them gets you for the night, but I'm sure that particular gentleman will be generous with the rest of his winnings.' He repeated the sentence in Spanish.

Her eyes went wide. Frightened.

'Now, now, you know we have an agreement. I wouldn't be too hasty in saying no.'

She shook her head and pleaded with him. He replied in a voice that seemed to chill her to the bone.

*'Pensar en el niño!'*

Audie knew *niño* meant boy, but couldn't tell if it was a threat or a statement. Belita wiped the back of her hand across her eyes, smearing a tear.

'Why are we doing this?' asked Audie.

'I'm just playing cards,' said Urban. 'You're the ones who want to fuck her.'

Audie couldn't look at Belita. She pulled back her shoulders and tried to maintain some dignity, turning away from the table, but her legs were shaking as she walked to the kitchen.

'I want her to watch,' said the mobster.

Urban summoned her back. Dealt the cards. Audie drew a seven and a king as his face cards. The flop brought nine, a queen and another seven. He was looking at a pair of sevens. The 'turn' and 'river' cards were flipped. Audie closed his eyes and opened them: an ace and another seven.

Urban didn't keep them waiting. He had two pair. They looked at Audie. Three sevens. The mobster crowed. 'Don't these ladies look pretty – especially when they come in threes?'

Audie stared at the queens on the table and felt his stomach spasm and clench. It wasn't losing the money that bothered him, it was the look on Belita's face – not shock or surprise or anger, but resignation, as though this was just another degradation in a long series.

Urban stood and stretched. His belly poked out of his unbuttoned shirt. He was philosophical about his loss. There would be other nights. Better hands.

'I hope you're not hung like a horse,' he said, slipping on his jacket. 'And I don't want her bruised or otherwise mistreated. Am I clear?'

The mobster nodded. 'I'm staying at the Park Hyatt.'

'Have her back here at noon.'

'I'm too drunk to drive.'

Urban glanced at Audie. 'You drive them. Make sure you bring her home.'

On the journey down the mountain, Belita sat close to the window as though trying to make herself smaller or to disappear completely. The mobster tried to make conversation, but she didn't answer.

'I know you speak English,' he said, slurring.

She kept her head down. Perhaps she was praying or crying. When Audie pulled up outside the hotel, he hopped out and opened the rear door like a proper chauffeur.

'I need a minute with Belita,' he said.

'What for?' asked the mobster.

'So I can arrange to pick her up.'

Audie took her to the far side of the car. She looked at him uncertainly. The lights from the hotel lobby reflected in her eyes.

'Make him a drink. Put these in it,' he whispered, pressing four sleeping pills into her hand and closing her fingers. 'Pretend you slept with him. Leave a note. Tell him he was good. I'll be waiting.'

An hour later Belita emerged from the hotel, ignoring the entreaties of cab drivers. Audie opened the back door for her but she chose to sit next to him in the front. They drove into the mountains and she didn't speak for ten miles, cradling herself in her folded arms. She spoke to him in Spanish.

'What would you have done if you had won me?'

'Nothing.'

'Why then?'

'It didn't seem right.'

'How much money did you lose?'

'I don't know.'

'I'm not worth it.'

'Why would you say that?'

Her eyes were brimming and she shook her head, unable to speak.

# CHAPTER 25

Houston Public Library on McKinney Street is the architectural equivalent of a love child conceived by a cement mixer and a cubist painter. Even with a newly cleaned façade and trees planted in the open spaces, the building has no warmth or charm.

A middle-aged woman behind the desk doesn't look up until Moss has finished speaking. She stamps a form and puts it in a tray and then shows him her blue eyes and bluer eye shadow. 'What for?'

'Pardon?'

'I heard what you wanted, I asked you what for.'

'I'm interested.'

'Why?'

'It's a private matter and this is a public library.'

Moss and the librarian stare at each other for a moment and she directs him upstairs to the eighth floor, where another librarian, who seems in a better mood, shows him how to read the index cards and fill out a request form for the *Houston Chronicle* from January 2004.

The microfilms are delivered from the basement archive. Moss looks at the boxes. 'What do I do with them?'

The male librarian points to a row of machines.

'How do I use them?' asks Moss.

The librarian sighs and takes the boxes from him, showing him how to fix the red spool and thread the film through the viewing window. 'This moves it forward. This moves it back. This is the focus.'

'Could I trouble you for some paper and a pen?' asks Moss, embarrassed by his lack of preparedness.

'We're not a stationery service.'

'I understand that.'

The librarian thinks the matter is settled, but Moss is still standing over his desk, waiting, which is something he's very good at. The paper is found, along with a cheap yellow pen.

'I want that back,' says the librarian.

'Yes, suh.'

Settled in front of a machine, Moss searches the editions of the *Chronicle*, concentrating on the front pages until he finds the first mention of the robbery. It's a headline:

## ARMORED TRUCK HIJACKING

Gunmen posing as a road construction crew hijacked an armored truck carrying

US currency in a daring daylight raid on the outskirts of Conroe, TX, late yesterday.

Two security guards were beaten and a third is missing after the Armaguard truck was ambushed while leaving a truck stop on the I-45, shortly after 3.00 p.m.

A gang of armed men dressed as highway crew forced two guards out of the vehicle, taking their weapons before hijacking the truck. A third guard was still inside when the gunmen drove off.

'Roadblocks were put in place within fifteen minutes, but we haven't had any sightings,' said Detective Peter Yeomans of Dreyfus County. 'Obviously our first concern is the whereabouts and welfare of the missing guard.'

Witness Denise Peters said the robbers were wearing reflective vests and hard-hats. 'I thought they were carrying shovels, but it was shotguns,' she said. 'They were using a concrete cutter and were holding up a STOP sign.'

Waitress Gail Malakhova said the guards had earlier been eating at the diner. 'They were laughing and joking, but soon after they left all hell broke loose. It was scary.'

Moss spools forward to the next day. January 28, 2004.

# FOUR DEAD IN ARMORED
# TRUCK HEIST

Four people are dead and another is fighting for his life after a bloody police shoot-out in Dreyfus County late yesterday. The dead include a female motorist, a security guard and two of the gang members who had earlier hijacked an armored truck carrying US currency. A further suspect in the robbery was shot by police and is listed in a critical condition.

The drama began just after 3.00 p.m. yesterday when the Armaguard truck was halted by fake road works just north of Conroe. Two guards were overpowered and a third was trapped in the back of the truck when it was hijacked and driven away.

Five hours later, two deputies from the Dreyfus County Sheriff's Office sighted the stolen truck in a rest area off Farm to Market 830, northwest of Conroe. When confronted by police, the gunmen fired shots and drove off at high speed. The police pursuit lasted more than twenty minutes and reached speeds of up to ninety mph along Old Montgomery Road before the armored truck lost control on the crest of a hill and crashed into an oncoming vehicle. The woman motorist was killed along with the guard trapped inside the overturned truck.

In the gun battle that followed, two gang members were shot dead and a third critically injured. A fourth suspect is believed to have escaped driving a dark-colored SUV, which was later found abandoned and burnt out near Lake Conroe.

For the next few days, the robbery remained front-page news, particularly when the size of the haul was confirmed on January 30. The *Houston Chronicle* reported:

## $7 MILLION STILL MISSING

### Armed Robber on Life Support

The armored truck hijacked near Conroe, TX, on Tuesday was carrying more than $7 million, making it one of the biggest heists in US history, according to the FBI, who are still trying to recover the money.

Four people died in the robbery, including a security guard and two armed robbers, while another of the gang is in a critical condition and may not regain consciousness according to doctors. The suspect, who has not been named, suffered massive head injuries and has been placed in a medically induced coma.

'He is on life support and his condition deteriorated further overnight,' a hospital spokesman said. 'Surgeons have operated to relieve pressure on his brain, but his injuries are extensive.'

The heist ended in a dramatic high speed chase and accident. Two gang members were shot dead by police and a security guard and woman motorist died at the scene. A fourth gang member is believed to have fled in a stolen dark-colored Land Cruiser that was later found abandoned and torched near Lake Conroe.

Forensic officers spent yesterday collecting evidence at the crash site and the road is expected to remain closed for another twenty-four hours.

Moss searches for more accounts of the robbery, but the reports thinned out over the following days. Janet Jackson's nipple-slip at Superbowl XXXVIII seemed to suck oxygen from the story, because nudity is more newsworthy than gun crime or theft. Police released the names of the dead gang members: Vernon Caine and his younger brother Billy, who came from Louisiana. They also named Audie Palmer and said that his brother Carl, a known fugitive and notorious cop killer, was a 'person of interest' in the robbery. Eight weeks after the shooting, Audie was taken off life support, but he didn't regain consciousness for another month.

Moss has been making notes as he reads, ruling

lines between people's names and drawing diagrams. He's enjoying using his brain. He wonders what he might have achieved if he hadn't grown up on the projects and started boosting cars aged eleven. Back then he thought his choices would always be in front of him. Now most of them lay behind.

He leaves the library with the pages folded in his shirt pocket. Following his hand-drawn map, he drives north along the I-45, before taking the south loop around Conroe and heading west, where he hooks up with Old Montgomery Road, a double-lane blacktop through dense strands of pine and oak.

He pulls over to the shoulder, resting his palms on the steering wheel. A solitary leaf spins out of the canopy above him. Ahead is a straight stretch of road, with a crest and a hard right-hander at the bottom of the dip. Moss gets out and walks, looking at a culvert full of muddy water and waist-high weeds with dense forest on either side. A power-line is strung between the trees and Moss notices a small cabin put together with scrap timber and sheet iron and frayed tar shingles. A natural creek runs along one side of the yard, which is overgrown and shaded by old oak trees and stumps of others that have fallen or been culled.

Moss jumps the ditch and follows a muddy track through the weeds until he reaches the front porch. He knocks. Nobody answers. As he steps back, he's sure that he's being watched, but he can't see any tyre tracks or footprints or signs of life. He walks around the house and finds a doorbell with a plastic button.

Pressing it with his thumb, he hears the unmistakable sound of a rifle being primed, the bullet sliding into the chamber. The door opens and a man is staring at him through the screen. He's wearing a pair of pants, belt hanging loose, and a potbelly poking out of an unbuttoned shirt like a pregnancy.

'You're one brave nigger,' says the man.

'Why's that?'

'Coming onto a man's property uninvited.'

'It's implied.'

'What?'

'You see your doorbell?'

'It don't work.'

'That don't matter. When a man has a doorbell it suggests that he gets visitors from time to time, so it's an implied invitation.'

'The fuck you talking about?'

'In a legal sense I had an implied invitation to ring your doorbell because otherwise you wouldn't have one.'

'I just told you, it don't work. Are you deaf?'

Moss isn't getting anywhere.

'How long you lived here, old-timer?'

'Thirty years.'

'You remember an incident about eleven years ago – an accident over yonder, behind the trees? The police were chasing an armoured truck. It crashed.'

'Not likely to forget.'

'You must have heard the shooting from here.'

'Heard and saw.'

'What did you see?'

The old man hesitates. 'I saw it all and I saw nothing.'

'What does that mean?'

'It means I mind my own business and I suggest you do the same.'

'Why?'

'Don't get me started.'

The two men seem to match stares, as though waiting for the other to blink.

'A friend of mine was involved,' says Moss. 'He said you could help me.'

'You're a liar.'

'What are you afraid of?'

The old man shakes his head. 'I know when to keep my mouth shut. You tell that to your friend. You tell him that Theo McAllister can be trusted.'

The door slams shut.

# CHAPTER 26

No mention was made of the poker game in the days that followed. Audie drove Urban to his various appointments and listened to his opinions and prejudices. He was less enamoured with his boss than before, but managed to pretend that nothing had changed between them. One morning they were driving to the largest of the farms. Urban sat in the middle of the back seat and Audie could see him in the rear-view mirror.

'I heard what you did for Belita the other night.' Urban said. 'That was very noble of you.'

'Did your friend say anything?'

'He said Belita was the best fuck he ever had.'

'The man has an ego.'

'He's not Robinson Crusoe.'

Audie drove through the gates of the farm. The limo kicked up dust that widened and settled on the dark green leaves of orange trees. Workers were spraying and weeding, moving between the rows. A quarter of a mile on they passed a cluster of rudimentary houses, built from wood scraps, chicken wire, stones and sheets of crumpled iron.

Washing hung from a makeshift line. A toddler was getting her hair shampooed in a tin bath. The big-hipped mother looked up, brushing hair from her forehead with a soapy hand.

'Did you fuck her?' asked Urban.

'No.'

'She said you didn't even try.'

'I felt sorry for her.'

Urban considered this. 'That's an expensive conscience you have.'

They pulled up outside a whitewashed hacienda-style farmhouse. Audie carried bags of cash into the house – money to pay wages to farm workers or to placate union officials or to corrupt politicians or pay off customs officers. From where Audie stood, Urban seemed to have tapped the artery of venality that existed in San Diego. He knew what wheels to oil, palms to grease and fundaments to lube.

'Moral outrage is a fickle beast,' Urban explained. 'That's why you can't always rely on tittie bars and lap dances to pay the bills. You need to diversify. Remember that.'

'Yes, sir.'

Audie deposited the cash on a polished maple desk and turned his back while Urban lifted a painting from the wall and spun through the numbers on a combination lock.

'I want you to take Belita shopping,' Urban said. 'Help her buy some classy clothes. Work stuff.'

'She cleans your house.'

'I'm promoting her. One of my couriers got beaten and robbed yesterday. Maybe he was telling the truth. Maybe he organised the whole shake-down. From now on Belita is going to do the money run.'

'Why her?'

'Nobody is going to suspect a pretty young woman might be carrying that much cash.'

'And what if somebody does?'

'You're going to look after her.'

Audie stuttered and started again. 'I don't under-stand why you want me.'

'She trusts you. So do I.'

Urban peeled off eight hundred-dollar bills from a bundle of cash. 'I want you to buy her some nice things – some of those fancy business suits you see women wearing, but no trousers, OK? I like her in skirts.'

'When?'

'Tomorrow. Take her to Rodeo Drive. Show her where the film stars live. I'd take her myself but I'm busy . . .' He paused before adding, 'and she's still pissed at me for the poker night.'

Audie picked Belita up after breakfast. She wore the same dress as the first time they'd met, covered with a light loose-weave cardigan. She kept her arms folded and sat demurely in the front passenger seat, her knees together, and a soft cloth bag on her lap.

Rather than drive the limo or the Cherokee,

Audie borrowed Urban's Mustang convertible in case Belita wanted him to drive with the top down. He pointed out landmarks and commented on the weather, occasionally sneaking glances at Belita. Her hair was held back in a tortoiseshell clasp and her skin looked like it had been cast in bronze and polished with a soft cloth. He began speaking Spanish to her, but she wanted to practise her English.

'You're from Mexico?'

'No.'

'Where?'

'El Salvador.'

'Down that way, isn't it?'

She stared at him. He felt stupid. He started again. 'You don't look very . . .'

'What?'

'It doesn't matter.'

'My father was born in Barcelona,' she explained. 'He came to El Salvador as a merchant seaman in his twenties. My mother was from Argentina. They fell in love.'

Audie drove north on the San Diego Freeway, hugging the coast for the first sixty-five miles – ocean to the left, mountains to the right. After San Clemente they turned inland, staying on the I-5 into downtown Los Angeles. Midweek, midsummer, and Rodeo Drive was full of tourists and out-of-towners and wealthy locals. There were liveried doormen at the hotels and tux-clad bouncers at the restaurants and every sign was clean and bright, as though it had been manufactured at some sterile plant in Silicon Valley.

During the drive, Audie had asked questions, but Belita didn't seem interested in talking about herself. It was as though she didn't want to be reminded of who she was or where she'd come from. So Audie talked about himself – how he went to college to study engineering but dropped out after two years and came to California.

'Why don't you ever go with the girls?' she asked.

'What?'

'The girls at the bar, they think you are . . . I don't know the word. *Una marica.*'

'What's that mean?'

'They think you like the dick.'

'They think I'm *gay*?'

She laughs.

'What's so funny?'

'The expression . . . your face.' Audie felt foolish and didn't say anything. In truth, he had no idea what to say. He had never heard anything so ridiculous. They drove in silence. He was seething, but soon he found himself snatching glances at her again, drinking her up, sipping the details, committing them to memory.

Audie thought she was a strange creature, like a wild animal hesitating on the edge of a clearing, unsure whether to emerge into the open. There was a haunting, almost magical sadness about her that seemed to empty the world; a sense that pain was a completion of her beauty and the only way to appreciate perfection was to recognise its impossibility; to see the flaws.

She pointed out the designer shops with familiar names like Armani, Gucci, Cartier, Tiffany and Coco Chanel. She spoke a sort of schoolbook English, testing each phrase as she strung the words together. Sometimes she asked if she had said something correctly.

He parked the Mustang and they walked along Rodeo Drive, past boutiques, courtiers, car showrooms, restaurants and champagne bars. In the space of a block Audie counted three Lamborghinis, two Ferraris and a Bugatti coupé.

'Where are the movie stars?' she asked.

'Who did you want to see?'

'Johnny Depp.'

'I don't think he lives in Los Angeles.'

'How about Antonio Banderas?'

'Is he from El Salvador?'

'No.'

She looked into the store windows where emaciated assistants were dressed in black, demonstrating an air of practised indifference.

'Where are all the clothes?' she asked.

'They only display a few at a time.'

'Why?'

'It makes them seem more exclusive.'

Belita paused to look at one particular dress.

'Do you want to try it on?' he asked.

'How much is it?'

'You have to ask.'

'Why?'

'You just do.'

She kept walking. It was the same at every store. She would look in the window or through the doors without ever venturing inside. They spent an hour walking the same three blocks, up and back. Belita didn't want to stop for a drink or coffee or something to eat. She didn't want to stay. Audie drove her along Santa Monica Boulevard past the Beverly Hills Police Station towards West Hollywood. They saw the Chinese Theatre and the Walk of Fame, which was crowded with Japanese tour groups following brightly coloured umbrellas and taking photographs with living statues of Marilyn Monroe, Michael Jackson and Batman.

Belita seemed to relax. She let Audie buy her some ice cream. She told him to wait while she went into a souvenir shop. Through the window, he saw her buying a T-shirt with a stencilled photograph of the Hollywood sign.

'It's too small for you,' he said, looking into her bag.

'It's a present,' she replied, taking it back.

'We still haven't bought you any clothes.'

'Take me to a mall.'

He drove her to a soulless concrete shopping plaza ringed by acres of parked cars and dotted with palm trees that looked fake but were probably real. Belita made Audie sit on a plastic seat outside the changing room. Going back and forth, she modelled for him, skirts and jackets, asking his opinion. He nodded each time, thinking she could have worn a burlap sack and looked beautiful. That's one of the things that Audie had never understood about women. So many of them felt they needed to get all dolled up in tight skirts and high heels, looking elegant as champagne flutes, when in reality they looked just as good in a T-shirt and faded pair of jeans.

Belita chose carefully. Audie paid. Afterwards he made her sit down at a restaurant with proper linen on the tables. He found himself feeling unaccountably happy in a way that he could not remember being for a long time. They spoke in Spanish and he watched the way the light played in her eyes and could not conceive of a more beautiful woman. He pictured them sitting at a little seafront café somewhere in El Salvador with the palms shifting above them and the sea a vivid blue, like those pictures you see in travel brochures.

'What did you want to be when you were little?' he asked her.

'Happy.'

'I wanted to be a fireman.'

'Why?'

'When I was thirteen I saw these firefighters pull three people from a burning building. Only one of the victims survived but I remember seeing those firefighters emerge from the smoke covered in soot and dust. They looked like statues. Memorials.'

'You wanted to be a statue?'

'I wanted to be a hero.'

'I thought you wanted to be an engineer.'

'That came later. I liked the idea of building bridges and skyscrapers – things that would outlive me.'

'You could have planted a tree,' she said.

'That's not the same.'

'Where I come from people are more interested in growing food than building monuments.'

Late afternoon, they battled the traffic on the journey home. The sun had dipped, painting a pathway across the ocean, arrow-straight, golden. But a storm somewhere had whipped up the waves, which were breaking on sandbanks offshore, spouting foam and mist.

'I want to walk on the beach,' she said.

'It's getting dark.'

'Please.'

He took the next exit onto the Old Pacific Highway and drove along a dirt track beneath the golden cliffs, pulling up in front of a deserted lifeguard tower. Belita left her sandals in the car. She ran across the stretch of sand, the sun shining through the thin fabric of her dress, accentuating every curve.

Audie had trouble pulling off his boots. He rolled up his jeans. He found her paddling in the white-wash, pulling the hem of her dress higher on her thighs to stop it getting splashed.

'Salt water is a great healer,' she said. 'When I was a girl I had surgery on my foot. My father took me to the ocean and I sat in a rock pool every day and my foot got better. I remember going to sleep to the sound of the waves. That's why I love the sea. Mother Ocean remembers me.'

Audie didn't know what to say.

'I'm going to swim,' she said, running back up the beach and unfastening her dress, pushing it down over her hips, dropping it onto the sand.

'What about your clothes?'

'I have new ones.'

She waded into the water in her underwear, gasping at the cold. She looked over a shoulder, a gesture he would never get over, a moment fixed in his mind – the perfection of her skin, the music in her laughter; her eyes brown in places that brown could only dream of reaching. And he knew at that precise moment that he would always yearn for Belita, whether they spent their lives together or if they parted that evening and he never saw her again.

She dived beneath a wave. He lost sight of her. Time passed. He waded deeper, calling her name. She still hadn't surfaced. He tore off his shirt and threw it behind him. Going deeper. Frantic. His feet slipped and he went under. The cold closed around him.

He saw her just before a wave crashed over him, forcing him under, spinning his body. He could no longer tell up or down. He hit his head on something hard. Spun. Kicked for the surface. Another wave pushed him under. He swallowed water, thrashing blindly.

Arms circled his waist. Words were whispered in his ear. 'Be calm.'

She pulled him backward until his feet found the bottom. He spluttered and coughed and felt like he'd swallowed a wave. Belita grabbed his face in her hands and Audie wiped his eyes and returned her stare, looking at her intently, engulfed by a strange, unsettling intimacy.

'Why didn't you tell me you couldn't swim?' she asked.

'I thought you were drowning.'

Belita's underwear clung to her the way it did when he first saw her at Urban's house. 'Why do you keep trying to save me?'

Audie knew the answer, but was frightened of the question.

# CHAPTER 27

Valdez has phoned Sandy four times since breakfast, reassuring her that everything was okay and Audie Palmer would be caught soon. Their conversations were short, tense, remote and sown with unspoken accusations and rebuttals. He wonders when their marriage became defined by the gaps and silences in between the words.

In the early days it had been different. He met Sandy in difficult circumstances. She was wearing a medical gown and sitting on the edge of a hospital bed, sobbing into the shoulder of a rape counsellor. Her clothes had been sent to the lab and her parents were bringing her fresh ones from home. Sandy was only seventeen and she'd been raped by a wide-receiver at an end-of-season party for her school football team.

Her parents were religious and law-abiding. Good people. But they wouldn't see their daughter raped all over again by a 'scumbag defence attorney', so the boy was never charged.

Valdez stayed in touch with the family and five years later he bumped into Sandy at a bar in

Magnolia. They started dating and got engaged and married on her twenty-third birthday. In truth the two of them didn't have much in common. She loved fashion and music and holidays in Europe. He preferred football and Nascars and hunting. He liked their sex to be serious, almost earnest, while she liked to laugh and tickle and be playful. He wanted her to be modest, well-presented and charming, while she wanted him to sometimes flip her over, plant her feet and take her from behind.

Sandy thought it was because of the rape that she couldn't get pregnant. Somehow her ovaries had been seeded with something noxious, which meant nothing could grow in her garden; or maybe it was God's punishment for her being promiscuous. She hadn't been a virgin when she went to the party. She hadn't been a virgin since she was fifteen. If only she'd waited . . . If only she'd been pure . . .

Valdez parks outside the Texas Children's Hospital and flashes his badge at the medical receptionist, asking to see Bernadette Palmer. Fingers tap on computer keys. Phone calls are made. Valdez gazes across the main foyer and remembers how many times he and Sandy walked through this place. They spent seven years trying to have a baby, visiting the Family Fertility Centre, going through the regimen of injections, egg harvesting and conception in a test tube. He grew to hate hospitals.

He grew to hate other people's children. He grew to hate the monthly cry of anguish he heard when Sandy's period came in.

The receptionist hands him a visitor's badge and directs him upstairs. She tells him to have a nice day, as though he might otherwise have forgotten.

Bernadette Palmer is on a break. Valdez finds her in the hospital's deli café on the sixteenth floor of the west tower. She doesn't look like her brother. She's tall and big-boned with a round face and strands of grey hair pulling out of her bun.

'Do you know why I'm here?' he asks.

'I already talked to the police.'

'Has your brother been in touch with you?'

Her eyes play hooky, going everywhere except his face.

'You know it's a criminal offence to help a fugitive?' he says.

'Audie served his time.'

'He escaped from custody.'

'By one lousy day – can't you just leave him alone?'

Valdez pulls up a chair and takes a moment to admire the view. It's not particularly beautiful, but he doesn't often get to see the city from this angle. From high up it looks less haphazard and he can see the general design – the small streets feeding into larger ones and the landscape divided into neat blocks. It's a shame that we can't see everything in life from above, to get our bearings and put things into perspective.

213

'How many brothers do you have?' he asks.

'You know how many.'

'One is a cop killer and the other a regular killer – must make you proud.'

Bernadette pauses and puts down her sandwich, wiping her mouth with a paper napkin. Folding it carefully.

'Audie isn't like Carl.'

'What does that mean?'

'You can eat from the same pot of chilli and still be different.'

'When did you last hear from Audie?'

'I can't remember.'

He gives her a long-lipped Coyote smile. 'That's strange. I showed your supervisor a photograph. She said somebody who looked just like your brother came to see you this morning.'

Bernadette doesn't reply.

'What did he want?'

'Money.'

'Did you give him any?'

'I don't have any.'

'Where is he staying?'

'He didn't say.'

'I could arrest you.'

'Go ahead, Sheriff.' She holds out her hands. 'Better cuff me. I might be dangerous. Oh, no, that's right – you prefer to shoot people.'

Valdez doesn't rise to the bait but would love to wipe that smile off her face with the back of his hand.

Bernadette folds the wax paper around her sandwich and dumps it into the trash. 'I'm going back to my ward. Sick kids need looking after.'

Valdez's phone is ringing. He looks at the lit screen.

*'Sheriff?'*

'Yeah.'

*'This is the Houston Dispatch Centre. You wanted to know if Audie Palmer's name came up. An hour ago one of our operators took a call from a woman who wanted to know if a reward had been posted on Palmer. She didn't give her name.'*

'Where was she calling from?'

*'She didn't say.'*

'What about a number?'

*'She used a cell phone. We triangulated the signal and traced it to a motel on Airline Drive, just off the North Freeway. I was going to call the FBI.'*

'I'll do it,' says Valdez.

The girls are watching music videos and dancing on the beds. Once lithe and bold, Cassie now has the making of a muffin top above the waistband of her jeans, but she knows how to move, holding her arms in the air and bumping hips with Scarlett.

'Have I missed the party?' asks Audie.

'Show us what you got,' replies Cassie.

Audie puts on his best moves, singing along to Justin Timberlake, but it's been so long since he danced that he comes across as gangly and uncoordinated. Both girls finish up collapsing with laughter.

Audie stops.

'Don't get self-conscious, keep going,' says Cassie.

'Yeah,' says Scarlett, who is mimicking his dance moves.

'I'm glad I could keep you entertained,' says Audie, falling backwards onto the bed. Scarlett jumps on top of him. He tickles her until she snorts. Then she shows him her latest drawings, propping her scrawny knees on the mattress beside him, rolling a putty-coloured ball of gum around her mouth.

'Let me guess . . . that's a princess.'

'Uh huh.'

'And that's a horse?'

'No, it'th a unicorn.'

'Of course it is. And who's that?'

'You.'

'Really? What am I?'

'You're the printh.'

Audie grins and sneaks a look at Cassie, who is pretending not to be listening. Scarlett's inner world seems to be populated by princesses, princes, castles and happy-ever-after endings. It's as though she's trying to wish another life into being.

Cassie is standing with her back against the closed curtains and her arms folded. Audie looks up at her. 'I didn't think you'd still be here.'

'We're leaving tomorrow.'

There is a long pause. 'Maybe you should think about going home.'

Cassie lowers her gaze. 'We're not welcome.'

'How do you know?'

'Daddy told me so.'

'And when was that?'

'Six years ago.'

'Man can change his mind a dozen times in six years. Does he have a temper?'

She nods.

'Has he ever hit you?'

Her eyes flash. 'He wouldn't dare.'

'Has he ever met Scarlett?'

'He came to the hospital but I wouldn't let him see her – not after the way he talked to me.'

'You sound a bit like him.'

A muscle twitches down the side of her jaw. 'I'm *nothing* like him.'

'You're quick to anger, obdurate, argumentative, intransigent.'

'I don't know what half them words mean.'

'You don't back down.'

She shrugs.

'Why not call him? Take the high ground. See what happens.'

'Maybe you should mind your own business.'

Audie leans across the bed and picks up Cassie's cell phone. She tries to snatch it back.

'I'll call him.'

'No!'

'I'll tell him you and Scarlett are okay.' He's holding the phone out of her reach. 'One phone call – what's the harm in that?'

She looks frightened, desperate. 'What if he hangs up?'

'It'll be his loss, not yours.'

Cassie sits on the edge of the bed, hands squeezed between her knees, skin pale. Sensing something important is happening, Scarlett crawls up next to her, resting her head on her shoulder.

Audie makes the call. The man on the end of the line answers gruffly, as though dragged away from his favourite TV show.

'Is that Mr Brennan?'

*'Who's this?'*

'A friend of Cassie's . . . Cassandra.'

There is a hesitation. Audie can hear Mr Brennan breathing. He glances at Cassie, whose eyes have filled with a fragile kind of hope.

*'Is she all right?'* asks the voice.

'She's fine.'

*'Scarlett?'*

'They're both OK.'

*'Where?'*

'Houston.'

*'My other daughter said Cassie had gone to Florida.'*

'She didn't make it, Mr Brennan.'

There is another long pause but Audie doesn't let it drag out. 'You don't know me, sir, and you have no reason to listen to me, but I believe you're a good man who has always tried to do his best by his family.'

*'I'm a Christian.'*

'They say time heals all wounds – even the

218

deepest ones. Maybe you remember why you and Cassie fought. I know how disagreements can escalate. I know how frustrating it can be when you think a person is losing her way and you want to stop her making a mistake. But you and I both know that some things can't be told or taught. Folks have to find out for themselves.'

'*What's your name, son?*'

'Audie.'

'*Why are calling me?*'

'Your daughter and granddaughter need you.'

'*She wants money.*'

'No, sir.'

'*Why hasn't she called me, herself?*'

'She's got a stubborn streak . . . in a good way. Maybe she gets that from you. She's proud. She's a good mother. She's been doing this on her own.'

Mr Brennan wants to hear more. His voice has grown thick and laced with remorse. Audie continues talking and answering his questions, hearing about arguments that seem less well defined after so much time has passed. His wife had died. He worked two jobs. He didn't give Cassie as much time as she deserved.

'She's here now,' says Audie. 'Would you like to talk to her?'

'*Yes, I would.*'

'Hold on.'

Audie looks at Cassie. Throughout the conversation she has looked hopeful, angry, scared, embarrassed, stubborn and ready to cry. Now she

219

takes the phone, holding it in both hands as though fearful it might drop and shatter. 'Daddy?'

A tear rolls down her cheek and hangs on the corner of her mouth. Audie takes Scarlett by the hand.

'Where are we going?'

'Out.'

He laces up her sneakers and leaves the room, walking down the stairs and past the swimming pool, which has tunnels of smoky blue light beneath the surface. They walk between the rows of parked cars and the palm trees, along the main road to the gas station, where he buys her a popsicle and watches her eat it from the bottom up.

'Why'th my mom alwayth crying?' she asks.

'She laughs too.'

'Not tho much.'

'Sometimes it's not easy being who we're meant to be.'

'Don't it jutht happen?'

'If you're lucky.'

'I don't underthtand.'

'One day you might.'

At some hour after midnight, Audie feels Cassie slip beneath the covers and press her nakedness against his. Sliding one leg across his body, she gets to her knees and straddles him, letting his whiskery chin rub against her cheek and her lips brush against his.

'We have to be quiet.'

'Are you sure?' he asks.

She searches his eyes. 'We're going home tomorrow.'

'I'm glad.'

Letting out a whistling breath, she lowers herself onto him, squeezing her pelvic floor muscles and making him groan.

Eleven years without a woman, but the muscle memory is there. Perhaps that's what people mean by animals behaving instinctively, knowing what to do without ever being shown. Touching. Kissing. Moving. Sighing.

And after it's over, she slips away, returning to the other bed. Audie sleeps and wakes, wondering if it could have been a dream.

The first time Audie made love to Belita they were in her room at Urban's house in the mountains. Urban had gone to San Francisco on 'family business', which Audie thought could be a euphemism for something else. Urban said San Francisco was full of 'fags and bumboys', but he could be equally insulting about Democrats, academics, environmentalists, TV evangelists, vegetarians, umpires, wops, chinks, Serbs and Jews.

For two months Audie had been taking Belita on Urban's money runs, picking up and dropping off cash. Her job was to make a note of the amount, write a receipt and take the money to the bank. Some days they had time to picnic at La Jolla Cove or Pacific Beach, drinking lemonade and eating sandwiches Belita made in the morning. Afterwards they would walk along the boardwalk past the souvenir kiosks, bars and restaurants, mingling with other pedestrians, cyclists and rollerbladers. Audie offered up information about himself, hoping she might do the same, but Belita rarely mentioned her past. Lying on a picnic blanket above La Jolla, he pushed his fingers into the air, making shadows that played across her eyelids. Then he picked wild daisies and threaded them together to form a crown that he placed upon her head.

'Now you're a princess.'

'With weeds on my head?'

'Flowers, not weeds.'

She laughed. 'From now on they're my favourite flower.'

Each afternoon he would drop her home, opening the car door and watching her walk up the path. She didn't turn or wave or invite him inside. In the hours that followed he would try to remember every detail of her face, her hands, her fingers, her chipped nails and the way her earlobes seemed to beckon his lips. But he kept changing small things depending upon how he felt that day. He could make her a virgin or a princess or a mother or a whore, not hallucinations but different lovers in the same woman.

Faint-hearted as usual, Audie didn't say anything. Afterwards, alone, he would speak his mind, eloquently, passionately, making his arguments.

Tomorrow, he told himself. Tomorrow would be the day.

Finally, one afternoon, he opened her door and before Belita could slip away, he grabbed her wrist and drew his body against hers, crushing her lips with an awkward kiss.

'Enough!' she said, pushing him away.

'I love you.'

'Don't talk such nonsense.'

'You're beautiful.'

'You're lonely.'

'Can I kiss you again?'

'No.'

'I want to be with you.'

'You don't know me.'

He put his arms around her. He kissed her hard and held her tight and tried to open her lips but they were pinched closed. He refused to let go and slowly he felt her body surrender and her teeth part and her head tilt back and her arms circled his neck.

'If I let you sleep with me, will you leave me alone?' she asked, as though terrified of what might happen if she ceded even that much territory.

'No,' he replied, picking her up and carrying her into the house. Stumbling into her bedroom they undressed urgently, clumsily, unbuttoning, unhooking, shaking, pulling, kicking, dancing on single feet, unwilling to let go of each other for even a moment. He bit her lip. She pulled his hair. He grabbed her wrists and held them above her head, kissing her like he wanted to steal her breath away.

The act itself was easy, quick, passionate, sweaty and frenzied, yet everything seemed to slow down and Audie was struck by how time seemed to drop away. He had been with women before, mostly ridiculous, fumbling encounters in dorm rooms beneath movie-star posters and photo collages of families. At college they tended to be arty girls who dressed in grungy clothes and read feminist treatises or Sylvia Plath poetry. He would spend the night and slip out before dawn, telling himself that they wouldn't mind if he didn't call them or text.

Other girls he had met had always tried to make themselves important with their flirting and their clothes and their secrets, but Belita wasn't trying to impress him or anyone. She was different. She didn't have to speak. They didn't have to know each other's thoughts. Yet with the barest movement of her eyes, or curl of her lips, or flash of her smile, she could move Audie, who felt as though he was staring into the depths of a well. All he had to do was fall.

What else does he remember? Everything. Every detail of her molasses-coloured skin, her smell, her haughty nose and heavy eyebrows, the faint sheen of perspiration on her top lip, the single bed, their clothes spread across the floor – her cotton dress, bleached by repeated washings, her sandals, her cheap blue panties, a chain around her neck with a small silver crucifix, how her breasts filled the hollow of his hands. How she mewled like a stranded kitten when she came.

'I am Urban's,' she said, absent-mindedly stroking his wrist.

'Yes,' Audie replied, without really listening. Her touch electrified him and paralysed him. Her hand in his, fingers entwined, all life reduced to that one soft, warm point of contact.

They made love again. She worried that Urban might come home and catch them together or that Audie would think her a whore, yet she seemed to crave the weight of his body between her thighs and the quickening of his breath against her ear and every slippery buck of his body.

Afterwards she got up to use the toilet. He sat on the edge of her bed, his eyes accustomed to the darkness. When she returned, he ran the tip of his finger along the nape of her neck and down the length of her spine, rising and falling over her vertebra. She shivered and her whole body seemed to ripple. She mumbled tiredly and curled into a ball. Slept. He did too, waking in the small hours. He could hear water running. She emerged from the bathroom, half-dressed. Pulled on her panties.

'You must go.'

'I love you.'

'Now!'

# CHAPTER 28

The Greater Third Ward in Houston has a small commercial district populated by moneylenders, taco stands, churches, skin joints and joyless bars, secured behind meshed windows and reinforced doors.

Moss pauses outside one of them, which has a sign above the window: FOUR ACES BAIL BONDS. Below is the poetic addendum – *Your baby's daddy sitting in jail? Sell your gold and post his bail.*

Cupping his hands around his eyes, he peers through the heavy-duty mesh. He can see display cases full of jewellery, watches and electric goods. A big Latina woman is washing the floor with a mop and a bucket of soapy water. Moss knocks, rattling the double locks. The cleaning woman opens the door a crack.

'I'm looking for Lester.'

'Mr Duberley ain't here.'

'Where is he?'

She hesitates. Moss peels a ten-dollar note from his wad of cash. She snatches at the money like it's about to fly away in a non-existent breeze and points across the road to a honky-tonk with a

226

single neon sign shaped like a naked cowgirl wearing a Stetson and twirling a lasso.

Moss turns back to the door, but it's already closed.

'Thank you, ma'am,' he says to nobody. 'Pleasure to meet you, too.'

He crosses the road and steps into the darkness of the bar, stumbling down the final two steps into a large room ripe with the smell of sweat, beer and deep-fried flatulence. The long counter runs the length of a mirrored wall with shelves holding bottles in all shapes and colours, some round, some slender, some with red wax seals or screw-tops.

Lester Duberley has both elbows on the bar and is hunching over a glass of crushed ice darkened with bourbon. He's a fat man with large-knuckled hands and clumps of grey hair sprouting from his ears. A paisley waistcoat cannot button over his gut.

Behind Lester's head, a topless girl in a sequined G-string and stilettos is gyrating on a ramp, her skin painted pink by the lights. She has large breasts, sagging slightly, bearing soft spidery stretch marks, whiter than the rest of her skin. Half a dozen men are sitting at tables in front of her, more interested in a second girl, similarly undressed, who is bending forward and peering through her spread knees.

Lester doesn't act surprised to see Moss. He barely reacts at all.

'When did you get out?'

'Day before yesterday.'

'Thought you were doing the full stretch.'

227

'Change of plan.'

Lester holds his glass against his forehead. Moss orders a beer.

'How long has it been?'

'Fifteen years.'

'You must be noticing a lot of changes. I bet you never even heard of an iPad or a smartphone.'

'I been in prison, not Arkansas.'

'Tell me who Kim Kardashian is.'

'Who?'

Lester slaps his thigh and laughs, showing his gold fillings.

One of the drunker patrons makes a lunge for the bendy stripper and the bouncer puts him in a headlock and drags him outside.

'I can't understand why they do that,' says Lester. 'The girl didn't mind.'

'Did you ask her?'

'This place has been raided twice in the past six months. Waste of taxpayer money if you ask me.'

'I didn't know you paid taxes.'

'I'm being serious. What people do privately is nobody else's business. If they want to spend their money on overpriced drinks in skin joints like this, why stop 'em? These guys are helping some poor girl feed her kids or put herself through school. What's so morally wrong with that in these tough economic times?'

'You want smaller government.'

'I'm a capitalist, but not the prissy, pussy-whipped form of capitalism they practise in this country. I want to see a pure form of capitalism. I want to see an America where if you have the money you can do whatever you damn well please. You want to concrete Kansas and you got the money to pay for it – go ahead. You want to frack for oil and gas? Pay the money and you can do it. Instead we have these rules and regulations and God-damn greenies and trade unions and Tea Party Neanderthals and bleeding-heart socialists. Let the fucking money decide.'

'Spoken like a true patriot,' says Moss.

Lester raises his glass. 'Amen to that!' He drinks and rolls his shoulders back. 'What do you want?'

'I need a meeting with Eddie Barefoot.'

'Are you crazy? You just got out.'

'I need some information.'

Lester crushes ice between his teeth. 'I can get you a phone number.'

'No, I want to see him.'

Lester looks at him dubiously. 'What if he don't want to see you?'

'Tell him I'm a friend of Audie Palmer's.'

'Is this about the money?'

'Like you said, Lester, it's always about the money.' Moss raises his beer and drinks it a long slow swallow. 'There's sumpin' else.'

'What?'

'I need a .45. Clean. With ammo.'

'Do I look like your regular punch?'

'I'll pay.'

'Yes you will.'

# CHAPTER 29

Valdez parks his pickup away from the motel and walks the final two blocks, washed by swirling air from passing trucks that are rumbling along the six-lane. Huddled in his jacket against the chill, he pauses at the entrance where the tops of palm trees are bending in the wind and the moon looks like a silver plate behind the swaying fronds.

The night manager is a middle-aged Hispanic man, sitting with his feet propped on the counter, watching a small TV showing a Mexican soap opera where the actors have hairstyles and clothes that are twenty years out of date and they talk as if they're about to fuck or fight each other.

The sheriff flashes his badge and the night manager looks at him nervously.

'You seen this guy?' asks Valdez, showing him a photograph of Audie Palmer.

'Yeah, I seen him, but not for a few days. His hair looks different now. Shorter.'

'Did he rent a room?'

'His girlfriend did. She's on the second floor. Got a kiddie with her.'

'What number?'

The night manager checks the computer. 'Two thirty-nine. Cassandra Brennan.'

'What sort of car does she drive?'

'Honda. Beat to shit. Loaded with stuff.'

Valdez points to the photograph again. 'When did you last see him?'

'I don't work days.'

'When?'

'Night before last. What's he done?'

'He's a wanted fugitive.' Valdez pockets the photograph. 'The rooms on either side – are they occupied?'

'Not since two days ago.'

'I need a key.' Valdez takes the swipe card. 'If I'm not back in five minutes I want you to call this number and say an officer needs help.'

'Why don't *you* call?'

'I don't know if I *need* help yet.'

Audie wakes with a strange certainty that he's been dreaming but with no memory of the dream. He feels the familiar ache of something that has just dropped off the edge of his consciousness, almost glimpsed but now lost. His past feels like that – a swirl of dust and litter.

He opens his eyes, not knowing if he has heard a sound or felt a change in the air pressure. Out of bed, he goes to the window. It's dark outside. Silent.

'What is it?' asks Cassie.

231

'I don't know, but I'm going to leave now.'

'Why?'

'It's time. You stay put. Don't open the door unless it's the police.'

Cassie hesitates and bites her bottom lip, as though trying to stop herself from saying something. Audie laces his boots and grabs his rucksack. He opens the door a crack, looking both ways along the breezeway. Nothing seems to move in the parking lot, but he imagines figures lurking unseen all around him. The reception area is partially visible but he can't see anyone behind the desk.

The breezeway angles to the right. Keeping close to the wall, he moves toward the stairs but hears someone coming. The nearest door is marked HOUSEKEEPING. Audie tries the handle, which rattles loosely. It's a cheap lock. He forces it with his shoulder and steps inside, pulling the door closed. There are wet mops and brooms standing upright in a trolley.

A shadow passes the slatted door. He waits a few more seconds; fear trapped in his throat. At that moment he hears someone yell 'Police!' and a woman scream. Audie is already running. At the bottom of the stairs he turns right and scurries crablike between parked cars until he reaches the rear wall. Up. Over. He lands heavily on the other side. Running again, he crosses a factory yard, finds an open gate to a slip road. He can hear people yelling. Popping sounds. Alarms. Curses.

★　★　★

232

Valdez had always subscribed to the belief that the course of a person's life is dictated by a handful of choices. These aren't necessarily right or wrong decisions, but each of them plots a different path. What if he'd joined the marines instead of the state police? He could have finished up in Afghanistan or Iraq. He could be dead. What if he hadn't been working the night Sandy was raped? He might never have met and comforted her. They might not have fallen in love. What if Max hadn't come into their lives? There are so many 'ifs' and 'buts' and 'maybes', but only a handful of them had ever really counted, because they had the power to change a life.

Pausing outside the motel room, he checks his service revolver but makes the decision to put it back in his shoulder holster. Instead he pulls a second weapon that he keeps strapped to his leg below his right knee. It was something he was taught early in his career by a sheriff who had survived the cost-cutting purges and political correctness of the nineties – always have a throw-down because you never know when it might come in handy. His is a small semi-automatic pistol with a broken handle wrapped in plastic tape. Without a history. Untraceable.

He looks over the balcony. The parking lot is empty. Palm fronds are waving dark shadows on the concrete around the pool. Pressing his ear to the door of 239, he listens. Nothing. He slides the swipe key over the panel. A red light blinks green.

The handle turns and opens a crack on a dark room.

A woman sits up suddenly, clutching a sheet around her. Wide-eyed. Wordless. Valdez scans the room, the beds, the floor, swinging the gun from side to side.

'Where is he?' he whispers.

The woman's mouth opens. No sound emerges.

A shadow steps from the bathroom. Valdez reacts instinctively and yells, 'Police!' Brightness leaps from the muzzle. The little girl gets thrown backwards, her blood spraying across a mirror. Her mother screams. He swings the gun. Fires again. A hole appears in her forehead. Her body slumps sideways, slipping off the bed, pulling the bedclothes with her.

It all happens in a moment, yet it plays out in slow motion in his mind – swinging the gun, pulling the trigger, feeling the weapon recoil and his heart jump with each impact.

The shooting has stopped. Valdez stands frozen, guilty of panicking, guilty of overreaching. He wipes his mouth with the back of his wrist and tries to think clearly. Palmer was here. Where is he? *What have I done?*

Someone is running down the stairs. Valdez goes to the window and sees a shadowy figure running across the parking lot. Kicking open the connecting door, he sprints through the adjoining room, yelling, 'STOP! POLICE! PUT YOUR WEAPON DOWN!'

He sprints along the breezeway, slipping his service revolver from its holster. Raising it above his head, he fires two shots in the air before leaping down the stairs and weaving between parked cars. He takes out his cell and hits 911.

'Shots fired. Officer in pursuit of armed fugitive . . . Airline Drive. Star City Inn. A woman and child have been shot. Paramedics needed.'

He jumps over a wall and runs on across a freight yard until he reaches a wide concrete culvert with a fetid stream running down the centre of the drain. Swinging his weapon from side to side, he looks left and right, turning in a full circle, still on the phone. 'I need backup and a chopper.'

'*Can you still see the offender?*'

'Affirmative. He's heading east along the edge of the culvert. I got factories on my right. Trees on the left.'

'*Can you give us a description?*'

'I know who it is – Audie Palmer.'

'*What's he wearing?*'

'It's too dark to see.'

Cruisers are being sent to East Whitney Street, Oxford Street and Victoria Drive. Soon he'll hear sirens.

Valdez slows and comes to a stop. He bends, hands on knees, panting. Moisture runs into his eyes and down the hollow of his back. His chest heaves and he spits bile onto the broken concrete beneath his shoes. Cursing. Shaking. He wipes his hand over his mouth again, trying to slow down his mind and keep things in perspective. He has to think. Breathe. Plan.

Using a handkerchief, he wipes his prints from the throw-down handgun. Barrel. Trigger. Guard. Safety. Holding it over the culvert, he lets go. The weapon bounces twice on the concrete and finds water.

He takes a falsetto gasp for breath and raises the phone.

'I think I lost him.'

Audie follows the culvert south, splashing through stagnant pools where rats screech and scurry into holes and shopping carts have committed suicide by leaping off the bridges.

Unused to such an open battleground, he has to fight the pull of the empty space around him, feeling it try to rip him apart and scatter the pieces. For years he had walls around him, boundaries and razor wire; something braced against his back, so he didn't have to fight on all sides.

How did the police know where he was? Cassie must have called someone. He doesn't blame her. How was she to know? She's young, already burnt out, no longer sure that she'll live forever, trying to bluff on a weak hand.

Audie has to keep moving forward because there is no way to back up or to start again. He heard shots being fired. The thought of it makes him feel dizzy, as though somebody has been shouting in his ear for hours and left him with an awful buzzing sensation in his head. He jogs past black sacks of rubbish, ripe as body bags, and flat-roofed warehouses with metal doors. The gabled roofs of buildings stand out in sharp definition against the wispy fog and a moon that looks like a cut potato. Pausing beneath a railway bridge, he takes off his boots and empties the water. Freight tracks lead east and west. He climbs out of the culvert and follows the railway, stumbling over the rough scree, heading toward the brightening sky.

Cassie and Scarlett will be okay. They've done nothing wrong. They didn't know he'd escaped from prison. He should never have asked for their help. He should never get close to anyone. Never make promises. That's how this started. He made a promise to Belita. Then he made a promise to himself that he wouldn't die in jail.

At the Kashmere Transit Centre, he catches a bus into downtown with the shift workers and early morning commuters, still half asleep, resting their heads against the windows. Nobody makes eye contact. Nobody speaks. It's not so different from being in prison, he thinks. You try to blend in rather than stand out.

Audie isn't particularly distinctive or unique or striking, so why is he somebody's punching bag, somebody's punch? Playing now at a screen near you – *Honey, I Butt-Fucked Junior.*

The bus drops him in the shadows of Minute Maid Park. Exhausted, he wants to stop moving, but his mind can't slow down. Lying down in a doorway he rests his head on his rucksack and closes his eyes.

# CHAPTER 30

Desiree Furness walks through the motel room, stepping over the body of a little girl, whose eyes are open in surprise. Strands of her blonde hair are clotted with blood and a raggedy doll with woollen hair is lying an inch from her open palm. Desiree has to fight the urge to pick up the doll and tuck it under the girl's arm.

The mother is lying between the bed and the wall. Naked. A slight beer pouch bulges low on her belly and a swirling tattoo is inked into the small of her back. Blonde. Freckles. Pretty. Arc lights have bleached everything in brightness, but can't remove the smell of bowels evacuated in the moment of death or the bloodstain on the wall above her head.

The forensic technicians still have to work to do. Three men and a woman, dressed in crisp white boiler suits, hairnets and plastic bootees, are setting up UV lamps to test the mattress for semen stains. Desiree gazes down at the two beds. Both have been used. The woman was shot as she tried to rise, but why was the little girl near the bathroom?

In a corner between the desk and TV she notices a wastepaper bin crammed full of fast food wrappings and magazines. There are brochures, Q-tips and wads of Kleenex; a box of breakfast cereal and an empty can of roach spray. A child's drawing is stuck beneath the edge of the mirror. Different coloured crayons were used to spell out the girl's name, Scarlett.

Outside, flashing lights are illuminating the motel in beats of colour. Onlookers have gathered in the parking lot, craning to get a better view of the police cruisers and ambulances. Some are taking photographs with iPhones. Others hunker down over the screens in texting position. A few of the local cops are peering into the room, wanting a glimpse of the dead and then wishing they'd kept away.

Desiree had been woken just after 5 a.m. and had driven halfway across the city to this cheap motel full of itinerants, pimps, prostitutes and the mentally defective – anyone who could produce a photo ID and pay forty-nine bucks a night. There are some field agents who dream about a case like this, an opportunity to investigate a multiple homicide, to catch the perpetrator and lock him in a cage. Desiree wants to go back to bed.

Other agents have partners, children and lives that approach normality. Desiree hasn't had a boyfriend since she dumped Skeeter, real name Justin, a year ago because he used funny voices and gave her pet names and talked to her like she was seven years old, even when she begged him to be serious. Eventually she wanted to scream at him, shake him, show him scenes like this one, but instead she told him to pack his things.

Crouching beside the girl's body, she notices several bloody boot prints on the carpet and examines the busted lock on the adjoining door, trying to recreate what happened in the room, but none of it makes sense.

She pushes a lock of hair from the child's eyes, wishing she could ask Scarlett questions, wishing the little girl could answer.

She peels off her gloves and goes in search of fresher air. More technicians are outside at the dead woman's car and dusting for prints along the breezeway, swapping small talk like this is just another day at the office. The man in charge is in his mid-thirties with a fleshy face and dark rings beneath his eyes. Desiree introduces herself but doesn't shake his gloved hand.

'What have you got?'

'Three, maybe four shots – two in the mother, one in the girl.'

'The weapon?'

'Possibly a .22 handgun, semi-automatic.'

'Where was the shooter standing?'

'Too early to say.'

'Speculate?'

'The mother was on the bed. The daughter came out of the bathroom. The shooter was probably standing in the middle of the room, closer to the window than the bathroom.'

Desiree turns away and runs her fingers through her hair. 'I want to see the ballistics report as soon as you're done.'

The spotlight from a TV camera blinds her momentarily. Reporters are yelling questions from the parking lot. There are news crews from local TV and radio stations. A chopper circles above, filming for the morning bulletins. One camera team is attached to the local homicide squad filming a reality TV show for a cable channel, turning cops into celebrities and spooking the public into buying more guns and burglar alarms.

Desiree finds Sheriff Ryan Valdez waiting in a spare motel room that has been commandeered by the homicide squad. He's lying on a bed with the brim of his Stetson pulled down like he's catching some shut-eye. He's surrendered his service revolver and his hands are wrapped in plastic bags, but somebody has brought him a coffee.

Although she has never met the sheriff, Desiree has already formed an opinion, which is heavily influenced by what she's just seen in the motel room. Valdez sits up and tilts his hat back.

'Why didn't you call for backup?' she asks.

'Nice to make your acquaintance,' he says. 'I don't believe we've been introduced.'

'Answer my question.'

'I didn't know if Audie Palmer was here.'

'The night manager identified him from the photograph you showed him.'

'He said he hadn't seen Palmer in two days.'

'So you decided to bust in?'

'I tried to make an arrest.'

Desiree stares at him, gripping her fists so tightly her fingernails cut into her palms. She produces her badge. Valdez doesn't appear to take any notice. He blinks at her with red-rimmed eyes, but his gaze seems to be summing her up and dismissing her without a second thought.

'Tell me what happened.'

'I announced myself, a woman screamed and I heard shooting. I came through the door, but they were already dead. He shot them in cold blood. Gunned them down. The man has no conscience.'

Desiree takes a chair and pulls it in front of the sheriff. He's bleeding a little from the corner of his mouth.

'What happened?' She points at his face.

'Must have been a tree branch.'

She sniffs and tastes something in her saliva, wanting to spit. 'What were you doing here, Sheriff?'

'A woman called Crime Stoppers asking if there was a reward out on Audie Palmer.'

'And you know this because?'

'A dispatcher told me.'

'This isn't your jurisdiction. You're the sheriff in Dreyfus County.'

'I asked to be kept informed. Palmer was outside my house. He talked to my wife and son. I have a right to protect my family.'

'So you decided to go all Charles Bronson on his ass?'

The corners of Valdez's mouth curl upward. 'Since you seem to know all the answers, Special Agent, why do you think Audie Palmer came looking for me? Maybe he's brain-damaged. Maybe he wants payback. I don't know what goes on inside the fucked-up head of a killer. I followed up a lead that the FBI failed to follow.'

'The FBI hadn't been informed. Now two people are dead and their blood is on your hands.'

'Not mine. His.'

Desiree feels a tension band pressing around her forehead. She doesn't like this man. Maybe he's telling the truth, but every time he opens his mouth, she sees a hole in a woman's forehead and a little girl lying in a pool of blood.

'Tell me the story again,' she says, wanting to know the exact sequence of events. Where was he standing when he heard shots fired? When did he open the door? What did he see?

Valdez gives the same account, describing how he announced himself and heard shots. 'I came through the door and saw the bodies. He'd gone through the connecting room so I went after him. I yelled for him to stop. Squeezed off a couple of shots, but he went over the top of the fence like he had wings.'

'Did you have your weapon drawn when you came through the door?'

'Yes, ma'am.'

'When you were chasing Palmer, how many shots did you fire?'

'Two, maybe three.'

'Did you hit him?'

'Might have done. Like I said, that boy can flat out haul ass.'

'Where did you lose sight of him?'

'He crossed the canal. I think I saw him drop something.'

'Where.'

'Near the bridge.'

'How far away was he?'

'Eighty, maybe ninety yards.'

'But you could see him in the dark?'

'I heard the splash.'

'And then you lost him.'

'I came back here and tried to help the woman and her little girl.'

'Did you move the bodies?'

'I think I turned the girl over to check her heartbeat.'

'Did you wash your hands?'

'I had blood on them.'

Valdez squeezes his eyes shut. A tear emerges and hovers in the wrinkles. He wipes it away. 'I didn't know Palmer was going to shoot them.'

A sheriff's deputy knocks on the door. Young. Fresh-faced. Grinning.

'Look what I found,' he says, holding a muddy pistol between his thumb and forefinger.

'Wow! Did you also find your brain?'

The deputy frowns, his smile gone.

Desiree opens a plastic Ziploc bag. 'It's evidence, you moron!' The muddy pistol is dropped inside. 'Show me where you found it.'

She follows him outside, walking between squad cars and ambulances, past the grief tourists, bystanders and rubberneckers. She can't hear the comments but she knows they're marvelling at her diminutiveness, telling jokes or making cooing sounds about the cute little FBI agent. Every day she has to contend with this, but Desiree knows that no amount of wishing will rearrange her DNA or take inches from her hips and put them on her legs.

The deputy leads her along the storm-water culvert behind a factory and a warehouse until they reach a concrete bridge. He shines a flashlight into the drain, revealing an oily puddle. Snapping on polyethylene gloves, Desiree slides down the sloped side and searches through the weeds, gravel, broken glass, discarded rubbers, beer cans, wine bottles and hamburger wrappers.

Her first station boss told her that most agents make the mistake of looking at events from the top down, when they should be doing the opposite. 'You got to *think* like a criminal,' he said. 'Get down in the gutter and look at the world through their eyes.'

Right now she's wading through putrid water in a stinking drain. The only way to look is up.

# CHAPTER 31

Audie hears a metal shutter being unlocked and rolled upward. Opening his eyes he sees a mobile taco stand painted in primary colours with a cartoon picture of a mouse with big ears and an oversized yellow sombrero. As a kid Audie used to watch cartoons with Speedy Gonzales, the fastest mouse in Mexico, who would always outwit stupid cats and save his village from the gringos.

'Rough night,' says the cook, who is opening plastic containers of sliced onions, peppers, jalapenos and cheese. He fires up the grill and wipes it down. 'You want me to fix you sumpin'?'

Audie shakes his head.

'How about a drink?'

Audie accepts a bottle of water. The cook is short and squat with an unkempt moustache and a soiled apron. He's still talking as he splashes water on the hotplate and scrubs it with a wire brush. A TV is bracketed to the wall above his head. It's showing Fox News – fair and balanced for those who like falling over. A woman reporter is doing a piece to camera, standing in front of crime-scene tape. In the background there are technicians in coveralls searching a Honda CRV.

*'Houston police are this morning hunting a dangerous fugitive following a double homicide at a city motel in the early hours. A mother and daughter were shot dead in an upstairs room at the Star City Inn on Airline Drive. Crime Scene Investigators are at the scene and the bodies are still inside.*

*The drama began just before five a.m. when guests heard several shots fired and police demanding that the gunman surrender . . .'*

Vomit rises into Audie's oesophagus and fills his mouth. He swallows, tasting whatever he ate yesterday. The bottle of water has dropped from his fingers and the contents are spilling into the gutter. Meanwhile, the footage switches to an eyewitness – a large white guy in a plaid shirt.

*'I heard these shots and someone shouting, "Stop or I'll shoot!" and then more shots. There were bullets flying everywhere.'*

*'Did you see the gunman?'*

*'Nope, I kept my head down.'*

*'Do you know anything about the victims?'*

*'A woman and her little girl: I seen 'em having breakfast yesterday. The girl was eating waffles, a sweet little thing, missing her front tooth.'*

Audie can't look at the screen any more. Cassie and Scarlett are alive in his mind, breathing not bleeding, and he doesn't want to believe differently. He wants to run. No, he wants to fight. He wants someone to explain.

*'The police have released the name and photograph of a man they wish to question . . .'*

He glances up at the screen and sees his police mugshot, which is soon replaced by an image from his high school yearbook. It's like he's aging backwards, his skin growing smoother, hair longer, eyes brighter . . .

The camera shot changes again to the exterior of the motel. Audie recognises someone in the foreground – the short frizzy-haired FBI agent who once visited him in prison. She had wanted to talk about the money, but they had finished up chatting about books and writers like Steinbeck and Faulkner. She told him he should read Alice Walker and Toni Morrison to get a female perspective on poverty.

The cook has been scrubbing the hotplate, taking no notice of the TV. He wipes his hands and looks at Audie. 'Are you crying?'

Audie blinks at him.

'I'll make you a breakfast burrito. Life is always better with food in your stomach.' The cook is putting onions and peppers on the hotplate. 'You doing drugs?'

Audie shakes his head.

'You a drinker?'

'No.'

'I'm not judging you,' says the cook. 'Every man got his vices.'

The TV news has moved on to a tornado in Oklahoma and the third game of the World

Series. Audie turns away, his face prickling, fever in his eyes. He can still feel Cassie's body against his and hear her breath in his ear and smell her sex upon his fingertips. This is his madness. His fault. Einstein said that the definition of insanity was doing the same thing over and over again and expecting the outcome to be different. Audie's life had been like that. Every day. Every relationship. Every tragedy.

Leaning into the gutter, his chest heaves and his nose runs and he hurts in places that he cannot name. Bereft and bewildered, he has lost control. Whatever plan he once had doesn't seem important any more. It doesn't seem possible.

Around him people carry on with their lives: commuters, shoppers, tourists, businessmen, boys in baseball caps, beggars in rags – people determined to be themselves, others trying to be someone else. Audie just wants to *be*.

# CHAPTER 32

Moss waits on the corner of Caroline and Bell streets watching vehicles being paused on red lights and shoved on by green. He looks at his cell phone. Nobody has called him yet. Maybe they were lying to him about the GPS tracking device. Glancing skyward, he looks into the blue white-welted sky and wonders if satellites are watching him now. He's tempted to wave or flip them the bird.

A six-door Autocrat pulls up at the kerb and a black chauffeur gets out and tells Moss to spread his legs and brace himself against the car. The chauffeur runs a metal detector up and down Moss's front and back, along his arms and between his legs. Moss left his .45 under the front seat of the pickup, wrapped in an oily rag, alongside a box of shells and a Bowie knife that Lester threw in for free.

The chauffeur nods to the car and the rear door opens. Eddie Barefoot is dressed in a dark suit with a flower in his lapel as though he's going to a wedding or a funeral. He could be anything from twenty-five to fifty, but his yellow curls and spindly legs give him an antique look, like someone who has stepped from a sepia photograph.

A former Miami wiseguy who came to Houston in the late eighties when the Bonanno crime family was expanding its interests away from southern Florida, Eddie built up his own crew, making a fortune from bank and mail fraud, drugs, prostitution and money-laundering. Since then he'd diversified into legitimate businesses, but there was still no serious action in eastern Texas that didn't get pieced to Eddie Barefoot. You paid your respects or you paid a percentage or you paid with broken bones.

The limousine is moving.

'I was surprised to hear from you,' says Eddie, adjusting the lapel flower. 'According to my sources, you are still in the big house.'

'You might want to change your sources,' says Moss, trying to appear relaxed, but scared that his voice might betray him. His eyes are drawn to the depression in Eddie's forehead. According to the story, a ball-socket hammer did the damage. And the man who delivered the blow, a business rival, was later buried up to his neck in sand and forced to swallow a live grenade. This could be a myth, of course, but Eddie had done nothing to correct the record.

'I also heard you went squeaky. The brothers thought you might have found God.'

'I went looking, but he'd left early.'

'Maybe he heard you were coming.'

'Maybe.'

Eddie smiles, appreciating the banter. His voice is steeped in the deep South. 'So how did you get out?'

'State let me go.'

'That's very magnanimous of the state. What did you give them in return?'

'Nothing.'

Eddie removes something from the back of his teeth with his little finger.

'So they just let you walk?'

'Maybe it was a case of mistaken identity.'

Eddie laughs. Moss decides he should join in. The car is speeding along a freeway.

'You know what's really funny,' says Eddie, wiping his eyes. 'You think I'm buying this bullshit. You have precisely fifteen seconds to tell me why you're here before I throw you out of this car. And just to be clear – we won't be slowing down.'

The smiles have gone.

'Two days ago, they dragged me out of my cell, put me on a bus and dumped me on the side of the road south of Houston.'

'They?'

'I don't know their names. I had a sack over my head.'

'Why?'

'I guess they didn't want me recognising them.'

'No, moron, why did they let you go?'

'Oh, they want me to find Audie Palmer. He broke out of prison three days ago.'

'I heard.' Eddie flicks a finger against his hollowed cheek, making a popping sound. 'You're looking for the money.'

'That's the idea.'

'Have you any idea how many people have tried?'

'Yeah, but I know Audie Palmer. I kept him alive inside.'

'So he owes you.'

'Yeah.'

Eddie's face breaks into a smile and he looks like he should be on TV playing a pimp or a drug lord on *Law & Order* or *The Wire*. The limousine is heading towards Galveston Bay, passing freight terminals and railway yards and acres of containers stacked like children's building blocks.

'What's supposed to happen when you find Palmer?' asks Eddie.

'They gave me a phone.'

'And then what?'

'My sentence is commuted.'

Eddie laughs again, slapping his thigh, hoedown style. 'You just take the fucking cake, boy. Nobody is going to give you a get-out-jail-free card with a record like yours.'

Despite the disparaging abuse, Moss can sense that Eddie is trying to work out who would run an operation like this without his knowledge. Who had the juice to get a convicted killer out of prison? It had to be someone with serious connections – a government employee in the Justice Department, or the FBI or the state legislature. A contact like that could be valuable.

'If you find Palmer, I want you to call me first, understand?'

Moss nods, in no position to argue. 'What do you know about the Armaguard truck robbery in Dreyfus County?'

'It was a clusterfuck. Four people died.'

'What about the gang?'

'Vernon and Billy Caine were part of a crew out of New Orleans. Brothers. They knocked over a dozen banks in California and then came east to Arizona and Missouri. Vernon was in charge. They had another regular, Rabbit Burroughs, who was supposed to be part of the armoured truck job but he got picked up for a DUI the weekend before the robbery. They had a warrant out for him in Louisiana.'

'Who else was in the crew?'

'They had someone on the inside.'

'A security guard?'

'Maybe.'

'What about Audie Palmer?'

'Nobody had ever heard of him. His brother Carl had a reputation for being a screw-up. He was dealing rock in the projects at seventeen – Mexican brown and crank, you name it – a finger in every pie. Later he ran with a crew in West Dallas, mainly cash-machine scams and mail fraud. Served five years in Brownsville. Came out with a bigger drug habit than when he went in.

A year later he shot an off-duty dick in a liquor store. Vanished.'

'So where is he?'

'That, my black friend, is the seven-million-dollar question.'

Eddie seems philosophical rather than aggrieved. Usually he'd know about a robbery of this size in advance, but Vernon and Billy Caine were out-of-towners and Carl and Audie were small fry who probably scoped out the job.

Eddie pinches his nose as if clearing his ears. 'You want my opinion? The money has long gone. Carl Palmer is either a mound in the desert or he's spent the millions trying to stay hidden. Either way he's been picked cleaner 'n a wishbone on Thanksgiving Day.'

'Where can I find Rabbit Burroughs?'

'Mostly he's operating on the straight, but he still has a couple of girls hooking out of a laundromat in Cloverleaf. He also works part-time mopping floors at a school in Harris County.'

A button is pressed. The limousine pulls over to the kerb. Massed water looms on three sides. They're on the edge of Morgan's Point, next to a container terminal with an industrial corsetry of cranes and derricks.

'This is where you get out,' says Eddie.

'How do I get back to my pickup?'

'Fifteen years inside, I thought you'd appreciate the walk.'

# CHAPTER 33

Desiree has been awake most of the night, going over the details of the shootings, hoping an answer might emerge from the static and white noise. She closes her eyes and has to force them open again. Someone is hovering behind her, leaning on a partition.

Eric Warner chews on a matchstick. 'I got a call from the Assistant Attorney General's office. Someone has filed a complaint about you.'

'Really? Let me guess – they say I'm too short for the rollercoaster?'

'It's not a joke.'

'Who?'

'Sheriff Ryan Valdez.'

'What did he say?'

'He claims you were abusive, heavy-handed and crude. He said you cast wild aspersions.'

'Did he actually use the word aspersions?'

'He did.'

'I called him a liar and he went and swallowed a thesaurus.'

Warner leans one buttock on the edge of her

desk and folds his arms. 'That sarcastic streak is going to get you into trouble.'

'If I gave up sarcasm that would leave interpretive dance as my only way of communicating.'

This time Warner smiles. 'You don't normally harass law enforcement officers.'

'The man had no right to be where he was. He should have called for backup. He should have notified the FBI.'

'You think that would have made a difference?'

'A mother and daughter might still be alive.'

'You don't know that.'

Desiree sniffs and scratches her nose. 'Maybe not, but I believe there's a thin line between cowboy cops and criminals and I think Valdez is dancing on that high wire, laughing at us.'

Warner tosses the chewed matchstick into a bin. He's got something else to say but takes no pleasure in the news.

'Frank Senogles is taking over the case.'

'What?'

'Seniority. It's now a double homicide.'

'But I'm still on the task force, right?'

'You'll have to ask him.'

There are many things Desiree wants to say, but she bites her tongue and stares at Warner, feeling disappointed and betrayed.

'You'll get your chance,' he says.

'I have no doubt about that,' she replies, glancing at the paperwork on her desk.

When she looks up, Warner has gone. At least she didn't embarrass herself by getting upset or pleading. She'll have to talk to Senogles . . . be nice to him. The two of them have a history, or what an independent observer might call a love–hate relationship: Senogles would *love* to get into Desiree's pants and Desiree *hates* his smugness and bullying ways. A lot of field agents are aggressive in their dealings with people, revelling in the power the badge gives them. They prod, cajole, lie and intimidate to get results, bragging about these things afterwards, as though they're in competition with each other. Who can clear up the most cases? Who can piss highest up the wall?

Being a woman automatically put Desiree at a disadvantage when it came to pissing and her height made her the constant butt of the jokes, but Senogles seemed to regard her very presence in the FBI as a personal affront.

The task force briefing is at midday. Senogles arrives in a flurry of swinging doors, handshakes, high-fives, telling everybody to gather round. Office chairs roll into position. When the circle has formed, he addresses the agents, appearing to grow in stature as he listens to the sound of his own voice. He's early forties with highlighted blue contact lenses, a blaze of bridgework and a JFK haircut.

'You all know why we're here. A mother and daughter are dead. Our prime suspect is this man, Audie Palmer.' He holds up a photograph. 'He is

258

a convicted killer and a fugitive, last seen on foot in this vicinity.' He identifies the area on a large map of Houston.

Senogles turns to another of the agents and asks about the deceased.

'Cassandra Brennan, aged twenty-five, born in Missouri, her father is a preacher. Her mother died when she was twelve. She quit school in ninth grade and ran away from home a couple of times. Later she trained as a beautician and make-up artist.'

'When did she come to Texas?'

'Six years ago. According to her sister she was engaged to marry a soldier who died in Afghanistan, but his family wouldn't recognise the relationship. Until a month ago she was living with her sister and working as a waitress, but there was a problem with the brother-in-law.'

'What sort of problem?'

'He took a little too much interest in Cassandra's welfare. Her sister told her to leave. Since then she's been living in her car.'

'Any other history?'

'Two outstanding warrants for unpaid parking fines and failing to repay $650 of a single-parent allowance that she was overpaid. Apart from that, no rap sheet, no aliases, no other immediate family.'

'How did she meet Palmer?'

'She's not on the visitors register at the prison,' says another of the agents.

'And she didn't come up in the earlier investigation,' adds a third.

'She would have been all of fourteen,' says the first.

'Maybe she was hooking out of the hotel,' says Senogles.

'Not according to the night manager.'

'Maybe he was getting a slice of the action.'

A photograph is pinned to a whiteboard – a shot from Cassie's high school yearbook. She looks coltish and shy, with white blonde hair and a fringe.

'State police are going door-to-door in the surrounding streets, using dogs to search yards and sheds. They're likely to pick up Palmer before we do, but I want to know where he's been, who he's contacted and where he got the gun. Talk to Palmer's family, friends, acquaintances – anybody who knew him or might offer him assistance. See if Palmer had any favourite places that he hung out as a kid. Did they ever go camping? Where does he feel comfortable?'

Desiree raises her hand. 'He grew up in Dallas.'

Senogles looks surprised. 'I didn't see you there, Special Agent Furness. Next time you'll have to stand on a chair.'

There is laughter. Desiree doesn't react.

'So what brings you here?' asks Senogles.

'I was hoping to be part of the task force.'

'I have enough people.'

'I've been keeping tabs on the original robbery and the missing money,' says Desiree.

'The money isn't the issue any more.'

'I've read Palmer's psych reports and prison files. I've talked to him.'

'Do you know where he is?'

'No.'

'Well, you're not much good to me.' Senogles slips the sunglasses from his forehead and puts them in a case.

Desiree remains standing. 'Audie Palmer's mother now lives in Houston and his sister works at the Texas Children's Hospital. Ryan Valdez was one of the law enforcement officers who arrested him eleven years ago.'

Senogles props one foot on a chair and rests his elbow on his knee, as though he's leaning on a fence. There are little webs of wrinkles in the corner of his eyes like hairline cracks in old china.

'What are you suggesting?'

'I think it's odd that Audie Palmer escaped the day before his release and then turned up outside the house of the officer who arrested him.'

'Anything else?'

'I also think it's odd that Valdez tried to apprehend Palmer without calling for backup after the motel night manager had positively identified Palmer from a photograph.'

'You think Valdez is dirty?'

Desiree doesn't answer.

Senogles gazes at the officers around the room. He seems to be caught in two minds. He straightens. 'Okay, you're on the team, but don't go anywhere near the sheriff. He's off-limits.'

Desiree tries to argue.

'Palmer was outside the man's house. Valdez had every right to be concerned. Remember who we're chasing here. If Palmer is launching some sort of revenge campaign, we should be looking at other people who could be targets – the judge, the defence attorney, the DA. They all have to be notified.'

'What about protection?' someone asks.

'Only if they request it.'

# CHAPTER 34

The old Granada Movie Theater in Jenson Drive has been derelict since the mid-nineties. Boarded up. Spray-painted. Stained with bird shit. Abandoned for the multi-plex half a mile away. It was built in the 1950s, when North Houston was the last major shopping area south of Humble and families made a Saturday morning ritual of grocery shopping while their kids watched a double feature.

Lamont's Bakery, where Audie had worked part-time during college, had been across the street, but was now a Chinese restaurant called The Great Wall. His boss at the bakery, Mr Lamont, had once told Audie how he met his namesake, the Texas war hero Audie Murphy, at the Granada Theater when he came to Houston to promote *To Hell and Back*, a movie about his life.

'That's why I gave you this job – you're named after the bravest man I ever met. You know what he did?'

'No,' said Audie.

'He stood on top of a burning tank firing a machine gun while flames were licking at his feet.

He was shot to shit but he refused medical attention, not stopping until his men were safe. Guess how many Krauts he killed.'

Audie shrugged.

'Go on, guess.'

'A hundred.'

'Don't be stupid!'

'Fifty?'

'Damn right! He killed fifty Germans.'

Audie promised Mr Lamont that he'd watch the movie one day, but had never got around to it. It was something else to regret.

Skirting the side of the theatre, he now climbs a fire escape and kicks at a padlocked door that bangs open on rotten hinges, knocking clumps of damp plaster from the wall. He searches the empty building, which smells of mildew and decay. The rows of seats have been ripped out and removed, leaving a sloping cavern strewn with scraps of carpet, twisted metal and broken light fittings. The walls, painted in dark greens and reds, still have decorative mouldings along the architraves and skirting boards.

This is where Audie tries to sleep, curled up in a fetal clutch, resting his head on his jacket. He has forgotten how old he is. He has to count back the years and comes to thirty-three. The night arrives, trembling and shimmering with lightning. It reminds Audie of all those nights in prison, curled on his rack, reliving tragedies against the brickwork.

'You're going to be scared,' Moss told him. 'So when you start getting scared, remember that the longest night is only eight hours and the longest hour is only sixty minutes. Dawn is always going to come – unless you don't want it to – but you got to fight against that thought. Give it one more day.'

Audie didn't think he would miss anything about prison – but he misses Moss. The big fella had been partly a bodyguard, partly a sponsor, mostly a friend.

They'll have questioned him about the escape. Maybe he copped a beating or two. It pains Audie to think about, but it was safer not to tell anyone about his plans – not even Moss. One day he'll write to him and explain.

Forcing his mind to move on, he thinks of Belita and remembers the first few months of their affair, marvelling at how vividly he can recreate particular moments. Love was an accident waiting to happen, he decided. It was like throwing a parachute out of a plane and jumping after it, convinced that you could catch it on the way down. He was falling but it didn't feel like a death plummet.

During those early days he saw Belita four or five times a week, driving her between pickups and drop-offs. They made love in the car and in Audie's room and at Urban's house when he was at a farm or away on business. Never overnight. Never falling asleep in each other's arms or waking up together in the morning. Instead they stole moments like thieves, staring at the ocean afterward, or the night sky or the ceiling of Audie's room.

'How many people have you ever loved?' she asked one day.

'Only you.'

'You're lying to me.'

'Yes.'

'It's all right. You can keep lying to me.'

'How many men have you loved?'

'Two.'

'Does that include me?'

'Yes.'

'Who was the other one?'

'It doesn't matter.'

They were lying in the back of Urban's SUV, parked above a beach where the surf curled and crashed on the sand, sucking to and fro like a mighty set of lungs. There were so many things that he wanted to know about Belita. Everything. He thought that if he gave up the details of his own life she might give up details of hers, but she had the ability to take part in long conversations while saying very little. At the same time her eyes, dark and unblinking, seemed to contain memories and knowledge that Audie couldn't begin to fathom or should leave well alone.

What had he learned? Her Spanish father had owned a little store in Las Colinas and her mother sewed the wedding dresses that he sold. They lived above the shop on two floors where Belita shared a bedroom with her older sister, whom she wouldn't speak of. She didn't like dogs, ghost stories, earthquakes, thrush, mushrooms, candy floss, hospitals, leaking pens, tumble driers, infomercials, smoke alarms, electric ovens and offal.

Her room told him nothing. It was uncluttered by personal possessions and most of the drawers were empty except for her underwear. The wardrobe had a half-dozen dresses, along with the clothes they had bought on their shopping trip.

When he asked her more questions about her family and where she grew up and when she came to America, she would react angrily. It was the same when he professed his love for her. Sometimes she accepted it and other times she called him stupid, pushing him away. She made fun of his youth, or diminished what they shared. Perhaps she hoped to drive him away, but it had the opposite effect because her mockery meant that she cared.

Belita glanced at Audie's wristwatch and said it was time to go. They had grown complacent, taking too many risks, riding their luck.

Audie hated dropping her at the house. He didn't know if she went to Urban's bed every night, but he feared as much and the thought of another man touching Belita made him groan into his pillow. Torn between jealousy and desire, he would lie in bed, his eyes closed, indulging in the cinema of his fantasies. He smelt Belita everywhere. She had scented his world.

'Do you like living like this?' he asked her, as

they drove along the ocean road. It was one of the half-days they sometimes managed to steal. That was how he measured his life now – in the hours he spent with Belita.

She didn't answer, her expression neutral.

He asked again. 'Do you like living with Urban?'

'He has been good to me.'

'He doesn't own you.'

'You don't understand.'

'Explain it to me.'

Audie saw the heat rise in her neck and cheeks.

'You're too young,' she said.

'No younger than you.'

'I have seen more.'

Audie turned his gaze toward the ocean for a moment. Frustrated. Sad. Confused. He wanted to ask if hidden love was still love or if it was like a tree falling in a forest when nobody is around to hear it fall. These moments with Belita seemed so real to him and everything else was an illusion.

'We could leave here,' he said.

'And go where?'

'East. I got family in Texas.'

She smiled sadly, as though listening to a like-able idiot.

'What's so funny?'

'You don't want me.'

'Yes I do.'

The window was open and the wind lifted her hair, blowing it into the corners of her mouth. She raised her knees to her chest and bowed her head.

'What happened to you?' he asked.

She didn't answer. Then he realised she was crying. Audie pulled to the side of the road. It was almost dark. He leaned across and kissed her cheek, saying he was sorry. Her skin felt almost cool. He brushed his fingertips over her face, through the hollows and grooves, as though reading her beauty like a blind man. And he understood for the first time that love could bring misery and cruelty and obliteration as easily as it brought goodness and joy.

She pushed his hands away and told him to take her home. Later he showered and stood for a long time motionless at the mirror, holding his toothbrush, not focusing on himself. He was haunted by Belita's face, which was so close yet so far away, looking through him and beyond him. Her eyebrows were so definite and strong, her lips slightly open, the smoothness of her skin, the brown of her eyes, the shallow panting of her breathing and cascade of sighs. He felt as though their passion could light up cities, yet she was already moving past him, using his body to make a journey to a distant place that he could never hope to reach.

Afterwards he went down the hallway to the payphone and called his mother in Dallas. He hadn't spoken to her in six months, but had sent postcards and a present for her birthday, a picture frame lined with seashells (which was bad luck according to Belita, who was full of superstitions).

He could hear the phone ringing and pictured his mother navigating the narrow corridor, avoiding the side table and the hat stand. There was an echo on the line. He wondered if the wires were actually carrying his words or turning them into signals.

'Are you alright?' she asked.

'I've met someone.'

'Where is she from?'

'El Salvador. I want to marry her.'

'You're too young.'

'She's the one.'

'Have you asked her?'

'No.'

Having fallen asleep at dawn, it is almost midday when Audie wakes. He wants to be outside feeling the sun on his skin and breathing in freedom while it lasts. Leaving the theatre, he walks the streets trying to clear his head. When he left prison he had a plan, but now he's starting to question if the price is too high. Two more innocents dead – how can any end justify those means?

He imagines that people are staring at him, pointing fingers, whispering behind their hands. He passes a man in a dressing gown and a young tattooed woman, brittle with fury, bawling beneath an upstairs window, telling someone to 'open the damn door'. He passes a burnt-out car, an abandoned fridge, discount stores, showrooms and a convoy of motorcyclists.

At some point he looks up and notices a church with a sign out front: IF YOU REALLY LOVE GOD, SHOW HIM YOUR MONEY. On the opposite corner is a small liquor store with a bright neon sign bolted above the door. Bottle after bottle stand upright on the shelves; spirits and liqueurs and fermented fruits that he has never tasted or heard of, yet he contemplates how easy it would be to drink himself to oblivion.

A bell jangles above his head. The aisles are empty. The store has a camera filming the entrance. Audie can see himself on a screen. He nods to the man behind the counter.

There is a pay phone. Audie thinks about calling his mother but instead asks directory assistance for a phone number and listens to it ringing. A receptionist answers.

'I need to talk to Special Agent Furness,' he says.

*'Who's calling?'*

'I've got information for her.'

*'You need to give me your name.'*

'Audie Palmer.'

The receiver is put down on a hard surface. Audie can hear muffled voices and people shouting down corridors. He looks at the cashier. Nods. Turns his back.

A woman answers.

'Is that Special Agent Furness?'

*'It is.'*

'I'm Audie Palmer. We've met before.'

*'Yes, I remember.'*

271

'I read those books you recommended. It took a while for the library to get hold of them, but I enjoyed them very much.'

*'You didn't call me for a book club meeting.'*

'No.'

*'You know we're looking for you, Audie.'*

'I figured as much.'

*'Give yourself up.'*

'I can't do that.'

*'Why?'*

'I still got some stuff I have to do, but you need to know that I didn't shoot Cassie and Scarlett. You have my word of honour. On my mother's life and my father's grave, it wasn't me.'

*'Why don't you come in and explain it to me?'*

Audie can feel perspiration dripping from his armpits. He holds the receiver away from his head and wipes his ear with his shoulder.

*'Are you still there?'*

'Yes, ma'am.'

*'Why did you escape, Audie? You only had one more day.'*

'I didn't steal that money.'

*'You fessed up to the robbery.'*

'I had my reasons.'

*'Why?'*

'I can't tell you that.'

Special Agent Furness unpicks the silence. *'I appreciate that you might have taken the fall for your brother or someone else, Audie, but in the eyes of the law everyone involved in a robbery is equally guilty*

272

*whether they did the hijacking, drove the getaway car or just made the phone calls.'*

'You don't understand.'

*'Then explain it to me. Why did you escape from prison? You were going to be released.'*

'I was *never* going to be free.'

*'Why?'*

He sighs. 'I have spent the past eleven years being scared, Agent Furness. Frightened of things that might happen. Frightened of things that did. Sleeping with one eye open. Keeping my back to every wall. But you know something – I've been sleeping just fine since I got out. I think I've come to realise that fear is the real enemy.'

She inhales deeply. *'Where are you?'*

'In a liquor store.'

*'Let me come and get you.'*

'I won't be here.'

*'What about Carl?'*

'He's dead.'

*'When?'*

Audie holds the phone tighter to his ear and squeezes his eyes shut until a kaleidoscope of coloured lights begins to swirl across his pupils. The lights fade and he pictures his brother sitting beside the river, his face slick with sweat, cradling a gun on his lap. Blood oozed through the bandages on his chest and Carl peered into the black water as though the river held the answer to life's most important question. Carl knew he wasn't going to the hospital. He wasn't going to escape to California and start a new life.

'That man I killed had a wife and kiddie on the way,' he said. 'I wish I could do things over. I wish I'd never been born.'

'I'm going to get a doctor,' Audie said. 'You're going to be all right.' But even as he spoke the words, Audie knew they weren't true.

'I don't deserve forgiveness or prayers,' said Carl. 'That's where I belong.' He motioned to the river, where the current sucked and coiled, oily black and unforgiving.

'Don't say things like that,' Audie said.

'Tell Ma I love her.'

'She knows.'

'Don't tell her what comes next.'

Audie wanted to argue, but Carl had stopped listening. He pointed the gun at Audie and told him to leave. He refused. Carl held the gun against Audie's forehead and screamed at him, spraying his face with bloody spit.

Audie got in the truck and drove away, bouncing along the rutted track, tears blurring his vision. He looked in the rear-vision mirror, but couldn't see anyone on the riverbank. For years he tried to convince himself that somehow Carl had escaped and was living out his life under a different name with a good job, a wife and a family, but deep down he knew what Carl had done. Special Agent Furness is still on the phone, wanting Audie to explain.

'Carl died fourteen years ago in the Trinity River.'

'*How?*'

'He drowned.'

'*We didn't find his body.*'

'He weighed it down with scrap metal and jumped into the river.'

'*How do I know you're telling the truth?*'

'Dredge the river.'

'*Why didn't you tell anyone?*'

'He made me promise.'

Audie is about to hang up.

'*Wait!*' says Desiree. '*Why did you go to the sheriff's house?*'

'I had to make sure.'

'*Make sure of what?*'

The line goes dead.

# CHAPTER 35

Moss doesn't find Rabbit Burroughs until late afternoon. The janitor is washing the floor of a school gymnasium, treating the mop like an anorexic dance partner. The place smells of sweat, Tiger Balm and something else that Moss recognises from his youth. Hormones, maybe. There's a girl sitting in the stands, playing with a cell phone. She's about thirteen. Overweight. Bored.

'Don't they have machines to do a job like that?' asks Moss, talking to the janitor.

'It's broken,' says Rabbit, turning slowly. He's wearing a short-sleeve Hawaiian shirt, a size too small so that his forearms stick out like Christmas hams, and his long hair is pulled back into a greying ponytail.

'School's finished. Everybody's gone home.'

'It's you I wanted to see.'

Rabbit shifts the mop from his left to his right hand. It can be a weapon now. He is sizing Moss up, deciding whether to fight or flee.

'I'm no threat to you,' says Moss, holding up his hands. 'How long you worked here?'

'Not your business.'

'Do they know you're a convicted felon?'

Rabbit blinks at him. His face looks feverish, the skin moist, his eyelids stitched open.

'I bet they have no idea.'

Rabbit has raised the mop in both hands.

'Relax. You're spilling water everywhere.'

Rabbit looks at the puddle.

'Who's the little girl?' asks Moss.

'She belongs here.'

'What does that mean?'

'Her mother is working. I look after her.'

'What does her mother do?'

'She's cleaning the restrooms.'

Moss wanders across the polished boards. He bounces an imaginary basketball and takes a shot, picturing it dropping into the basket. The place has an echo. He has done a little research on Rabbit and knows he's done two stints in state pens, the longest six years. He also did some time as a juvie for postal fraud and drug possession. But a rap sheet can't tell you anything about how a man was raised – if his father was a violent drunk or if he was ugly, poor or stupid.

Rabbit is an alcoholic. Moss can tell. Red blood vessels are etched against the whites of his eyes and dried mucus has crusted in the corners of his mouth. There are different styles of drunks. Some get bombed in the excitement of the moment, high spirits; others drink to escape. Alone. Soaking.

'Tell me about the Dreyfus County truck robbery.'

'Don't know what you're talking about.'

'You were part of the gang.'

'Not me.'

'You got picked up for DUI before the robbery.'

'You're mistaken.'

Rabbit is mopping again, moving with far more energy than before, doing a foxtrot rather than a waltz. Moss steps closer. The mop swings towards his head. He ducks it easily and twists it out of Rabbit's hands, snapping it across his knee. The girl looks up. The incident happened so quickly she missed it. She looks back at her phone.

Moss hands Rabbit the two broken pieces and the janitor holds them like cheerleading pompoms.

'They're going to make me pay for that.'

Moss reaches into his pocket and pulls out a twenty. He tucks it into the pocket of Rabbit's Hawaiian shirt. Resigned to the situation, Rabbit takes a seat on one of the bleachers and pulls a flask from his pocket. Unscrewing the lid, he upends the metal container and swallows. His eyes go watery. He wipes his lips.

'Y'all think you can frighten me. Y'all think I'm nothin' but a broken-down wreck, but I won't be intimidated. Do you know how many times people have come asking me about that robbery? I been threatened, beat up, burnt with cigarettes, harassed and victimised. The FBI still pulls me in for questioning every couple of years. I know they're listening to my phone calls and checking my bank accounts.'

'I know you don't have the money, Rabbit. Just tell me about the robbery.'

'I was sitting in a county jail.'

'You were supposed to be driving the car.'

'Supposed to be, but I weren't there.'

'Tell me about Vernon and Billy Caine.'

'I knew 'em.'

'You robbed banks with them.'

Rabbit takes another swig from the flask. 'I met Billy in juvie and we stayed friends. I didn't know Vernon until Billy called me one day, out of the blue, and said he had a job. I'd just got laid off work and had car payments due. Vernon was the boss. He had this modus operandi where he and Billy would go into a bank separately and wait in different queues. They let people slip ahead of them, so that each reached a window at roughly the same time, carrying a folded newspaper or a magazine with a gun tucked inside. Only the teller could see it. They didn't shout, or yell at people to lie on the ground, or fire shots in the air. Instead, they spoke very softly, instructing the tellers to fill the bags with cash. Then they walked out, cool as you like, and I drove off. We must have done thirty or forty banks like that, starting in California, moving east.'

'What about the job in Dreyfus County?'

'That was a whole other kettle. Vernon knew a guy who worked at a security company that had a contract to collect cash from banks and brokerages.'

'Scott Beauchamp?'

'I never met the guy.'

'He was the guard who died in the robbery.'

Rabbit shrugs. 'Maybe he was the inside man, maybe he wasn't. Vernon didn't say. It was a perfect set-up. Twice a month the armoured truck visited the banks and collected the damaged bills – the ones that get torn or go through washing machines or get stuff spilt on 'em. The cash is taken to a data-destruction facility near Chicago. The Fed burns the money in a big fucking incinerator. Do you believe that? Vernon knew the timing and the route the truck took, so we planned to hijack the shipment, tie up the guards, blow the back doors and take off with the cash, which was unmarked and untraceable. Nobody even knew the serial numbers. It's not like we were stealing from anyone. The money was gonna get burned anyway, right?'

'How did Audie Palmer get in on the job?'

'Vernon must have found him.'

'You ever meet Palmer?'

'Nope.'

'What about his brother?'

Rabbit shakes his head. 'I never heard of neither of 'em until the job went pear-shaped. I was cut up, I tell you, losing Vernon and Billy like that. Billy was a little spacey. He dropped some acid when he was a teenager and it made him paranoid, but he was a good kid. Dated my little sister for a while.'

'What about since then – any word about Carl?'

'I heard he was in South America.'

'You think he took the cash?'

'That's what the cops said. I figure I must be owed at least half a mill.'

'Why?'

'Vernon promised me a cut even when I couldn't do the job. Now look at me – I'm fucking cleaning floors and babysitting Princess Fiona.'

The girl raises her head and calls out in a whiny voice, 'I'm hungry.'

'Get sumpin' from the machine.'

'I got no money.'

Rabbit searches his pockets. There's only the twenty. He looks at Moss. 'Got anything smaller?'

Moss gives him a five-dollar bill. The girl takes it and tosses her hair. Rabbit watches her go, paying too much attention to her hips.

'Where did you say her mother was?'

'Workin'.'

'You might want to keep your eyes on the floor.'

'Nothin' wrong with looking,' says Rabbit, grinning. 'Then I go home and screw her mother with the lights off.'

Moss grabs him by the shirt, popping buttons that bounce off the sprung floorboards. Rabbit's toes are scrabbling for purchase. 'It was a joke,' he whines. 'Where's your sense of humour?'

'I think I might have lost it up your ass. Maybe I should stick my boot up there and look for it.'

Moss shoves him backwards over the bench and

walks out of the gymnasium, passing the girl at the bottom of the stairs. She's eating a packet of potato chips, licking her fingers.

He stops. Turns. 'He ever touch you inappropriate-like?'

She shakes her head.

'What are you going to do if he does?'

'Cut his pecker off.'

'Clever girl.'

# CHAPTER 36

Audie has spent two hours waiting outside Bernadette's apartment, watching the street and studying the darkened windows, half expecting to see SWAT teams crouching in stairwells and the silhouettes of sharpshooters on the rooftops. Dusk is gathering and the neighbourhood is marbled with shadows as rain clouds move sporadically across the sun.

Residents have come and gone. A woman passes him now, walking a reluctant dog that is too lazy to sniff a hydrant or too fat to cock a leg. A tall thin man in a black suit is smoking on a stoop and staring at the ground between his shoes as though reading a chalk message scrawled on the concrete.

Audie crosses the road, trying to look as though he belongs when he's not sure where he belongs any more. There are cars parked in bays between the dusty shrubs and verdant strips of lawn that seem to be chemically coloured rather than natural. He stops beside a vehicle that is wrapped in a blue plastic cover that ripples in the breeze as though there might be something alive underneath.

Crouching and reaching beneath the fabric, he runs his fingers across the top of each tyre, searching for the keys. Bernadette promised. Perhaps she changed her mind. He looks again, lying on his stomach. A flash of silver catches his attention. The key is lying on the bitumen behind the wheel. He crawls under the chassis.

Behind him he hears footsteps on the pavement. He rises to his haunches, expecting to see a dozen guns pointed at him. The man from the steps is standing over him, blocking out the sun. He's tall with a long nose and a ribbon of hair under his chin that must have started as sideburns and turned into a beard. The cuffs of his trousers are tucked into his boots.

'Howdy.'

Audie tries to smile and nod.

'You lost something?'

'My keys.'

The man draws on his cigarette. The glowing end flares. Audie can't see his eyes but instinctively he knows them to be dull and cruel – the sort of eyes he'd seen on prisoners in prison yards that nobody would approach unless accidentally and never more than once.

Audie begins pulling the cover from the car, a Toyota Camry, almost new. The man crushes the cigarette beneath his boot.

'I want you to throw me the keys.'

'Why?'

'Certain things have to be done. Don't make

'em any harder.' The man's hand is in his jacket pocket. 'If I pull this out, I use it.'

Audie throws him the keys.

The man walks to the rear of the car and opens the trunk. The lid hinges open.

'Get in.'

'No.'

The hand appears, a gun at the end of it, the barrel like a small hollow black tube, aiming at Audie's chest.

'You're not a cop.'

'Get in.'

Audie shakes his head and watches the gun rise from his chest to his forehead.

'They said dead or alive, amigo. Makes no difference to me.'

Audie bends toward the trunk and the gun swings into the back of his head. He doesn't see flashing lights or fireworks. In that brief moment, the darkness narrows to a small white point and fades completely as though someone had turned off an old black and white TV set.

Sometimes Audie imagines he is living somebody else's dream. At other times, he contemplates the possibility of a parallel universe in which Belita is living in California, cleaning house for Urban Covic, sleeping in her master's bed. In this parallel universe, Carl is fixing engines at their daddy's garage and cigarettes aren't carcinogenic and Bernadette's husband isn't a violent drunk and Audie is an engineer working for a foreign aid agency building sewage and water systems.

People talk about there being sliding doors or forks in the road when lives take a different course. Sometimes it's only later, in retrospect, that we recognise we even had a choice. Mostly we are victims of circumstance or prisoners of fate.

When Audie looks back he can pinpoint the day when he came to such a fork in the road. It was a Wednesday morning in mid-October when he arrived to pick up Belita from the big house and she walked to the car wearing dark glasses and a straw hat. He opened the door. She took her seat. Then he noticed her left eye, which was swollen and half closed, already changing colour.

'What happened?'

'Nothing.'

'Did he hit you?'

'I made him angry.'

'He had no right.'

Belita gave him a pitying smile, as though he were a little boy who could never know the ways of the world, never understand what it was like to be a woman, to be her. She got out of the car, chose to sit in the back. They drove in silence, no ease between them, no warmth in each other's company, no opportunity for Audie to relax and soak up her beauty.

Had Urban discovered their affair? Had she been punished? Beaten? Audie felt his vision blur and he wanted to tear down Urban's world – smash every gaming table, jukebox, liquor bottle and fruit tree.

He and Belita spoke only a handful of words that day. She collected the money, filled out the receipts and wrote the deposit slips. By three o'clock they were back at the house. Audie opened her door and reached for her hand. She ignored it. Then he noticed she was wearing something new. Instead of her small silver cross on a chain, she had a pendant around her neck that looked like it could be an emerald.

'Where did you get it?'

She didn't answer.

'Did he give it to you? Was it before or after he hit you?'

She refused to listen.

'Did he fuck you first?'

She spun around and slapped him across the face. She would have struck him again, but he grabbed her hand and tried to pull her close. Kiss her. She fought back. He screamed a question at her.

'Why?'

'He rescued me.'

'I can rescue you.'

'You can't even rescue yourself!'

She fought his hands away and disappeared into the house.

For the next four weeks Belita put space between herself and Audie. She created traps, laid spikes, poisoned conversations. If she wanted distance, he would give it to her, he told himself, but his heart gave a different answer. He saw Belita everywhere . . . in everything. And the thought of anyone else having her made his cheeks burn and chest ache and it felt like the essence of his life was draining away.

One Saturday at Urban's house in the hills, he stripped to the waist and worked on the fountain, which had stopped running a few weeks earlier. Wading into the scum-coloured water, he reached the statue of a nymph with apple-sized breasts, wide hips and a wreath around her head.

The tiles were bright blue, missing in places. He began to scrape the muck from the outlets, using the blade of his penknife. Belita watched him from the veranda. She told him to put on his shirt or he'd get sunburnt. It was the first time she had acknowledged him in a month.

The blade slipped and sliced into his hand. He looked at the cut. Raised his hand. Blood ran down his wrist.

'You idiot!' she cried in Spanish.

Moments later she appeared with a first-aid box. Bandages. Disinfectant.

'You may need stitches.'

'I'll be fine.'

She cleaned the cut and staunched the bleeding.

'Are you angry with me?' he asked.

She didn't answer.

'What have I done to upset you?'

'You must keep this dry.'

'Do you love me?'

'Don't ask.'

'I want to marry you.'

'Stop! Don't say it.'

'Why?'

'I will be sent back one day.'

'What does that mean? Tell me. Why are you so scared?'

'I have lost everything before – it cannot happen again.'

And then she told him the story, describing how the earth bucked and reared and people flipped over like tortoises trapped on their backs and buildings crumbled like biscuits and the sound was like the roar of a locomotive rushing through a tunnel. Forty seconds. That's how long it took for the mountain to come down the hillside and sweep away four hundred houses in Las Colinas, east of San Salvador. The death toll was higher because most people were sleeping.

Belita's husband dragged her outside. He went back for her brother. And a third time for her sister, but neither of them came out. Instead four floors of reinforced concrete collapsed like a concertina, leaving rubble and a cloud of dust. For eight days they dug, pulling out occasional survivors from different buildings, but mostly bodies. They dug with their bare hands until the sidewalks were covered in corpses and the smell was an abomination. They pulled an eight-year-old girl from a basement. An elderly couple were found cradling each other, encased in mud like they'd been cast in bronze.

Both of Belita's parents were dead. Her husband, her sister, a dozen neighbours . . . all swept away. Belita and her brother were all who remained of the family. Oscar was sixteen. She was nineteen and pregnant. The bulldozers were still clearing the rubble when they decided to go north to America. What other choice did they have? They were homeless. Destitute. Bereft.

So they crossed a thousand miles of jungle, mountains, rivers and desert, travelling in the back of trucks or by bus or walking. In Mexico they paid two 'coyotes' to take them across the border to guide and guile them through the desert into Arizona. They walked at night, carrying bottled water, blindly slashing their skin on fences of barbed wire and thorny shrubs. They ran from border agents and were captured. Tied up. Thrown into a van and then into jail, where they slept on a bare floor for three nights before a bus took them back to Mexico.

The second time they tried to do it alone, but bandits found them as they waited to crawl through a hole in the fence. They were stripped naked and their possessions taken. Belita tried to cover her breasts and hide her pregnant belly. The men debated whether to rape her.

'She's pregnant, man,' one of them said.

'The pregnant ones are the best,' replied the

other. 'They hump like minxes because they want a daddy to stick around for their baby.'

He touched her stomach. Oscar threw himself across the gap. He died before he could strike a blow.

'Shit man, look what you did.'

Oscar lay on the ground, blood crawling from his nose. Belita knelt in the dirt next to him, rocking over his body. The bandits left her. She looked at the hole in the fence and the desert beyond. She looked at the way she'd come. Pulling on her clothes, she crawled through the gap and expected to die that night.

They were the darkest hours, crossing the desert without food or water, battling the night-time cold, the insects, the sharp stones; throwing her body into ditches when the border patrol ATVs came past. She walked until sunup and then midday, until a truck driver gave her water and drove her as far as Tucson. For two nights she slept in an abandoned car. Another was spent on a mound of sawdust at a timber yard and the next in a freight car on a railway siding. She ate dog food and went bin diving. She hitched rides and walked until she reached San Diego.

A cousin had told her there was work picking fruit, but few of the foremen wanted to employ a pregnant teenager. She washed clothes and cooked at a pickers' camp until her waters broke and she gave birth in a hospital corridor, waiting for a bed.

That was three years ago. Since then she had

picked crops, washed clothes, cleaned floors and worse, always *sin papeles*. Undocumented. Unregistered. Invisible.

There were no tears as Belita told Audie this story. She didn't seek his sympathy or try to shock him. And even when she spoke of the day two men took her from the field, blindfolded and gagged her, threatening her life unless she agreed to work in a brothel, she did not rail at the injustice. Her past was a life, not a parable, and no different to thousands of other illegals pushed by poverty and pulled by hopes.

Audie held himself motionless as Belita spoke, as though frightened she might stop talking and equally frightened of what else she might say . . His hand rested next to hers, but felt too heavy to lift and take her fingers into his. And so she continued, her eyes saucer-like and full of a terrible gravity, drawing him into a story that was not his yet he feared losing himself in the details.

She finished.

A groan escaped his lips in a voice he did not recognise. 'Where is your son?'

'My cousin is looking after him.'

'Where?'

'In San Diego.' She ran her finger over Audie's bandaged hand. 'I see him on Sundays.'

'Do you have a photograph?'

She took him inside to her bedroom and opened a drawer, showing him a picture in a small silver frame of a little boy, nestled in her lap, her chin resting on the top of his head, his hair falling to just above his eyes that were browner than brown, just like his mother's. Someone had scrawled a message across the bottom of the image: *Life is short. Love is vast. Live like there's no tomorrow.*

Belita took the photograph back and said no more. The story had been told. Now he knew.

# CHAPTER 37

Sitting at the window of a Fourth Ward motel Moss watches the peculiar mix of addiction and prostitution pass by – the people left behind by the latest boom or washed ashore like debris after a storm. In Texas, money doesn't so much churn as trickle down, urinal style, and people will happily pat a man on the back if he's lucky enough to make it, but resent any suggestion they should help him to get there.

The motel room has paisley curtains and nylon carpets and black girls hanging from the adjacent balconies, watched over by pimps who are loitering in the street outside. A century ago Houston was full of bordellos and opium dens. Even the well-to-do women of the city would partake in a pipe to settle their constitutions. Now the drug dealers are usually black teenagers with faces full of arrogant self-regard and designer pockets full of the latest technology.

At dusk Moss goes looking for a bar and some-where cheap to eat. Cars and cabs are jostling like people ready to fight. He enters a place and orders a beer, taking a seat with his back to the door.

This is the sort of dive he used to drink in when he was underage using his older brother's ID.

He watches the bubbles rise in the frosted glass and takes another mouthful, swirling it around in his mouth. The beer doesn't taste as good as it did when he was a teenager, forbidden fruit and all that, but he finishes it anyway because it's been such a long time between drinks.

At some point Moss wants to be outside again. Shoving his hands in his pockets, he walks past factories and car yards and fast food joints that cling to the six-lane like grease. When he reaches an intersection, he glances at a newspaper vending machine. Audie Palmer's face is staring out from the front page – the lopsided grin and floppy bangs.

## TWO DEAD IN HOUSTON MOTEL SHOOTING

Moss can't read below the fold and doesn't have any change. He asks a passer-by, who steps around him like he's contagious. Moss tries to force open the hinged lid of the vending machine. His frustration seems to reach a critical mass and he kicks the metal box. He kicks again and again, until the hinges buckle and break. He picks up a newspaper from the wreckage, shakes it open and reads the details, not wanting to believe that Audie could shoot dead a mother and daughter.

Maybe he finally cracked, thinks Moss, aware of his own hair-trigger temper and how often he had seen it happen before. An inmate gets a letter from his wife or girlfriend. She's leaving him. She's shacking up with his best friend. She's run off with his savings. That's when some men lose the plot. They string a noose around the bars or saw away at their wrists with a razor blade, or pick a fight with the meanest motherfucker in the yard or take a run at the wire and get riddled with bullets.

Maybe that's why Audie Palmer broke out of prison. He was always looking at that photograph in his notebook, running his fingers over a woman's face, or being woken by his own screams, his chest heaving and face dripping with sweat. Love will do that to a man – drive him crazy. It doesn't make him blind or indestructible, it makes him vulnerable. It makes him human. It makes him real.

The honky-tonk has a string of coloured electric bulbs that crisscross the outside courtyard, strung from a trellis with a gnarled grapevine. A band is playing, dressed in matching cowboy shirts, singing a Beach Boys song with a slide guitar that sounds like someone is stomping on a live cat.

Moss weaves between shoulders, passing a table of women who are dressed in identical pink T-shirts and ballet tutus. One of the number is wearing a bridal veil pinned to her head and an 'L-plate' strung around her neck. She's gyrating on the dance floor with a bottle of beer in each hand.

Finding a spare foot of space, Moss leans against the wall, propping one foot on the vertical, nodding his head to the music. He feels a vibration in his pocket. It takes him a moment to work out that his cell phone is making an unaccustomed sound. He fumbles for the right button, his fingers too big for the small keys. Holding the phone cautiously to his ear, he listens, but can't hear anyone over the music.

'Hold on,' he says, pushing through the crowd to the restroom. He takes a stall. The back of the door is decorated with graffiti and drawings of genitalia. Someone has scrawled: *I had to overcome a happy childhood to get this fucked up.*

'You're supposed to be looking for Audie Palmer,' says a voice.

'Maybe I *am* looking.'

'He must be living with the Beach Boys.'

Moss wants to drop the phone into in the toilet bowl and flush it like a turd.

'Palmer has been located,' says the voice. 'I want you to pick him up.'

'Where is he?'

'I'll text you the directions.'

'You'll what?'

'Send you a message, dipshit!'

'If you got Audie, why do you need me?'

'Do you want to go back to prison?'

'No.'

'Then do as you're told.'

Ever since childhood Audie had been terrified of being trapped in confined spaces. Carl once locked him inside an old chest freezer during a game of hide-and-seek. Audie almost suffocated before being let out.

'You were squealing like a girl,' Carl said.

'I'm going to tell Daddy.'

'Do that and I'll put you back in there.'

Audie wakes now like a blind man entering his first day without sight, hoping the world might suddenly reclaim its colour and light. The drumming of the tyres on the road is sending vibrations through his shoulder and hip. His wrists and ankles are fettered with plastic ties and each breath contains a dirty mixture of exhaust fumes and his own body odour. Trying not to panic, he pictures a happier time – a game of baseball, high school, the regional championships, two home runs, both disappearing over left field. He punches the air as he rounds first base and high-fives his teammates on the run home. He can see his daddy sitting in the bleachers, accepting the plaudits of well-wishers and other parents, soaking up the vicarious fame. Another scene shimmers and takes shape – the state fair in Dallas; fireworks are exploding above the Ferris wheel and Butch Menzies rides a three-hundred-pound Brahman called 'Frenzy', sticking like a burr to its rippling back as it twists, rears and bucks.

Periodically the car pauses, perhaps at stoplights. Audie can hear the radio playing: a country and western song about a lonely cowboy and a woman who did him wrong. Why do women always get the blame, he wonders. He doesn't think Belita was the architect of his woes. She saved him. She took a boy with no prospects and gave him a reason to care. Why else would he still be here?

The car dips off the edge of the road and bounces heavily along a track that rises and falls. The tyres are flinging small rocks against the wheel wells and chassis. Audie feels around for a weapon. The spare wheel is beneath him. Rolling into a ball, he uses his fingers to pull back the nylon matting. He runs his palms around the edges of the wheel rim, which is held down by a central bolt, screwed in place by a wing nut.

He tries to loosen the nut, but the lurching of the car scrapes his knuckles against the sharp metal, stripping skin. He tries again, feels it slacken, but he can't lift the tyre because his own weight holds it in place. It's useless. Foolish. He can't do it. He tries again. His left shoulder feels ready to pop.

The car is slowing down. Stopping. The engine is idling. Boots move over the ground and the latch pops open. The trunk lifts. Audie breathes in the cool nocturnal smell of a forest. The tall man is silhouetted against the sky and the trees. He grabs Audie by the collar and hauls him backwards over the lip, dumping him onto the dirt. Audie groans and turns his head, looking at the nearest trees, which are dull silver in the headlights. They're in a clearing on the edge of a dirt road. Audie can see the old stone foundations of a house or a mill, long gone. Stringy weeds are pushing up through the rubble.

The tall man cuts the plastic tie around Audie's ankles, but leaves his wrists cuffed. Then he opens the passenger side door and pulls out a shovel and a twelve-gauge sawn-off shotgun. He motions for Audie to start walking, pushing him into the arc of light. They move through the knee-high weeds. A bird explodes out of the branches above them. The tall man swings the shotgun into space.

'It's just an owl,' says Audie.

'Who the fuck are you – Al Gore?'

They reach a sandy wash behind the remnants of the house. The foundations consist of concrete blocks partially buried in the dirt. One of them has a metal ring embedded in one end. The tall man hooks up a chain and makes Audie kneel. He wraps the chain around Audie's right ankle, securing him to the concrete block like a dog on a leash. Then he cuts the plastic on Audie's wrists and steps back. Audie stands, massaging his chafed skin. The shovel lands next to him.

'Dig.'

'Why?'

'It'll be your grave.'

'Why would I dig my own grave?'

''Cos you don't want mountain lions, coyotes and vultures predating upon your body.'

'I'll be dead – won't bother me.'

'That's true, but this way you buy a little time. You say a little prayer. You say goodbye to your mama and your friends. You won't feel so bad about dying then.'

'That's your theory?'

'I'm a big-hearted guy.'

Resting his foot on the top edge of the shovel, Audie grips the shaft with both hands and drives the blade deep into the soft sand. He can feel his heart beating against his ribs and a vinegary smell rising from his armpits. His mind ticks over as he digs, evaluating what can be lost or gained from using up his energy.

The chain gives him about a fifteen-foot circle. Testing his boundaries, he feels the cement block move slightly as he reaches the end of the restraint. The tall man is sitting on a slab of stone, leaning back with his cowboy boots crossed and the shotgun resting in the crook of his left forearm.

Audie pauses and wipes his forehead.

'Did you kill them?'

'Who?'

'The woman and her daughter?'

'I don't know what you're talking about.'

'At the motel.'

'Shut up and dig.'

The moon breaks out from behind a cloud, creating shadows beneath the trees and a soft halo around the upper branches. The hole is getting deeper but the sides keep collapsing because the soil is coarse and dry. The tall man lights a cigarette. He seems to exhale more smoke than he inhales.

'I'm just asking if you prefer shooting women and children,' says Audie, pushing his luck.

'I never shot no woman or child.'

'Who do you work for?'

'Anyone who pays.'

'I can pay you more. Don't you know who I am? Audie Palmer. You ever heard of the Dreyfus County truck robbery? Seven million. That was me.' Audie shifts his leg. The chain rattles against the block. 'They never recovered the money.'

The tall man laughs. 'They told me you'd say that.'

'It's true.'

'If you had that sort of money, you wouldn't be living in shitty motels and you wouldn't have done ten years in a federal prison.'

'How do you know I was living in a shitty motel?'

'I watch the news. Keep digging.'

'I got friends who can pay you.'

The gun muzzle swings across Audie's chest and drops lower. 'If you don't shut up I'm gonna shoot you in the leg. You can dig and bleed at the same time. Dirt needs a bit of moisture.'

The tall man's phone is ringing. He keeps the gun trained on Audie, while he reaches into his pocket and flips it open. Audie ponders whether he could flick a blade full of sand in the man's eyes. Maybe he could make the trees if he carried the cement block, but what then?

He can only hear half the conversation.

'When did you call him . . . and he's coming

here . . . how much does he know? Fine. Cost you double.'

The call ends and the tall man steps to the edge of the hole.

'It's not big enough.'

Moss follows the directions he's been given, driving east out of the city before leaving the interstate and taking a series of back roads that grow more narrow and rutted. Eventually he enters an area of dense pine forest, crisscrossed by fire trails and dried-up creek beds. He checks the odometer. He was told it was three miles from the last turn-off. There are fresh tyre tracks in the dust. Slowing down he kills the engine and headlights and coasts down the next hill in neutral. As he peers into the darkness, his eyes pick up a faint flickering light through the trees.

He pulls over and slowly opens the door. The engine makes a pinging sound as it cools. He takes the .45 from beneath the seat and tucks it into the back of his jeans before closing the door with a muffled click. His eyes become accustomed to the darkness as he sets off along the road, heading in the direction of the light. This feels more like an ambush than a prisoner transfer. Wetting his lips, he smells the pine needles and hears the sound of a shovel stabbing into earth.

Moss is not a lover of the countryside. He's city born and bred, preferring to know the proximity of his nearest takeout than seeing newborn lambs gambolling in a meadow or a field of wheat shivering in the breeze. The countryside has too many things that buzz, bite, slither or growl; and it also happens to be full of murderous hicks who think lynching black men should still be a recognised sport, especially in parts of the South.

Ahead, he can see a clearing. A silver sedan is parked on the far side, shining headlights across a dry wash covered in stunted shrubs and weeds. Two men. One of them is sitting on a rock, the other digging a hole.

Seeking higher ground, Moss climbs up a slope, concentrating on his footing. He can hear the shovel rise and then fall. A loose rock rolls from under his feet, triggering a small rockslide that echoes as it tumbles into the wash.

The sitting man jumps to his feet and peers into the darkness, holding a sawn-off shotgun in his fists.

'That weren't no owl,' he says.

'Could have been anything,' says the man digging the hole. Moss recognises the voice. It's Audie Palmer. In the bleaching light, Audie's skin looks sallow and the concavities beneath his eyes are like dark stains. But the eyes themselves are what shock him the most. Once almost fizzing with life and energy, they now stare out from some interior place like a frightened animal or a beaten dog.

Moss lies on the crest of a ridge and peeks from between two boulders, still warm from the heat of the day. Audie is still digging. The other man is the same tall streak of misery that was outside Audie's mother's place, the ex-con with cruel eyes and a ridiculous beard. He's moved to the edge of the light, still swinging the shotgun from side to side.

'Is someone there?'

Moss shrinks down, the rocks cutting his knees and the heels of his hands. He takes a stone and throws it over his head like he's tossing a grenade. The tall man swings the shotgun toward the sound and fires off a shot that explodes in the stillness like cannon fire.

When the noise dies, he crouches behind the crumbling foundations of the building.

'I know you're there,' he yells. 'I mean you no harm.'

'Is that why you started shooting?' replies Moss.

'You shouldn't sneak up on a man.'

'I was told you were expecting me.'

'Is that Mr Webster?'

Audie has stopped digging. He stares up the slope as though trying to place the voice.

'Why didn't you just announce yourself?' asks the tall man.

'You looked a little trigger-happy.'

'I mean you no harm.'

'Then you'll put the gun down.'

'Why would I do that?'

'So you'll see the sun come up.'

Audie is still gazing up the ridge. 'When did you get out, Moss?'

'Few days ago.'

'I didn't know you were up for parole.'

'Neither did I.'

'How you been?'

'Good. I managed to see my old lady.'

'Guess you had some catching up to do.'

Moss laughs. 'We tore up the sheets. I'm still feeling sore.'

The tall man grunts. 'What is this – a PTA meeting?'

Moss ignores him.

'Hey, Audie! They're saying you killed a woman and child.'

'I know.'

'Did you do it?'

'No.'

'I figured as much. Why are you digging a hole?'

Audie motions to the tall man. 'He said it was a grave.'

The tall man interrupts. 'I was only trying to keep him busy till you got here.'

'I'm supposed to make it big enough for two,' yells Audie.

'He's talking horseshit, amigo,' says the tall man, who swings the shotgun at Audie.

Moss is contemplating his next move as he works his way further along the ridge to get a better look at the tall man. He peers over the edge of a rock, trying not to create a silhouette against the sky, still pointing his .45, the hammer on full cock, the barrel trembling because he's holding the grip so hard. From this distance, he's not likely to hit anything unless it's by accident.

'You gonna pick him up, or what?' yells the tall man, his voice bouncing weirdly off the trees.

'We got some shit to talk about first,' Moss replies. 'How about you put the shotgun down? I conversate best when I don't have a gun pointed at me.'

'How do I know you're not armed?'

'You'll have to take my word for it.'

The tall man moves into the glare of the head-lights. He holds the shotgun above his head and places it on the hood of the Camry. He raises his empty hands. 'I done put it down.'

'You wouldn't lie to a fella, would you?'

'Not me, amigo.'

'I wish you'd stop calling me that. It's not like we're pen-pals.'

Moss tucks the .45 into his jeans and gets to his feet, brushing the dirt from the front of his shirt. He slides down the slope, not taking his eyes off the shotgun or the tall man.

Audie can feel the muscles in his neck begin to knot and twist. He's trying to figure out how Moss got released from prison and what he's doing here. He bends down and massages his ankle where the chain is rubbing against his shin. The tall man tells him to get in the hole.

'No.'

'I'll shoot you.'

307

'What with?'

Moss is still fifty yards away. Audie can't see his features, but recognises his walk. Edging closer to the concrete block, Audie picks up the chain in his hands, looping it in his opposite fist like a lasso.

The two men are closer now. Moss shakes out a handkerchief and wipes his forehead with his left hand. His right hand is resting on his hip. The tall man has lit a cigarette and is standing with the headlights behind him, letting them shine in Moss's eyes.

'How do you two know each other?' he asks.

'We go way back,' replies Moss.

'Where you parked?'

'Over the ridge a ways.'

There is a long silence. The tall man truncates it. 'So how do we do this?'

'You hand Audie over and fuck off.'

'You asking me or telling me?'

'If it makes you feel any better you can tell people I asked you.' Moss glances at the chain around Audie's ankle. 'I'll need the keys.'

'Sure.'

The tall man reaches for his back pocket. Instead he draws a pistol that was tucked in his waistband. In the heartbeat it takes to clear his hip, Audie flings the chain, which curls through the air and snaps back again, striking the gun hand. The round goes past Moss's head and hits something harder than bone, issuing a spark. The second shot is closer to the mark, but Moss has taken cover behind a boulder. He goes down hard, twisting his knee, cursing and returning fire without aiming. Both men are shooting at each other.

Audie reloops the chain over his forearm and bends to pick up the concrete block, staggering under the weight. He stumbles toward the vehicle, cradling the rock like he's heavily pregnant or expecting a bullet in the back at any moment. The lactic acid is building up in his muscles, making his forearms burn, but he keeps running until he reaches the Camry. He drops the concrete block and picks up the shotgun, priming it with one hand and aiming it across the hood.

The tall man sees him at the last moment and rolls into the hole. Audie bellows at both of them to hold their fire. Silence follows, except for Audie's breathing and the blood in his ears.

'You got him covered?' yells Moss.

'I got *both* of you covered,' says Audie.

'I came here to help you.'

'That remains to be seen.'

Audie raises his head above the level of the side window and checks the interior of the car. The engine is still running.

'OK, I'll tell you what's going to happen. I'm going to drive away from here and you two can kill each other for all I care.'

'You get behind that wheel and I'll shoot you,' replies the tall man.

'You could try, but this shotgun is more likely

to hit you than the other way round.' Audie looks at his ankle. 'Where are the keys?'

'I'm not giving 'em to you.'

'Suit yourself.'

Audie crouches and picks up the block. He opens the car door and heaves it inside. Then he crawls over the top of the rock and squeezes behind the steering wheel.

The tall man is yelling at Moss to do something.

'What am I supposed to do?'

'Shoot him.'

'*You* shoot him.'

'He's getting away.'

'I'll shoot him if you tell me why that hole got dug big enough for two people.'

'It's like I said, I was keeping him occupied.'

Audie slams the Camry into reverse. The headlights swing over the ground, away from the hole where the tall man is hiding and past the pile of boulders where Moss has taken shelter, onto the dirt road that leads through the pine trees. He waits for the sound of more gunfire, breaking glass.

Nothing. He breathes. He sighs. Sweat cools on his face.

A cloud of dust is floating into the trees as Moss listens to the car labouring up a grade, grinding loose rocks beneath the tyres.

'So, amigo, what happens now?' yells the tall man.

'I should shoot you and bury you in that hole.'

'What makes you think I won't shoot you?'

'You're out of bullets.'

'That's a big call.'

'I counted.'

'Your math is shit. Maybe I got another clip. Maybe I reloaded.'

'I don't believe so.'

'Maybe *you're* out of bullets, amigo, and you're trying to bluff me.'

'Maybe.'

Moss stands, pain flaring in his knee. He limps from the cover of the boulders and walks toward the tall man, who is just a shadow lying in the freshly dug hole. The moon makes a timely appearance so he can see more clearly.

'We're amigos,' says the tall man. 'We both want to get the job done. Put the gun down.'

'I'm not the one who's out of ammo.'

'You keep saying that, but it's not true.'

Moss is close enough to see the tall man's strange beard. 'What were you gonna to do to me and Audie?'

'I was gonna hand him over.'

Moss raises the .45. 'I want a straight answer or your brains will be flying out the back of your head.'

The tall man is still aiming at Moss. He pulls the trigger and hears a dull click. He drops the weapon is disgust.

'On your knees! Hands behind your head!' says

311

Moss, who is now standing at the edge of the hole. He circles the kneeling man. 'You still haven't answered my question.'

'OK, OK, I was supposed to kill you . . . something about loose ends.'

'Who gave the order?'

'I don't know his name. He gave me a cell phone.'

'Are you lying to me?'

'No it's the God honest truth.'

'Whenever somebody starts using God as a character reference it usually means they're lying.'

'I swear to you.'

'Where's the cell?'

'In my pocket.'

'Toss it to me.'

The tall man takes a hand from his head and retrieves the phone. He throws it to Moss. It's the same shitty make and model as the one he was given.

'What did the guy look like?'

'I didn't see his face.'

Moss closes one eye and gazes along his forearm, his finger stroking the trigger.

'What you are fixin' to do?' the tall man asks.

'I haven't decided.'

'If you let me walk away, you won't see me again. I won't keep looking for Audie Palmer. You can have him to yourself.'

'Lie down in the hole.'

'Please, sir, don't.'

'Lie down.'

'I got a mother. She's seventy-six. She's hard of hearing and cain't see real good, but I call her every evening. That's why I would never have hurt Audie Palmer's mama. I was told to threaten her, but I couldn't do it.'

'Shut up, I'm thinking,' says Moss. 'One part of me says I should shoot you, but that's how my problems started. Every time I fronted the parole board the chairman would ask me if I was sorry for my crimes and each time I put my hand on my heart and told him that I'm a different person now, more circumspect and tolerant, slower to anger. If I shot you now I'd be proving myself to be a liar. There's also the other problem.'

'What's that?'

'I'm out of bullets.'

Moss swings his fist in a short sharp arc and the handle of the gun strikes the tall man's temple, causing spittle to fly from his mouth. His body topples forward into the hole and lands with a thud. He'll wake in the morning with a bump and bad memories, but at least he'll wake.

# CHAPTER 38

Out on the road, the Camry is just another vehicle on another journey. Audie steers with both hands on the wheel, trying to overcome the urge to drive too fast and risk drawing attention to himself. He keeps glancing in the mirrors, convinced he's being followed or that every set of oncoming headlights is making directly for him, seeking him out, illuminating his soul.

At some point he turns off the sealed road and passes a barn and a pasture with horses and a water tank. Up the slope he can see the silhouette of a house with darkened windows and fancy railings around the porch. He drags the block from the passenger seat and rests the chain across the edge of a rock. Pressing the barrel of the shotgun against the links he turns his face away before pulling the trigger. The noise hurts his ears and fragments of rock hit the back of his head. He tosses the smoking chain aside.

Back behind the wheel, he returns to the four-lane and thinks about Moss. At first sight of him Audie had wanted to run through the weeds and hug him. He wanted to dance around and laugh and afterwards they'd get drunk and swap stories and as they reminisced the prison years would become nothing and everybody dead would be alive to them, jumping and beating inside their chests so hard they would need another drink to slow the feeling down.

In prison they called Moss the big fella, because he had the physical presence and the reputation that allowed him to circumvent most of the daily squabbles for territory and control. Moss didn't ask for the name or take advantage of his status. Sometimes Audie wondered if he had willed Moss into being because he so desperately wanted to connect with another human being – one that didn't want to fight him or kill him.

What was Moss doing out of prison and how did he find Audie in the forest? Was he still a friend or working for someone else?

Staring at the white lines of the road, Audie feels stricken with shame and guilt and unrelieved anger. His plans are falling apart. He can picture Cassie and Scarlett, their faces still animated and laughing, now dead because of him. He didn't pull the trigger, but he's still to blame. He's a fugitive. Battered like a piñata. Flushed like a turd. Beaten. Stabbed. Choked. Burned. Shackled. What more can they do to him?

Audie had never been a hater, because when people hate with too much energy it's normally something about themselves they hate the most.

But ever since he lost Belita, anger seems to have become his most pervasive emotion, like a default setting on a machine. He knows when it began: New Year's Eve, 2003, when the future announced itself and forced him to make a decision.

Urban had decided to throw a party and Audie had spent weeks running errands, organising caterers, setting up tables and picking up parcels. Extra staff arrived to help with the party. Marquees were raised in the garden and coloured lights threaded around the branches until the trees twinkled like constellations. Caterers brought in truckloads of food and set up a temporary kitchen. A pig was skewered on a metal pole and hung over a charcoal pit, turning slowly and dripping fat that sizzled in the coals, the aroma mingling with the scent of blossoms from the flower arrangements.

Audie hadn't seen Belita since Christmas Day, when he drove her to Mass. She wouldn't let him come inside the church and she wouldn't let him touch her afterward because it was a holy day, she said, and God might be watching. Audie didn't mind. He had discovered the pleasure of contemplating Belita's body without possessing it. He knew her so intimately that he could close his eyes and picture the smooth dents on top of her shoulders, scalloped in the bone, and imagine his tongue tracing those hollows. He could feel the curve of her waist, the weight of her breasts, and hear her quickening breath when his fingers played certain notes.

Later Belita would tell Audie about her conversation with Urban before the party on New Year's Eve. She'd been seated at her dressing table watching Urban in the mirror as he opened a velvet-lined box and took out a necklace with a fire opal surrounded by a circle of small diamonds.

'Tonight I will introduce you to everyone,' he told her in Spanish.

'And what will you say of me?'

'I'll say you're my girlfriend.'

She was still staring at him. His cheeks grew hot.

'That's what you want, isn't it?'

She didn't answer.

'I can't marry you. Twice bitten, you understand, but you'll have everything a wife has.'

'What about my son?'

'He's happy where his is. You can still see him on weekends. Holidays.'

'Why can't he live here?'

'People would ask questions.'

The party began at dusk. Audie's job was to direct traffic through the big stone gates and park the cars. Most of them were expensive. European. He could see Urban mingling with guests, shaking hands, telling them jokes, playing the genial host. At eleven Belita brought him a plate of food. Her silk dress had a translucent black veil across the high part of her breasts and seemed to stroke every dip and curve of her body. Held up by shoestring straps, lighter than air, it looked like at any moment it would slide down and pool around her ankles.

'Marry me instead,' he said.

'I'm not going to marry you.'

'Why? I love you. I think you love me.'

She shook her head and glanced over her shoulder at the party. 'I can't remember the last time I danced.'

'I'll dance with you.'

She stroked his cheek sadly. 'You have to stay here.'

'Can I see you later?'

'Urban will want me.'

'He'll be drunk. You could sneak out.'

She shook her head.

'I'll wait for you near the gates,' said Audie as she walked away.

He spent the rest of the evening listening to the music and watching Belita dancing with her hair tied up and her chin held high and her hips moving like water and every man watching her like moths drawn to a porch light.

At midnight he heard 'Auld Lang Syne' and saw the fireworks explode in balls of dripping light across the ridge, setting dogs barking and horns blaring.

The last of the revellers had gone by four. Urban waved them goodbye. Drunk. Swaying. Audie closed the gates and collected empty bottles discarded along the driveway.

'Did you have a good time?' asked Urban.

'Parking cars?'

He laughed and put his arm around Audie. 'Why

don't you go down to the Pleasure Chest? Choose a girl. On me.'

'Happy New Year,' said Audie.

'And to you, son.'

He waited outside the gate for Belita. The trees in the garden were still twinkling with fairy lights. An hour passed. Two. Still he waited. Still she didn't come. He had a key and let himself in the rear door of the house, creeping along the hallway to Belita's room, where he undressed and slipped into bed, not wanting to wake her. Rather than touch her skin, he held the edge of her nightdress in his fingertips and watched the way her chest lifted and fell as she breathed, barely making a sound.

He fell asleep.

She woke him soon after. 'You must leave.'

'Why?'

'He's coming.'

'How do you know?'

'I just know.'

She looked at the door. 'Did you leave it open?'

'No.'

Now it stood gaping blackly.

'He's seen us.'

'You don't know that.'

She pushed Audie out of bed and told him to dress. He crept through the house barefoot, carrying his socks and shoes. He heard a radio playing in one of the rooms. Smelled coffee. He slipped through the kitchen and down the steps, gingerly dancing over the sharp gravel on the drive.

He drove back to his room. It was New Year's Day and the streets were almost deserted. A handful of cars were parked outside the bar. Some of the girls must be earning overtime, thought Audie.

As he stepped through the door into his room he was shoved from behind. Three men forced him down. Tape was wrapped around his head, across his mouth and eyes, screeching as it was ripped from a spool. Hooded and bound, he was dragged down the stairs and bundled into the back seat of a car. He recognised the voices. Urban was driving and two of his nephews were sitting on either side of Audie. He knew them only by their initials – J.C. and R.D. – and their matching skinny-leg jeans and snap-button shirts. They also sported designer stubble that magazines had once suggested was fashionable, but Audie suspected appealed more to homosexuals than to women.

Audie's mouth had gone dry and he could feel the skin on his face shrinking. Urban knew. How could he know? He saw them together. The strongest urge was to deny everything. Then he considered falling to his knees and confessing. He could live with the guilt. He could take his punishment – as long as Belita was spared.

Audie tried to keep track of the corners, but there were too many of them. One of the cousins joked to the other. 'He's lucky he's not in Mexico or they'd find his head in a ditch.'

The car pulled off the road. The ruts were so

deep the chassis bashed against the earth and the wheels slid sideways into potholes. They stopped. Doors opened. He was dragged outside. Forced to kneel.

Urban spoke. 'We don't choose the moment of our births, son, but the hour of death can be predetermined by a bullet or some other lethal intervention.'

He pulled off the hood and the sudden brightness stung Audie's eyes. He blinked it away and saw the hewn rock wall of a quarry with water pooled at the base, forming a small lake, blacker than sump oil.

The tape was ripped away, tearing at his hair and skin. Urban had taken Audie's wallet. He pulled out the driver's licence and social security cards, dropping them in the dirt. He found a photograph of Belita – one taken in a photo booth at Sea World with Belita sitting on Audie's lap. Urban tossed the picture into the water, where it spun like a floating leaf, pushed by the breeze. Squatting next to Audie, he draped his hands on his thighs.

'Do you know why you're here?'

Audie didn't answer. Urban signalled his nephews, who pulled Audie to his feet. Urban punched him hard in the solar plexus so that Audie's whole upper body jackknifed forward and he cried out.

'You think you're smarter than me,' said Urban.

Gape-mouthed, Audie shook his head.

'You think I'm some ignorant spick, who doesn't

know the difference between his ass and a hole in the ground.'

'No,' Audie gasped.

'I trusted you. I let you get close to me.'

Urban's voice shook and his eyes shone. He nodded to his nephews, who dragged Audie to the edge of the water, forcing him to kneel. Audie could see his reflection in the smooth, glass-like surface; see himself aging, growing old in the space of a few seconds. He saw his father's white hair. Wrinkles. Disappointment. Regret.

His face touched the water and the image dissolved. He attempted to twist away from the hands, but they pushed his head deeper. He kicked with his feet and tried to keep his mouth shut, but soon his body cried out for air and his brain reacted instinctively. He drew breath, flooding his lungs. Air bubbled from his mouth past his eyes. His head was jerked upward. He coughed and spluttered, his mouth opening and closing like a dying fish. They plunged him forward again and leaned their weight on the back of his neck, pushing his head so deep that his forehead touched the bottom. The more he struggled, the weaker he grew. He grabbed at their legs and belts, trying to crawl up their bodies like a man clinging to a rope on a cliff face.

He lost consciousness and didn't remember being dragged from the water. When he came to he was lying on his stomach, spitting water, his whole body heaving. Urban squatted next to him, cupping the back of Audie's neck in a fatherly way. He pressed his mouth closer, his breath like a feather against Audie's skin.

'I let you come into my house, eat my chow, drink my booze . . . I treated you like a son. I would have made you one. But you betrayed me.'

Audie didn't answer.

'Do you know the story of Oedipus? He murders his father and marries his mother and brings disaster upon his kingdom, all because of a prophecy made when he was born. The old king tried to stop it happening. He took the baby and abandoned it on a mountainside, but a shepherd rescued Oedipus and raised him, so he grew up and he fulfilled the prophecy. I do not believe in these myths, but I can see why they last. Perhaps the old king should have killed Oedipus. Perhaps the shepherd should have minded his own business.'

Urban squeezed Audie's neck more firmly. 'Belita loved me until you showed up. I rescued her. I educated her. I gave her clothes and put a roof over her head.' He waved his finger back and forth. 'I could have filled her stomach with balloons of cocaine and sent her back and forth across the border, but instead I let her share my bed.'

He looked at his nephews and back at Audie, raising his voice again. 'If I ever see you again, I will have you killed. If you ever come near Belita, I will have you both killed. If you want to be a martyr, I can arrange that. If you want to die like Romeo and Juliet, I can make that possible. But it will not happen quickly. I have associates who can keep someone alive for weeks, drilling holes through bones, pouring acid onto skin, scooping out eyes, severing limbs. They enjoy it. For them it is natural. You will plead for death, but it won't come. You will renounce everything you have ever believed. You will give up your secrets. You will beg and plead and promise, but they will not listen. Understand?'

Audie nodded.

Urban looked at his fists, examining the broken skin, then he turned and walked toward the car.

Audie called after him. 'I'm owed money.'

'That has been forfeited.'

'What about my things?'

'I hope they're flammable.' Urban had opened the car door. He took his coat from the seat and shrugged it on, tugging at the sleeves. 'If I were you, I'd forget about Belita. She's been used more often than a jailhouse condom.'

'Then let her go.'

'What sort of signal would that send?'

'I love her,' blurted Audie.

'That's a wonderful story,' replied Urban. He nodded to his nephews and each of them swung a boot into Audie, one kicking his stomach, the other his back. The pain almost shook loose his bowels.

'Have a nice life,' said Urban thickly. 'Be thankful.'

# CHAPTER 39

In the basement of the Dreyfus County Criminal Court there are records of every case tried before a judge dating back 150 years: legal briefs, trial transcripts, exhibit lists and statements – a vast repository of bleak stories and black deeds.

The woman sitting behind the screen is called Mona and her hair is darker than midnight, piled so high it makes her look top-heavy. She sets aside a half-molested sandwich and looks up at Desiree. 'What can I do for you, sugar?'

Desiree has filled out a form asking for archival material.

Mona looks at the request. 'This might take a while.'

'I'll wait.'

Having countersigned the form and stamped it twice, Mona rolls it into a tube and tucks it inside a canister, which is popped into a chute and sucked downward. She tucks a pen behind her ear and studies Desiree more closely. 'How long you been with the Bureau?'

'Six years.'

'They make you jump all the hurdles?'

'A few.'

'I bet they did. I bet you had to be twice as good as any man.' Mona gets up and leans forward, glancing at Desiree's shoes.

'Is something wrong?'

Mona looks at her sheepishly and points out the waiting room.

Desiree takes a seat and flicks through several out-of-date magazines, periodically checking the watch on her wrist, which belonged to her father. He gave it to Desiree on the day she graduated, telling her that she had to wind it up every night and think of her parents when she did.

'I was late for work only once in my working life,' he had told her.

'On the day I was born,' she replied.

'You know the story?'

'Yes, Daddy,' she laughed. 'I know the story.'

The cavernous archive smells of copier fluid, floor polish, paper and leather bindings. Dust motes are trapped in the bright beams of light that angle from the high windows.

She gets a coffee from the machine, but flinches at the first taste. Discarding the cup, she chooses a soft drink. Her stomach rumbles. When did she last eat?

Mona calls her name and slides a dozen folders through an opening in the screen.

'Is that all?'

'Oh, no, sugar.' She points behind her. A trolley

is stacked with boxes. 'And I got two more just like that one.'

Desiree finds a desk in the reading room and pulls out a pad. She begins reading about the robbery, laying it out page by page, threading the details together as if editing a film, cutting and splicing the footage in her mind. Photographs. Timelines. Autopsy reports. Statements.

The truck was hijacked just north of Conroe shortly after 3 p.m. The security firm Armaguard had a contract to collect the damaged bills from banks and credit facilities, which were then to be delivered to a data-destruction facility in Illinois.

The delivery schedule and route were changed every two weeks, which meant that somebody tipped them off. The guard who died in the robbery, Scott Beauchamp, was suspected of being the inside man, but no evidence was presented at the trial. His phone records and movements were investigated as agencies searched for the final gang member and the missing money, but the only evidence against Beauchamp was circumstantial.

Audie Palmer pleaded guilty, but refused to reveal the names of anyone else involved. He didn't give up his brother or implicate the security guard. Because of his injuries it was three months before police could interview Audie and another eight months before he was well enough to stand trial.

Desiree turns to the witness statements. According to police logs, at approximately 20.13 – five hours after the hijacking – a DSCO patrol deputy and his partner on a routine patrol observed an armoured truck parked on the northern service road of the I-45 at League Line Road. While running the licence plate, the deputy noticed a dark-coloured SUV pull up with a single occupant. The rear doors of the armoured truck were opened and bags were transferred between the vehicles.

The deputy called for backup, but their cruiser was spotted and both suspect vehicles took off at high speed.

Desiree reads the transcript of the radio communications, noting the names of the officers involved: Ryan Valdez and Nick Fenway were the first responders. A second cruiser, driven by Timothy Lewis, joined the pursuit.

The first radio message was timed at 20.13 hours on January 27.

> **Deputy Fenway:** 1522, suspicious vehicle parked on Longmire Road near Farm Market 3083 West. Investigating.
> **Dispatcher:** Copy that.
> **Deputy Fenway:** We have an armored vehicle, licence plate November, Charlie, Delta, Zero, Four, Seven, Nine. It's parked on the shoulder. It could be from that robbery.
> **Dispatcher:** Copy that. Any occupants?
> **Deputy Fenway:** Two, possibly three males. White. Medium build. Dark clothing. Deputy Valdez is trying to get closer . . . Shots fired! Shots fired!

**Dispatcher:** Officers under fire. All units. The corner of Longmire Road and Farm Market Road West.

**Deputy Fenway:** They're getting away. In pursuit!

**Dispatcher:** Copy that. All available units, all available units. Police pursuit in progress. Shots fired. Approach with caution.

**Deputy Fenway:** Passing Holland Spiller Road. Seventy miles per hour. Light traffic. They're still shooting . . . We're coming up to League Line Road. Where are the cars?

**Dispatcher:** Still five minutes away.

**Deputy Lewis:** 1522 where do you need me?

**Deputy Fenway:** Come down League Line Road. You got spikes?

**Deputy Lewis:** Negative.

**Deputy Fenway:** The truck just crossed League Line Road. Still heading north.

**Dispatcher:** We got eyes coming in from the west.

The pursuit continued for another seven minutes as the patrol cars and armoured truck reached speeds of up to ninety miles per hour. At 20.29 this happened:

**Deputy Fenway:** He's lost it! The truck is over! Sliding! Shit! I think he hit something.

**Dispatcher:** Copy that.

**Dispatcher:** Give me a location.

**Deputy Fenway:** Old Montgomery Road. A quarter mile west of the RV Park. They're shooting at us! Shots fired. Shots fired . . .

**Deputy Lewis:** I'm coming.

**Deputy Fenway:** (unintelligible).

**Dispatcher:** Can you repeat that 1522?

**Deputy Fenway:** Leaving the vehicle. Under fire.

(Four minutes of silence follow with the dispatcher trying to raise the officers.)

**Deputy Fenway:** Three suspects down. We got a seriously wounded security guard and a vehicle on fire. Code 4.

**Dispatcher:** Copy the code 4. We have fire and paramedics responding.

Desiree goes back and reads the first statements made by the responders and notices how often they used similar phrases and almost identical language to describe the events, as if they might have swapped notes or agreed on a story. It was common practice among law enforcement officers, who wanted to ensure that nobody jeopardised any subsequent trial. The pursuit ended when the armoured truck failed to take a bend and tipped over, slamming into a car, which burst into flames, killing the lone driver. Audie Palmer and the Caine brothers tried to shoot their way out.

According to their accounts, Deputies Fenway and

Valdez were pinned down by heavy gunfire. They took cover behind their vehicle, returning fire, but were outgunned and vulnerable until Deputy Lewis arrived. He reversed his car into the line of fire, allowing his colleagues to take up better positions.

In total more than seventy rounds were fired by the three deputies. All three suspects were hit, two of them dying at the scene and a third being critically wounded. According to Dreyfus County Coroner Herman Willford, Vernon Caine had died from a gunshot to the chest and his younger brother Billy was hit three times – the leg, chest and neck. Both bled to death at the scene. Audie Palmer was shot in the head. The security guard Scott Beauchamp, who had been bound and gagged inside the truck, died from injuries sustained in the crash.

Desiree takes out five albums of crime-scene photographs and scans the images quickly before going back to study particular pictures more closely. Both police cars are visible, blocking the road, along with the twisted wreckage of the truck and burned-out car. The truck's doors are bust open. Blood has pooled inside. Using the drawings and computer simulations, Desiree creates a mental diorama where she can place each of the 'players' at the scene.

There are gaps in the albums – more numbers than there are images. Either they were mislabelled or somebody has removed them. By 2004, most police cruisers in Texas were equipped with a camera and a hard-drive recording system. These could either be turned on by the officers or triggered automatically when the cruiser reached a certain speed. Newer systems record constantly and download via Wi-Fi whenever the cruiser returns to headquarters.

During disclosure, the defence had asked about the dashboard cameras and been told that the two cruisers didn't carry such equipment. This detail snags in Desiree's mind. She goes back through the photographs. The police cruiser driven by Fenway and Valdez is shown parked diagonally across the road. The windshield is shattered and holes are punched through the outer metal skin of the doors.

Using a magnifying app on her cell phone, she hovers over the image, focusing on the dashboard of the cruiser, noticing the telltale bump above the windscreen. A camera. Desiree jots down the code on the photograph, putting a question mark alongside it in her notebook.

Studying more of the images, she can see the wreckage of a burned-out car in the background. A charred body is just visible in the upturned wreck, which is so twisted and bent by heat and collision that it looks like a piece of abstract sculpture.

Desiree looks for details of the vehicle – a 1985 Pontiac, Californian plates. According to the autopsy report the driver was female, mid-twenties. The photographs show her charred corpse locked in a pugilistic pose with flexed elbows and clenched fists, caused by the shrinkage of body tissues and muscle due to the severe heat. There was no evidence of alcohol or drug use or childhood fractures.

Without a face or fingerprints, police had difficulty identifying the victim, which led to a nationwide search of DNA and dental databases. Later the hunt was expanded to include international agencies like Interpol and organisations dealing with undocumented immigrants. Desiree looks for a chain of ownership. The Pontiac 6000 was first sold by a dealer in Columbus, Ohio, in 1985, and resold twice more. The last registered owner was a Frank Aubrey in Ramona, southern California.

Desiree picks up her iPhone and calls a colleague in Washington. She and Neil Jenkins went through training together, but Jenkins had shown no desire to work in the field. He wanted a desk job at 935 Pennsylvania Avenue, preferably in the data surveillance section where he could eavesdrop on other people's conversations.

True to form, Jenkins wants to shoot the breeze, but Desiree doesn't have time.

'I need you do a vehicle history search. It's a Pontiac 6000, 1985 model. California plate 3HUA172.' She rattles off the VIN number. 'The car was destroyed in an accident in January 2004.'

'*Anything else?*'

'A woman was driving – see if they ever identified her.'

'*Is it urgent?*'

'Call me back.'

Desiree moves on to the security guard who died in the robbery. Scott Beauchamp was a former marine who did two combat tours in the Gulf and one tour in Bosnia. He resigned his commission in 1995 and had worked for Armaguard for six years. Police suspected an inside informant, but couldn't link Beauchamp to the gang through phone records; however a fuel receipt put him in the same truck-stop diner as Vernon Caine a month before the hijacking. A waitress positively identified Beauchamp from a photograph, but couldn't remember seeing the two men talking.

Desiree discovers a DVD at the bottom of the box. She crosschecks the evidence label with the list of exhibits. It's Audie Palmer's arraignment hearing.

She goes back to Mona, who looks surprised to see her.

'You been here for six hours.'

'I'll still be here tomorrow.'

'We close up in forty-five minutes, so unless you brought a sleeping bag . . .'

'I need a DVD player.'

'You see that room over there? You'll find a computer inside. Here is the key. Don't lose it. And you got till six or you come back tomorrow.'

'Understood.'

Desiree fires up the computer and can hear the DVD spinning as the screen blinks to life. A fixed camera shows Audie Palmer in a hospital bed, his head swathed in bandages, tubes sticking from his nose and his wrists. She had already read the medical reports. Nobody had expected Audie to survive. Surgeons had to glue his skull together like a jigsaw puzzle, using fragments of bone and metal plates. Audie lay in a coma for three months, showing minimal brain activity for the first few weeks. Specialists debated whether to pull the plug, but Texas only executes people on death row, not when they're brain-dead, because it might mean culling most of their politicians.

Even when Audie came out of the coma doctors doubted if he would ever talk or walk. He proved them wrong, but it was another two months before he was strong enough to be arraigned at a bedside hearing.

The footage shows a defence attorney, Clayton Rudd, sitting next to Audie, who is communicating by spelling out short messages on a borrowed Ouija board. The district attorney was Edward Dowling, now a state senator, who wore a surgical mask as though frightened of catching germs.

Before convening the arraignment, Judge Hamilton asked Dowling why the local DA's office was prosecuting Palmer. 'The defendant could have been tried under federal or state laws, your honour, but it's my understanding that a conflict of interest arose,' said Dowling, sounding deliberately vague.

'What conflict of interest?'

'A possible witness being a blood relative of a senior federal official,' replied Dowling. 'That's why the FBI recommended the DA's office handle it.'

Judge Hamilton looked satisfied and asked Mr Rudd if his client understood the purpose of the proceedings.

'Yes, your honour.'

'The man can't state his full name for the record.'

'He can spell it out.'

'Mr Palmer, can you hear me?' asked the judge. Audie nodded.

'I am going to arraign you today on charges that include three capital murder offences, hijacking a vehicle and second-degree vehicular homicide, is that clear?'

Audie groaned and squeezed his eyes shut.

'These offences have maximum penalties that include the death sentence or life imprisonment without parole or any terms of years. Do you understand these charges and the maximum consequences?'

Slowly and deliberately, Audie moved his hand to the word 'yes' on the Ouija board.

Judge Hamilton turned to Dowling. 'You can proceed.'

'This is the matter of the people of Texas versus Audie Spencer Palmer. Case number forty-eight, docket six-hundred and forty-two.'

The DA took ten minutes to list the murder and robbery charges before outlining the prosecution case. Palmer was accused of conspiring with others to steal seven million dollars belonging to the US Federal Reserve.

Judge Hamilton spoke. 'Sir, you have been charged with capital and felony offences. I must advise that you have certain entitlements. You have the right to be represented by an attorney and Mr Rudd has been appointed for you at public expense, but if you wish to hire your own attorney you may do so. Are you happy for Mr Rudd to represent you at today's arraignment?'

Audie indicated yes.

'Do you wish to enter a plea?'

Audie began spelling out a response, but Clayton Rudd reached across the board and stopped his trembling hand. 'Let the record reflect that my client pleads not guilty,' he said, glancing at Dowling, as though seeking his approval. He leaned back to Audie. 'Best keep our powder dry, son.'

'What about bail?' the judge asked.

'The state opposes bail,' said Dowling, 'These are capital crimes, your honour, and the money is still missing.'

'My client isn't leaving the hospital any time soon,' replied Rudd.

'Does he have family?' asked the judge.

'His parents and sister,' said Rudd.

'Any other ties to the community or significant assets?'

'No, your honour.'

'Bail is refused.'

The DVD ends. Desiree presses the eject button and slips the disk into the plastic sleeve, returning it to the box.

It was five more months before Audie Palmer came to trial at Dreyfus County Courthouse. By then he faced a different judge and Clayton Rudd had done a deal with the DA's office, downgrading

the capital murder charges to second-degree homicide in return for a guilty plea on all counts. Audie
didn't dispute any of the facts and declined to
make a statement in mitigation.

The *Houston Chronicle* reported the verdict:

A 23-year-old man was yesterday convicted
of armed robbery and second-degree
murder for the botched 2004 hijacking of
an armored truck that left a security guard
and female motorist dead, along with two
of his accomplices.

Judge Matthew Coghlan sentenced Audie
Palmer to ten years in prison after he
pleaded guilty to all charges, including the
theft of $7 million in US currency, which
was never recovered.

Before delivering his sentence, Judge
Coghlan criticized District Attorney Edward
Dowling for not bringing first-degree murder
charges against Palmer for his role in the
deaths. 'These were capital offences and
in my opinion today's verdict is an insult
to the law enforcement officers who risked
their lives to bring this offender to justice.'

Outside the court, FBI Special Agent
Frank Senogles told reporters that the
FBI had conducted more than a thousand
interviews in connection with the robbery
and had focused its attention on relatives and
known associates of the gang, but the

338

money had proved impossible to trace because no serial numbers were kept of cash that was destined for destruction.

'I can assure people that we have an open file and regular conversations with the state and county police over strategy and tactics. We have not changed our minds about the people responsible, but as time passes the case becomes harder to solve without public help.'

Desiree is surprised to see Frank Senogles being quoted. Why hadn't he mentioned that he was involved in the original inquiry? The FBI had headed the investigation, which meant Senogles would have interviewed Ryan Valdez and the other deputies. He would also have talked to Audie Palmer, yet when Desiree claimed to know more about the case than anyone else, Senogles didn't correct or contradict or belittle her, which he normally wouldn't hesitate to do.

Turning the page, she finds another news story.

GOVERNOR PRAISES HEROIC COPS

By Michael Gidley

Despite coming under fire, Dreyfus County Sheriff's Deputies Ryan Valdez, Nick Fenway and Timothy Lewis did not waver in coming to each other's rescue after a

339

dramatic high-speed pursuit of a stolen armored truck.

Thanks to their heroism, the three officers are alive today and a dangerous criminal is behind bars. For their bravery on that chaotic day in January 2004, deputies Valdez, Fenway and Lewis today received the Star of Texas Award – the state's most prestigious honor, recognizing "acts of heroism above and beyond the call of duty."

Gov. Rick Perry and Attorney General Steve Keneally presented the awards at a Capitol ceremony, praising the officers for their outstanding bravery and public service.

The photograph shows all three deputies in uniform, standing beside Governor Perry, smiling for the camera. Fenway, Valdez and Lewis look slightly uncomfortable in the pose, but the Governor is feeding off the shine. In the background, caught in profile as he turned away from the camera, is Frank Senogles. There is a radio in his hand. Perhaps he was part of the security detail.

Desiree hits redial on her phone.

'There's something else,' she tells Jenkins. 'I need to find two state police officers: Nick Fenway and Timothy Lewis. Both of them worked for the Dreyfus County Sheriff's Department in 2004.'

# CHAPTER 40

Invisible within the bowels of the Old Granada Theater, Audie curls in a ball and tries to sleep, but he keeps dreaming of the Trinity River on a stormy day a dozen years ago. Standing close to the edge of the water, he stares into the depths as lightning springs and crackles from dark bulbous clouds above his head. Suddenly a skeleton surges from beneath the surface, carried on a black wave. Within the ribcage is a seal-like creature with sharp white teeth. Trapped. Shrieking to be released. The skeleton slips back beneath the surface, leaving nothing but ripples. Other things rise from the river, new horrors lifted from the blackness, reaching out for Audie, demanding to be freed.

His eyes snap open and a scream dies in his throat. Sitting upright, he catches sight of a reflection in a shattered mirror and can't recognise himself, this haggard shadow, this joke of a man, this wretch . . .

The night is over. Audie leans against a damp wall and writes a list of the things he needs. Other people would be running. They would be selling their watch, the gold in their teeth, a spare kidney; they would be catching a bus to Mexico or Canada

341

or working passage on a container ship or swimming to Cuba. Perhaps he desires his own destruction, although Audie doubts he has the necessary moral fibre to support a death wish.

What else to put on his list?

- Masking tape
- Sleeping bags
- SIM cards
- Water

He remembers making a similar list, nursing different bruises, after being beaten up by Urban's nephews and told never to see Belita again. He had booked into a cheap motel near the Mexican border, where he lay in bed like a hospital patient waiting for the truth to make its rounds. Occasionally, he crawled to the bathroom and spat blood into the sink, sucking on a broken tooth. On the fourth day it took him an hour to walk two blocks to a pharmacy and liquor store, where he bought painkillers, anti-inflammatory drugs, icepacks and a bottle of bourbon.

He floated back to the motel on a cocktail of drugs and booze. Along the way he thought he saw Belita. She was walking toward him, her skirt billowing one moment, hugging her thighs the next. Her hair was swept back and held in place by a clasp which he knew was tortoiseshell because it was the only thing that survived her journey from El Salvador.

She walked so elegantly with her back straight and chin held high, and pedestrians seemed to make way for her, stepping aside and smiling. She was only fifty yards away when he called out. She didn't respond. He tried to run and called her name again. She didn't pause or miss her stride.

'Belita,' he cried, louder this time. She quickened her step and crossed the road. A car braked. A horn blasted.

'Belita!'

She stopped. Turned. How thin she'd grown. How old. It wasn't Belita. The woman told him to get lost, but less politely. Audie backed away, palms open, incapable of speech.

Back at the motel he made a list of things he needed. He knew the details of Urban's accounts, the bank branches, account names and numbers. On Friday January 9, a man wearing dark glasses and a baseball cap walked into eight branches and made an equal number of withdrawals of a thousand dollars each. This man could have taken ten or twenty times that amount – he could have taken it all – but he took what he thought he was owed and a little extra for his injuries. That's what the man told himself as he filled out the different withdrawal slips and forged Urban's signature. Afterwards, he bought himself some new clothes and searched the classifieds for a second-hand car.

'One more time,' Audie told himself, he had to see her one more time. He would not beg, he would simply ask, knowing that his pride would survive even if his heart broke into a thousand pieces.

Arriving at the church an hour before the morning service, he parked the car in a nearby cul-de-sac and waited for the doors to open. He had a small overnight bag in the trunk, along with the cash. A smudge of the city skyline was just visible above the rooftops and he could hear the highway less than a block away. Would she come, he wondered. Would Urban let her?

When the priest opened the doors, Audie sat in the shadows of the baptismal area, watching the parishioners arrive. Belita was among the last. The nephews had driven her, but waited outside smoking and listening to the radio. Audie hadn't noticed the young boy. He was sitting four rows from the front, next to a moon-faced Hispanic woman with dyed black hair poking from beneath a colourful scarf that did nothing to soften her features.

Belita dipped her finger into the holy water and made the sign of the cross, keeping her eyes down as she passed him. She genuflected and moved along a pew, wrapping her arms around the boy, who sank into her embrace as though falling into freshly driven snow.

Only thirty or so people had come to Mass. Audie slid into the pew behind Belita and sat so he could see one side of her face. She wore a faded blue sundress, which was tight across her belly, and scuffed white sandals that had a gold buckle above her toes. The smudge of dirt on her cheek

344

turned into an old bruise when he looked more closely. She had taken a fist, which was his fault as surely as if he had delivered the blow himself. The boy next to her wore shorts, long socks and polished black shoes. His legs stuck straight out and he clung to her arm, raising his face to hers, his eyelashes as thick as epaulettes.

Everybody stood. The procession began. A portly priest made his way down the central aisle to the sound of an organ and a mumbled hymn. A young boy and girl, brother and sister perhaps, were dressed in white robes and carrying a Bible and a candle. Belita turned to watch. She spied Audie. He saw relief in her eyes and then fear. She turned away. The woman in the scarf glanced over her shoulder and seemed to understand. Her features hardened. This must be Belita's cousin, he thought, the one who looks after her boy.

Audie's eyes hadn't left Belita. 'I need to talk to you,' he whispered.

She said nothing. The priest had reached the altar, where he took the Bible and placed it on the pulpit. The hymn had almost finished. Voices rose more confidently in the final chorus.

Belita made the sign of the cross. Audie now stood directly behind her, his chin almost touching her shoulder. He could smell her perfume. No, it was something else. Not soap or shampoo or talcum powder, but something earthy and raw, her own essence. He was a fool to think he could ever live without her.

The young boy was kneading the folds of Belita's dress with one hand and holding a stuffed bear in the other. He had a hymnbook balanced on his lap and he was pretending to read the words.

'Come away with me,' Audie whispered.

Belita ignored him.

'I love you,' he said.

'He will kill us both,' she murmured.

'We can go far away. He'll never find us.'

'He will *always* find us.'

'Not if we go to Texas. I have family there.'

'That's the first place he'll look.'

'We'll hide from him.'

They were trying to talk in whispers, but people were beginning to notice. Belita's cousin turned and confronted Audie.

'*¡Fuera! ¡Fuera! Usted es el Diablo.*'

She poked at his chest and waved him away. Someone hushed them. The priest looked over the top of his glasses.

Audie leaned closer, his breath on the back of Belita's neck. 'You have taken so many chances to get here. You deserve more than this. You deserve to be with your son. You deserve to be happy.'

A tear hovered on the edge of her lower eyelash and her hands fluttered across the soft swelling of her stomach.

'Life is short,' said Audie.

'Love is vast,' she whispered.

His chin was resting on her shoulder. 'If you leave through the side door, follow the fence and you'll find a gate. Don't let them see you. I'll be waiting. I have a car and money.'

When the sermon finished, Audie slipped away and went back to the Pontiac. There was a skate park over the road with a concrete half-pipe spray-painted with graffiti. Skateboarders rocked back and forth, doing aerial manoeuvres and then resting on the platforms above. Audie's tongue explored his mouth in search of moisture. What if she didn't come? Why should she trust him? He had made his move, a fluky play, more in blind hope than real expectation.

The mass ended. Nobody came. Audie drove slowly past the church and saw the nephews escorting Belita to the car. She hugged her boy, who clung to her leg, burying his face in the folds of her skirt, not wanting her to go. She crouched and brushed hair from his eyes. He cried and she cried and the car doors clunked shut and soon she was gone.

Audie sat staring at the scene for a full minute, as though waiting for the actors to return. Surely this couldn't be the end. Bereft, he lifted his face to the sky like a slave contemplating freedom and looked straight into vast blue heavens that mirrored his own emptiness. 'OK, show me something,' he wanted to scream. 'Show me how I get through this.'

Somebody knocked on the side window. The sour-faced cousin was motioning at Audie, wanting him to lower the glass. She was holding the boy's hand.

'Write down your address,' she said in Spanish.

Audie searched desperately for a pen . . . paper. He found the bill of sale for the car and jotted down the name of the motel. Room 24.

'She will contact you.'

'When?'

'Beggars must be grateful.'

Waiting sounds like a passive thing, but it wasn't for Audie. His vigil was as fraught and strenuous as anything he had ever done. He paced. He reasoned. He did push-ups. He ignored the TV. He didn't sleep. Time could not be killed. He could have plunged a stake through its heart, diced it up, burned it, buried it deep, but it still would have lived.

He waited three days until he got a message from Belita's cousin, and another two days before he stood at the Greyhound Bus station on National Avenue and watched a coach empty, staring at the faces. What if she had missed the bus? What if she'd changed her mind?

But then she took the final step and stood between the coaches, a small suitcase in her hand. Audie was suddenly speechless. Dumb. The distance between them seemed immense. She smiled. Gaunt. Tired. Beautiful. She was clutching an ugly orange suitcase and pressed against her belly was a small boy. Clearly terrified, he was dressed in beige corduroy trousers, a T-shirt and bright red sneakers.

Audie didn't know what to say or do. He took Belita's suitcase. Put it down. Hugged her. He squeezed her too tightly.

'Steady,' she said, pulling away.

He looked crestfallen. She took his hand and placed it on her stomach. His eyes asked the question.

'It is yours,' she said, waiting for his reaction.

He bent and scooped her up, hugging her hips and raising her high in the air so that his face pressed into her abdomen and he could kiss her stomach through the cotton of her dress. She laughed and told him to put her down.

The young boy was standing next to the suitcase. He had hair the colour of cooking chocolate and those unbelievably brown eyes.

'How-do,' said Audie. 'What's your name?'

The young boy looked at his mother.

'Miguel,' she said.

'It's nice to meet you, Miguel.'

Audie shook the boy's hand. Miguel looked at his fingers afterward, as though worried Audie might have stolen one.

'Nice shoes,' said Audie.

Miguel looked at his feet.

'Very red.'

Miguel turned one leg inwards to get a look at the shoes himself and then put his face back in his mother's skirt.

They left that evening and drove until after midnight. Miguel slept on the rear seat, hugging a battered bear that he carried with him everywhere. He wasn't very big for his age and his thumb went automatically to his mouth when his eyelids began to droop.

They drove with the windows open and talked about the future. Belita told him stories about her childhood, dropping details like breadcrumbs, wanting him to follow the trail and ask her questions. At other times they didn't need to speak. She leaned her head on his shoulder or brushed her fingers against his thigh.

'Is this what you want?' she asked.

'Of course.'

'You love me.'

'Yes.'

'If you lead me on, or let me down, or run away . . .'

'I won't.'

'And we'll be married?'

'Yes.'

'When?'

'Tomorrow.'

A song came on the radio.

'I'm not listening to country music,' she said. 'And I'm not getting married in the Elvis Presley chapel.'

'Really?'

'Really.'

'OK.'

# CHAPTER 41

In the light of the morning, Desiree pours herself a bowl of Grape-Nuts and slices a banana on the top. She has to call her parents and tell them that she won't be coming over tomorrow. Saturday is normally when she visits, sitting down to a home-cooked meal before watching her father referee a football game from his armchair, yelling at the screen and throwing imaginary penalty flags.

Steeling herself, she makes the call. Her mother picks up and recites her phone number before asking, 'How can I help you?' in a posh accent that sounds like an affectation. Her mother is also inclined to order food in the same accent as the waitress or waiter who is serving and doesn't understand how this might be construed as being patronizing or demeaning to the server.

'It's me,' says Desiree.

'*Hello, dear, we were just talking about you, weren't we Harold? It's Desiree. Yes, DESIREE, she's on the phone.*'

Her father is deaf without his hearing aid and Desiree suspects that he leaves it turned off on purpose so that he doesn't have to listen to her mother.

'*I just bought a ham*,' her mother says. '*I was gonna bake it the way you like – with the mustard and honey glaze.*'

'I can't make it home,' says Desiree. 'I have to work.'

'*Oh, that's a shame . . . Desiree won't be coming, Harold. SHE HAS TO WORK.*'

'*But we're having baked ham*,' her father yells in the background, as though everybody else is deaf.

'*She knows, Harold, I just told her.*'

'*Has she found herself a boyfriend?*' he asks.

'*He wants to know if you've found a nice man*,' says her mother.

'Tell him I got married and had twins. Timon and Pumbaa. Pumbaa farts a lot, but he's very sweet.'

'*I wish you wouldn't joke about it*,' her mother says.

From the background, her father yells, '*Tell her it's okay if she's a lesbian. We don't mind.*'

'*She's not a lesbian*,' scolds her mother.

'*I'm just saying that if she is a lesbian, we won't mind*,' says her father.

'*Don't tell her that!*'

Soon they're arguing.

'I have to go,' says Desiree. 'Sorry about tomorrow.'

She hangs up and collects her things. Leaving the apartment, she descends the outer stairs and waves to her landlord Mr Sackville, who is twitching his curtains. Weekend traffic is light as she drives into the northern suburbs of Houston.

Half an hour later she reaches Tomball and parks outside a neat blue and white bungalow with an emerald-green lawn and garden shrubs pruned to look naked and cold. Nobody answers the front-door chime. Desiree can hear the sound of children squealing and laughing in the rear garden. She unlatches the side gate and walks along a path around the house.

Balloons and streamers decorate a trellis above an outside patio. Children and grandchildren are running between the trees, chasing a dog. Women are chatting around a table, beating eggs for French toast and making batter for pancakes. The few men present have convened around the barbecue, that great leveller of social class and status, where a man is judged on how often he turns a steak rather than how much he earns or what car he drives.

Former Dreyfus County pathologist Herman Willford, now retired, sits on a folding director's chair, cradling a plastic plate on his lap. His trousers are belted high on his waist and a cardigan buttoned across his chest. He looks at the children, flinching at every squeal like the noise sets his teeth on edge.

A matronly woman approaches Desiree, wiping her hands on an apron. She looks at the badge.

'This is a family gathering.'

353

'It's important. I wouldn't bother him otherwise.'

The woman sighs, but Herman looks almost relieved to be given a leave of absence. He takes Desiree into the house and offers her a libation. She declines and he makes small talk, complaining about being old and impatient and wanting everyone to leave.

'That's the problem with family,' he says, his eyes sharp beneath busy eyebrows. 'You can't retire from them.'

Desiree has brought crime-scene photographs and maps with her. She spreads them on a coffee table in the living room. The old pathologist examines them almost lovingly, as though remembering a time when he felt more youthful and useful.

'You're asking me about where the fatal shots were fired from?'

'I'm trying to understand the sequence.'

'Vernon and Billy Caine were killed by police-issue weapons. Vernon was shot in the neck and Billy through the heart.'

'What about Audie Palmer?'

'It was close range.'

'How close?'

'Three, maybe four feet away.' The old pathologist picks up a photograph. 'From the angle of the shot, I'd say he was shot from the front.'

'Did you find the bullet?'

'There were entry and exit wounds, but the shell wasn't recovered.'

'Is that unusual?'

'There were seventy shots fired that day – not every shell was retrieved.'

'Can you tell me which officer shot him?

'Not with any certainty.'

'Why not?'

He chuckles. 'I try not to perform autopsies on people who survive.'

'Why was he found so far away from the others?'

'According to the police statements he was trying to escape.'

'He was shot from four feet away.'

He shrugs.

'And his hands were burned, how do you explain that?'

'A gas tank ruptured and burst into flames.'

'Why just his hands?'

The pathologist sighs. 'Listen here, Special Agent, what difference does it make who fired the shot or how his hands got burned? He lived. My job was to tell the coroner how those people died.'

'The woman was never identified, don't you find that strange?'

'No.'

'Really?'

'Take a trip down to any county morgue and you'll find unclaimed bodies.'

'How many are unidentified?'

'You'd be surprised. In Brooks County they found a hundred and twenty-nine bodies last year. Sixty-eight are unidentified – most likely illegal immigrants who died in the desert. Sometimes they only find the bones. That woman was burned beyond recognition. We couldn't even reconstruct her face because the intense heat caused so many fractures. There was no conspiracy, Special Agent. We just couldn't give that poor woman a name.'

Desiree notices Willford's daughter peering at her from the cracked door, as though ready to intervene to protect him. Collecting the photographs, she thanks the pathologist and apologises for interrupting his brunch.

Outside a child screams and tears follow. Willford sighs. 'They say grandchildren are a blessing but mine are holy terrors. It's like being locked in an insane asylum full of midgets.' He glances at Desiree. 'No offence meant, ma'am.'

# CHAPTER 42

Audie watches Sandy Valdez through the large glass windows into the fitness centre where she's running on a treadmill, her hair bouncing on her shoulders.

Some time later she emerges, showered, wearing white golfing shorts and an expensive-looking sleeveless top that fits loose, yet shows off her breasts. Her tanned legs stretch from sockless sneakers. She picks up a coffee to go. Window-shops. Tries on a shirt.

Audie glances up from a newspaper, watching her move through the brightly lit atrium and ascend on the escalator. They're under a clear dome of the shopping mall where water streams down a glass wall into a pool that's supposed to represent a rainforest. She waves to a friend on the down escalator. They signal each other. Phone. Coffee. Catch-up. Later.

In another shop, Sandy chooses a skirt and blouse and goes into the changing room. She emerges a few minutes later and goes back to the rack, looking for a different size.

Audie has survived without luck for so long that

he hardly recognises when it arrives. Sandy has left her gym bag in the changing room. Slipping inside the cubicle, he unzips the bag and takes her cell phone.

An assistant walks past. 'Can I help you?'

'My wife needs her phone,' he says, motioning to Sandy, who is studying a label. At that moment she turns and starts walking toward the changing room. Another shopper has attracted the assistant's attention. Audie lowers his head and passes within a foot of Sandy, expecting a shout of alarm or someone yelling for the police. Fifteen . . . twenty . . . thirty feet . . . he's outside the shop . . . on the escalator . . . across the concourse.

Minutes later he's sitting behind the wheel of the Camry, scrolling through Sandy's text messages until he finds one from the boy. He hits the reply option and types:

*Change of plan. We want you home. I'll pick you up from school in fifteen minutes. Mom xx.*

He presses 'send' and waits. The phone vibrates with a new message:

*What's up?*

*I'll explain later. Meet you in the parking lot.*

Audie searches the contacts list again and punches in a new number. A woman answers. Bright. Breezy.

*'Oak Ridge High School.'*

'This is Sheriff Ryan Valdez,' says Audie, lengthening his vowels.

*'How can I help you, Sheriff?'*

358

'My son Max is a junior. He needs to come home. I'm picking him up in a few minutes.'

*'Did he lodge a permission slip?'*

'No. That's why I'm calling.'

*'Your wife told us there was a security issue.'*

'That's why it's important we pick him up. I'm calling on my wife's cell phone.'

The secretary checks the number. *'Very good. I'll get Max out of class.'*

Audie hangs up and drops the phone in his lap. Pausing at the next stoplight, he reaches behind him and pulls the sawn-off shotgun from under his rucksack on the seat. He has three shells. Rolling them in his palm, he feels the coolness of the curved metal edges.

Pulling into a parking spot near the school gates, he lets the engine idle and watches the main doors. The sky is the purest blue, not cobalt or vapour-laden or discoloured by smog.

His cell phone chimes. Max texts: *Where are you?*

*Walk to the exit.*

*You have to sign something.*

*Tell them I'll do it later. We have to hurry.*

Moments later he sees Max push through the heavy glass doors and jog down the steps. He's wearing a baseball cap low over his ears and is moving with gangly teenage awkwardness, searching for his mother's car.

Audie triggers the hazard lights. Max moves closer. He crouches to look through the tinted glass. The window glides down.

'Get in the car.'

The boy blinks at him. His eyes drift down to the shotgun on Audie's lap. For a fleeting moment he seems to consider running.

'I have your mom,' says Audie. 'How else could I set this up?'

Max hesitates. Audie shows him Sandy's phone. 'Get in the car, I'll take you to her.'

The boy looks over his shoulder. Uncertain. Scared. He climbs into the passenger seat. Audie slides the shotgun onto the floor next to his left hand and pulls away from the kerb. The doors centrally lock. Max tries the handle.

'I want to talk to Mom.'

'Soon.'

They're driving north along the I-45, keeping to the centre lane. Audie checks the mirrors, occasionally slowing or accelerating, making sure they're not being followed.

'Where is she?'

Audie doesn't answer.

'What have you done to her?'

'She's fine.'

Audie moves to the outer lane. 'Give me your cell.'

'Why?'

'Just do it.'

Max hands it over. Audie winds down the window. He tosses Sandy's and then Max's phones onto the hard shoulder of the freeway where the devices shatter and the pieces bounce and skip across the asphalt.

'Hey! That was my cell!' cries Max, looking out the back window.

'I'll buy you another one.'

Max looks at him murderously. 'You're not taking me to Mom, are you?'

Silence.

Max pulls at the door handle and begins yelling. He hammers on the window, screaming at passing vehicles. The drivers ignore him, locked in their own little worlds. He lunges for the steering wheel. The Camry slews across two lanes and almost swipes the safety rail. Vehicles swerve out of the way. Horns blare. Max is still gripping the wheel. Audie elbows him in the face and the boy falls back into his seat, holding his nose, blood running through his fingers.

'You could've killed us,' yells Audie.

'You're gonna kill me anyway,' Max hiccups.

'What?'

'You're gonna kill me.'

'Why would I do that?'

'Revenge.'

'I don't want to hurt you.'

Max lowers his hands. 'What do you call this?'

Audie's heart is still racing. 'I'm sorry I hit you. You frightened me.' He pulls out a handkerchief and hands it to Max. The teenager holds it on his nose.

'Tilt your head back,' says Audie.

'I know what to do,' Max replies angrily. They drive in silence. Audie checks the mirrors again, wondering if the near-accident was caught on any camera or reported by another driver.

Max's nose has stopped bleeding. He touches it gingerly. 'My daddy says you stole a lot of money. That's why he shot you. He's going to catch you again. This time he'll kill you proper.'

'I'm sure he wants to.'

'What's that supposed to mean?'

'Your daddy wants me dead.'

'So do I!'

He slouches, dropping his chin to his chest, staring at the passing fields and farmhouses.

'Where are we going?'

'Somewhere safe.'

# CHAPTER 43

Desiree knocks on the door of a simple wooden cottage in Conroe. She hears a woman yelling inside, telling someone called Marcie to 'turn the music down' and 'don't let the dog out'.

A teenager opens the door a crack. She's wearing skintight cut-off jeans and a Minnie Mouse T-shirt. A dog is scrabbling on the wooden floor, trying to squeeze between her legs.

'We're not buying an'thang.'

Desiree shows her badge.

Marcie yells over her shoulder. 'Ma! It's the Feds.'

*This girl watches too much TV.*

Marcie grabs the wet-looking dog by the collar and drags it along the hallway, leaving Desiree standing on the doorstep. A woman appears, wiping her hands.

Desiree holds up her badge. 'I'm sorry to bother you.'

'In my experience when people say something like that, they're not sorry at all.'

Mrs Beauchamp pushes strands of hair from her

eyes with the back of her wrist. She's wearing shorts and an oversized denim shirt that is dotted with wet spots. 'I've been washing the dog. He rolled in something dead.'

'I wanted to ask you a few questions about your late husband.'

'He's been gone twelve years in January, can't get much *later* than that.'

They move to a cluttered living room. Magazines are gathered off the sofa to make room. Desiree sits. Mrs Beauchamp glances at her wrist, but she's not wearing a watch.

'I've been taking another look at the Armaguard hijacking and robbery,' says Desiree.

'He's out, isn't he? I saw the news.'

Desiree doesn't reply.

'I still get folks looking at me funny . . . in the supermarket, or at the gas station, or when I pick up Marcie from school – they're all thinking the same thing: that I know where the money is.' She laughs sarcastically. 'Do they think we'd live like this if I had all those millions?' The rims of her nostrils whiten, as though she remembers another unfinished thought. 'They blamed Scotty.'

'Who blamed him?'

'Everyone – the police, the neighbours, complete strangers, but especially Armaguard. That's why they refused to pay out his life insurance. I had to sue them. I won, but the lawyers finished up with most of the money. Thieving scum!'

Desiree listens quietly while the woman tells her

about the robbery, how she heard the news of the hijacking on the radio and tried to call her husband.

'He didn't answer. When Marcie came home from school I lied to her and said her daddy had been in an accident. I couldn't tell her what had happened. The County coroner said he died from his injuries. He died trying to protect that money. He was a goddamn hero and they made him out to be a villain.'

'What did the police say?'

'They started the rumours. There was never any evidence but they decided to smear someone because they couldn't recover the money and Scotty wasn't around to defend himself.'

'Did he normally make the run to Chicago?'

'He'd done it five, maybe six times.'

'Always a different route?'

She shrugs. 'Scotty didn't talk to me about work. He was ex-military. When he fought in Afghanistan he wouldn't tell me about his deployments. It was operational. Secret.'

Mrs Beauchamp stands and pulls open the net curtain. 'He wasn't even supposed to be doing that run.'

'Why?'

'One of the trucks was damaged in an accident, so they missed a previous delivery. Scotty was due a vacation, but they asked him to make the run.'

'Who asked him?'

'His supervisor.' She wipes a spot of dirt from her cheek. 'That's why there was so much money in the truck. It was four weeks' cash instead of two.'

'How did the truck get damaged?'

'Somebody put the wrong gas in the tank.'

'Who?'

'I don't know – some apprentice or general moron.' Mrs Beauchamp drops the curtain. 'I work two jobs – both of them barely above minimum wage, but I still get people looking at me funny if I buy something new.'

'They must have had a reason for suspecting your husband.'

The woman scoffs and screws up her face. 'They had a photograph taken at a gas station a month before the robbery. Have you ever seen that picture?'

Desiree shakes her head.

'Well, you go and look at it! My Scotty is holding a door open for a man to walk through. That man was Vernon Caine. Scotty could have been saying, "How do you do?" They could have been talking about the weather or the football scores. Doesn't mean Scotty was one of the gang.'

She's building up a head of steam. 'He fought for his country and died for his job and they treat him like some scumbag criminal. And then that boy went and fessed up, but got ten years instead of going to the chair. Now he's running around, free as a bird. If I sound bitter and twisted – it's because I am. Scotty won medals. He deserved better than this.'

366

Desiree averts her eyes, not knowing what to say. She apologises for taking up Mrs Beauchamp's time and wishes her a happy Thanksgiving. Outside, the day seems brighter and the trees a darker green against the blue. Desiree puts in a call to Jenkins in Washington, asking for a list of employees at Armaguard, including the name of the supervisor in January 2004.

'That was eleven years ago,' he replies. 'There might not be a record.'

'I don't expect there will be.'

# CHAPTER 44

Moss parks the pickup behind a row of storefronts with offices on the upper floors. He leans back in the seat and closes his eyes, feeling as if his brain has been wrung out and hung up to dry in the blazing sun. It's his first hangover of the century and he could happily wait another hundred years.

They'll know by now – the people who broke him out of prison. They'll know that he doesn't have Audie Palmer, which means they'll report him missing or worse. Whatever happens, this isn't going to end in early release. Either he'll be recaptured or killed – buried in a forest or the desert or dumped in the Gulf. According to the stories, Eddie Barefoot has a novel way of getting rid of bodies. He hires a portable wood-chipper and has it towed to a desirable location. The very thought of that crimson arc staining the ground makes Moss want to heave.

The big question is why? Why do they want Audie dead? Things would be easier to accept if he understood the reasons. Maybe he'd be willing to forgive and forget if somebody could just explain.

He keeps remembering the way Audie had looked in the clearing. Hunted. Scared. In all their time together in prison, Moss had never seen Audie look flustered or frightened. He was simply noble where others were not. It was like he'd been living ever since Adam bit the apple and Eve had covered up. He could not be surprised or shocked because he'd seen it all before.

Moss looks down at his bare arms. Sunshine is streaming through the window, but he still feels cold. He wants to be with Crystal . . . to hold her . . . to hear her voice.

There's an old phone booth on the corner. He fumbles in his pocket for spare change and slips inside, follows the instructions. She answers on the third ring.

'Hey, babe?'

*'Hey yourself.'*

'How ya doing?'

*'You sound drunk.'*

'I've had one or two.'

*'Is everything OK?'*

'I found Audie Palmer, but I lost him again.'

*'Are you hurt?'*

'No.'

*'Are you in trouble?'*

'I don't think things are going to work out like I planned.'

*'I hate to say I told you so.'*

'I know. I'm sorry.'

*'Why do you assume I blame you?'*

'You should.'

'*What are you going to do now?*'

'I'm not sure.'

'*Give yourself up. Tell the police what happened.*'

'I would if I knew who I could trust. Listen, I want you to go and stay with your folks for a few days.'

'*Why?*'

'I don't trust these people and I want to be sure you're safe.'

Glancing out the window, he notices an overweight man in a business shirt and blue tie pull up in a Mercedes. He gets out and takes a coat from a hanger and picks up his briefcase before walking up the steps, locking the car door over his shoulder.

'I got to go, babe,' Moss says.

'*Where?*'

'I'll call you later.'

Moss jogs across the street and takes the stairs two at a time, jamming his foot in the sprung door before it automatically closes. The lawyer has tucked the briefcase under his chin and is fumbling with a heavy set of keys and a double lock.

'Clayton Rudd?'

The attorney turns. In his mid-sixties with a potbelly and shock of white hair, Clayton Rudd's most memorable feature is a southern moustache that twirls at each end like he's selling fried chicken. He's wearing a suit that might have fitted a younger version of himself, but now the buttons

370

are pulled so tight they could take someone's eye out.

'Do we have an appointment?'

'No, suh.'

Moss follows Rudd into the office where the attorney hangs up his coat and takes a seat behind a desk. His pale protruding eyes seem to rove around, not settling on any object for more than a moment.

'Talk to me, son. What slings and arrows of outrageous fortune have brought you here?'

'Pardon?'

'Have you sued? Injured? Wronged?'

'No, suh.'

'Well, why do you need a lawyer?'

'It's not about me, Mr Rudd. I'm here to talk about Audie Palmer.'

The attorney stiffens and his eyes go wide behind his rimless glasses. 'I don't know anyone by that name.'

'You represented him.'

'You're mistaken.'

'The Dreyfus County truck robbery.'

Out of view, Rudd uses his foot to slide open the bottom drawer of his desk.

Moss raises an eyebrow. 'If you're considering pulling a gun out of that drawer, Mr Rudd, please reconsider.'

The attorney looks into the drawer and slides it closed. 'You can't be too careful,' he says apologetically. 'Are you a friend of Mr Palmer?'

'We're acquainted.'

'Did he send you?'

'No.'

Rudd eyes the telephone. 'I'm not supposed to discuss cases. Lawyer–client privilege. You understand? Audie Palmer has no right to complain. He was lucky.'

'Lucky?'

'To have me! I got him the deal of a lifetime. He could have gone to the chair, but he got ten years.'

'How did you manage that?'

'I did my job well.'

'I hope he thanked you.'

'They rarely do. When a client gets off he thinks he's beaten the system. When he goes down he blames me. Either way I never get the credit.'

Moss knows this to be true. Every con will tell you he was stitched up by his lawyer or framed by the cops or just plain unlucky. None of them ever admits to being stupid or greedy or vengeful. Audie was the exception. He didn't talk about his conviction or complain about the verdict. He helped other prisoners with their appeals and to lodge petitions, but had never once mentioned his own circumstances.

'Have you any idea why Audie would escape the day before his release?'

Clayton Rudd shrugs. 'The boy has more metal in his head than a toaster.'

'I think that's wrong,' says Moss. 'I think he

knew exactly what he was doing. Did he ever mention the money?'

'No.'

'And I reckon you didn't ask.'

'That's not my job.'

'Excuse my language, suh, but I think you're full of shit.'

Rudd leans back and laces his fingers on his chest. 'Let me tell you something, son. Fate was working its sorry ass off when Audie Palmer got ten years.'

'Why wasn't he charged with capital murder?'

'He was but I pleaded it down.'

'That was one hell of a plea bargain.'

'Like I said – I did my job.'

'Why did the DA's office agree? Why would they?'

The attorney sighs wearily. 'You want to know what I think? I think nobody expected Audie Palmer to survive. They didn't *want* him to. Even when by some miracle he lived, the doctors said he'd be a cabbage, which is why the DA suggested a deal. By pleading guilty we saved the state the cost of a trial. Palmer agreed.'

'No, it was more than that.'

Rudd stands and opens a filing cabinet. He pulls out a legal folder that looks heavier than a sandbag. 'Here! You can read about it yourself.'

The file has newspaper clippings from the trial, along with a photograph of Audie sitting next to Clayton Rudd in the courtroom, his head still swathed in bandages.

'I couldn't put him on the stand because he couldn't speak properly. Reporters were baying like rabid dogs, wanting him to get the death penalty because an innocent woman died along with a security guard.'

'Folks blamed Audie.'

'Who else could they blame?' Rudd looks at the door. 'And now if you excuse me, I have work to do.'

'What happened to the money?'

'That's one more question than you're allowed. Don't let the door hit you on the ass.'

# CHAPTER 45

The Law Enforcement Complex for Dreyfus County is located at No. 1 Criminal Justice Drive – an ambitious address that could be seen as a statement of intent or one of wishful thinking. The building looks modern and functional, but lacks the architectural charm of the older-style police stations and county courthouses and city halls that have mostly been sold off because the land is worth more than the history.

Desiree uses the side mirror of her car to check herself. Audie Palmer's phone call has been exercising her mind. He denied shooting the mother and daughter but he didn't beg to be believed or plead for understanding. It's as though he didn't care less if Desiree took his word for it or not. He also said that his brother was dead and if she wanted the proof she could dredge the Trinity River.

Why tell her that now? Why not reveal it eleven years ago when it could have done him some good? Yet something about Audie's frankness and lack of guile made her *want* to believe him.

She recalls the moment she stepped into the

motel room. There was something about the scene – aside from the senseless violence – that struck a dissonant chord. Why would Audie kill Cassie and Scarlett? Perhaps he blamed Cassie for calling the police, but why shoot her at that moment – just as Valdez knocked on the door and announced his presence?

According to the sheriff's account, Audie squeezed off three shots, killing two people, then broke down the adjoining door, fled through the next room, along the breezeway, down the stairs and across the parking lot, fully clothed, leaving no personal possessions behind in the motel room where he'd spent the previous two nights. All this in the time it took the sheriff to knock on the door, announce himself and use the entry card. It defies logic. It mocks common sense. No wonder she can't shake her doubts.

Sheriff Valdez has an office on the fourth floor with a view over a nondescript factory with no sign on the gate or indication of what it might store or manufacture. Valdez doesn't look up when Desiree knocks and enters. He's talking on the telephone and hoops his hand in the air, motioning Desiree to take a seat.

The call ends. The sheriff leans back in his chair.

'I hope I haven't caught you at a busy time,' she says.

'It's hard to be busy when you're suspended. Any officer who discharges a weapon must be stood down pending the completion of the investigation.'

'They're the rules.'

'I know it.'

Desiree has taken a seat. She rests her handbag on her knees, clutching the top with both hands. It embarrasses her a little because it makes her feel like Miss Marple bringing her knitting along to the interview. She puts the bag on the floor between her feet.

The sheriff laces his fingers behind his head and studies her. 'You don't particularly like me, do you, Special Agent?'

'I don't trust you, there's a difference.'

Valdez nods as though his trustworthiness were only a matter of semantics. 'Why are you here?'

'I wanted to apologise. Aparently you took offence at my line of questioning the other day.'

'You were out of line.'

'I was just doing my job.'

'It's not right that you talk to people the way you do, especially a fellow law enforcement officer. You treated me like human refuse . . . like a criminal.'

'The sight of that young woman and her daughter, lying dead, I guess I lost my sense of perspective.'

'Yes you did.'

Desiree has rehearsed what she's going to say to Valdez, but the words keep getting caught in her throat like she's trying to swallow unbuttered bread.

'I'm not very experienced at seeing death so close up,' she says. 'You're obviously accustomed to it.'

'Meaning?'

'The armoured truck robbery was a bloodbath by all accounts. What did it feel like to shoot those boys?'

'I was doing my job.'

'Talk me through the robbery again.'

'You've read the files.'

'You gave a statement about an SUV parked next to the armoured truck, but the original radio dispatch doesn't mention any SUV.'

'It was parked on the far side of the armoured truck. We didn't see it at first.'

'That sounds plausible,' says Desiree.

'Plausible? It's the goddamn truth!'

Desiree hides any inkling of pleasure she obtains in getting under the sheriff's skin. 'I was hoping to speak to Lewis and Fenway.'

'They no longer work for the county.'

'I would appreciate your help in providing phone numbers or contact addresses.'

There is a heartbeat of silence. Desiree glances out the window where dust and smoke from a distant fire has smudged the light and turned it golden.

'I can give you an address for Lewis. You got a pen and paper?' says Valdez.

'I do.'

'Magnolia Cemetery, Beaumont, Jefferson County, Texas.'

'What?'

'He died in a light plane crash.'

'When?'

'Six, maybe seven years ago.'

'What about Fenway?'

'Last I heard he opened a dive bar in the Florida Keys.'

'Address?'

'Nope.'

'How about a name?'

'I think he called it the Dive Bar.'

His sarcasm ignites something in Desiree. 'Whatever happened to the dashboard footage?'

Valdez hesitates but recovers, flexing his lower jaw. 'Footage?'

'The crime-scene photographs show a camera on the dashboard of your cruiser. I couldn't find any reference to there being footage.'

'The camera wasn't working.'

'Why?'

'One of the many bullets that were being fired in our direction must have disabled it.'

'Is that the official explanation?'

Valdez seems to chew hard on a ball of anger, rolling it around like a loogie in his cheek. He forces a smile. 'I don't know about the official explanation. I didn't pay much attention. I guess I must have been too busy dodging bullets fired by men who wanted to kill me. Have you ever been shot at, Special Agent?' He doesn't wait for her to answer. 'No, I don't expect so. People like you live in privileged seclusion in your ivory towers, separated from the facts and practicalities of the real world. You carry a gun and a badge and you chase white-collar criminals and tax cheats and federal fugitives, but you don't know what it's like to face down a meth addict swinging a machete or a drug dealer with a semi-automatic. You've never worked on the front line. You've never dealt with the dregs. You've never put your life on the line for a colleague, or a buddy. When you've done any of those things you can come back and question my actions and my motives. Until then you can get the fuck out of my office.'

Valdez is on his feet. The muscles in his neck are bulging hotly and sweat is beading his forehead.

The phone on his desk is ringing. He snatches it out of the cradle.

'What do you mean? . . . I didn't call them . . . And the school let him go?' He glances at Desiree. 'OK, OK, calm down . . . talk me through it again . . . where did you last have your phone? . . . which means it was probably stolen . . . Stay calm, we'll find him . . . I know . . . It's going to be fine . . . I'm going to call the school. Where are you now? . . . I'll send a cruiser to pick you up.'

He lowers the phone, cupping the mouthpiece. 'Somebody phoned my son's high school pretending to be me.'

'When?'

'Forty-five minutes ago.'

'Where is your son now?'

'They don't know.'

# CHAPTER 46

udie takes the South Freeway through the outskirts of Houston into Brazoria County. At Lake Jackson he turns west on the 614 toward East Columbia. A rusted pickup in front has a bumper sticker across the back window: *Secede or Die: Texas Patriot.* The driver tosses away a cigarette, which bounces and sparks across the blacktop.

Most of the farms look neat and prosperous. The fields are full of sunflowers, cotton and the broken stalks of harvested corn. They pass silos and windmills and barns and tractors; people going about their daily lives, oblivious to an ordinary-looking Camry carrying a man and a teenage boy.

Once or twice Audie sneaks a glance at Max, seeing the buds of spittle in the corners of his mouth and the red rims around his eyes. The teenager is frightened. He doesn't understand. How could he? Children normally grow up believing the world is a certain way. They hear fairytales and watch feel-good movies where every orphan finds a family and every stray dog finds a home. There is a moral to these stories. Good things happen to good people and love always finds a way, but for a lot of kids reality is less glossy and wholesome because they learn about life via a swinging belt or a swishing cane or a cocked fist.

Audie had an uncle on his mother's side, who used to enjoy dragging Audie onto his lap at family gatherings. He'd tickle him with one hand, while jamming his other thumb into Audie's ribs until the boy thought he might faint with the pain.

'Listen to him,' his uncle would say, 'he doesn't know whether to laugh or cry.'

Audie had never understood why his uncle chose to hurt him; what pleasure he could have taken in torturing a young boy. Now he glances across at Max and hopes he avoided sadistic uncles and school bullies and others who prey on the vulnerable.

Two hours after leaving Conroe, they reach Sargent – which is little more than a collection of buildings spread out along Caney Creek, which meanders for miles in wide looping turns until it reaches the Gulf coast. By road the journey is almost dead straight until the bitumen crosses a swing bridge and stops abruptly at Sargent Beach.

Reaching the T-junction, Audie turns east along Canal Drive, following the single-lane that is spider-webbed with heat cracks and crumbling in places. The road continues for another three miles along the beachfront. Slowly the houses begin to thin out. Most of them are holiday places built on stilts because of the king tides and storm swells that bring seawater sloshing almost as high as the floorboards. They are shuttered up for the winter; the flagpoles bare and deck furniture stored inside or tied down, while boats are garaged in sheds or anchored in front yards.

Flanking the road to the left is a large canal that carries dredging barges and pleasure cruisers along the Intracoastal Waterway. Further inland are marshes and mile upon mile of treeless prairie and wetland dotted with shallow ponds and narrow watercourses. In the strange twilight, Audie can see ducks moving in a V-formation across the sky, as though forming an arrow that points to a distant shore.

On the opposite side of the road the long flat beach is dotted with clumps of seaweed and ribbed by tyre tracks. Audie gets out of the car and scans the empty beach. The light is fading the air the colour of dirty water. He walks to the passenger side and opens the door.

'Why have we stopped?' asks Max.

'I'm going to find us somewhere to sleep tonight.'

'I want to go home.'

'You're gonna be fine. This'll be like a sleepover.'

'What am I – nine?'

Audie ties the teenager's hands with a roll of masking tape. Then he nudges him forward, pointing toward the beach.

They approach a darkened house that is shielded by sand dunes and low scrubby trees. Crouching in a hollow above the tideline, Audie watches for ten minutes, looking for any sign of activity.

'You have to promise that you'll stay here and be quiet. Don't try to run. Otherwise I'll take you back and lock you in the trunk.'

'I don't want to go in the trunk.'

'OK, I won't be long.'

Max loses sight of Audie in the gloom and expects to feel relieved, but the opposite is true. He doesn't like the dark. He doesn't like how it amplifies the sound of the insects or his own breathing or the waves against the shore. Looking across the beach, he can see lights out to sea that could be a ship or an oil platform, something moving slowly or not moving at all.

Why isn't he more frightened of this man? Once or twice he has snuck a glance at Audie, secretly studying his face, trying to work out what makes a killer, as though he might see it in his eyes or written on his forehead. It should be obvious – the hatred, the blood lust, the thirst for revenge.

All through the drive, Max has been making mental notes of the signs and landmarks, plotting their location in case he gets a chance to call the police. They headed south out of Houston and then turned west through Old Ocean and Sugar Valley to Bay City.

Audie had tried to make conversation, asking about his parents.

'Why do you want to know?'

384

'I'm interested. Do you get on with your daddy?'

'Yeah, I guess.'

'Do you do stuff together?'

'Sometimes.'

*Not much. Not any more.*

Now crouching in the dark, listening to the waves, Max tries to remember a time when he and his daddy were close. It might have been different if Max had played Little League or basketball or liked dirt biking. He wasn't even very good at skateboarding – not compared with Dean Aubyn or Pat Krein, boys in his class at junior high. Max didn't have much in common with his daddy, but that wasn't the main reason they'd drifted apart. It was the arguments he hated most. Not his own, but those that he listened to at night, lying motionless in bed.

*You should have seen yourself! Really! You were flirting with him. I know what I saw. Jealous? Me? Never. Why would I be jealous of a barren cold bitch like you?*

These fights ended with thrown objects or slammed doors and sometimes with tears. To Max it seemed like his father believed that his wife and son were unappreciative and ungrateful, perhaps even unworthy, but the arguments rarely lasted until the morning. Breakfast would see normal service resumed, his mother packing his daddy's lunch and kissing him goodbye.

Max misses them both and wants his daddy to come. He imagines a convoy of police cruisers

385

with flashing lights and screaming sirens, hurtling down the road toward him, while the blades of a chopper thump the air and a team of Navy SEALs comes roaring onto the beach in inflatables. He cocks his ear for a moment, but doesn't hear any sirens or helicopters or boats. Cautiously, he begins moving along the path, looking over his shoulder, wondering if Audie is watching. He reaches the car and pauses for a moment, sipping the darkness. The road is another hundred yards away. He can flag down a car. He can raise the alarm.

Running now, he has a gait almost like a gallop because his wrists are bound together and his arms can't swing freely. Suddenly he trips over something and tumbles face first into the sand.

'Now that was a proper face-plant,' says Audie, stepping from behind a fence, resting the shotgun on his shoulder. Max spits sand from his mouth.

'You said you wouldn't hurt me.'

'I said I didn't want to.'

Audie helps him stand and brushes him down. Max angrily pushes the hands away, not wanting Audie to touch him. They turn back along the path, approaching the house from the beach side, climbing the steps to a rear deck that overlooks the ocean. The railings and banisters have been stripped of paint and varnish by a combination of salt, wind and sunlight.

After checking the shutters and outside doors, Audie wraps his coat around his forearm and drives his elbow through a small square pane of glass above the doorknob. Reaching inside, he flips the latch and pushes the door open, telling Max to watch his step because of the broken glass. He makes him sit at the kitchen table and then moves quickly through the house, searching each room. The place feels musty and closed up. Sheets have been thrown over the sofas and the beds are stripped and covered in plastic.

Audie finds a magazine cradle with maps and old newspapers, which are three months out of date. There are family photographs on the mantelpiece and in some of the bedrooms. Father. Mother. Three children. Toddlers transformed into teenagers over the course of a decade or more.

He turns on the fridge and checks the cupboards for dried foodstuffs and non-perishables. Without turning on the light, he opens a single shutter on the seaward side of the house and looks across the Gulf at the oil platforms that could be cities floating in the air.

Max hasn't said a word. Audie finds linen in storage trunks and lights the pilot light on the water heater.

'It's going to take a few hours to heat up,' he says. 'We might have to shower in the morning. There are some clothes in the wardrobe.'

'They don't belong to us.'

'That's true,' says Audie. 'But sometimes necessity requires the breaking of rules.'

'Do I have to be tied up?'

Audie considers the question. Inside one of the bedrooms he had seen a tambourine on a shelf. He fetches it to the kitchen and tells Max to stand before taping the instrument between the teenager's knees. He can't move without making a jangling sound.

'I want you to sit in that armchair. If I hear you moving, I'm going to tie up you hands *and* feet. Understand?'

Max nods.

'Are you hungry?' Audie asks.

'No.'

'Well, I'm going to fix something anyway. You can eat if you want to.'

He discovers a box of fusilli pasta in the pantry and dumps the contents into a saucepan of boiling water. Then he finds a can of tomatoes, some herbs, garlic powder and seasoning. Max watches him cooking.

Later they eat in silence at the kitchen table. The only sound is the occasional jangling of the tambourine and of forks scraping on plates.

'I'm not a very good cook,' says Audie. 'I haven't had much practice.'

Max pushes his plate to the centre of the table. He flicks his bangs from his eyes and looks at the scars that seem to be crosshatched on Audie's forearms.

'Did you get those in prison?' he asks after another minute of silence.

Audie nods.

'How?'

'People get into disagreements.'

Max points to the back of Audie's right hand where a scar runs from the base of his thumb to his wrist. 'How did you get that one?'

'A shank made from a melted toothbrush.'

'And that one?'

'Cut-throat razor.'

'How did someone get a razor?'

'One of the guards must have smuggled it in.'

'Why would they do that?'

Audie looks at him sadly. 'To kill me.'

Rinsing their plates in the sink, he glances out the window, studying the sky. 'We might get a storm tonight, but if it clears up tomorrow, we could go fishing.'

Max doesn't answer.

'You know how to fish, don't you?'

He shrugs.

'What about hunting?'

'My daddy took me once.'

'Where?'

'Up in the mountains.'

Audie thinks about Carl and the hunting trips they took as teenagers. Always nerveless on the trigger, Carl showed no emotion, not even a flicker, as he made the shot. Ducks, squirrels, white-tailed deer, doves, rabbits, geese – his face was always a mask, whereas everything that Audie killed would twitch with his nervousness and bleed with his anxiety.

'Are you going to shoot me?' asks Max.

'What? No!'

'Why am I here?'

'I wanted us to be friends.'

'Friends!'

'Yeah.'

'You're fucking crazy!'

'Don't curse. We have a lot in common.'

Max scoffs dismissively.

'Have you ever been to Las Vegas?' asks Audie.

'No.'

'I once got married in Vegas. It was eleven years ago. I married the most beautiful woman . . .' He pauses, recalling the moment with a wrinkled smile. 'It was in one those chapels you read about.'

'Like the Elvis Presley chapel?'

'Not that one,' says Audie. 'It was called the Chapel of the Bells on Las Vegas Boulevard. They had an "I-Do Service" that cost $145 with music and a marriage certificate. We went shopping beforehand. I thought she wanted to buy a dress, but she was looking for a hardware store.'

'Why?'

'She bought two yards of soft woven rope. And she told me I had to find thirteen gold coins and give them to her. "They don't have to be real gold," she said. "They're symbols."'

'Symbols of what?' asks Max.

'They were supposed to represent Jesus and his disciples,' Audie replies. 'And by giving her the coins, I was saying that I would look after her and her little boy.'

'Boy? You didn't mention any boy.'

'I didn't?' Audie traces a scar on his forearm. 'He was my best man. I let him hold the wedding ring.'

Max doesn't reply, but for a brief instant Audie senses that the teenager might remember. The moment passes.

'What was his name?'

'Miguel – it's the Spanish version of Michael.'

Again nothing.

'During the ceremony, Belita tied the soft cord around my wrist and then her own. She said it signified our infinite bond because our fates were now tied to each other.'

'Sounds pretty superstitious,' says Max.

'Yeah,' says Audie, as the first distant flashes of lightning chase away the shadows. 'I guess she was superstitious, but she didn't believe that evil lay in things, only in people. A place could not be tainted, only a soul.'

Max yawns.

'You should get some sleep,' says Audie. 'Big day tomorrow.'

'What's going to happen?'

'I'm going to take you fishing.'

# CHAPTER 47

Police cruisers are parked in the driveway of the Valdez house and unmarked cars line both sides of the street. Detectives are going door to door and a forensic team has taken fingerprints and hair samples from Max's bedroom.

Voices are raised in the kitchen. Accusations. Recriminations.

'We don't know it was Audie Palmer,' says Desiree, trying to cool tempers.

'Who else would it be?' says Valdez.

'He's threatened us already,' echoes Sandy, dabbing her eyes with a tissue.

'How did he threaten you?'

'By turning up here, of course . . . and by talking to Max.'

Desiree nods and looks at Senogles, who is perched on a stool, stroking his chin, playing the wise man.

'That doesn't explain why he'd kidnap Max,' says Desiree.

Sandy loses her temper. 'Have you been listening? Ryan shot him. Ryan arrested him. Ryan got him locked away.'

392

'OK, I understand that, but it still doesn't make sense.' Desiree tries another angle. 'How old is Max?'

'Just turned fifteen.'

'Did you ever mention to Palmer that you had a son?'

Valdez shakes his head.

'Did you have any contact or correspondence with Palmer after his conviction?'

'No. What are you getting at?'

'I'm trying to figure out why Palmer turned up here last Sunday. And if Max was the target, why not take him that first day? Why wait until now?'

Valdez blinks at her angrily. 'The man is crazy! Brain-damaged!'

'Not according to the psychiatrist who treated him in prison.' Desiree tries to keep her voice calm and even. 'What did he talk to Max about?'

'What difference does that make?'

'I'm trying to establish his motives.'

Valdez throws up his hands. 'We should have had protection. You should have provided us with a safe house.'

Senogles answers. 'I would have given you protection, Ryan, but you didn't ask for it.'

'So it's my fault, Frank?'

'You said you could look after things.'

The two eyeball each other. Desiree wonders when they started using first names; perhaps during the original investigation.

'Max should never have gone to school,' says

Sandy, sobbing into her husband's chest. 'This is my fault. I should have listened to you.'

Valdez puts an arm around her. 'It's nobody's fault. We're going to get him back safe and sound.' He glances at Senogles. 'You tell her, Frank.'

'We're going to do our very best.'

Senogles stands and rubs his hands together. 'OK, this is what we know. Sandy and Max's cell phones were both transmitting for ten minutes after Max left the school. The last signal has been traced to Interstate 45, about sixteen miles north of Woodlands. We're studying footage from the Interstate and the shopping mall to see if we can identify what vehicle Palmer is driving. Once we know that we can trace his movements on traffic cameras and narrow down the search area.' He looks at Sandy. 'We need a recent photograph of Max to give to the media. And we may also decide to hold a news conference. Would you be prepared to make a statement?'

Sandy looks at her husband.

'It can generate more publicity,' says Senogles. 'The emotional plea for help from the family: please give our boy back . . . that sort of thing.'

Desiree adds, 'Does Max have any medical conditions? Allergies?'

'He's asthmatic.'

'Medication?'

'He has some with him.'

'Do you know his blood type?'

'What difference does that make?'

394

'It's just a precaution,' explains Desiree. 'We brief paramedics and doctors so they're prepared.'

Sandy lets out another sob and Valdez glowers at Senogles. 'Get her out of here, Frank.'

Senogles motions Desiree to the sliding door, ushers her onto the patio. When they're alone, he turns and gazes over the swimming pool, his face bathed in an alien blue glow from the sub-merged lights.

'I think you're treating these people like they're guilty of something.'

'I don't agree.'

'I also think you get moist for Audie Palmer. Am I right? Do murdering scumbags get your juices flowing, Special Agent?'

'Who the hell are you to ask me that?'

'Your goddamn boss is who I am, and I think it's time you accepted that fact.'

Desiree is standing away from the light, her hair hanging against her cheeks, her eyes bright in the shadows.

'Audie Palmer isn't brain-damaged. He's highly intelligent, almost off the scale. Why does he risk coming back here if he has all that money from the robbery at his disposal? Why risk kidnapping a sheriff's son? None of it makes sense. Unless . . .'

'Unless what?'

Desiree pauses and blows a puff of air past her nose, lifting a strand of hair on her forehead.

'What if there was no fourth man? What if the police took the money?'

'What?'

'Hear me out.'

Senogles waits.

'Imagine for a moment that Palmer and the gang hijacked the armoured truck but the police stumbled upon them before they could unload the cash. There was a high-speed chase, a shoot-out. The gang was dead. The money was there for the taking.'

'What about Audie Palmer?'

'He was part of the gang.'

'He would have fingered them.'

'They shot him. They didn't expect him to live.'

'But he did.'

'Maybe that's why he came back – he's looking for his share.'

Senogles shakes his head, wiping his lips with his thumb and forefinger. 'Even if what you're saying were true – which it's not – Palmer would have called his lawyer and tried to cut a deal.'

'Maybe that's exactly what he did – he got ten years when it could have been worse.'

'Not the ten years he served. They were the toughest.'

Desiree tries to argue, but Senogles interrupts. 'You're talking about a conspiracy that involves police officers, the district attorney's office, defence counsel, the coroner, maybe even the judge.'

'Maybe not,' says Desiree. 'A file goes missing. Charges are changed.'

Lifting one foot, Senogles rubs the polished toe of his shoe against the back of his trouser leg.

'Can you hear yourself?' he asks, his voice shaking with anger. 'Audie Palmer is a cold-blooded killer and you keep trying to make excuses for him. In case you've forgotten – he pleaded guilty. He admitted to the crime.' Senogles clears his nose, hawking phlegm into the garden. 'You think I'm tough on you, Agent Furness, and here's why. I deal in facts and you deal in fantasies. Grow up. You're not seven years old playing with your My Little Pony. This is real life. Now I want you to go inside and tell those good people that we're going to do everything we can to get their son back.'

'Yes, sir.'

'I didn't hear you.'

'Yes, sir!'

# CHAPTER 48

The storm arrives in the early hours, sweeping across the Gulf and hurling rain and salt against the windows and sending a chill wind beneath the doors and through cracks in the floorboards. Lightning ripples behind distant clouds, framing them momentarily. As a kid, Audie used to love nights like this one, lying in bed, listening to the rain rattle against the windows and gurgle down the gutters. Now he sleeps on the floor because his body has grown accustomed to hard surfaces and thin blankets.

For a long while, he watches the boy sleeping, wondering where he goes in his dreams. Does he visit willing girls, or hit home runs, or score winning touchdowns?

Growing up, Audie was told he could be anything he wanted: a firefighter, policeman, astronaut, even the President . . . Aged nine he had wanted to be a fighter pilot, but not like Tom Cruise in *Top Gun*, which looked like a computer game rather than combat. Instead he wanted to be Baron Von Richthofen, the legendary German flying ace.

He had a comic book about the Red Baron and one particular drawing stuck in his mind. It showed the Baron saluting a flaming Sopwith Camel as it plunged toward the earth. Instead of looking triumphant, he seemed to lament the loss of a brave opponent.

When Audie finally nods off, he dreams about the journey from Las Vegas to Texas, through Arizona and the mountains of southern New Mexico. They stopped at tourist spots along the way like the Children's Museum in Phoenix, Montezuma Castle near Camp Verde and Carlsbad Caverns in the Guadalupe Mountains. They spent two nights at a guest ranch in New Mexico where they rode horses and rounded up cattle. Audie bought Miguel a cowboy hat and a toy six-shooter in a faux leather holster.

Usually they stayed at roadside motels and or in campground cabins. Sometimes Miguel slept between them and on other nights they had a second bed. Belita woke one morning and slapped Audie in the face.

'What was that for?'

'I dreamed you'd gone,' she said.

'What?'

'I dreamed I woke up and you'd gone.'

He put his arms around her and rested his head against her stomach, smelling the clean cotton of her nightdress. She crossed her arms and lifted the dress, revealing herself. Then she put his hand where it would do most good and they made love slowly. When the moment came, Belita clung to him as though he could stop her falling.

'Will you always love me?' she asked.

'Always.'

'Don't I make a good wife?'

'The very best.'

On the fifth day they crossed the state line into Texas. The sky stretched ahead with pale trails, jets so high they couldn't be seen. Miguel had grown more talkative, laughing at Audie's jokes and riding high on his shoulders. At night he wanted Audie to read him bedtime stories.

Belita didn't mind. She watched over both of them, never fully relaxing, always checking the security chain was latched on the door. Only in sleep did she unwind, breathing so faintly that Audie took her pulse by pressing his fingers gently against her neck, so he could feel the blood circulating beneath her skin with the fluidity of a song.

Up until then, Audie didn't believe it possible that someone could die of love. He thought it was a fate invented by poets and writers like John Donne and Shakespeare, but now he understood what they meant by such suffering and wouldn't have swapped the delights of it for anything in the world.

Outside the wind has grown stronger, rattling the windows. Lightning flashes and almost instantaneously thunder splits the air. Max sits bolt upright and flings himself out of bed, crashing into the wardrobe door. Audie catches him as he bounces off, lifting him in a clumsy clean-and-jerk. Hugging him. Holding him off the ground because his feet are still twirling in a running motion, the tambourine jangling between his knees.

Max is coughing and gulping at the air, as though trying to bite off chunks and swallow it more quickly.

'Are you OK?'

He can't answer.

Audie eases the boy down onto the bed. His face is pale and sweaty, his chest tight, his lips tinged with blue.

'Where's your asthma pump?'

He grabs at Max's schoolbag and searches the pockets. The teenager has started to wheeze.

'Just try to relax. Breathe slowly,' says Audie.

He tips up the bag and shakes it, emptying the contents. The asthma inhaler bounces on the floorboards. Audie scrambles on his hands and knees. He shakes it hard and forces the nozzle between Max's lips and teeth. The boy doesn't react.

'C'mon, take it.'

Max turns his face away.

'Don't do this to me,' says Audie.

He grips the boy's head, putting the inhaler between his lips, pressing the nozzle. He waits for Max to inhale and then pinches his nose, forcing him to hold his breath.

Eventually, he lets him breathe normally. Max

relaxes. His chest loosens. His eyes are closed, his cheeks wet.

'I want to go home.'

'I know.'

Thunder rumbles above them. 'I hate storms.'

'You've been that way since you were little,' says Audie.

'How do you know?'

Audie sighs, frightened of going forward. Perhaps he has no choice. Max sits up against the headboard, breathing normally now.

'You knew I was asthmatic.'

'Yes.'

'How?'

Closing his eyes, Audie can still picture the place: a roadside motel outside of Thoreau in New Mexico – one of those one-story breeze-block complexes built so you could park out front of your room. The parking lot was packed with long-distance rigs, 4WD pickups, RVs and campers. The receptionist buzzed and fussed like she was battery-powered and freshly charged, even at midnight.

'Get that little 'un to bed,' she said. 'Breakfast is served until ten. We got a swimming pool, but it could be a mite chilly until noon.'

Audie carried Miguel to the room and put him into the smaller of the beds. He marvelled at how fragile the child seemed, how perfectly formed. The room was less than twenty yards from the highway and every set of headlights slid across the walls and every passing truck rattled the light fittings and sounded ready to come crashing through the front wall.

Despite the noise, they slept. Each new day took them further away from California, but neither could shake the feeling that Urban Covic was searching for them.

At some point Audie woke to the sound of a half-scream. Miguel was twitching in the midst of a nightmare, his chest heaving and compressing like he was fighting for every breath. Belita took an asthma inhaler from her bag and put a mask over Miguel's mouth and nose, holding it there until she knew the medication had reached deep into his lungs. Then she rocked him on her breasts, cooing while he sobbed against her neck until he fell asleep, curled in a ball, his face polished by the passing trucks.

'You have to promise me something,' she said afterwards, as she rested her head on Audie's chest.

'Anything.'

'I don't want *anything* – I want *something*.'

'OK.'

'Promise me that you'll look after Miguel.'

'I'm going to look after you both.'

'But if something happens to me—'

'Nothing is going to happen to you. Don't be so gloomy.'

'What is gloomy?'

Audie tried to explain, but couldn't think of a word in Spanish.

Belita told him to be quiet. 'Promise me on fear of death . . . on your mother's life . . . as God is your witness . . . Promise me that if something happens to me, you will look after Miguel.'

'I don't believe in God,' Audie joked.

She pinched his bottom lip until it bruised. 'Promise me.'

'I promise.'

The wind rises in furious gusts, making the walls groan. Max is sitting against the headboard, waiting for Audie to answer his questions, but Audie has lapsed into silence, eyes closed, twitching at some memory. The teenager almost feels sorry for him but can't explain why. It's like he's broken. No, he's trapped. He's like a rabbit caught in a snare, thumping at the ground with its legs, fighting against the wire even as it pulls tighter.

'What day is your birthday?' asks Audie.

'February 7.'

'What year?'

'2000.'

'Where were you born?'

'Texas.'

'What's the first thing you remember?'

'What do you mean?'

'Your earliest memory.'

'I don't know.'

'Have you always lived in the same house?'

'Yeah.'

'Have you ever been to California?'

'No.'

Audie rolls off the bed and retrieves his backpack. Tucked inside one of the many pockets is a photograph of a woman standing beneath an arch of flowers, holding a small bouquet. Just visible, peeking out from behind the folds of her dress, a young boy smiles shyly at the camera.

Audie hands it to Max. 'Do you know who that is?'

The boy studies the image and shakes his head.

'That's my wife.'

'Where is she now?'

'I don't know.'

Audie takes the photograph from him, holding it gently between his thumb and forefinger. His eyes are glistening. He puts the photograph away and goes back to his sleeping spot on the floor.

'You were going to tell me how you knew me,' says Max.

'It can wait till tomorrow.'

# CHAPTER 49

Valdez takes his car keys and leaves the house, ignoring the huddle of reporters who have gathered at the end of his driveway. He heads west toward Magnolia, still smarting over an argument with Sandy. That woman has a sharp tongue and suspicious mind. One minute she's blaming herself and the next she's blaming him.

Things were less complicated when he was single. Back then he only had to worry about himself. Now he feels like there's a chain around his neck and no matter how high he flies he will always be dragged back to earth by a casual tug of her wrist.

Victor Pilkington lives in a mansion overlooking Old Mill Lake. It's a southern gothic-style structure with wrap-around verandas on both floors, painted to make it look like a wedding cake. The old-world façade camouflages a state-of-the-art house with a poolroom, a private cinema and a gun safe that can be turned into a panic room or a bomb shelter.

A black woman answers the door. She has kept house for the Pilkingtons for twenty years, but rarely speaks unless spoken to first. Some domestics try to ingratiate themselves with a family, but this one drifts through the house like a ghost who doesn't know what else to do.

She takes Valdez into the living room. Moments later, double doors open and his Aunt Mina swishes into the room wearing a long nightgown. She's his mother's older sister, mid-forties, sculptured but softening at the edges. She throws her arms around him and sobs.

'I'm so sorry – I heard the news. It's shocking, just plain shocking.' She doesn't want to let him go. 'How's Sandy? Is she holding up? I was going to call her, but one doesn't know what to say.' She runs her hands from his shoulders down his forearms. 'Max is such a beautiful boy. I'm sure it's going to be fine. The police are going to find him. They're going to catch that terrible man.'

Valdez has to force his way out of her grip.

'Where Victor?'

'In his office.' She glances at the stairs. 'Neither of us could sleep. Go on up.'

Pilkington is watching a fight on pay TV. He leans forward in a big leather armchair, dipping his shoulders as though throwing punches. 'Come on, hit him, you pussy!' He waves at Valdez to take a seat, not looking away from the screen. Then he adds, 'Take a deep breath, Ryan. Don't come in here angry.'

'What in *fuck's* name are we going to do?'

Pilkington ignores him. 'You know the problem

407

with boxers today? They're not willing to come forward and get hurt. Take this kid – he's Puerto Rican. He wins this fight and he could get a crack at Pacquiao, but the only way he's going to last two rounds against Manny is if he gets in close and takes some hurt.'

'Did you hear what I said?'

'I heard you.'

Pilkington gets up. Stretches. Pours a coffee from a glass pot. Doesn't offer. Although only fifteen years separate them, Pilkington is Valdez's uncle on his mother's side. Age hasn't diminished the older man physicality.

'How is that gorgeous wife of yours?' he asks.

'Christ! Are you listening to me?'

'Don't use the Lord's name in vain.'

'Our son is missing and you're acting like nothing is wrong.'

Pilkington ignores the statement. 'You married a keeper there. Do you know how I know?'

Valdez doesn't answer.

'Her smell.' Pilkington drops a lump of sugar in his coffee. Stirs. 'Human beings aren't so different to dogs. The first thing that comes to us is a sense of smell. It's a primary instinct. Immediate. Powerful. Understand?'

*No*, thinks Valdez, who doesn't understand. Pilkington could fuck a roast turkey for all he cares, so long as he keeps clear of Sandy . . . and helps find Max.

The fight has finished. The Puerto Rican kid

lost. Pilkington turns off the TV and takes his coffee to the window where an antique telescope is aimed at the houses opposite.

'This is your fault.'

'What?'

'Palmer. You should have neutralised this issue when you had the chance.'

'Don't you think I've tried! Half the scum in that prison took money to kill him.'

'Your excuses count for shit, Ryan. What did you suppose was going to happen when Palmer got out? Did you think he was going to buy a sweater vest and take up golf?'

'I don't think you should lecture me.'

'What?'

'I don't like being lectured.'

'Is that right?'

'What did you do in the war, uncle? How many shots did you fire?'

Pilkington picks up a paperweight of a grizzly bear, weighing it in his hands. Valdez is still talking, venting his anger, nose to nose with the older man.

'I don't like being lectured by someone who gets other people to do his dirty work and then complains about the stench.'

He opens his mouth to say something else, but doesn't get the chance. Pilkington swings the paperweight underarm, sinking it into the younger man's stomach, sending him to his knees. With surprising speed for a big man, he holds the bronze bear above Valdez's head.

'For a man with no cows you talk a lot of bullshit, Ryan. You'd be nothing without me. Your job and your fancy house and your property portfolio that nobody knows about – that was *my* doing. I got Frank put in charge, and he's covering your ass, but I'm not going to waste any more of my political capital on you. You should have silenced Palmer when you had the chance.'

'What am I supposed to do now?' says Valdez, still struggling for breath.

'Find him.'

'On my own?'

'No, Ryan, you have the combined resources of county, state and federal agencies. I think that should be enough. And when you find him, I'm going to make sure the job gets done properly.'

'And my boy?'

'You should hope he doesn't get in the way.'

# CHAPTER 50

Desiree's second-floor apartment is opposite Milroy Park in Houston Heights, down a narrow lane and up a flight of wooden stairs. According to her rental agent the floor space is a thousand square feet, but she doubts this every time she tries to rearrange the furniture.

As she climbs the wooden steps, she has a sudden feeling that there's something she's forgotten. She checks her handbag. Her keys. Her phone. Nothing amiss.

Reaching the landing, she notices the door slightly ajar. She stands very still, and wonders if her mother could have visited. She has a key but normally phones first. Surely she would have closed the door.

*Who else has a key? Her landlord Mr Sackville could be making an inspection. He might be inside now, trying on her underwear.*

Slipping her Glock semi-automatic from a holster, she contemplates calling it in, but she can't be sure it's not a false alarm. Imagine the laughter if she's wrong. Senogles would never let her live it down.

411

She presses her ear against the door and listens for footsteps or movement or chatter. Her mother would have switched on the TV, which is worshipped like a deity at her parents' place.

Nudging the door with her foot, she steps into the short entry hall. The gun is warm and weirdly sticky in her hand. At the far end of the hall there is a living room and a thin galley kitchen. The bedroom is on the left and bathroom to the right. She has lived in this apartment for three years. Now she sees it differently. The shadows have become hiding places and the corners are blind.

She searches the bedroom first, swinging the gun from side to side, checking behind the door. The long narrow room has a queen-sized bed pressed into the far corner, a wooden dresser and wardrobe and large red chair. Everything is as she left it, with her dry-cleaning draped across the bed, the black jacket and trousers, still in plastic. On the nightstand is an antique silver picture frame with a black and white photograph of her mother and father, taken on their wedding day.

Across the hall is the bathroom. The sink is cluttered with shampoos, bubble baths and talcum powder. More products line the glass shelf where she has a wicker basket full of those complimentary mini-bottles you get at hotels. The shower curtain is closed. Did she do that? Did the curtain just move?

Reaching behind her with her left hand, she turns on the overhead light. The white curtain is

412

translucent. There are no shadows. The bath is empty. A tap drips.

She turns and moves back into the entry hall and on to the living room. There is a sofa, an armchair, a coffee table and a bookcase with books that she wants to read by authors she thinks she *should* have read. She looks at a pile of unfolded washing, the basket of ironing and the breakfast dishes in the sink – evidence of neglect or single-mindedness, she doesn't know which.

Wasn't there a folder on the coffee table? It had copies of crime-scene photographs from the armoured truck robbery, specifically the images showing the dashboard cameras on the police cruisers. Statements. Notes. Clippings.

She scans the room. The folder is not on the bookshelf or benches. Did she take it into the bedroom? She drops to one knee and looks under the sofa and beneath the coffee table. Pressing her cheek to the floor, she feels a faint breeze. A window must be open – or perhaps the sliding door to the balcony.

In the same breath it occurs to her that she rarely unlocks the sliding door unless it is to water her lone plant. She should have checked the balcony. This is her last thought before a shadow moves across the light and an object strikes the back of her head.

Moss wakes an hour before dawn with a bottle of bourbon propped in his armpit and a smudged

413

glass on the pillow next to his head. Lying very still, he hears the slow beat of his own blood and the wind gusting outside. He doesn't remember falling asleep, just the disjointed dream – a parade of faces from his prison years. They say that a killer dreams about the people he murdered, but Moss has never thought twice about the man he beat to death with a barbell in the exercise yard. It's not that Dewie Heartwood didn't deserve it, but Moss is older now, wiser, more self-possessed.

Stumbling into the darkened bathroom, he bends to suck water from the tap, soothing his parched mouth. Outside he can hear homeless voices fighting over cardboard boxes or cigarette butts.

In the bedroom, he turns on the TV. The small screen fizzes and blinks. A woman is delivering a traffic report, making it sound life-changing. The image shifts and two newsreaders report the day's top headlines.

'*A fugitive wanted for the murders of a Houston mother and child is believed to have kidnapped a sheriff's son who was last seen leaving his high school yesterday afternoon.*'

Moss turns up the volume.

'*Audie Palmer escaped from a federal prison a week ago and is now at the centre of a massive manhunt involving police, FBI and the US Marshals Service.*

'*The missing boy, aged fifteen, is Maxwell Valdez, the son of Dreyfus County Sheriff Ryan Valdez, who arrested Palmer more than a decade ago after an*

414

*armoured truck robbery. The family is expected to hold a media conference later today . . .'*

Moss isn't concentrating on the rest of the bulletin. He's trying to work out why Audie would do such a thing. During all those years in prison, Audie was the cleverest man Moss had ever met. He was Yoda. He was Gandalf. He was Morpheus. Now he'd become a walking suicide note. Why?

Moss's brain hurts and it's not just the bourbon. Motivation is overrated as a controlling force in human affairs, he decides. Shit just happens. There's no logic. No grand plan.

He fumbles for a bottle of aspirin in his jacket pocket and crunches two tablets between his teeth. Then he drops to the ground and rips out fifty push-ups that make his headache even worse. Flexing his muscles, he looks at himself in the mirror, aware of how soft he's growing.

He showers, shaves and pulls on his jeans, buttoning his shirt. Picking up his jacket, he hears paper crumple in the pocket. His fingers find the notes that he made at the library. He reads them again, trying to make sense of the robbery and its aftermath. The names and dates have been smeared by Moss's sweat. He remembers meeting the old man who witnessed the shoot-out and who had rambled on about keeping his mouth shut.

Theo McAllister had been frightened – but not of Moss. What scares a man who lives alone in the woods with a shotgun next to his door?

# CHAPTER 51

Desiree sits on the edge of the sofa, holding an icepack to the back of her head. A female paramedic shines a penlight into her eyes, asking her to look up and down, left and right.

'How many fingers am I holding up?'

'Not counting your thumb?'

'How many?'

'Three.'

Senogles is watching from the balcony. 'You should have checked the balcony door first,' he says, masterfully stating the obvious.

Desiree doesn't answer. Her tongue is swollen. She must have bitten it when she was bludgeoned.

'Why didn't you call it in straight away?' asks Senogles.

'I wasn't sure.'

He looks around her apartment, running his fingers along the titles in her bookshelf. Philip Roth. Annie Proulx. Toni Morrison. Alice Walker.

'It was probably some crack addict.'

'Crack addicts don't normally pick the lock,' says Desiree, fighting another wave of nausea.

'And you said nothing was taken.'

'Except for the file.'

'Of photographs and statements that shouldn't have been here.' Senogles is now studying her cookbooks. 'You do realise that I'm in charge of this investigation? You take orders from me.'

'Yes, sir.'

Desiree knows the dressing down is coming and that self-preservation requires that she remain silent and suck it up. At the same time she's trying to understand why somebody would take the file. Who knew that she had copies of crime-scene photographs and statements? Her name was in the register at the records office. She visited Herman Willford. She asked Ryan Valdez about the dashboard cameras.

Senogles is still talking, but Desiree holds up her hand. 'Can we take this up again later? Right now I need to throw up.'

Finally the paramedics and forensic technicians leave and Senogles tells Desiree not to come into the office in the morning.

'Am I suspended?'

'You're on sick leave.'

'I feel fine.'

'Then you're suspended from active duty until further notice. And don't bother calling Warner. He approved my decision.'

After showering, she sits on the edge of the mattress, her thoughts creaking in the darkness. Padding barefoot through the apartment, she gets another icepack from the fridge. Her cell phone shows two missed messages. She calls her voicemail and hears Jenkins in Washington:

'That vehicle you wanted to me to trace – the 1985 Pontiac 6000. It was first sold in Ohio in 1985 and had three former owners. The last one was a guy called Frank Robredo in San Diego, California. He buys up used cars and turns them around. Says he sold the Pontiac to a guy who paid him nine hundred bucks in January 2004. He signed the pink slip and provided a bill of sale and lodged the release of liability form within five days, but the transfer was never completed because the purchaser didn't visit a DMV office to lodge the transfer application or pay the fees. He didn't remember the guy's name, but he does recall talking to a Dreyfus County deputy who told him the buyer had used a fake name. I've contacted the Californian DMV to see if they still have the original paperwork. I'll let you know how it's going.'

The message ends and another begins. Jenkins again:

'California DMV came back to me about the Pontiac 6000. The digital version of the paperwork is missing, but they're searching for the hard copies. Here's the really weird thing – somebody else has been asking for the same thing. It was six months ago. The request came from a prison librarian at Three Rivers FCI.'

Desiree looks at the time. It's too late to call the prison. The message continues:

'I also chased up those names you gave me. Timothy Lewis died in a light plane crash seven years ago. I

418

*can't find anything on Nick Fenway owning a bar in Florida but I'll keep trying.'*

The message ends. Desiree gazes out the window at the quiet street. Audie Palmer had access to the library computer, but why would he be interested in the Pontiac? This entire case is riddled with discordant notes like a child plinking the keys of a piano, making noise instead of music.

Sitting at her desk, Desiree unpacks her satchel and takes out her iPad. She runs through her old emails. One of them has an attachment – Palmer's prison file, along with the names of people who visited him over the past decade.

She scans the list, which runs to barely half a page. Audie's sister visited him a dozen times. There are eight other names. One of them is Frank Senogles, who must have interviewed Audie when he was in charge of the cold case. He visited the prison three times: twice in 2006 and, strangely, only a month ago. By then he had handed the file to Desiree. Why talk to Audie when it was no longer his cold case?

She looks at the other visitors on the list. One of them, Urban Covic, used a Californian driver's licence as identification. Desiree types his name into a search engine and comes up with a businessman from San Diego. Covic is quoted in several articles about a golf course development called Sweetwater Lake that drew protests from a local environmental group who claimed it would threaten a local wetland. The group's headquarters was firebombed and there were allegations of illegal donations to city counsellors.

Desiree logs into the FBI database, typing in her username and password. She carries a fob on her keychain, which generates a random number, providing an extra layer of security. Having gained access, she searches for Urban Covic and finds an immediate match. Covic has four aliases and according to intelligence reports, he once worked for the Panaro crime family in Las Vegas but broke with the family in the mid-nineties when Benny Panaro and his two sons were convicted of racketeering.

Since then Covic had made a fortune running nightclubs and skin joints in San Diego before branching out into construction, property development and farming.

Why would Urban Covic be visiting Audie Palmer in prison?

The file contains a list of addresses and known associates for Covic, including telephone numbers. Desiree looks at her watch. It's approaching midnight. Still 10 p.m. in California. She calls. A man answers, grunting rather than greeting.

'Is that Urban Covic?'

*'Who wants to know?'*

'I'm Special Agent Desiree Furness of the FBI.'

There is a heartbeat of silence.

*'How did you get this number?'*

'We have it on file.'

Another pause.

'What can I do for you, Special Agent?'

'Ten years ago you visited a federal prison in Texas. Do you remember?'

'No.'

'You went to see a prisoner by the name of Audie Palmer.'

'So?'

'How do you know Palmer?'

'He once worked for me.'

'In what capacity?'

'He was my gofer. If I wanted something he'd go fetch it for me.'

'How long did he work for you?'

'I can't remember.'

Covic sounds bored with the conversation.

'So he wasn't particularly valuable as an employee?'

'No.'

'But still you travelled halfway across the country to visit him in prison.'

Silence greets the comment. Covic sighs. 'If you're about to accuse me of something, Special Agent, I suggest you piss or get off the pot.'

'Audie Palmer was convicted of hijacking a truck and stealing seven million dollars.'

'Nothing to do with me.'

'So you visited Audie Palmer as a friend?'

'A friend!' Covic laughs.

'What's so funny?'

'He stole from me.'

'What did he steal?'

'Something I cherished very dearly – along with eight thousand dollars.'

'Did you report the robbery?'

'No.'

'Why not?'

'I decided to handle it myself, but as it turned out, I didn't have to bother.'

'Why not?'

'Audie Palmer fucked up all by himself.'

'So why did you visit him?'

'To gloat.'

# CHAPTER 52

Awake now, Audie stares at the ceiling and feels dazed at the preposterousness of what he has done – kidnapping a boy, expecting another wrong will somehow balance all the others and make things right. Odds don't change because a coin has landed on the same side a dozen times or more. And there is no invisible set of scales or grand ledger that has to be balanced over the course of a lifetime.

When people survive a disaster – a flood or a hurricane – they are often asked by reporters how they coped. Some of them credit God for answering their prayers or say it 'wasn't my time', as though each of us carries a hidden expiry date. Normally, they have no answer. No secret. No special skill. That's why so many survivors feel guilty. They didn't earn their good fortune by being braver, or cleverer, or stronger. They were simply lucky.

Out of bed, Audie goes to the kitchen and looks out the window. He can see the burnished tufts of grass, clinging to the dunes, and feel the wind still pummelling the house, beating against the shutters. Mornings like this one, raw and untouched, seem like a victory over the night.

A toilet flushes and he hears the tambourine. Max leans barefoot against the doorframe, his hair tousled and his face creased from the pillow.

'You want some breakfast?' asks Audie. 'We got instant coffee, but no milk.'

'I don't drink coffee.'

'Good to know.'

Audie stirs powdered eggs into a bowl and continues talking. 'Did you sleep OK? How was the mattress? I can get you another blanket.'

Max doesn't answer.

'We don't have to talk,' Audie says. 'I'm used to having one-sided conversations.' He tips the eggs into a hot skillet. 'I'm sorry I don't have any bread, but I found some crackers.' He glances out the open shutter. 'I know I promised to take you fishing, but there's still a lot of wind. Storm hasn't quite blown through. I listened to the news on the radio. There's another late-season storm off Cuba. They're saying it might turn into a hurricane, but they don't expect it to head northwest any time soon.'

'I don't want to go fishing. I want to go home,' says Max.

Audie sets down a plate in front of him. They eat in silence. When the meal is finished, Audie washes and dries the plates. Max hasn't moved.

'You were going to tell me today.'

'That's true.'

Audie glances around the room as though trying to calculate the dimensions. He goes to his bag, takes out his notebook and shows Max the same photograph.

'Remember I told you I was married?'

The teenager nods.

'It took me a long while to find this. The photographer at the wedding chapel lost his job for being a drunk and left Las Vegas. He didn't leave a forwarding address. Then he went travelling in Europe for a few years. He thought of tossing his old digital files, but he kept a few disks in a storage cage.'

Max frowns, but something, somewhere, seems to register. 'Why are you showing me this?'

'That's you,' says Audie, pointing to the boy in the photograph.

'What?'

'You were only three. And that woman who's holding your hand is your mom.'

Max shakes his head. 'That's not Sandy.'

'Her name is Belita Ciera Vega and she's from El Salvador.'

Another silence, longer this time.

'Your full name is Miguel Ciera Vega,' says Audie. 'You were born at San Diego Hospital on August 4, 2000. I've seen your birth certificate.'

'My birthday is February 7,' says Max, growing upset. 'I'm American.'

'I didn't say you weren't.'

'I'm *not* illegal. I got a mother and a father.'

'I know you do.'

'But you're saying I'm adopted.'

'I'm saying this is your mother.'

'This is bullshit,' yells Max. 'I've never been to Las Vegas or San Diego. I was born in Houston.'

'Let me explain—'

'No, you're telling lies!'

'You had a favourite toy when you were little – do you remember? It had a purple bowtie and black button eyes and you called it Boo Boo, like Yogi's little friend.'

Max hesitates. 'How do you know that?'

'It only had one ear,' says Audie. 'You sucked the other one off, just like you sucked your thumb.' Max remains silent. 'We were on our way from California to Texas. We stopped off to get married in Las Vegas and then drove through Arizona and New Mexico. We visited a whole lot of places. Do you remember visiting Carlsbad Cavern? There were stalactites and stalagmites. You said it looked like pink ice.'

Max shakes his head as though trying to rid himself of an idea.

Audie starts at the beginning, trying to tell the story in the same words that Belita used – describing the earthquake and the loss of her husband, her parents and her sister. He recounts the exodus and the trek across the desert and the death of her brother and the journey to California. Audie's own eyes begin to fill with tears, but he doesn't stop because he's frightened the language will leave him, the words of love and loss.

'She was pregnant with you,' he says. 'You were born in San Diego, but I didn't meet you until later. By then I'd fallen in love with Belita. It felt so easy, like forgetting yourself and thinking only of someone else. We ran away together – escaping from a bad man. We were coming to Texas to start a new life. She was going to have another baby. Our baby. A brother or sister for you . . .'

As he talks Audie can see himself reflected in the boy's eyes and begins to wonder if he's making a mistake. He is reframing Max's history, tearing down everything the teenager has ever known or trusted or believed in.

'You're wrong,' Max whispers. 'You're lying.' The statement is full of cold certainty and hatred and Audie feels a terrible vertigo, as though he were being swept into a gigantic maelstrom that can only cause destruction.

During all his years in prison, Audie had pictured Miguel growing up, riding his first bike, losing his first tooth, heading off to school, learning to read and write and draw and a thousand other everyday rituals. He had imagined taking him to a ball game and hearing the clean sharp crack of wood and feeling the surge of the crowd as the ball climbed into the heavens and fell into the forest of upraised arms. He imagined meeting his first girlfriend, buying him his first beer, taking him to his first rock concert. He thought of them travelling to El Salvador together and looking for Belita's extended family and walking along the beach that she walked upon as a child. He wanted to climb the towers, ride the rapids, stare at the sunsets, read the same books, watch the same movies, break the same bread and sleep under the same roof.

It was bullshit. Ruined. Too much time had passed.

Max will not thank him for having saved his life – he will blame him for having wrecked it.

# CHAPTER 53

The media conference starts badly when reporters, photographers and camera crews are kept waiting in the rain because the school won't let them into the auditorium until Senator Dowling arrives. The Senator apologises to the damp faces and begins to make an education announcement, but the reporters want to ask about the kidnapping of a Dreyfus County Sheriff's son.

'I know the sheriff in question,' the Senator says. 'He's an old friend and I want to reassure Ryan Valdez and his family that we will do everything in our power to get his boy back to him.'

Senator Dowling returns to his prepared speech, but another reporter yells a question. 'Why wasn't Audie Palmer charged with murder one when you were prosecuting him as the district attorney in Dreyfus County?'

Dowling rubs his mouth with the flat of his hand and the microphone picks up the scratching of his whiskers against his palm.

'Excuse me, but I'm not about to revisit history and conduct a post-mortem on every case I ever prosecuted.'

'Did Audie Palmer bribe state officials to face lesser charges?'

'That's a ridiculous lie!' The Senator stabs his finger at the questioner, his face reddening. 'I didn't make that decision. I didn't sentence Audie Palmer. And I am not going to justify every action I took as a DA. My record speaks for itself.'

An aide steps close and whispers something in his ear. Dowling nods and his mouth flexes uncertainly before he speaks again, adopting a softer tone, full of candour and integrity.

'Y'all need to understand something. For you it's just another story, but for this family it is their son. Before you start pointing fingers at people, you should spare a thought for that poor boy out there in the clutches of a killer, and for his family waiting and praying for news. There will be plenty of time to review this case when the boy is home, God willing, safe and well. And as an elected official, I am going to do everything in my power to make that happen.'

Ignoring further questions, he walks away from the rostrum and is hustled through a side door into a corridor where he launches into an expletive-riven tirade about 'fucking journalists, blood-sucking leeches and pariahs'.

The target of his anger changes when he sees Victor Pilkington huddled beneath an umbrella outside the main doors. He tells his minions to 'fuck off' and drags Pilkington down the steps to a waiting limousine. A chauffeur tries to follow them both with a second umbrella and Dowling tells him to 'take a walk'.

He pushes Pilkington into the car.

'You said this was under control.'

'In essence,' says Victor.

'In essence?'

'We had a minor setback.'

'He kidnapped the fucking boy! If that's your idea of minor, you're looking through the wrong end of the fucking telescope. We don't have any leverage against him.'

'The police are doing everything they can.'

'That's so fucking reassuring. What if he talks?'

'Nobody will believe him.'

'Christ!'

'Relax.'

'Don't tell me to relax. I've had Clayton Rudd on the phone, bleating about needing protection. Said he had some negro in his office asking him questions about Audie Palmer. And now I've got reporters asking me about why I didn't call for the death penalty when I had the chance. I'm not carrying the can for this.'

'Nobody has to carry the can.'

'One man. One solitary fucking individual.'

'Can I just say, I—'

'No! Shut the fuck up! I don't care how much money you spent on my campaign, Victor. I'll give it all back. I don't want to see you again. I don't want to hear from you. You find this fuck and then we're finished.'

# CHAPTER 54

Moss parks the pickup in a grove of pine trees eighty yards from the shack and follows a path through the waist-high grass until he reaches the porch. The wind has dropped and the rain has stopped, but the sky is still the colour of a soggy cigarette. He wipes the palms of his hands on his pants legs before pulling open the screen door, propping it with his foot. He knocks. The inner door opens suddenly. Two eyes peer from the dark interior like pale clouds, shifting shape as the light catches in them. Momentarily startled, Moss stumbles backward and the screen door slams shut.

'You again! You're just itching to get shot.' Theo McAllister is holding a rifle in both hands. He's wearing a woollen hat with strands of grey hair poking from the edges. 'What you want?'

'I have another question.'

'Fuck off!'

'It's about the boy.'

Theo hesitates and his eyes narrow. 'How do you know about the boy?'

'Same way you do.'

'Did the sheriff send you?'

'Yeah.'

'What does he want?'

'Your continuing cooperation.'

Moss has no idea what they're talking about – but he's seeing how far he can take it before Theo realises that he's fishing without bait.

The old man studies him, scratching an insect bite on his neck. 'Well you'd better come inside.'

Moss follows Theo down a dark hallway that smells of cooking oil and coffee grounds. The living room is washed in the blue light of a TV screen. An Asian woman sits in an armchair, watching a comedy with canned laughter. She's half the old man's age, dressed in denim shorts and a singlet.

'Is the sheriff offering more money?'

'Is that what you want?'

'I got a new wife to look after. Lost my first one three years ago. Got this one from Asia, but she's still American, you know what I'm saying – made sure of that.'

The kitchen floor is filthy, the linoleum lifting in places, newspaper yellowing underneath.

'You tell the sheriff I haven't told a single solitary soul about the boy. Not one. I kept my side of the bargain.'

'You got paid.'

'Not enough.'

'How much more do you want?'

Theo scratches his neck again and ponders a figure. 'Two thousand.'

433

'That's steep.'

'I'm not threatening, mind you. Don't go giving him that impression. It's just a request. I don't want to appear ungrateful.'

'So I'm clear – you want the sheriff to give you more money to keep quiet about the boy.'

'Yeah.'

Theo walks to the sink and turns on the tap, getting himself a drink of water in a jam jar. It dribbles down his stubble and lands on the buttons of his checked shirt. He refills the jar and offers it to Moss.

'No thanks,' says Moss. 'Where did you find the boy?'

Theo empties the jar. 'Yonder.' He points through the tattered curtains. 'Little lost thing – filthy as could be – no more'n three or four, wearing a cowboy hat and this plastic silver gun in a holster. It's a wonder he didn't perish out there. He could have fell into a stream, or broke a leg, or got run over by a car. He was just a slip of a thing. Muddy. Wet. I looked at him and said, "Where did you come from, little hero?" but he didn't say a word.'

Moss watches the man's face change as he tells it. 'Was he hurt?'

'Not that I could see.'

Theo puts a thumb to his nostril and hawks on the other one, rattling the sink.

'Where did he come from?'

He taps the side of his nose. 'I got my suspicions, which I keep to myself.'

Moss nods. 'Show me where you found the boy.'
'Why?'
'I'm interested.'
Theo takes Moss outside and they walk along the fence line, through a gate hanging off one remaining hinge. They push through high weeds and brambles.

'I used to keep my dogs out here. I bred 'em for huntin'. That boy could have been eaten if they were hungry enough, but he was sitting in there amongst 'em like he belonged to a litter. Filthy. Didn't say a word. Figured he must have been out there all night.'

'What did you do?'

'I took him home and gave him something to eat. He had cuts and bruises all over his legs. I kept thinking his mama was gonna come along any minute and knock on the door, but she never did. So I turned on the TV news and listened. I figured that if someone had lost their little boy they'd call the police or send out a search party. You know what I mean?'

Moss nods. 'So what did you do?'

'I had the sheriff come to see me about the robbery and the shooting. He was only a deputy back then.'

'So this was the same day as the shooting?'

'No, the next day . . . or maybe the one after.'

'You said you saw the shoot-out.'

'I saw flashes in the dark.'

'And that's when you met the deputy Valdez?'

435

'He said I was going to get a reward and he helped me write a statement.'

'About the boy?'

'And the shooting.'

'What did he tell you?'

'He told me that if anybody came asking questions about the boy, I was to tell 'em that I found him somewhere else.'

'Where?'

'Two mile from here – at the reservoir.'

'He say why?'

'Nope.' Theo slides the woollen cap off his head and looks back at the house and the trailer and the rusting truck bodies. 'That's when he gave me a reward. I got two thousand dollars for finding the little cowboy and the paper wrote a story about me.'

'Did you ever see the boy again?'

Theo shakes his head. 'I saw the deputy's picture in the paper. He got a bravery medal for shooting them armed robbers.'

'And you haven't seen him since?'

'He drops by every few years. That's how I know he got promoted to sheriff. I think he's hoping I might be dead, but I keep hanging on. This is the first time he's sent someone else. He must trust you a lot.'

'Guess he does.'

# CHAPTER 55

The sun is yellow and high in the sky, raising steam from the deck and making the blacktop shimmer. Max is sitting on the sofa, bent over the photograph of Belita. Audie watches him from the armchair. Waiting. If he squints he can still see the boy, aged three, pretending to read a hymnbook next to his mother in church. Grown up now – almost a man. Audie wasn't there to read him bedtime stories or put Band-Aids on his cuts or explain that sometimes life is tragic and sometimes it's wonderful.

'So you're saying this is my *real* mother and she's an illegal immigrant from El Salvador?'

'Undocumented.'

'And I was born in San Diego?'

'Yes.'

The teenager leans back and stares at the ceiling.

Audie keeps talking. 'She was beautiful, with long black hair that shone in the sunlight, and flecks of gold like honeycomb in her eyes.'

'Where is she now?'

Audie doesn't answer. This is the moment he has dreaded since he contemplated kidnapping

437

Max. It's the point of no return. He either tells the story or he remains silent.

'I wasn't sure if I'd ever get to meet you. I thought I'd get shot during the escape or drown in the lake or they'd recapture me before now. That's why I wrote it down so that if something happened to me, there was a chance you might still learn the truth. You can read it yourself or you can burn it. It's your decision.'

He hands the notebook to Max, who doesn't take it.

'Tell me the story.'

'Are you sure?'

'Yeah.'

And so Audie speaks from memory and from the heart, bringing past events to life:

On the last day they drove past Austin and headed east along the 290, passing through Elgin, McDade and Giddings. At Brenham they took the 105 toward Navasota and then Montgomery because Audie wanted to show Belita the lake where he went fishing as a boy.

The urgency had gone and they took the back roads, through farmland and wineries, driving with the windows open and radio playing, singing songs about cowboys being home on the range. Miguel had never seen a buffalo. Audie pointed one out.

'It's a hairy cow,' said the boy. They laughed.

Audie asked Miguel if he could count to ten.

He did.

'Do you know your alphabet?'

Miguel shook his head. 'I know my ABCs.'

'That's the same thing.'

Again they laughed and Miguel frowned because he couldn't understand what was so funny.

Yet despite the cheerfulness and good humour, Audie felt more and more disconcerted as the miles ticked by. They were getting close to Lake Conroe – a place that he couldn't separate from his brother Carl, because so many memories of his childhood were attached to the lake; some of the happiest days of his life – before Carl went to prison and the tumour showed up in his daddy's lungs. Fishing. Swimming. Canoeing. They cooked over a campfire and told ghost stories and jokes, or played hide-and-seek with flashlights.

A mile from the turn-off, Audie drove over a bridge. There was a picnic area set amid trees. A small wooden pier, bleached by the sun, divided off a section of the lake where a floating platform had been moored a hundred yards from shore. The water was black and cool and felt almost silken on Audie's fingertips.

For lunch they ate a picnic on the shores of Lake Conroe, opposite Ayer's Island. Afterwards they threw their bread crusts to the ducks and bought ice cream. Miguel stood on Audie's lap dripping chocolate down the front of his shirt. He refused to take off his cowboy hat or his gun. Later they looked at the boats moored at the marina, wondering what famous people might own them.

Audie put his arm around Belita and rolled her plaited hair around his fist. She looked fresh and young and beautiful.

'Do you believe things are meant to be?' she asked.

'Like fate?'

'Yes.'

'I think we make the best of our bad luck and the most of our good luck.'

Audie squeezed her tightly and she squeezed him back and he felt the movement of her hip beneath her skirt.

'You seem sad today. What are you thinking about?' she asked.

'My brother Carl.' Audie kissed her hair. 'We used to come here when we were kids. I thought it would be nice to see it again, but now I can't wait to leave.'

'There is a saying in El Salvador that memories keep us warm,' she said, stroking his cheek, 'but I don't think that applies to you.'

It was late afternoon before they got on the road again. Audie planned to stop on the outskirts of Houston. He would call his mother in the morning. He didn't want to visit her until he was sure that Urban hadn't sent someone ahead to wait for him.

'I need to do a wee,' said Miguel.

'Can you hold on?'

'What do I hold?'

Audie pulled off the road. 'OK sport, we're going to do it behind a tree.'

440

'Like cowboys.'

'Yep, just like cowboys.'

They walked through the trees in the damp air, over a layered mat of dead leaves and pine needles. Mosquitoes rose in clouds from their footsteps.

'Do you want me to hold you?'

'No.'

Miguel stood with his legs apart, pushing out his groin, watching the thin golden stream splash against a tree trunk.

'This is how big boys do it,' he said.

'Yes it is,' said Audie.

The boy began to say something, but Audie's attention was elsewhere. From somewhere that seemed to be high in the air, he heard the sound of sirens.

'Is that a fire-truck?' asked the boy.

'I don't think so,' said Audie, who had looked over his shoulder, but couldn't see further than the bend in the road.

The sirens were getting closer. Audie couldn't tell which direction at first. He looked at Belita, who waved from the passenger seat of the Pontiac. Then he turned his head and saw a truck, the twin headlights blazing. It took a moment to realise how fast it was travelling, too quickly to take the bend. It veered to the wrong side of the road and the near-side tyres dug into the soft shoulder. The driver overcorrected and the truck slewed to the left. Audie could picture the man at the wheel, wrestling to get control and then throwing

441

up his arms in that strange way people do when they're trying to ward off a collision. It was too late. The truck tilted on two wheels for a moment and then toppled over, sliding sideways along the two-lane.

One moment the Pontiac was beside the road and the next it was gone. Audie heard the crunch of metal and convulsions of sparks and a booming sound. Time slowed down. Time stood still. With extraordinary effort, he bent and lifted Miguel, cradling him under his bottom like a toddler. He ran back through the trees until he reached the edge of the road.

He could see the truck, but not the car. He set Miguel down on his feet and grabbed his forearm, his fingers digging into the scant flesh. 'Stay right there. Put your hand on the tree. Don't let it go.'

'Where's Mommy?'

'Did you hear what I said?'

'Where did Mommy go?'

'Don't move.'

*Oh God! Oh God! Oh God!*

Running. Stumbling. He climbed the rise, trying to comprehend what had just happened. His eyes had been deceived. He would reach the car and find that everything was OK.

There were sirens and swirling lights behind him. The truck was lying on its side, ripped open as if something had exploded inside. Audie tried to breathe but his breath would not come. He saw the upturned Pontiac thirty yards further along the road. It didn't look like a Pontiac any more. It didn't look like a car. The twisted mound of metal had two wheels still turning in the air.

Audie screamed a name. He tried to open the remnants of a door, which seemed to be welded shut by the force of the impact. Lying flat on the road, he bent his body and slithered through the shattered rear window, across the collapsed roof of the Pontiac. Fuel soaked the front of his shirt and glass cut into his hands and knees.

Amid the confusion of torn wiring and twisted seats, he saw an arm and a hand with blood running down the fingers. For a split second he thought there was no body.

Gripping the seat above him, he dragged himself forward, almost dislocating his shoulder. Then he saw her. Her body was wedged beneath the dashboard, concertinaed unnaturally. He reached out and touched her face. Her eyes opened. Alive. Frightened.

'What happened?'

'An accident.'

'Miguel?'

'He's fine.'

Fumes stung Audie's eyes and caught at the back of his throat, making him want to gag. He could hear the leaking fuel sizzling as it spilled onto hot metal.

'Can you move your legs?'

She wiggled her toes.

'What about your fingers?'

She moved her fingers. Her arm was broken. Glass had lacerated her cheek and forehead.

She tried to move, but her legs were pinned by the crushed dashboard. Audie heard gunshots. There were two men in the truck. They had managed to crawl from the window and drop to the ground.

One of them spun around and then collapsed, clutching at his neck, blood running through his fingers. The other was hit almost at the same time, a bullet smashing into his knee. The uniformed police officer had a gun gripped in both hands, angled upwards. He had a stiff military-style haircut and deeply tanned skin.

Audie was peering through the shattered windows of the Pontiac below the still spinning tyre. He noticed a second deputy about thirty yards away, on the far side of the truck. One of the wounded men tried to stand. He looked helplessly at Audie, his eyes jittering, a pistol dangling uselessly from his hand. The deputy fired. Two slugs found their mark, knocking the man backwards, decorating his shirt with scarlet flowers. The last shot spun him around and he simply sat down on top of his legs, as though his skeleton had vanished.

The officer still hadn't seen Audie. His colleague yelled. The deputy holstered the gun and disappeared from view. Audie was about to call out, but something made him stop. He saw the two officers again. This time they were carrying sealed canvas sacks toward the open trunk of a police cruiser. They would make the journey again and again. One of the bags caught on a snagged spur of metal and ripped open, spilling banknotes that were caught by the breeze, skipping across the tarmac where they wrapped around weeds and were pinned against tree trunks.

There were more sirens.

Audie crawled back toward Belita, pulling himself along with his arms and elbows. Her head was twisted at an odd angle by the compressed roof. Audie reached for her hand. His fingers took hold of her wrist. He pulled and heard her grunt in pain.

Audie retreated and yelled to the deputies. One of them turned and walked toward him. There were ironed creases in his trousers. Black leather shoes. Audie looked up. The deputy's pale cheeks were red with exertion. He lowered a sack of money to the ground.

'We have to get her out,' pleaded Audie.

The officer turned. 'Hey, Valdez?'

'What?'

'We got a problem.'

Valdez joined him, crouching and resting his arms on his thighs, a revolver dangling from his right hand with the barrel slanted downward. 'Where did he come from?'

His partner shrugged.

Valdez leaned closer, his breath sour and a tiny web of saliva stretching and breaking between his lips. He turned his head and saw Belita trapped in the wreckage. He scratched his chin.

Audie grabbed the deputy's shirt, knotting the fabric in his fist.

'Help her!' he cried.

In the same instant the road shimmered and the air filled with a whooshing breath as a blue flame slid across the tarmac from the ruptured fuel tank of the truck. Belita's eyes were frozen wide.

'Fire!' yelled Audie, repeating it over and over. He crawled back into the twisted debris, reaching for Belita, trying to pull her toward him. He screamed at the officers to help, but they stood and watched with their hands at their sides. Audie retreated and ran to the far side of the wreckage. Ripping off his shirt, he beat at the flames but his hands were suddenly on fire. He dropped the shirt but kept trying to pry the metal apart with his fingers. The heat forced him back. Valdez picked up his hat and put it on his head. The other deputy lifted the bags of cash.

Belita's screams softened and died. Audie collapsed on his hands and knees, sobbing. Blood ran in strings down his blackened thumbs. He became aware of a deputy standing over him. Valdez dumped the spent brass and began to reload. He stood over Audie and pointed the gun at his forehead, his eyes clean of emotion, a man who knew that reason and logic had no place in an unreasonable world.

Audie turned his head and saw Miguel standing in the trees still wearing his cowboy hat and holding his bear. He tried to shrink inside his own skin, to squeeze all awareness and sensation from his mind, to become nothing but dust that would float away on the breeze and re-form later into his body and soul, allowing him to become whole again.

'Don't take this personally,' the deputy said as he pulled the trigger.

Max remembers. Somewhere deep inside his head there are doors and windows opening. Papers blow off desks. Dust rises. Machines hum. Phones ring. Single frames are threaded together like film being spliced, rewound and replayed. Images of a woman in a floral dress, who smelled of vanilla and mangoes, who took him to a fairground where there were coloured lights. Fireworks.

Yet even as his mind opens, Max tries to close it down. He doesn't want a different past. He wants the one he knows – the one he's lived. Why are there no pictures of him as a newborn, he wonders. He had never really questioned it before but now he mentally studies the photo albums that Sandy keeps in a drawer of her dresser, turning the pages in his mind. There are no shots of him swaddled in a cotton blanket, or being nursed in a hospital bed.

His parents had never talked about his birth. Instead they used terms like 'when you came along' and 'we waited a long time for you.' They talked about having IVF. Miscarriages. He was loved. He was wanted.

This man is making up stories. He's a killer! A liar! Yet there was something about how he told the story that Max knew was genuine. Audie spoke as if he had been there since the very beginning.

'Are you all right?' asks Audie.

Max doesn't answer. Without a word, he goes to the bathroom and scoops water into his mouth, trying to take away the taste. He stares at his reflection in the mirror. He looks like his father. They have the same olive skin and brown eyes. Sandy is fairer, with blonde hair and freckles, but that doesn't mean anything. They're his parents. They raised him. They love him.

He closes the lid of the toilet and sits down, holding his head in his hands. Why did this man, this stranger, have to tell him? Why couldn't he be left alone?

When he was young he wanted to be a cowboy. He had a silver gun that fired caps and a cowboy hat with a star on the hatband. He had a teddy bear with a purple bowtie. These things he knows to be true, yet he has become a different person in the past few hours.

He had been born in San Diego. He had travelled to Texas. He had seen his mother die.

# CHAPTER 56

Desiree walks across her office foyer, passing a woman who is about her age, well-dressed, pretty, busy. She is someone who probably has plans for the weekend. Perhaps she will see a movie with her boyfriend or have a drink with a girlfriend. Desiree has no such arrangements, which should depress her more than it does.

Somebody has taped a newspaper clipping on a whiteboard near the water cooler – a photograph taken outside Star City Inn. Desiree is visible, two feet shorter than the detective standing next to her, pointing at something on the second floor. The speech bubble says: *'It's de plane, boss! It's de plane!'*

Desiree doesn't tear the cutting down. Let them have their fun. She's not supposed to be in the office, but she knows that Senogles left an hour ago and she doubts anyone else cares whether she recuperates at home or at her desk.

Her phone is ringing.

*'Is that Special Agent Furness?'*

'Who's calling?'

'*You probably don't remember me. We talked at Three Rivers prison. You wanted to know about Audie Palmer.*'

Desiree frowns and looks at the caller ID number. 'I remember you, Mr Webster. Do you have some information about Audie?'

'*Yes, ma'am, I think I do.*'

'Do you know where he is?'

'*No.*'

'What did you want to tell me?'

'*I think he might be innocent of that robbery they said he done.*'

Desiree sighs internally. 'And what has led you to this startling conclusion?'

'*That boy he kidnapped. I think he belonged to the woman who died in the robbery – the one they never identified.*'

'What?'

'*I think she had a kid with her. Don't ask me why he wasn't in the car when it got hit. Maybe he got thrown clear. He didn't get found until a few days later.*'

'How do you know this?'

'*I just talked to the man who found him.*'

'On the phone?'

'*No, ma'am.*'

'He came to the prison?'

'*I'm not in prison any more.*'

'You had a life sentence!'

'*They let me go.*'

'Who?'

'*I don't know their names. They said that if I found*

450

*Audie Palmer, they'd get my sentence commuted, but I think they were lying to me. I think they're going to kill Audie and they're gonna kill me for talking to you.'*

Desiree is still getting her head around the fact that Moss Webster isn't in prison.

'Wait! Wait! Go back!'

*'I'm gonna run out of spare change real soon,'* says Moss. *'You gotta listen to me. The man I spoke to said a deputy told him to lie about where he found the boy. The police said it was miles away, but it was just near the shootings.'*

'Go back to the beginning – who let you out of prison?'

*'I don't know.'*

'Did you see these men?'

*'I had a hood over my head. They're gonna say I escaped, ma'am, but I didn't. They let me go.'*

'You got to come in, Moss. I can help you.'

Moss sounds on the verge of tears. *'Audie is the one who needs help. He deserves it. I'm going back to prison regardless, if I live that long. I wish I'd never become friends with Audie. I wish I could help him now.'*

There is a beeping sound on the line.

*'I'm outta change,'* says Moss. *'Remember what I said about the boy.'*

'Moss? Give yourself up. Take down my cell phone.' She yells the number but doesn't know if he heard the last digits before they're cut off and the line goes dead.

She contacts the switchboard and asks if the call can be traced. The operator comes back with a location: a payphone at a supermarket in Conroe. By then Desiree has managed to get Chief Warden Sparkes on the phone from Three Rivers prison.

'*Moss Webster was transferred out two days after Audie Palmer's escape,*' he says.

'Why?'

'*They don't always tell us why. Prisoners are moved around all the time. Could be operational or on compassionate grounds.*'

'Somebody must have approved this,' says Desiree.

'*You'll have to talk to Washington.*'

An hour later – having made a dozen calls – Desiree is still on the phone. 'This is horseshit!' she yells, berating a junior staffer at the Bureau of Federal Prisons, who must regret having returned her call. 'Why was Moss Webster transferred from a high-security Federal Prison to a holiday camp in Brazoria County?'

'*With all due respect, Special Agent, the Darrington Unit is a prison farm, not a holiday camp.*'

'He is a convicted killer serving a life sentence.'

'*I can only tell you what I have in front of me.*'

'And what's that?'

'*Webster used a homemade knife to threaten and disarm a US marshal during a rest stop at a Dairy Queen in West Columbia. The marshal was unharmed in the escape. State police have been informed.*'

'Who authorised the transfer?'

'*I don't have that information.*'

'Why wasn't the FBI notified of his escape?'

'*It's in the system.*'

'I want to see statements from the marshal and any other witnesses. I want to know *why* he was being transferred. I want to know who gave approval.'

'*I've made a note for the director. I'm sure he'll look at it first thing Monday morning.*'

Desiree can hear the sarcasm in the bureaucrat's voice. She slams down the phone and considers hurling it across the room, but that's something a man would do and she's sick of men.

Instead she goes back over what Moss told her. Logging into her computer, she calls up information on missing children.

*Do you have any idea, Mr Webster, how many children go missing every year in Texas?*

She narrows the search to Dreyfus County in January 2004 and comes across a story in the *Houston Chronicle*:

## BAREFOOT BOY FOUND WANDERING

A small boy dressed as a cowboy was found beside Burnt Creek Reservoir in Dreyfus County on Monday, showing signs of having spent all night in the wild, police say.

Aged between three and four, the child was discovered by Theo McAllister and his dog Buster on the eastern edge of the reservoir.

'We were just walking along the track and Buster found this bundle of rags under a bush. I got closer and realized it was a little boy,' Mr McAllister said. 'He was a hungry little hero so I gave him some food. When I couldn't find his mama, I called the police.'

The boy was taken to St Francis Hospital where doctors said he was dehydrated, cold and suffering scratches and bruises, indicating he had spent the night outdoors.

Deputy Ryan Valdez said: 'The boy is clearly traumatized and hasn't been able to talk to us yet. Our first priority is to find his mother and to provide whatever support she needs.'

Desiree calls up a map. Burnt Creek Reservoir is almost two miles from where the shooting took place. According to the timeline, the boy was found three days later. There's nothing to link the two events except for Ryan Valdez . . . and Moss Webster's phone call.

Almost a week later a second story appeared in the *Chronicle*.

## LONESOME COWBOY MYSTERY

State and Federal authorities have stepped up efforts to solve the mystery of a young boy wearing a cowboy hat found wandering near Burnt Creek Reservoir in Dreyfus County last Monday.

The boy, aged about four, is described as being olive-skinned with brown eyes, dark hair, 35" tall, weighing 33lbs. He was found wearing blue elastic-waist jeans, a cotton shirt and a cowboy hat.

Authorities are now utilizing the FBI's NCIC system along with the National and Missing Unidentified Persons System (NamUs) in the hope of locating the boy's parents or guardians.

Deputy Sheriff Ryan Valdez is heading the investigation. 'It's been difficult because the boy hasn't uttered a word. We figure he doesn't speak English or he could be traumatized. For the moment we're calling him Buster after the dog that found him.'

Desiree puts in a call to the Department of Family and Protective Services in Dreyfus County. She has to explain herself three times before she's put through to a caseworker who has been with the department since 2004.

'Make it quick, I'm busy,' the woman says, standing on a noisy street. 'I got four police officers with me and we got to rescue a kid from crackhead central.'

Desiree talks in shorthand. 'January 2004 – a boy, aged about three or four, was found wandering alone near a reservoir in Dreyfus County. Whatever happened to him?'

'You mean Buster?'

'Yeah.'

She yells at someone to wait. 'Yeah, yeah, I remember that one. Odd case. Kid never said a word.'

'Did you find kin?'

'Nope.'

'So what happened?'

'He was fostered.'

'By whom?'

'I'm not supposed to give out details like that.'

'I understand. I tell you what. I'll put a proposition to you – if I'm wrong, you hang up. If I'm right, you stay on the line.'

'I might hang up anyway.'

'The boy was fostered by a deputy sheriff and his wife. I think they later adopted him.'

There is a long pause. Desiree can hear her breathing.

'I think that's long enough,' the woman says.

'Thank you.'

# CHAPTER 57

The sun appears briefly from behind broken clouds, creating shadows on the water that look like prehistoric sea monsters moving beneath the surface. Audie and Max sit on the deck overlooking the beach, where gulls float against the breeze.

'How did it feel to get shot?'

'I don't really remember.'

'It must have been an accident,' says Max. 'They thought you were one of the gang.'

Audie doesn't answer.

'My daddy wouldn't have done it on purpose. It was a mistake,' says Max. 'And he didn't take that money. If you talk to him he'll help you.'

'It's too late for that,' says Audie. 'Too many people have too much to lose.'

Max picks at the flaking paint on the armrest of his chair. 'Why didn't you say something sooner?'

'I was in a coma for three months.'

'But then you woke up – you could have talked to the police . . . or a lawyer.'

Audie remembers waking up in the hospital, slowly becoming conscious of his surroundings.

He would hear nurses talking to each other or feel their hands washing him, but it was like a scene snipped out of a drunken dream. When he opened his eyes for the first time, he could see only vague shapes and swirls of colour. The brightness was too much for him and he went to sleep. The periods of consciousness grew longer, unpunctuated stretches that shone like tunnels of light with dark shadows moving within the glare. Silhouettes. Angels.

Audie opened his eyes again some time later and saw a neurologist standing beside the bed talking to a group of interns. One of the interns was asked to do an examination of the patient. A young man with curly hair bent over the bed and was about to pull open Audie's eyelid.

'He's awake, Doctor.'

'Don't be ridiculous,' said the neurologist.

Audie blinked and triggered a commotion.

Unable to talk, he had a tube in his mouth and another in his nose, which felt like it was being dragged back and forth through his lungs. When he turned his head he could make out orange dials on a machine near the bed and a green blip of light sliding across a liquid crystal display window like one of those stereo systems with bouncing waves of coloured light.

Beside his head was a chrome stand holding a plastic satchel of liquid that trailed through a pliable tube and disappeared under a wide strip of surgical tape wrapped around his left forearm.

There was a mirror on the ceiling above the bed. He could see a man lying on a white sheet, pinned like an insect mounted on cardboard, his head swathed in bandages that covered his left eye. The image was so surreal that Audie thought he might already be dead and this was an out of body experience.

Weeks passed like this. He learned to communicate by raising his bandaged hands or blinking his eyes. The neurologist visited him almost every day. He wore jeans and cowboy boots and called himself Hal, and would talk slowly, mouthing the words, as though Audie had the mental age of a five-year-old child.

'Can you wiggle your toes?'

Audie did as he was asked.

'Follow my finger,' said Hal, moving it from side to side. Audie moved his eyes.

He scraped a hooked metal tool along Audie's arms and the soles of his feet.

'Can you feel that?'

Audie nodded.

By now they had removed the tubes from his mouth and nose but his vocal cords were bruised and he couldn't speak. Hal pulled up a chair, sitting on it backward, draping his arms over the backrest.

'I don't know if you can understand me, Mr Palmer, but I'm going to explain what happened. You were shot. The bullet entered from the front and travelled the length of the left side of your brain before exiting through the back of your head. It could take months before we determine the extent of any permanent damage, but the fact that you're still alive and communicating at all is a darn miracle. I don't know if you're a religious man, but somebody somewhere must have been praying for you.'

Hal smiled reassuringly. 'Like I said, the bullet passed through the left hemisphere of your brain, which is better than it going through both. A brain can sometimes tolerate losing one half – it's like a twin-engine plane losing only one engine. In your case the slug missed the high-value real estate, so to speak, your brain stem and thalamus.

'That left side of your brain controls language and speech, which is why it might take some time for those things to recover, or it could never happen. In a few days' time, I'll organise an MRI scan and we'll start running some neurological tests to test how your brain is functioning.'

Hal took hold of Audie's hand. Audie squeezed his fingers.

A few hours later, Audie woke in a darkened room with the only lights coming from the machines. There was a man sitting beside his bed. Audie couldn't turn his head to see the face.

The figure leaned forward and put his fist against the bandages around Audie's head, pressing into the shattered bone. If felt like a grenade disassembling his skull.

'Can you feel that?' spoke the voice.

460

Audie nodded.

'You can understand me?'

He nodded again.

'I know who you are and where your family comes from, Mr Palmer.'

The fist continued to twist against his head, grinding the broken bone and metal plates. Audie's arms were waving in the air as though his motor controls had been cut.

'We have the boy. Do you understand? If you want him to live, you do as I tell you.'

The pain was so great, Audie struggled to hear what was being said, but the message still made it through.

'You keep your mouth shut. Understand? You plead guilty or the boy dies.'

A heart monitor began beeping an alarm. Audie lost consciousness. He didn't expect to wake up. He didn't want to wake up. He told himself he wanted to die and he relived the accident, listening to Belita's dying screams and seeing Miguel's face. He woke every night to this same dream until he was too frightened to sleep and would instead stare at his reflection in the mirrored ceiling, his throat undulating softly, swallowing saliva.

'Who was he?' asks Max.

'An FBI agent called Frank Senogles.'

The teenager stares at Audie as though trying to decide if he's exaggerating or making up answers as he goes along.

'You're telling me you went to prison because of me?'

'You didn't put me in prison.'

'But you did it because they threatened me?'

'I made a promise to your mother.'

'You could have told the police.'

'Really?'

'You could have proved to them who you were.'

'How?'

'They would have believed you.'

'I couldn't speak. And by the time I could the evidence had been twisted or lost or manufactured. I had no way of proving my innocence – and if I tried they were going to kill you.'

Max gets to his feet, pacing angrily. 'You're wrong! This is fucked! My dad would never hurt me. He'd kill anyone who did. He's gonna kill you when he finds you . . .' Max squeezes his eyes shut, grinding his molars, his face twisted in fury and disgust. 'My father won a bravery medal. He's a goddamn hero.'

'He's *not* your father.'

'You're a fucking liar! You're wrong! I was happy. I'm loved. You had no right to kidnap me.'

Max storms into the house and slams the bedroom door. Audie doesn't try to follow him. His entire relationship with the boy feels detached, like he's holding a camera up to his eye, recording events but not taking part in them. He and Max are in the same place, but they're not connected. The soft rope was cut a long while ago – in that moment when flames engulfed the Pontiac and Belita screamed his name.

What did he expect the boy to do? What else could he have said?

For eleven years people have wanted Audie to keep his mouth shut – to fade into the background, to disappear, to die . . . He might have granted their wish if they had left him alone. He could have succumbed to one of the many attempts made on his life or fallen victim to the endless reel of violence that played out every day in prison. However, he could not give up on the memory of Belita, who still hypnotised him and drew him like a sleepwalker toward the precipice. He had promised her.

It's not that Audie had been passive. First he punished himself, taking every beating and humiliation because the pain he suffered helped mask the pain that he truly felt. But there came a point when turning the other cheek became problematic because both sides of his face were bruised and both his eyes were closed. He knew he was doing the penance for somebody else's sins. He was a rat thrown into a python's cage, slowly being crushed by the weight of his grief and a promise he made.

He couldn't tell Max about being beaten, stabbed, burned and threatened. And he didn't mention that a month before he was due to be released, the same man who had visited him in his hospital bed came to Three Rivers. He sat on the far side

463

of a Perspex screen and motioned for Audie to pick up the phone. He brought it slowly to his ear. It was an odd feeling to hear that voice again and remember when they last spoke.

The man scratched idly at his cheek with four fingers. 'Do you remember me?'

Audie nodded.

'Are you afraid?'

'Afraid?'

'Of what's waiting on the other side.'

Audie didn't answer. Light-headed, shaking, he seemed unable to keep the receiver to his ear, but he was pressing it so tightly it caused a bruise that he felt for weeks.

'I'm impressed,' said the man. 'If someone had told me that you'd still be alive after ten years inside, I'd have called him a goddamn retard. How did you survive?' The man didn't wait for an answer. 'What's the world coming to when you can't find a competent fucking killer in a prison?'

'The competent ones don't get caught,' said Audie, trying to sound fearless when his heart hammered against his ribs like a cat trapped in a trashcan.

'We even tried to get you a new trial, but the US Attorney got cold feet.' The man tapped his fingers against the screen. 'So now you think you're getting out of here. How long you think you'll last? A day? A week?'

Audie shook his head. 'I just want to be left alone.'

The man reached inside his jacket and took out a photograph, holding it up to the Perspex. 'Recognise him?'

Audie blinked at the image of a teenage boy in shorts and a T-shirt.

'We still have him,' said the man. 'If you so much as breathe in our direction . . . understand?'

Audie hung up the phone and hobbled back to his cell with his head bowed, wrists and ankles chained, desperate as a condemned man. That night he raged and his anger felt good, cleansing, excoriating, scouring away the scar tissue. For far too long he had been fighting ghosts, but now the ghosts had names.

# CHAPTER 58

Audie hears a car approaching, idling roughly as it rocks over the potholes. From the kitchen window, he spies an old Dodge pickup splashing through puddles left by the storm. It pulls up on the windward side of the house and reverses up to the door of the boatshed.

An old man gets out. He's wearing coveralls and work boots and a Houston Oilers cap, bleached of colour. The Oilers left Houston in 1996, but for some the memory will never dim. He unlocks the shed and takes the cover off an aluminium dinghy, folding the tarpaulin neatly before hooking the trailer onto the tow ball of his pickup.

He's a neighbour or friend, borrowing the boat. Maybe he won't come up the stairs. He might not have a key. Where's Max? He's in the bedroom listening to music on his iPad.

The old man carries an outboard motor from the back of the pickup to the dinghy, where he hooks it over the stern and tightens the bolts. Next comes a fuel tank and tackle box. When everything is stowed, he gets back behind the wheel, but then glances up and notices the open shutter. Scratching his head, he gets out of the Dodge and walks across the lawn.

Audie picks up the shotgun and holds it against his side. It could still be OK. He'll blame the storm for opening the shutter. As long as he doesn't check the door . . . He's at the top of the steps now. Wood creaks beneath his weight. He closes the shutter and checks the hinges. Nothing appears broken or bent. He moves along the deck to the door. Still four paces away, he sees the shattered square of glass.

'Bloody kids,' he mutters, reaching through the broken pane and slipping the bolt. 'How much damage did you little bastards do?'

Pushing open the door, he steps inside and looks into the twin black holes of a shotgun about an inch from his forehead. He staggers on rubbery legs, the colour draining from his face.

'I'm not going to hurt you,' says Audie.

The old man tries to respond, but his mouth opens and closes like he's talking in a language a goldfish might understand. At the same time his hand slaps against his chest above his heart, making a hollow thudding sound.

Audie lowers the gun. 'Are you OK?'

The man shakes his head.

'Your heart?'

He nods.

'Do you have pills?'

Another nod.

'Where?'

'Pickup.'

'Dashboard? Glovebox? Bag?'

'Bag.'

Max comes out of the bedroom, still bashing the tambourine between his knees. He sees the old man and stops jangling.

'He's got a heart problem,' says Audie. 'There are pills in his pickup. I need you to get 'em right now.'

Max doesn't question the order. The tambourine bashes all the way down the stairs and across the lawn, before going quiet. Audie can't see the pickup because the shutter has been closed.

He gets a chair for the old man and makes him sit down. His face is sallow and wet with sweat and he's staring at Audie like he's looking at the ghost of Christmas Past.

'What's your name?'

'Tony,' he croaks.

'Is it a heart attack?'

'Angina.'

Max opens the door of the pickup and searches until he finds an old sports bag. The keys are hanging in the ignition. This could be his chance. He could take the rig and be long gone before Audie got down the stairs. He could flag someone or find a phone. He could rescue himself and be a hero. Maybe Sophia Robbins would go out with him.

468

He's contemplating these things as he searches through the bag and his fingers close around a cell phone. Next to it is a plastic bottle of pills. Glancing back at the house, Max opens the phone and keys a text message to his father's cell:

*This is Max. I'm OK. Beach house. East of Sargent, between Gulf and a canal. Blue house. Shingle roof. Deck. Boatshed.*

He turns the phone off and tucks it into the crotch of his underwear. He takes the pills and shuts the door, glancing along the beach. Half a mile west he can see a 4WD carving donuts in the sand.

'Did you find the pills?' yells Audie. He's standing on the deck.

'Yeah, I found them.'

Max holds up the bottle, shaking it above his head.

'Bring me the whole bag.'

'OK.'

Audie gets Tony a glass of water. He opens the bottle.

'One or two?'

Tony raises two fingers. Audie puts the pills in his palm and watches them being swallowed and washed down.

'Is he going to be OK?' asks Max.

'I think so.'

'Maybe we should call an ambulance.'

'Let's give him a minute.'

Tony opens his eyes and looks almost serene, loaded up on whatever drug keeps his heart beating regularly or stops the pain. He smiles at Max and asks for another glass of water.

'Heart disease,' he explains, still heavy-lidded. 'They say I need a bypass but I don't have no insurance. My daughter's been saving but it's gonna cost $159,000. She's doing two jobs now but I'll still be dead twenty years before she can pay for it.'

He wipes his face with a handkerchief, which is little more than a rag. 'That's why I go fishing, to put a bit of food on the table. I borrow the Halligans' boat, which they don't know about.' He looks up at Audie. 'Guess they don't know about you neither.'

Audie doesn't answer.

'So who are you and what're you doing here?'

He studies Max and Audie, his eyes travelling south until he spies the tambourine between Max's knees. An idea occurs to him and his eyebrows jump. 'You're that boy they looking for. It's all over the news.' He frowns at Audie. 'And they say you're a killer.'

'They're wrong.'

'So what are you going to do with me?'

'I'm thinking.'

'I won't be going fishing.'

'Not today. When was your daughter expecting you home?'

'Around dusk.'

'Do you have a cell?'

Max interrupts. 'There's none in the bag.' He glances at Tony and something passes between them.

'My daughter keeps wanting me to carry one,' says Tony, 'but I never got the hang of them.'

'You feeling better?' asks Audie.

'I'll be fine.'

'You should take him to the hospital,' says Max.

'If he gets worse,' says Audie, checking the windows and flipping the safety on the shotgun.

'What about my daughter?' Tony asks. 'She'll be worried 'bout me.'

Audie look at his watch. 'Not until dusk.'

# CHAPTER 59

Desiree runs the gauntlet of reporters and TV camera crews who dance around her like dogs waiting to be fed. Their broadcast vans and media cars are blocking the street outside the Valdez house, drawing spectators and grief tourists who have come to watch the news being made.

A police family liaison officer opens the door with one hand resting on her sidearm. Sandy Valdez is standing behind her in the hallway. Eyes wide. Hopeful. She's dressed in a faded T-shirt and jeans, her feet bare, hair tousled, face free of make-up, showing her lack of sleep. They talk in the living room where the curtains are closed and blinds lowered. Desiree sits. Eschews coffee.

'Is your husband at home?'

Sandy shakes her head. 'You can't ask someone like Ryan to sit still. He wants to be out there shaking the trees and yelling from the rooftops.'

Desiree says she understands, although Sandy seems to doubt that.

'Why didn't you tell us that Max was adopted?'

Sandy pauses with the tissue beneath her nose. 'What difference does it make?'

'Did you withhold the information on purpose?'

'No! Of course not!'

'When did you adopt him?'

'When he was four – why is that important?'

Desiree ignores her question. 'Through an agency?'

'We went through all the proper channels, if that's what you're asking.' Sandy perches on the edge of the sofa, her knees together, working the soggy tissue in her fingers until it starts to break apart. 'Ryan said he'd been abandoned. Somebody found him wandering in the woods. Dirty and freezing. Ryan took him to the hospital and tried to find his momma. Afterwards he stayed in touch with the DFPS.'

'You fostered him and then adopted him?'

'We'd been trying to start a family. We went through it all – injections, egg harvesting, IVF – but nothing worked. We'd never really talked about adoption until Max came along. It was like God delivered him to us.'

'Does Max know?'

Sandy glances at her hands. 'We were planning to tell him when he was old enough.'

'He's fifteen.'

'There was never a right moment.' She changes the subject. 'Do you know he never uttered a single word for five months. Not a sound. Nobody knew his real name. We called him Buster for a long

473

time – after the dog that found him – but then he started talking and said his name was Miguel. Ryan didn't want to call him that, so we settled on Max and the little boy didn't seem to mind.'

Desiree doesn't answer. 'Did Miguel tell you his surname?'

'No.'

'Did he say where he came from?'

'Once or twice he would point at pictures or say something that could have been a clue, but Ryan said we shouldn't push him.' Sandy screws up her eyes. 'I used to be so scared that somebody would come looking for him. Every time I heard the phone ring or a knock at the door – I thought it was going to be his mother wanting him back. Ryan said it wouldn't make any difference because Max was legally ours now.'

She looks at Desiree, her eyes brimming. 'Why are we being punished? We did a good thing. We're good parents.'

Audie looks in the kitchen cupboards, stocktaking. He's going to run out of time before they run out of food. Tony is watching him, his face pale but no longer shiny with sweat.

He's a talker – making observations that segue into stories about his life. Maybe he's read somewhere that hostages should try to bond with their kidnappers. Either that or he's trying to bore Audie to death.

'You ever serve?' he asks.

'No.'

'I was in the Navy – too young to fight the Krauts or the Koreans, too old for Vietnam. They made me a welder. Used to do the plumbing and insulate the engine rooms with asbestos. That's how Maggie died – my wife. They said I brought it home on my clothes and she washed 'em and the fibres got in her lungs. Didn't affect my lungs but it killed her. That what people mean when they say sumpin' is ironic?'

'I don't think so.'

'Just bad luck I guess. I'm not complaining.' He pauses, his lips thin lines. 'No fuck it! I *am* complaining, it's just nobody ever listens.'

'Don't you get medical insurance if you're a veteran?' asks Audie.

'I didn't serve overseas.'

'That doesn't seem right.'

'Knowing what's right don't make it happen.'

Tony flinches and thumps his chest as though restarting a non-existent pacemaker. He should be in a hospital or at least see a doctor. Audie doesn't want another death on his conscience. The next part of his plan was always going to be problematic. It could be argued that he didn't bother with an exit strategy because he didn't expect to get this far. Max knows the truth now. He may not believe some of the details, but he has that choice. It's like taking a kid to church and Sunday school, giving him a faith he can accept or reject.

Audie has a hundred and twelve dollars left. He

counts the money and puts it in his front pocket. Unzipping his rucksack, he takes out his cell phone and installs a new SIM card before turning on the power and looking for a signal. First he calls the Texas Children's Hospital and asks for his sister. Bernadette is on the ward. Somebody has to fetch her.

Audie glances at Tony. He and Max are talking to each other. Nodding. Maybe they're plotting. It won't matter soon.

'It's me. I can't stay on the line very long.'

'*Audie? The police have been here.*' Bernadette is cupping the phone and whispering.

'I know.'

'*Are you going to hurt that boy?*'

'No.'

'*Give yourself up. Let him go home.*'

'I will, but I need you to do something for me. That file you've been keeping for me, do you still have it?'

'*Yeah.*'

'I want you to give it to someone. Her name is Desiree Furness. She's a Special Agent with the FBI. You have to give it directly to her – not anyone else. Face to face. You understand?'

'*What do I say to her?*'

'Tell her to follow the money.'

'*What?*'

'She'll understand when she reads the file.'

Bernadette's voice is shaking. '*She's gonna want to know where you are.*'

'I know.'

'*What do I say?*'

'Tell her the boy is safe and I'm looking after him.'

'*You're going to get me into more trouble. I keep telling people that you're a good person, but then you prove me wrong.*'

'I'll make it up to you.'

'*How are you gonna do that if you're dead? Let that boy go home.*'

Where's home, wonders Audie. 'I will.'

Ending the call, he makes another. The only person he can vaguely trust is the one who helped him survive in prison. He doesn't understand how Moss got out of Three Rivers and managed to find him, but the grave that Audie was digging in the woods was supposed to be for both of them.

A woman answers: '*Harmony Dental Service.*'

'I'm looking for Crystal Webster.'

'*Speaking.*'

'My name is Audie Palmer – we've met once or twice before.'

'*I know who you are,*' says Crystal, nervously.

'Have you heard from Moss?'

'*He calls me most days.*'

'Do you know why they let him out of prison?'

'*He was supposed to find you.*'

'Then what?'

She hesitates. '*Hand you over. They said he could have the money if he found it.*'

'There *is* no money.'

'*Moss knows that, but he was hoping they might commute his sentence if he did what they asked.*'

'What does he think now?'

'*He knows they were lying.*'

Audie gazes out the window where seagulls are floating above the waves, beating their wings and uttering strange deep-throated cries. Sometimes they sound just like human babies.

'When you hear from Moss, tell him I have a plan. I want him to come and get the boy. He can take the credit. Give him this address. I'll be here for another six hours.'

'*Can he call you?*'

'I'll be turning this cell phone off.'

'*Is the boy OK?*'

'He's fine.'

'*Why shouldn't I just call the police right now and tell 'em where you are?*'

'Ask Moss. If he agrees, let him call the police.'

Crystal thinks about this for a while. '*If my Moss gets hurt, I'm gonna come looking for you myself. And let me promise you, Mr Palmer, I'm a lot scarier than he is.*'

'I know that, ma'am. He told me so.'

# CHAPTER 60

Pilkington raises his eyes to the scudding clouds, squinting into the glare. The air has a damp feral odour with a breeze blowing out of the west. Two vehicles stand on the narrow access road to his house, parked in the scant shade of a dead tree with branches like bleached white bones on a dry lakebed.

'We're going to do it properly this time,' he says, chewing on the sodden end of an unlit cigar. 'Nobody cuts and runs.'

He glances at Frank Senogles, who is checking a rifle, raising the telescopic sight to his right eye, closing his left. Valdez shuts the trunk of the car and unzips a black rifle case. There are two other men wearing black cargo pants with pockets stitched on the thighs. Mercenaries with made-up names, Jake and Stav, they won't speak unless they have something to say. They'll do their job as long as they're paid. Jake has long hair tied back in a ponytail, but he's receding at the front, as if the tide were going out leaving his eyebrows behind. Stav is shorter and swarthier, with a buzz-cut and a nervous habit of wiping his mouth with the back of his wrist. He has scars down his neck like a burns victim.

Pilkington can't help staring at the buckled skin.

'You got a problem with my face?' asks Stav.

Pilkington looks away, mumbling an apology. He doesn't like to be pushed. He doesn't like losing control of things. This isn't his world. His father had gone to prison for securities and wire fraud and had emerged with an unexpected respect for criminals and miscreants. In that violent world, people valued power more than money. Violence was an end not just a means. Wield a bigger stick. Hit harder. Hit sooner. Hit more often.

Pilkington slaps his gloved hands together as though geeing up a little league team. 'All for one and one for all, eh?'

Nobody answers.

Senogles glances angrily at Valdez. 'Well, I think the guy who created the problem should fix the problem.'

'I shot the guy in the head,' counters Valdez. 'What else was I supposed to do?'

'Shoot him twice.'

'Stop your bickering,' says Pilkington.

'Palmer is like a fucking vampire,' says Valdez. 'You can stab him in the heart, burn him and bury him, but somebody keeps digging him back up and bringing him to life.'

'So the prick is hard to kill,' says Jake.

'He bleeds like anybody else,' replies Stav, who

slips his arms into a black bulletproof vest and fastens the Velcro straps.

'What if the kid remembers?' asks Senogles.

'He won't,' replies Valdez.

'Why else would Palmer take him? He must want the kid to back up his story.'

'Max wasn't even four years old – nobody is going to believe him.'

Senogles isn't convinced. 'What about DNA tests, eh? What if Palmer can prove he wasn't part of the robbery?'

'He can't.'

Valdez removes and reattaches an ammunition clip to an automatic pistol. Senogles looks at Pilkington, wanting reassurance.

'Max won't say anything. He's a good boy,' says the older man.

'He's a loose fucking end.'

Valdez interrupts. 'Nobody touches him, OK? I want that agreed.'

'I'm not agreeing to anything,' counters Senogles. 'And I'm not going to prison because you adopted some spic kid.'

Valdez body-slams the agent against the truck, which rocks from the impact. His forearm is forced against his throat.

'He's my fucking son! Nobody touches him.'

Senogles matches his stare, neither man blinking or backing down.

'OK, let's relax,' says Pilkington. 'We got a job to do.'

Valdez and Senogles eyeball each other for another few seconds before Valdez loosens his grip and they shove each other apart.

'OK, Frank, talk us through this,' says Pilkington.

Senogles unrolls a satellite map on the hood of a Ford Explorer.

'We think the house is here, on Canal Drive. There's only one road in or out. Once we seal it off he'll be trapped unless he has a boat.'

'Does Palmer know we're coming?' asks Pilkington.

'Unlikely.'

'Is he armed?'

'We're going to assume so.'

'What's our cover story?' asks Pilkington.

Senogles answers. 'The family got a ransom demand and Sheriff Valdez took matters into his own hands because he was concerned for Max's safety.' He turns to the others. 'I was never here, understand? If we get stopped, the sheriff does the talking. No cell phones, no pagers, no GPS trackers, no transponders, no identification – keep your weapons hidden.'

'I need my cell in case Max calls,' says Valdez.

'OK, just your phone.'

Inside Valdez's head is nothing but conflict and doubt. Every killer has to live with images he cannot expunge from his dreams – murder scenes that are indelibly inked onto his subconscious. For three nights he had been visited by the images of

482

Cassie Brennan and her daughter Scarlett. He didn't know either of them when he shot them dead. He thought Audie was in the bathroom but it was the little girl. Once she was dead he had to kill the mother. It was the only choice.

And now he can't tell anyone, not his wife or his colleagues or his priest or his bartender. Audie Palmer is to blame. It has nothing to do with the money – that was spent long ago. This is about Max, the boy who had saved his marriage, the boy who had made his family complete. Yes, they could have tried again, and there were adoption agencies and surrogate services, but Max had been delivered to them by chance, the happiest of accidents and the answer to his prayers.

Now Audie Palmer has him. The big question is why. If he had wanted to kill Max he could have done it that first day outside the house. No, he'd *never* kill the boy – that's the whole point – but what if he tells Max what happened or helps him remember? What if he turns Max against the people who raised him?

If only Audie Palmer had died when he was supposed to.

# CHAPTER 61

Bernadette Palmer is still wearing her nurse's uniform, a brightly coloured shirt and tailored trousers, as she waits in the foyer of the FBI building.

*Just look for the shortest person you've ever seen,* Audie had told her.

*That must be her,* thinks Bernadette, as Desiree Furness comes out of the elevator. Even in high-heeled boots, the Special Agent doesn't come up to Bernadette's chest, yet everything about her is in proportion, like a scaled-down model of the real thing.

Desiree suggests they sit down. They take a seat at opposite ends of a leather sofa. People glance at them as they walk toward the elevators, making Bernadette feel self-conscious. The sooner this is over the better. She retrieves a manila folder from her shoulder bag.

'I don't know what it means or why it's important, but Audie told me I had to give it to you and nobody else.'

'You've heard from him.'

'He called me at work.'

'When?'

'An hour ago.'

'Where was he? Did you tell the police?'

'I'm telling you.'

Desiree opens the file. The first document is a birth certificate from El Salvador for someone called Belita Ciera Vega, born in April 30, 1982. Her parents were a Spanish-born shopkeeper and an Argentinian-born dressmaker. The next document is a wedding certificate that also features Belita, issued by a chapel in Las Vegas in January 2004. The name of the groom: Audie Spencer Palmer.

Desiree looks up from the file. 'Where did you get these?'

Bernadette seems to think about the implication of the question, plainly wondering if she's going to get in trouble.

'Audie sent them to me. We had a system. He had this email account and he gave me the password and the user name. Every week I would log on and he would have left messages for me in the draft folder. Sometimes there were documents attached. I had to print everything out and double-delete the messages. I couldn't tell anyone. And I could never use the account for anything else.'

Desiree can picture exactly how it was done. Audie set up an anonymous Gmail or Hotmail account using a computer in the prison library. Leaving messages in the draft folder is an old trick used by terrorists and teenagers to avoid detection because these communications are never sent and therefore leave a fainter digital trail.

There is a photograph in the file showing Audie standing beneath an arch of white and pink flowers. His arm is around a young woman's waist and a small boy is peeking from the folds of her dress.

'Did you know your brother was married?'

Bernadette shakes her head.

'Do you know this woman?'

'No.'

Desiree finds a birth certificate from San Diego County. A boy was born on August 4, 2000. First name: Miguel. Surname: Ciera Vega. Father's name: Edgar Roberto Diaz (deceased).

Flicking more quickly now, she scans the rest of the folder, which contains Texas land record searches, copies of title deeds, receipts, financial records, company returns and magazine articles. It must have taken years to collate.

One name keeps coming up in the documents: Victor Pilkington. It's a familiar name to anyone who has grown up in Texas. Desiree has a particular family connection. Her great-great-grandfather, Willis Furness, was born on a Pilkington plantation in 1852 and worked in the family's fields for nearly fifty years. His wife, Esme, a wet nurse and seamstress, probably suckled Victor Pilkington's grandfather or darned his socks.

The Pilkingtons had produced two congressmen and five state senators before their empire crumbled during the energy crisis in the mid-seventies.

The family's fortune was wiped out and one of them – Desiree can't remember who – went to prison for securities fraud and insider trading.

In recent years, Victor Pilkington had restored some of the family's status by making a fortune in property deals and corporate raiding. Among the cuttings there is a photograph of him smiling at the cameras outside Houston's Museum of Fine Arts, where he chaired the Latin American fund-raising gala. Black tie. White teeth. Hair an oily wave. Another story shows him throwing the ceremonial opening pitch at a Rangers game, his baseball uniform still bearing creases from the box. The media had nicknamed him 'The Chairman' and Pilkington played up to it, always being photo-graphed with a cigar in his fist, unlit. He married a society girl with a double-barrel surname, whose father had been partying with George Bush Jnr on the night he got picked up for drunk driving in Maine in 1976.

Wealth begets wealth, Desiree knows that, but she's never envied such moneyed elites, who tend to be phenomenally dull and ignorant of the lives of others and blind to the beauty of the natural world. She glances again at Audie's folder. Some of the documents mention shell companies and offshore accounts. She's going to need a forensic accountant to explain them.

Near the end of the file, she comes across a piece of paper that slips from between two others and rocks like a falling leaf to the floor. It's not a full page. Somebody has torn off the lower half. The heading reads:

## CALIFORNIA DEPARTMENT OF MOTOR VEHICLES.

## NOTICE OF TRANSFER AND RELEASE OF LIABILITY

It takes a moment for Desiree to recognise the significance of the document, which mentions a Pontiac 6000 with the same make, model and licence number as the car that burst into flames and incinerated a woman driver in Dreyfus County in 2004. The car was purchased in San Diego, California, on the 15th of January 2004, from Frank Robredo at a cost of $900. The man who purchased it gave his name as Audie Spencer Palmer.

Desiree turns the page over. It's a photocopy, but doesn't look like a forgery.

'Do you recognise this signature?'

'That's Audie's.'

'Do you understand what it means?'

'No.'

Desiree understands. Scooping up the folder she leaves Bernadette in the foyer and walks briskly to the elevator. Details are rapidly falling into place. More than she can handle. She feels like a bridesmaid trying to catch the bouquet at a wedding, but the bride keeps throwing dozens of

488

them and Desiree can't hold them all in her arms. The woman in the car was Belita Ciera Vega, Audie's wife. The boy in the photograph is most likely her son.

Desiree has reached her desk. She opens the folder again and stares at the wedding photograph, studying the young boy. His features are more Spanish than Salvadorean. Belita's father was from Spain and her mother from Argentina. She calls up a photograph of Max Valdez as a teenager and compares the two. Take away the years – it's the same boy. How is that possible?

Valdez organised the adoption. He had contacts within the DA's office, lawyers and judges, people who could smooth the path. Nobody came forward to claim Miguel. His father died in an earthquake. His mother perished in a burning car. Audie lay in a coma, never likely to recover. The medical records show that he was shot from close range, almost point-blank. It was almost as though somebody tried to execute him. Yet he survived. He witnessed what happened. How do you silence a man like that?

'Working late?'

Desiree gasps and snaps the folder shut. She'd been concentrating so hard that she hadn't heard Eric Warner approach.

'Christ, you're jumpier than a virgin at a prison rodeo,' he says, walking around her desk.

'You surprised me.'

'What are you reading?'

'An old case file.'

'Any news on Palmer?'

'No, sir.'

'I was looking for Senogles, he's not answering his phone.'

'I haven't seen him since last night.'

Warner takes a roll of antacid tablets from his pocket and peels off the paper wrapping. 'I heard about the break-in. Are you feeling OK?'

'Fine.'

'I thought you were told to stay at home.'

'Yeah. Can I ask you a question?'

He pops a tablet on his tongue. 'Depends.'

'Why did you put Frank in charge of this investigation?'

'He was more senior.'

'Any other reason?'

Warner puts his hand in the air, a stop sign. 'Did I ever tell you that I met JFK? My father worked on Kennedy's security detail – not the final one, thank God. I don't think he could have lived with that. I was just a boy. One of my favourite Kennedy quotes was when he said politics was just like football – if you see daylight you go through the hole.'

'It was political?'

His smile looks ironically sad. 'Isn't everything?'

# CHAPTER 62

Before leaving the stilt house, Audie strips the beds, washes the dishes and flushes the toilets again for good measure. Then he collects some clean underwear and a rain jacket, shoving them into a pillowcase.

'I'm just borrowing these things,' he tells Max. 'I'll return them.'

'Where are you going?'

'I haven't decided yet.'

'Do you even know what you're doing?'

'I started with a plan.'

'What plan?'

'To keep you safe.'

'How's that working out for you?'

Audie laughs and Max joins him and Audie feels a surge of warmth and relief. In prison he used to imagine moments like this, but nothing is ever exactly as we picture it – life splinters and smears the most ordinary of dreams – but this one feels like it's almost right.

'So what happens to me?' asks Max.

'A friend of mine is coming. He'll make sure you get home.'

Tony is watching from a chair at the kitchen table. His hands are taped in front of him, so he can reach a glass of water and his pills. Audie has loosened the tape around his ankles.

'What about me?' he asks.

'I'll drop you at a hospital.'

'I don't want to go to the goddamn hospital. They'll just tell me what I already know.'

Audie ponders the growing darkness. The western horizon is streaked with red and orange, like somebody has sliced open a sack of burning coals. He picks up his bag and the pillowcase. 'I'll put these in the car and come back for you, Tony.'

'You gonna steal my rig?'

'I'll leave it somewhere safe.'

Max glances nervously at the shuttered windows. Ever since he sent the text message to his father he's felt something gnawing at his insides like a hungry rat is trying to get out. He doesn't know if he's done the right thing. His father will be proud of him. He'll backslap and brag to his buddies. He'll say that Max kept his head just like his old man did during that shoot-out.

'Don't leave!' he blurts.

Audie pauses at the door. 'Moss is going to be here soon.'

'I don't want to be left alone.'

'I could stay with him,' says Tony. 'Either that, or you let me take the boy. You'll get a head start before I call the police.'

492

Audie lifts his bag onto the kitchen table and unzips a pocket. He takes out the cell phone, along with a fresh SIM card.

'As soon as we're gone, you can call your mom.'

Max doesn't answer.

'What's the matter?' asks Audie.

'Nothing.'

'Are you sure?'

Max nods without conviction. He can feel Tony's cell wedged in his underwear and can picture the police coming. He wants to tell Audie what he's done, but he doesn't want to disappoint him.

'Try not to worry,' says Audie. 'Things'll work out.'

'How do you know?'

'For you they always have.'

# CHAPTER 63

The dented paint-skinned blue pickup pulls up alongside Desiree as she nears her car in the underground parking garage. She turns her head and almost topples over when she spies the man behind the wheel.

Wobbling for a moment, she tries to straighten, but one of her heels is caught in a ventilation grate. She attempts to pull it out, but has to hop backward a step and twist her boot.

'Need a hand?' asks Moss, who has one arm draped over the wheel and the other resting along the top of the passenger seat.

Desiree wants to pull her gun from her holster, but it's going to look clumsy and unprofessional because she has Audie Palmer's folder in her arms. If she drops the papers, they'll blow everywhere.

'What are you doing here?' she asks.

'Get in.'

'Are you surrendering?'

Moss seems to ponder this. 'OK, we can call it that, but first I need you to come with me.'

'I'm not going anywhere with you.'

'Audie needs our help.'

494

'I'm not here to help Audie Palmer.'

'I know that, ma'am, but he's out there on his own and people are trying to kill him.'

'What people?'

'I think it's the men who really stole that money.'

Desiree blinks at Moss, feeling like he's been reading her mail. 'Did you break into my apartment?'

'No, ma'am.'

'Are you armed?'

'Nope.'

She's managed to free her heel from the grate. Desiree reaches for her pistol and points it through the open passenger window. 'Get out of the vehicle.'

Moss doesn't move.

'I will shoot you if I have to.'

'I don't doubt that.'

Moss glances out the windshield and raises his eyes as though frustrated by how the day has gone so far.

Desiree doesn't lower her weapon. 'Tell me where he is. We'll take it from here.'

'I know exactly what you'll do,' says Moss. 'You'll tell your boss and he'll call a meeting and then he'll brief a SWAT team and they'll recce the area and study satellite images and set up roadblocks and evacuate the neighbourhood. Meanwhile, all they'll ever find of Audie Palmer is a bloodstain. If you're not coming, I'm going alone.'

'You can't just drive away. You're under arrest.'

'Guess you'll have to shoot me.'

Desiree runs her fingers through her hair, gingerly touching the bump on her head. Every fibre of her training tells her to arrest Moss Webster, but her gut is saying something different. In the previous twenty-four hours, somebody has broken into her place, knocked her unconscious and stolen her files. Her boss has lied to her and done nothing but try to bench her from the beginning or given her pointless errands to keep her out of the way. If she's wrong about Audie Palmer it will be the end of her career. If she's right she won't be thanked. Every which way she loses.

Getting into the car, she buckles her seatbelt and rests her .45 on her lap, pointing at Moss's crotch. 'You so much as run a stop sign and I'll blow your balls off.'

# CHAPTER 64

The two Ford Explorers pull onto the shoulder of a dirt road and stop beneath a copse of low scrubby trees a hundred yards from the house. The sky is the colour of dishwater and the ocean dark grey topped with strips of froth. Rain coming. Sun disappearing. Time pressing.

Senogles gets out of the vehicle and rests a rifle over the hood, pressing his cheek to the wooden stock, feeling the cold hard smoothness against his skin. Steadying his pulse, he runs the scope along the walls of the house, paying special attention to the windows and doors. The place looks shuttered. Empty.

'You sure this is it?'

Valdez nods and raises his binoculars. The coastline looks deserted. The only lights he can see are perched on the mast of a dredging barge moored in the canal and a couple of ships moving across the Gulf.

'How are we going to do this?' he asks.

'First we need to make sure they're still here.'

Senogles walks to the other car and talks to Jake and Stav, telling them to scout ahead to the far side of the house. They check their two-way radios and move off along the edge of the canal, soon disappearing in the gloom. Valdez and Senogles stay in the open where beads of rain cling to their hair and bulletproof vests. Pilkington hasn't left the car. He's acting like he's in charge, but Senogles is running the operation.

Valdez peers through the binoculars again. The pulse in his throat is beating slowly. He remembers what it was like on the night of the robbery; how they waited for the truck to arrive, his sphincter tight, hands damp on the wheel. His uncle had spent four years setting up the opportunity, putting someone inside the security company and waiting for them to reach a senior position. It was Pilkington who discovered the delivery route and the timetable, but Valdez had recruited Vernon and Billy Caine, dumb and dumber. That's one of the advantages of being in law enforcement – the people it brings you into contact with: the shysters, second-story creeps, money launderers, safe-crackers, gunrunners, carjackers and thieves.

When the Caine brothers hijacked the armoured truck and parked on the shoulder of an isolated road, they expected to meet a getaway car. Instead it was an ambush. The execution was clumsier than anyone planned, but the outcome the same. Audie Palmer was the joker in the pack – the wildcard that no one allowed for. Wrong place. Wrong time. Almost silenced. Not quite.

The others blamed Valdez. Fenway the drunk,

Lewis the gambler, both dead now because they were foolish and splashed cash around. They were supposed to launder the money through Pilkington's land deals, but couldn't wait to show off. Unexpected wealth draws attention. Cover stories are necessary. Care.

'Someone is coming out.'

Senogles looks through the scope of the rifle, one eye closed. 'That's Palmer.'

'I can't see Max.'

'He must still be inside.'

Palmer is walking down the stairs and across the lawn toward a Dodge pickup with a boat trailer attached. He opens the door and throws a bag inside before arranging a blanket on the passenger seat.

'Looks like he's fixin' to leave,' says Senogles, whose finger is poised on the trigger, eyes dilated. 'We should take him out now.'

'Wait till he gets closer.'

Palmer moves around the boat, uncoupling the trailer. He wipes his hands on his jeans. The shot is easier to take. Senogles eases off the safety and places the crosshairs between Palmer's eyes before lowering the sight to his chest, trying to make sure he doesn't miss. He breathes, taking air into his lungs deeply and letting it out slowly. Then he takes a second breath, shallower this time, and lets it out halfway, judging the distance and the wind and the roll of Palmer's gait. He blinks, resets his mind. Blinks again. Pulls the trigger.

★　　★　　★

Audie has unhitched the boat trailer, checked the tyres and pondered how much gas Tony has in the tank. He doesn't want to have to fill up until he's well away from the coast. It doesn't seem right to run off after going to so much trouble to find Max and tell him the truth, but he'll be safe when Moss gets here, safer than he is now.

Special Agent Furness will have the file by now. She'll know what to do. Unless he's misjudged her, of course, in which case there's little that Audie can do except to keep running until they hunt him down. It wouldn't matter so much if it were just him they wanted, but Max knows the secret now. Valdez raised him as a son. Will he protect him like one?

A small bright flash registers in Audie's peripheral vision. In the same instant a bullet tears through his left shoulder, blowing his clavicle apart like a sledgehammer hitting a watermelon. He hears only the percussion as it exits, thwanging into the metal boat and detonating like a firework next to his ear. He falls to the ground and clutches his left arm. Sticky. Wet.

The shooter has changed his line of fire and gone to work on the boat, punching holes through the metal. Audie crawls under the trailer and forward until he's below the driver's door of the Dodge.

Another round comes in from a different direction, closer to the beach. They're not going to keep missing. His left arm is useless. Opening the door, he reaches up and turns the key in the ignition. The engine sparks and rumbles. Two rounds blow out the glass in the driver's door. Audie puts the car into 'drive' and takes off the handbrake. It begins to roll forward. Running and crouching, he keeps his head below windshield level. The right front tyre makes a popping sound, then the rear one. The car slows. Audie breaks cover and heads for the stairs, taking them three at a time.

Wood splinters near his right hand. He's on the deck, sprinting for the door. If they lock him out he's dead. It opens. Collapsing inside, he pulls Max down with him and slides across the floor, cutting the tape on Tony's legs, telling him to lie flat. The old man is yelling, wanting to know who's shooting.

'Did they hit my rig? What about the boat? I'm gonna lose my job if they mess up that boat.'

Audie crawls to the living room and presses his back to the far wall. He lifts his head and peers through the slatted shutter. A hundred yards away he can see the box-like silhouettes of two vehicles. There are no lights except for a dredger further along the canal. Straight lines of drizzle form a nimbus around the glowing filament.

'Your arm,' cries Max.

Audie is trying to keep pressure on the wound. It exited clean, but he's going to bleed out if he doesn't staunch the flow.

'Find me a sheet,' he says. Max obeys, hunching over to pull open the linen cupboard. 'Tear it into strips. There's a first-aid box in the bathroom with gauze bandages.'

Audie bunches the gauze in his fist, packing the entry wound, telling Max to do the same with the exit hole. Then he wraps multiple strips of sheeting beneath his arm and over his shoulder while others are bound around his chest. Already the blood is soaking through.

'It's my fault,' sobs Max. Pale. Tearful.

Audie stares at him.

'I sent my dad a message. I told him where I was.'

'How?'

'Tony had a cell phone in his bag.' Max reaches down the front of his trousers and retrieves the phone. 'I'll talk to him. I'll tell them not to shoot.'

'It's too late now.'

'He'll listen to me.'

Max punches the number but Audie takes the phone. Valdez answers.

'*Max?*'

'No, it's me.'

'*You fuck, I want to speak to Max.*'

'He can hear you.'

'*Max. Are you OK?*'

'You have to tell them not to shoot, Dad. It's all been a big mistake.'

'*Shut up! Has he hurt you?*'

'No. You got to stop shooting.'

'*I want you to listen. Don't believe a word he says. He's lying to you.*'

'Did you adopt me?'

*'Shut up and listen!'*

Valdez is yelling. There are muffled voices in the background, people arguing. Audie turns off the speaker and raises the phone to his ear. 'You don't have to yell at the boy.'

The comment lights a fire under Valdez. *'He's my goddamn son and I'll tell him what I please.'*

'You'll tell him lies.'

*'You're a fool! You're gonna get him killed. Why couldn't you just keep your mouth shut?'*

'You mean like last time?'

Valdez has walked away from the car. Audie can see the brightness of the cell phone pressed against the sheriff's ear.

*'This is how it's going to go down. You're going to walk outside with your hands in the air.'*

'It's not that simple.'

*'Sure it is.'*

'There's someone with us. He's a local. He looks after places when folks lock 'em up for the winter. You just shot up his rig.'

Valdez doesn't answer.

'He's got a heart condition, and he's not doing so good. If you come storming in here, you're going to kill him.'

*'His death will be on your hands.'*

'You mean like Cassie and Scarlett's?'

Audie hears an intake of breath. He shouldn't be goading this man, but he's angry that innocent people are dying around him. He glances out the

503

kitchen window toward the beach and sees two heads, stooping but not stooping low enough, as they run between the dunes. Moving closer. They're dressed in black, wearing balaclavas with only their eyes showing. *Night-fighting shit.*

'*Send him out,*' says Valdez. '*I'll make sure he gets to the hospital.*'

Audie looks at Tony, who is sitting with his back to the kitchen bench.

'I don't trust you.'

'*You want to help the guy or not? You got thirty seconds.*'

He hangs up. Audie watches Valdez walk back to the cars, where he discusses something with the others. Audie drags himself across the floor next to Tony.

'Are you OK?'

'Fine. You heard him, they're not going to shoot me.'

'He's lying.'

'They're the police!'

'No, they're not.'

'My dad is a county sheriff,' protests Max.

Audie wants to argue but knows that Tony is no safer inside the house than outside. Any moment they're going to come in with guns blazing, shooting anything with a pulse.

Tony shakes two pills into his hand and swallows them dry. 'If it's all the same to you, I'd prefer to take my chances with them than with you. The odds are better.'

# CHAPTER 65

Seated beside Moss in the pickup, Desiree thinks of every law that she's breaking. She has ignored protocols, disobeyed orders and jeopardised her career, yet everything about this case has altered her perception of normal. The man next to her should still be in jail or in hand-cuffs. He swears blind he didn't escape. Whoever set him free had influence, connections. They didn't want the money, according to Moss, they wanted Palmer dead.

'Did you steal this pickup?' she asks, speaking for the first time since they left the outskirts of Houston.

'No, ma'am.' Moss looks hurt by the accusation. 'They gave it to me.'

Desiree opens her cell phone and calls Virginia, asking for a status update on Moss Webster and asking them to run a motor-vehicle check on the Chevy.

She looks at Moss. 'You lied to me. It was stolen from a garage near the Dairy Queen after you escaped.'

'What?'

'I'm sitting in a stolen pickup.'

'Give me some credit. You think I'd steal a shitbox like this? Makes me look like a redneck. And I didn't escape – they let me go!'

'According to you.'

'I wouldn't be seen dead driving a Chevy.'

She waves her gun. 'Well, I could test that theory.'

They fall into a sullen silence until Desiree changes the subject and asks about the old man who found the boy.

'Theo McAllister's place is set back from the road,' explains Moss, 'but it was near enough for him to hear the shooting and see the burning car. He found the boy the next day.'

Moss taps his hands loosely on the steering wheel. Desiree likes men with big hands.

'That's when I got to thinking: what if the boy belonged to that woman, the one who was never identified?'

'How do you know about her?'

'I read about it in the papers.'

'She has a name now.'

Moss glances at her.

'Belita Ciera Vega.'

His eyebrows arch.

'You've heard it before?'

Moss looks back at the road. 'Audie used to have these nightmares. Not all the time, but often enough. He'd wake up screaming, crying out a name. That was the one: Belita. I used to ask him about her but he said it was just a dream.' He glances at Desiree. 'You think he's that boy's real father?'

'Not according to the birth certificate.'

Desiree falls silent and begins adding more details to the picture forming in her mind. Audie and Belita were married in a chapel in Las Vegas. Five days later they were in Texas. If Audie took part in the robbery, why bring his wife and the boy along? More likely, they were bystanders – caught up in the outcome. Perhaps Audie and the boy were thrown clear by the impact, or they'd stopped by the side of the road and weren't in the car. Nobody came forward to claim Belita's body. Audie was in a coma. The boy was too young to help.

Moss breaks the silence. 'Why didn't Audie tell someone about the boy?'

'Maybe they threatened him. Maybe they threatened the boy.'

Moss whistles through his teeth. 'That's got to be one precious child.'

'Why?'

'You didn't see what they did to Audie in prison. He swam through an ocean of shit when most men would have happily drowned.'

Desiree ignores him for a moment, still developing the story in her mind. She and Moss had been working toward the same end but approaching the search from different angles. Together they had created a compelling story, but that didn't make it true.

Audie Palmer saw the accident and shootout. He watched his wife die. There were seven million reasons to clean up and remove any witnesses, which meant killing Audie or silencing him. They tried both.

There were three deputies involved in the shooting. One is dead, another missing, and the third is Ryan Valdez. DA Edward Dowling is now a newly elected State Senator. Frank Senogles ran the original investigation and is now a Special Agent in Charge. Who else might be involved? The conspiracy relied upon Audie Palmer's silence. They must have used the boy as leverage, which is why they kept him close . . . very close.

What about the other gang member? In the original statements the two deputies claimed a dark-coloured SUV was parked alongside the armoured truck and the bags of cash were being transferred. The SUV sped off and was later found burnt out near Lake Conroe. These elements of the story were only added after the shooting. The deputies could easily have searched the dispatcher's log for reports of stolen and burned-out cars and chosen one to link to the robbery.

There was never a description of the missing gang member. Nobody claimed to have seen Carl Palmer. It was always an assumption, which the police helped foster by creating rumours, third-hand accounts and reports from unnamed sources. Somebody leaked Carl's name to the media and the story took on a life of its own. Soon it became accepted as fact, backed up by periodic 'sightings' of Carl in places like Mexico and the Philippines. There were never any photographs or fingerprints. Each time Carl would mysteriously slip away before the FBI could confirm his identity. Somebody like Senogles could have planted the stories. By keeping this fictitious gang member alive it stopped anyone looking more closely at the robbery.

Desiree's mind comes back to the present. The sun is a fading spark on the horizon and farms have given away to wetlands, canals and shallow lakes. Short grasses are bent by the wind and the air blooms with the smell of salt and rain. Big sky. Big land. Big sea.

# CHAPTER 66

'Let me take the boy with me,' says Tony, rubbing his hands over his head as though his whole scalp itches.

'He'll be safer here,' says Audie, his voice sounding hollow and brittle. He takes a reflective vest from Tony's bag. 'You should wear this.'

Standing unsteadily, Tony slips it over his shoulders.

'They won't shoot you,' says Max, looking at Audie for reassurance. 'My dad is out there. He's a sheriff.'

Tony looks at the teenager and smiles. 'A braver man would offer to stay here.'

'You're brave enough,' replies Max.

Audie wants to stop Tony, but he doesn't have any arguments left. Staying is no safer than leaving. In the same breath he thinks of Scarlett and Cassie in the motel room and wonders if it would have made a difference had he stayed. Could he have protected them?

Tony motions to Audie's shoulder where blood is leaking through the bandages and running down his forearm. There are droplets like beads of mercury on the polished wooden floorboards.

'I'm a little confused about what you're hoping to achieve here, son.'

Audie opens his palms and stares at them. 'I'm trying to keep Max safe. And I'm trying to keep you safe. And I'm hoping to stay alive. Which bit confuses you?'

'The third part, I guess. I'm seventy-two. Widowed. Retired. Unemployable. Ex-Navy. I got a dodgy ticker and it takes me an hour to pee. I don't have a son, only daughters, but I'm not complaining. They've been good to me. I've seen you with Max and I know you'd never set out to hurt him.'

'Thank you,' says Audie.

'No point thanking me.' Tony glances back at Max. 'Good luck, young 'un.'

Tony crosses the deck and walks slowly down the stairs, feeling for each step in the darkness. When he reaches his pickup, he pauses to examine the bullet holes and curses under his breath. He walks toward the road, the footing firmer, the pain in his chest getting worse.

Panic is the enemy. That's what his old drill sergeant used to say. Panic is what takes over when fear renders your brain useless. Where are the police cars? Why haven't they come out to get him?

In that instant, a blast of light almost knocks Tony backward. He raises his hands to shield his eyes but sees nothing but red circles burned onto the back of his lids.

'Stop there,' says a voice.

'I'm not armed.'

'Hands on your head.'

'Hey, I'm going blind here. Can you turn down the lights?'

'Kneel down.'

'My knees aren't what they were.'

'Do it.'

'I'm just the caretaker. You don't have to bother with me. I'm no problem. The boy's safe.'

'What's your name?'

'Tony Schroeder.'

'How do you know Audie Palmer?'

'I don't know him. I just met him. I came to check on the house after the storm. You shot up my rig and the Halligans' boat. I hope someone is going pay for that.'

'You should have stayed out of this, old-timer.'

'What do you mean?'

From a distance Audie hears a dull wet popping sound and sees the red mist of blood in the brightness of the headlights. Tony collapses to the asphalt, his head tilted sideways like a man in search of a pillow to lie upon.

Max watches it happen and screams. He bolts for the door and Audie has to throw out his good arm, catching the teenager in mid-flight, lifting him off his feet.

'They shot him!' screams Max, blinking at Audie incredulously. 'They shot Tony!'

Audie doesn't know what to say.

The teenager is sobbing. 'Why? He didn't hurt anybody. He was kneeling down. They shot him in the head.'

Audie knows they're removing witnesses and finishing the job they botched eleven years ago. Max is kneeling on the floor, slumped over like a puppet with cut strings. Audie's heart aches. He wants to run his thumb over the boy's lower lip and wipe away the errant tear.

Outside the headlights have been turned off. They'll be coming now. Audie sits beside Max, feeling empty inside, hollowed out. Despite the sense of urgency, his body is ready to give up. Blood loss. Hope lost. The quest over. Even if he managed to get to the beach, what then? Would they let Max live?

The teenager has stopped crying. He's sitting, braced against the wall, knees bent, staring at the cell phone.

'I remember,' he whispers hoarsely. 'You were kneeling down and someone was standing over you pointing a gun at your head. You were looking at me . . .'

'You have to run, Max.'

'He won't shoot me.'

'You don't know that.'

There is someone on the stairs outside. Audie looks out the kitchen window and sees the outline of a head appear above the deck. Rising to one knee, he primes the shotgun and rests it on the sill.

'I'll try to draw their fire. Once I'm gone I want you to run.'

'Where?'

'You can swim across the canal. Stay hidden.'

'You can't go out there.'

'I don't have a choice.'

Moss crosses the swing bridge and eases the pickup onto Canal Drive, heading east past a handful of houses that are mostly closed up for the winter. Away from the brightness of the headlights, he can just make out the whitewashed shore and the darker shade of the sea.

The houses begin to thin out and disappear. The canal and coastline converge to create a narrow strip of land less than a hundred yards wide in places. Although only a few feet above sea level, there are still swales and humps that could hide a man if he was lying down. The air is laced with salt and woodsmoke and the stench of rotting seaweed. Perhaps someone has lit a campfire or teenagers are drinking on the beach.

Moss slows. Ahead, just visible past a bend, he notices the rear red reflectors of two vehicles blocking the road. He flicks off the headlights and rolls to a stop, turning off the engine. At that same instant Desiree turns her head.

'Did you hear that?'

*Gunfire.*

They listen. The next shot is louder, followed by a short burst of semi-automatic gunfire that sounds

514

like firecrackers exploding in an empty paint tin. Desiree opens her cell phone and calls for backup. It's too dark for Moss to see her features, but he can hear the tremor in her voice.

He peers out of the windshield. Each time the wiper blade sweeps across the glass the scene comes into focus. A pair of binoculars would have been handy.

Desiree unzips her boots. 'You stay here.'

'Where are you going?'

'Out there.'

'Are you crazy?'

Desiree holds up her pistol. 'I know how to use this.'

'These guys aren't going to swap phone numbers.'

'Neither am I.'

Moss watches her move away. Reaching below the seat, he finds the big revolver wrapped in the oily rag. He unfolds it gently on his lap and weighs it in his hand, remembering when he first held a firearm, aged thirteen. He liked the way it made him feel – six inches taller and forty pounds heavier, no longer weak or insignificant. The gun gave him gravitas. The gun made him more articulate. The gun gave him courage. This was imaginary and fleeting, of course, but it took a lot of lean years in prison for him to realise that.

Desiree is thirty yards in front of him, moving further away. She looks twelve years old in her stockinged feet. Looking left and right, Moss scans the low shrubs and chooses to take the beach side, finding a path through the dunes.

Feeling too exposed, Desiree navigates the shallow ditch and climbs a hummock. Down on her belly, grasses tickling her chin, she slithers across the clumpy ground to within thirty feet of the two Ford Explorers. At first glance the vehicles had looked empty, but now she notices a figure sitting in the passenger seat with the door partially open, smoking a cigar. Lying flat, she digs her forearms into the sand and aims her pistol at the man's head, her finger tightening on the trigger.

'FBI! Hands on the dashboard.'

His head jerks around with an expression of amazement, as though the Virgin Mary had suddenly appeared before him. One hand rises, the other falls.

Moss is watching from the opposite side of the car. He can't see the man's face, but senses what's coming next. This guy is going to roll the dice. Maybe he thinks Desiree won't fire. Maybe he believes that he's faster.

In one movement, the man raises a machine pistol above the level of the window. The weapon needs two hands to hold it steady, but he's only using one. He presses the trigger and the pistol jumps, raking the grassy hummock with a staccato burst. Desiree fires twice, hitting him under the armpit and again in the neck. The man falls sideways, half in the car and half out, his face illuminated by the interior light.

Moss sprints from his hiding place and leaps over the ditch. When he reaches Desiree she's bleeding onto her blouse.

'It's only a nick,' she says, showing Moss her forearm. Slightly deafened by the noise, she doesn't realise she's shouting.

Moss looks at the body. 'Who is it?'

'A man called Victor Pilkington.'

More flashes pierce the darkness. The sounds arrive a moment later. Moss helps Desiree stand. She barely reaches his waist. She points to his .45. 'You said you weren't armed.'

'I lied, ma'am.'

She shakes her head. 'Come on.'

# CHAPTER 67

Audie can't see the shadows outside any more. They're probably braced against the walls, waiting to come through the windows and the door. His shotgun is resting on the windowsill, aiming at the top of the stairs.

'Get ready to run.'

'I'm scared,' says Max.

'I'm sorry I made such a mess of things. I should have left you alone.'

He hears a burst of gunfire in the distance. At the same time a dark shape appears on the deck. He pulls the trigger and hears someone grunt and collapse backward down the stairs. Audie doesn't wait. He flings open the door and sprints across the deck, planting his good hand on the railing and swinging his legs over the top. The drop is about fifteen feet. He lands heavily, knees buckling into his stomach. Lying on his back, winded, he sucks in air.

Stencilled against the horizon he sees the silhouettes of two figures breaking cover and running toward the house. Another shooter stands on the beach, arm extended, preparing to fire. Audie scrambles up and starts to run. Fear hums in his sinews. Reaching the dunes, he throws himself over the top and tumbles down the other side. The ocean is eighty yards away, the beach deserted with seaweed clinging to the tideline. What's across the water? Cuba, Mexico, Belize. Places he'll never see. A world of countless millions of people, living in the heat and the light, while he is a universe of one, alone on the beach, a lighthouse whose light cannot be relit.

Looking up and down the sand, he's filled with a desperate, almost suffocating sadness and sense of abandonment. Why does the world have so little need of him? What can't it just be ambivalent?

He groans, climbs to his feet and starts running along the beach. Bullets are kicking up sand and whizzing past his ears. They're not firing wildly. There is a gap between each burst. These aren't nickel-and-dimers, they're professionals who take aim. They've come to do a job.

He zigzags as he runs and falls into another swale, holding his useless arm, staring skyward, considering his choices or lack of them.

*Give up.*

No.

*Get up.*

Can't.

Glancing back the way he's come, he sees shadows hiding in the ragged clumps of grass where the insects have gone silent. Spectres. Ghosts. Furies.

Impatient gods. The men are reloading. Waiting for him.

Moss and Desiree have reached the house and are crouching beneath the deck, smelling the cold mineral odour of cement and the tropical ferns. Someone is lying at the base of the stairs, holding his face. Moaning. There are voices above. Two people are coming down the stairs – a teenage boy and someone holding a machine pistol.

'Do as you're told.'

'You shot him!'

'Shut up!'

Desiree recognises the older voice. Moss is standing directly beneath the stairs as they descend. He reaches through the bare wooden steps and grabs an ankle. Valdez pitches forward. Max has to leap out of the way. Desiree steps from the shadows and presses a gun to the sheriff's head.

'Don't move!'

'Thank God, you're here,' he says. 'We found Palmer. He's getting away.'

Desiree looks at the boy. 'Max?'

The boy nods.

'Are you all right?'

'You gotta help Audie,' he cries, pleading with them. 'They're going to kill him!'

Desiree has never heard a voice this fraught and desperate, this real. It makes her turn and look in the direction of his outstretched hand. In that instant Valdez reaches for the machine pistol and

520

spins on his back, feeling for the trigger. But Moss has seen it coming. He pushes Max aside and fires a round into the sheriff's chest. The .45 doesn't penetrate the vest, but Valdez drops the pistol and curls into a ball, groaning and nursing his ribs.

When Moss looks up, Max has gone, sprinting toward the beach.

'Stop him,' says Desiree. 'He'll get himself killed.'

Moss picks up the machine pistol and gives chase, running hard through the soft sand. For the best part of fifteen years he has kept his temper under control, but now that genie is out of the bottle. It's not about slaking a bloodlust or quenching a thirst; it's about living instead of rotting away in prison; it's about one crowded hour being worth more than a lifetime of the commonplace or the mundane.

He hears the sound of an engine and ahead of him an ATV soars over the top of a dune, front wheel airborne and then the rear. They went back for a vehicle, which is now churning through sand, using a spotlight to search for Audie. The beam sweeps back and forth, briefly trapping a lone figure, running over the dunes. He looks like a wounded duck, flapping through the ragged grass.

The shotgun dangles from Audie's damaged arm. He has one shell left. Swapping hands, he turns and fires, almost falling. The round goes high. Stumbling into a swale, he gets a mouthful of sand as lights sweep above his head. These people aren't going to cut and run. They're going to hunt him down.

Ahead there are fences erected across the beach in a staggered formation to stop erosion. Seaweed has clumped at the base of them, marooned by the tide. Audie uses them as cover, running between each new section of fence. Closer to the water he notices an odd mound that looks like a beached whale until he realises that someone has pulled a boat onto the sand, or maybe it broke loose from a mooring and washed ashore. Audie throws himself down behind the fibreglass dinghy, holding his shoulder. The shotgun is still dangling from his useless hand. He has to pry his fingers open.

The ATV has stopped further up the beach. The spotlight is searching for him, sweeping back and forth over the dunes.

He hears footsteps . . . someone is running headlong toward him. He grips the shotgun by the warm barrel, ready to swing it like a club.

*I'll take one of you bastards with me!*

He swings it hard, but at the last moment lets go of the shotgun, which spins past Max's head and splashes into the water. The teenager collapses next to him, sucking air into his lungs.

'You were supposed to go the other way.'

'I think my dad is dead.'

Audie doesn't ask what happened. They're not going to let either of them live now.

'I'll draw their fire. You head for the canal.'

'Come with me.'

'No.'

'Why not?'

'I can't swim.'

Max looks at Audie's shoulder, then at the boat. He stands and tries to drag the dinghy to the water, but it's beached high and dry. He rocks it from side to side. Max pulls. Audie pushes. Slowly it begins to inch down the natural camber of the sand. The vehicle has reached the fences and the spotlight sweeps across the dunes and down to the water's edge.

Max is standing in the shallows. They wait for the next swell and make one last effort. The boat slides away and Audie falls flat on his face, swallowing a mouthful of water. Max drags him up and rolls him into the dinghy, before pulling the boat deeper, wading until he can't touch bottom and then kicking his legs.

Audie looks over the gunwale and sees the vehicle pull up. A moment later a beam of light fills his vision and a burst of gunfire splinters the fibreglass, creating a spider-web pattern across the stern. Audie yells to Max to get down and flattens himself against the bottom boards, lying in a puddle of rainwater. More rounds rip through the hull. He crawls back and yells for Max but can't see him.

The teenager appears on the port side of the dinghy, water dripping off his face.

'We're too close to shore.'

Audie looks at the beach. The vehicle is no further away. The current is dragging the boat sideways. One shooter is running along the sand while someone else controls the spotlight. More bullets strike the hull. Audie lies face down on the deck, his shirt already wet, his cheek pressed into a deeper puddle. Salt water. They're sinking.

There's a lull in the shooting. He rolls over the side, holding on with his good arm. He and Max both kick, but the boat is wallowing, already too heavy. Inexplicably, the spotlight swings away and the bullets start to miss. Audie looks at the beach and notices someone running across the sand like a broken field quarterback, crashing through bushes and grasses.

Moss Webster is on the charge. It's like that scene in *True Grit* where Rooster Cogburn puts the horse's reins in his mouth and gallops into a blaze of bullets, with a rifle in one fist and a pistol in the other, yelling, 'Fill your hand, you son of a bitch.'

Ignoring the incoming fire, Moss looks like a man who doesn't care, a man angry beyond reason. The spotlight tries to catch up with him, but the figure behind the light starts dancing like a puppet as bullets rake across his chest.

The other shooter tries to counter, but he's caught in the beam of the headlights, a human wraith exposed by the brightness. Moss fires until the machine pistol is empty and tosses it aside.

He walks forward, aiming and firing, aiming and firing.

The shooter is crouched in a classic pose, just like they teach the experts at Quantico, but it doesn't do him any good. A bullet hits him in the throat and he flutters and falls, his blood finding the sand.

Silence follows. Only the bow of the dinghy is above the water. Audie holds on with one hand, resting his chin on the edge. The water is very cold and the current is pulling at his legs, trying to drag him under.

'We have to swim,' says Max.

'You go. I'll stay here.'

'It's not far.'

'My shoulder is a mess.'

'You can kick.'

'No.'

'I'm not leaving you here.'

Audie remembers what his father told him about clinging to the wreckage. He had to hold on like a limpet but he didn't know what a limpet was.

'*OK, you hang on like a one-armed man clinging to a cliff while he's being tickled.*'

'*I'm ticklish.*'

'*I know.*'

*You got to hold on like a frightened kitten on a sweater.*

*You got to hold on like a baby being breastfed by Marilyn Monroe.*

So he clings to the dinghy until his fingers grow

numb and his good arm can't hold on any longer. Exhausted and barely conscious, he doesn't feel his fingers release and he doesn't scrabble for a handhold or grope for one more lungful of air. Instead he slips beneath the surface, tired of fighting, wanting to sleep.

He drifts downward, looking up at the dinghy, wondering if it's possible to see the stars from under the water. Then she appears, the same angel that came to him on the night he escaped from Three Rivers and swam across Choke Canyon Reservoir. She's dressed in a translucent white robe that floats and sways around her as though she's falling in slow motion.

His heart soars. As long as she's here, he won't die alone. Belita wraps her legs around his waist and pulls his head to her breasts. He can feel the heat of her body and the softness of her hair brushing back and forth across his face.

Their future unfolds before him – waking on cotton sheets, listening to the ocean breaking against the shore. Breakfast at a café in the mercado, eating tortillas and fried plantain. Swimming in the bottle-green waves and lying on the sand until the sun drives them indoors to the cool of a shuttered room where they will make love under the blades of a spinning fan . . .

'You have to go back,' she whispers.

'No. Please let me stay.'

'It's not time.'

'I kept my promise. He's safe now.'

'He still needs you.'

'I've been lonely.'

'You have him now.'

She kisses him and he sinks deeper, happy to drown in her arms, but a fist grabs hold of his shirt collar, a forearm reaches around his neck and strong teenage legs drag him upwards, kicking hard for the shore.

# EPILOGUE

It's a strange thing for a man to sign a visitor's book and enter a prison where he has spent nearly a third of his life. And even stranger to walk down the long narrow visitors' room, past Perspex screens where prisoners are waiting to meet wives, mothers, sons and daughters.

Audie feels quite nervous as he takes a seat and looks up and down the rows, where children are fidgeting on their mothers' laps or being held up to the screen to plant kisses on the clear plastic.

Moss appears and pulls up a seat, hunching down to fit his big frame in the viewing window. He picks up the telephone, which looks like a toy in his fist.

'Hey!'

'How you doing, big fella?'

Moss grins. 'Cooler than a polar bear's toes. How's the shoulder?'

Audie holds up his left arm, which is still in a sling. 'My NBA career is through.'

'You white guys can't jump anyways.' Moss leans back in his chair, resting his legs on the narrow table. 'How did you get here?'

'Agent Furness drove me.'

'Where is she?'

'Talking to the chief warden, but she's going to come and say hello. She thought we needed some time together.'

'I hope she doesn't think we're gay.'

'You, maybe.'

'Yeah, you try saying that when I'm out of this place.'

'And when will that be?'

'I got a good chance of early parole, according to my attorney, especially after I gave evidence to the Grand Jury about Valdez and Pilkington.'

'How early?'

'Before I'm fifty, which ain't that long relatively speaking.'

'Speaking of relatives, how's Crystal?'

'Oh, she good. You just missed her. She wore one of my favourite dresses – one that showed off her titties.'

'Don't let Special Agent Furness hear you talking like that.'

'Hell, no.' Moss grins. 'You see the TV news?'

'Yeah.'

He's talking about Senator Dowling's arrest. Surrounded by TV cameras and baying reporters, he was led across the pavement by two FBI agents, one of them so small you could only see the very top of her head. A Grand Jury had just charged him with judicial corruption and perverting the course of justice.

Clayton Rudd had rolled over faster than a rotisserie chicken, giving evidence against Dowling and Valdez. Pilkington and Senogles were the architects, according to Valdez, who told the Grand Jury he was a mere pawn in the robbery, under the spell of his uncle, who threatened him with exposure and ruin. 'I didn't kill anybody,' he shouted to reporters as he was led away from the courtroom.

It could be another year before he comes to trial. How many other people will be caught in the net by then? Or maybe the establishment will close ranks and try to limit the damage.

Max is back living with Sandy, but only because Valdez was denied bail. She claims she knew nothing about the robbery and the cover-up and Audie believes her.

'You're going to be a rich man,' says Moss. 'Ten years for a crime you didn't commit – they're gonna give you millions.'

'I don't want their money.'

'Sure you do. Shit! Give it to me.'

'Look what happened the last time folks thought I had money.'

'Yeah, but this time it's different. You're innocent.'

'I was *always* innocent.'

A baby has started crying further along the row of visitors. The young mother unbuttons one side of her blouse and starts to breastfeed, but the guards tell her that she'll have to feed her baby elsewhere. Grudgingly, she says goodbye and carries the infant to the waiting room or the public toilet or the broiling heat of her car.

'Ever think you'll have kids?' Audie asks.

'I like making 'em,' replies Moss, 'but I'd be a bit scared of raising 'em. It's not like I've set a good example.'

'You'd be a good father,' says Audie. 'Better than most.' He pauses to clear his throat. 'I haven't had a chance to thank you for what you did.'

'I didn't do anything.'

'You know what I mean. All my life people have been putting themselves out for me and I don't know what I ever did to deserve saving.'

'You did plenty,' says Moss, leaning forward, a moist sheen making his eyes shine. 'I remember when you first arrived. You didn't look like much. We took bets on how long you'd survive.'

'Did you have money on me?'

'You cost me twenty bucks and two Mars bars. Nobody knew what you were capable of, but you showed 'em.'

Audie draws a deep breath. 'I didn't set out to—'

'Let me finish,' says Moss, squeezing his eyes shut. 'You know what it's like in this place – every day's a test. The monotony. The violence. The misery. The loneliness. It builds up inside a man's chest like a scream. Sure you hear the occasional joke or get a food parcel or a letter or a visitor – things that make life bearable for a few hours – but that ain't enough. Then you came along, Audie. I know you didn't set out to be noble or honour-able, but that's the strange truth of it. Terrible things happened to you. You fought and couldn't stop it, but you rose above. You gave us somebody to look up to. We were weak men, treated like animals, but you proved to us that we could be more.'

Audie tries to swallow the lump in his throat and is grateful when Desiree appears in the visitor's room, ignoring the whistles and catcalls of the prisoners as she passes their windows. She picks up the second phone.

'You look like you've grown taller,' says Moss.

'And you're fatter than I remember.'

Moss sucks in his stomach. 'Must be all the fine cuisine we get in here.'

Audie offers his chair to Desiree. 'You can stay,' she says.

'No, I'm going to stretch my legs.' He glances around nervously. 'I keep thinking they're going to realise they've made a mistake and lock me up again.'

'Nobody is going to lock you up.'

'All the same.'

Audie spreads out his right palm and places it on the Perspex screen, waiting for Moss to do the same until their fingers match up on either side.

'You stay safe, big fella. Say hi to Crystal for me.'

'I will.'

Audie walks along the windows, noticing how

some of the visitors turn and stare at him. He hears chairs being pushed back and the sound of someone clapping their hands together. Turning, he glimpses Junebug on his feet behind the window. Klutz is at the next, then Sandals and Bowen and Little Larry and Shoats. They stand and applaud, hard men serving hard time, and the sound begins spreading like a wave through Three Rivers, reaching distant cells where inmates bang cans against the bars and stamp their feet and chant Audie's name, which resounds in his ears and blurs his vision on the short walk, which has taken him eleven years to make.

The sky is clear blue, combed through with clouds that look like seed balls ready to scatter in the first gust of wind. But there's not a breath of it and barely a sound except for the traffic noise and the birds in the trees. Audie steps out of the car, feeling the heat radiating from the asphalt. A cemetery spreads out ahead of him with thousands of head-stones, dotted in neat rows like baby teeth with gaps in between filled with flowers instead of gold.

Sandy Valdez gets out of the driver's seat and waits for Max to join her.

'Do you want to do this alone?' she asks.

'No,' says Audie, looking at Max.

'I'll wait here,' she says, squeezing Max's hand.

They walk beneath the trees, staying in the shade, until they reach a corner of the cemetery where the lawns are less kempt and a wire fence flanks a four-lane road. The clearing is dotted with small mounds of soil. Audie consults a map that was given to him by the Dreyfus County Coroner's office.

'This is the place,' he says. There are no head-stones. No flowers. The only markers are a dozen square metal plates that are stuck on spikes into the earth, almost hidden by weeds. Each one is stencilled with a number. Audie has to search for the right one. He finds it: UJD-02052004. Kneeling down, he begins to pull weeds from around the marker. He should have brought flowers. On a nearby grave, a jam jar contains the remnants of perished blooms. Audie tosses the dead stalks aside and polishes the jar on his shirt. He begins picking at the scrawny daises that have avoided the mower by growing close to the fence.

Max joins him, and soon they have a small collec-tion in the makeshift vase. Using just his good hand, Audie digs his fingers into the soil, half burying the jar so it doesn't topple over. He had wanted to give Belita so much, but this is all she has – an unmarked grave, a stencilled number, daisies in a jam jar.

'I'm sorry we couldn't come sooner,' he whis-pers, imagining her lying beneath him, her head on a pillow. 'They're your favourite flower, remember?'

Audie glances up at Max. 'I brought Miguel.' Max looks embarrassed and unsure of what to do. Should he kneel down? Should he say a prayer?

'He saved me from drowning,' says Audie, still talking to Belita. 'It must run in the family.' He begins telling her the story, explaining how Max had swum Audie to shore and dragged him onto the beach as police cruisers arrived and a helicopter hovered overhead. Audie was barely conscious but can remember the bright lights and people yelling. Moss was ordering others around and standing over Audie as though keeping guard.

It was eighteen hours before Audie next opened his eyes. He was lying in the hospital with his arm in a sling and Special Agent Desiree Furness beside his bed.

'How can one man be so unlucky and so lucky?' she asked.

'I guess I broke a mirror and found a horseshoe on the same day,' he said, floating on painkillers.

It was Desiree who found Belita. Dreyfus County had a special corner of a cemetery set aside for bodies that were unclaimed or unidentified.

'Why is there no headstone?' asks Max, wiping the sweat from his top lip.

'Nobody knew her name except me . . . and I couldn't tell them,' replies Audie, rubbing his dirty hands on his jeans.

'Are you gonna say a prayer?'

'I don't really know how to.'

'I'll do it,' says Max, kneeling next to him and making the sign of the cross. He asks the Lord to bless Belita and keep watch over those who loved her. Audie says amen, his heart caught somewhere between his diaphragm and his throat. He looks at the barren square of earth and knows that it will never be big enough to hold the history buried beneath.

We get given our faces, thinks Audie, but we inherit our lives, our happiness and our unhappiness. Some get a lot, some get a little. Some savour every morsel and suck the marrow out of every bone. We take pleasure in the sound of rain, the smell of cut grass, the smiles of strangers, the feeling of dawn on a hot day. We learn things and realise we can never know more than we don't know. We catch love like a cold and cling to it like wreckage in a storm.

'We should get her a proper headstone,' says Max, helping Audie to stand. 'What do you think it should say?'

Audie ponders this for a moment and realises that he's always known the epitaph: 'Life is short. Love is vast. Live like there's no tomorrow.'